QUEENS OF THEMISCYRA

HANNAH LYNN

Text copyright © 2022 Hannah Lynn

First published 2022

ISBN: 978-1-915346-06-3

Imprint: Medusa Publishing

Edited by Carol Worwood and Joel Hames-Clark
Cover design by Books Covered

To Laura and Stephie,
Two warrior women.

ANCIENT GREECE

PART I

CHAPTER 1

*H*er blade whistled through the air, sure and unwavering, first through the warrior's leather armour, then through the soft flesh of his belly. A spray of blood arced upwards as he toppled from his horse. Already racing away, Hippolyte paid him no heed. Her mare's hooves churned the dry earth beneath them, sending up clouds of dust as the Queen locked her aim on her next victim. Within moments, he too lay face down in the dirt.

From all around came the clang of metal—swords against shields, arrow heads against breastplates—and the stench of blood, bitter and cloying, hung densely in the arid air. The aroma was one she knew well. One of battle. Of sweat and pain. Burning skin under the glare of Helios's sun. Of horses slick with perspiration. But above all else, it was the stench of victory.

Their adversaries, who only an hour ago had been screaming in rage and fervour, were now crying in fear, begging for mercy, choking as they drowned in their own blood. If they were fortunate, her women would offer them a swift death.

Flies had already arrived in their droves, settling on open wounds, buzzing on the corpses already greying in the dirt.

By the time the last scream had faded, and the sun had reached its zenith, the earth was crimson with the blood of the fallen.

Hippolyte cast her gaze across the scene. These were young men. Some barely in their teens. It was a weak king who thought to send such boys to face her and her warriors.

"Back home to Pontus and Themiscyra, my Queen?"

Hippolyte turned to face Penthesilea. Her sister sat upright upon her horse, her embroidered tunic, leather trousers, and boots—the traditional warriors' garb—possibly even more stained with the colour of battle than Hippolyte's own. The Princess's bow was stowed in a sling on her back, an elegant weapon with its double curve, smaller than those their enemies favoured. Smaller than those that littered the ground around them.

The bow had been carved, planed and strung by Penthesilea's own hand. Wood and bone, shaved off in the finest of slivers, imperceptible to some yet enough to shift the weapon's balance and ensure the truest aim. Hippolyte could not imagine how many arrows had been loosed from it that day, how many bronze tips had met their target, piercing hearts or skulls. Penthesilea's arrows did not miss.

"Back home to Themiscyra, Sister," the Queen replied. "Although first we must collect our payment."

It was a handsome settlement, the largest they had received in some months. The bulk was in metals—gold, iron, bronze—that would be hammered out or melted down, but there were other items too. There were jewels, both raw stones and those already cut and polished. There was pottery. There was even a lyre, and although she herself did not play,

Hippolyte knew many of her women would strike a fine tune from it.

Within the city walls, the King had thanked them profusely, bowing low to the ground in the awkward, angular movements of one unaccustomed to such humility, even more so towards women. Hippolyte was almost as uncomfortable with the display as he was. After, settled into a more reposeful posture, he asked if they wished to stay the night. Most kings prayed she would refuse and offered only out of courtesy, and this was the case today. She could not help but note a flash of relief dart across his face when she declined his offer and found herself feeling a pang of sympathy for the man. This was unlikely to be the last battle they fought for him.

Their saddlebags full and their horses rested, they began the ride east, back to the region of Pontus and their citadel home, Themiscyra.

The journey to the edge of the Black Sea would take two days at a leisurely pace. If needed, they could ride at a gallop and without stopping unless it was unavoidable—that was the way they had ridden to reach here—but the women and the horses had earned a little respite.

Blue skies, littered with feather-like clouds that hovered motionless in the still air, stretched above them as they rode. On a clear day like today, from its southernmost point, they could see all of Anatolia. To the north, beyond the Sea of Marmara, was Thrace, and west, across the Aegean, lay Thessaly and Athens. They had travelled to these places and further still. They had travelled to Thebes and the Peloponnese, called to fight for kings who might otherwise have lost their lands. Called to rain their arrows on armies with whom they had no quarrel. And they had been paid handsomely for it. Sometimes the battles would come one after another, and they would race from one beleaguered land to the next, always ready, always victorious. But for now, they were headed home to rest, basking in the scent of the ferns that littered the hillsides around them.

The women chattered as they rode. There was always a rush that came after battle. The adrenaline that had lent them such force and ferocity now drew words from their lips as quickly as the blood had spilled from their enemies. Such exuberant conversation between her women might endure for miles, over plains and through valleys, across rivers and around grand lakes. Yet inevitably, at some point before the sun set on that first day after a battle, a quiet would descend, in which they recalled those they had lost. Those that had been granted the most honourable of deaths. A warrior's death. An Amazon's death.

"Four women made their first kill today."

It was Antiope who spoke to the Queen through the quiet.

"Four who can ride with us to the Gargareans next spring."

"That is good news. I will meet with them personally upon our arrival home."

Shortly after they halted at a shallow lake that had survived the droughts of summer. Shingle shimmered beneath the surface as the women knelt to wash the blood and grime from their skin and watched as swirls of red eddied from their palms.

While Hippolyte and her sisters considered Themiscyra their home, this was not the case for all Amazons. Certainly, most dwelt within the city walls, with the luxuries and protection provided by so many warriors living in close proximity, but there were those who found such a life constrictive and claustrophobic. These nomads spent their time outside of battle wandering the steppes and camping out beneath the stars. They hunted with bow or spear, preferring to make small fires and pick the meat from the bones of the birds and beasts they had caught. They craved solitude, returning to join the rest of the warriors only on those occasions that required them to do so. At festivals, or to fight or to embark upon the annual spring-time trek south to the Gargareans. There was no enmity between the two groups of women. The Queen had no prefer-ence in how they lived and did not judge one way of life more favourably than another. Each woman could choose to spend her days living as she preferred, and would therefore fight with all the more determination to preserve that way of life when the time came.

By the time they had pitched their bivouacs, the sun had long since sunk below the horizon, and streams of stars glimmered above them. A chorus of cicadas hummed and buzzed, a counterpoint to the chatter of the women. Lying on her back in the grass, her sword by her side, Hippolyte listened. This was her favourite time—the night after a battle had been fought and won. The women would regale their comrades with stories: how their opponents had fought, how close those enemy blades had come, boasting of the mounted attacks they had mastered. The Queen would seal it all away in the back of her mind.

They had lost a dozen women that day. Nothing, when set against the hundreds of deaths their opponents had suffered but more than was acceptable. They had brought the bodies with them, wrapped tightly in linen, to be returned to their homes in Pontus. They would perform a proper burial there, committing the women to the land, along with their weapons and all the honour they deserved.

Next time, Hippolyte told herself as the fire sizzled and spat, she would not lose any. And she would offer a greater sacrifice to her father. Her immortal father, Ares, the God of War.

~

ON THE SECOND DAY, the sky had brightened to the point of brilliance, Helios's glow so radiant they were forced to pull their caps lower on their heads and squint so much their eyes were mere slits. The grass was short, brittle and brown, and the horses flicked their tails, agitated by a heat that caused the flies to buzz in swarms and their coats to darken with sweat. Spring was a swift season in these parts, with lush green turning dusty and arid almost overnight. Heat rippled from the ground, blurring the air immediately above it. This part of the journey would end soon enough, though. The further northwest they travelled, the cooler it would become. And by nightfall, Pontus, and perhaps even Themiscyra, would be in view.

Hippolyte considered the harshness of life in a place such as this, for there could be little to hunt, nothing to fish and no prospect of farming such lands. She had seen mules, grey and hunched, long eyelashes drooped and blinking, but no horses. The leaves were already browning on what few trees there were, whose brittle twigs were too weak to bear the meanest of fruit.

As was often the way when she passed through such lands, Hippolyte thanked the gods for all they had been given in Pontus and Themiscyra and vowed once again to present a sacrifice to her father upon her arrival home.

Hour after hour, they rode without stopping, even when the sun reached its apex. There was nowhere to stop, no shade to be found at this time of day. On they went, until clouds began to form above them. Thick and white, like freshly plucked down, they cast thick shadows on the earth. Small at first, they ripened as she watched. Swelling with water, their edges glimmered as they muted the sun's rage.

They would burst soon, Hippolyte thought, staring up at them, and bring water in great sheets, bridging the void between sky and earth. As a child, she had loved to race ahead of a downpour, and if she failed to outrun it, would stop and lift her head to greet the refreshing rain and let it flow across her face, its coolness replenishing her. Her memory stirred with more moments from her childhood, she and Penthesilea riding out for days, living only on the rabbits that they caught or the berries they could forage. This was before Ares had chosen her instead of her sister to rule the Amazons, despite Hippolyte not being the eldest. Only once had Hippolyte succeeded in drawing blood against Penthesilea in battle. A nick. Nothing more. But that had been enough for Ares to name her Queen.

But now she dwelt on the times before that, when they would train and spar and ride from dawn until dusk, unburdened by the cares of leadership. They spent their time learning about their land. Practising on horseback those acrobatics that would one day be put to use in battle. But this had been one of their favourite games: to watch clouds thicken, to stand completely motionless beneath them. There they would wait while they grew greyer and greyer until they had swollen so fat, they could no longer contain all the moisture within them. At that point, the instant when the clouds cracked apart and unleashed a deluge, the girls would squeeze their thighs into their horses' flanks and fly in an attempt to outride the rain.

Sometimes they made it. Sometimes they would reach shelter before the storm caught them, or else keep riding at such pace that the clouds would, in time, lose their weight and have nothing left to drown them with. But more often than not they ended the game drenched. Soaked to the skin by the downpour. Hair plastered to their heads. Their horses sodden from ear to hoof. And they would laugh as the icy water ran down their spines. Afterwards, they would build a fire and dry their leathers before riding back to Themiscyra and their mother, to continue their training.

Noting again how the clouds were burgeoning above them, Hippolyte signalled to the women to pick up their pace, urging her own bay mare into a soft canter and then faster still, until she was galloping. Slicing through the grass.

The air drew through her hair like a comb as she closed her eyes and lifted her head to the sky. Not even the thrill of battle could compare to this, to the thunder of hooves on the earth beneath her and the cold blast of air needling her skin. The laughter of the women as they rode was more melodious than any lyre. More tuneful than any flute. All were now following her lead. Galloping as if their very lives depended on it.

A glance behind her brought a smile to her lips. Several of the women were taking advantage of the opportunity to practise their horseback combat positioning, twisting to face behind them or else balancing on their knees as their horses sprinted across the ground, their feet barely grazing the short stubble beneath their hooves. Some, however, Hippolyte saw were grieving, remembering those who had been lost: daughters, sisters, mothers. She would let the mourners ride out first in the next battle. Let them drown their pain in the blood of others.

As they approached the coast, the rain came, but rather than the downpour she had hoped for, it fell as a light shower that formed perfect droplets on her skin and clothes, before evaporating into nothing.

It was here, where the foaming waves crashed against jagged cliff edges, that the horses picked up the scent of home. Their pace quickened without instruction from their riders.

Their nostrils flared as they turned in unison like a flock of birds, the pull of home upon them, the certainty that there was nowhere else on Earth quite like it.

The citadel of Themiscyra had been built on the steppes of Pontus, with views out over the Black Sea. The land that surrounded it was an oasis, regardless of the time of year. It did not suffer droughts or floods. Their animals did not get plagued by mites or vermin, and the forests that filled the far regions to the east were as bountiful as the sea to the north. Birds, rabbits, wild pigs and mouflon made their homes above and below the ground, their songs and snuffles providing choruses day and night, their tracks weaving among the thick layers of foliage of the forest floor. Had they chosen to do so, the two-thousand-strong Amazon women might have picked a different-coloured fruit for every day of the week, although no food was ever more satisfying than that from a hunt. Yes, they would hunt that evening, Hippolyte thought as she rode ahead of her sisters and the other women. A good hunt to celebrate their victory and to find an adequate sacrifice. They would need to salt and dry more meat too, preparing for the long trips that might await them.

The Queen's mind was so lost in thoughts of home and the future that it took her a moment to notice the flashes of light on the peak of a hill several miles to the east. And even when she did see it, within a blink she had disregarded it—as if it were some trick of the evening light, like rays reflecting off a puddle, or caught on the sheen of iridescent wings. Small lakes and tributaries littered the land, though generally at lower levels than this. Birds, however, could be found everywhere. It was likely to be a bird.

"My Queen."

Antiope had sped from behind to catch her.

"Did you see that? Did you see the light?"

"I did."

Hippolyte was about to dismiss any concerns her younger sister might have had when it flared again. Her heartbeat quickened. It was no accident. It was a sure and certain signal, a flash of polished bronze, from one of the many mirrors placed along the tops of the steppes so that the women could communicate with each other. But the pattern of flashes was one they had never used before, one they had never had cause to use before.

It was well-known throughout Anatolia and the whole of Greece that if anyone was in need of the services of the Amazons, the women would hear of it one way or another, but it would always be their decision as to whom they aided. Sometimes money played a part, but often it was the righteousness of the cause that made the choice for them. Never did anyone other than the Amazons themselves set foot on the silver sands of their beaches or ride the dense forests to reach the steppes of their home. To do so would certainly bring about an intruder's demise. But in spite of this, the sequence of flashes came for a third time, and it could mean only one thing.

Outsiders had come to Themiscyra.

CHAPTER 2

"It must be a mistake," Antiope said. "An accident. A ship that has got lost, perhaps?"

There was no fear in her voice, only confusion. Confusion Hippolyte could feel herself. The single, short flashes of light had each lasted the same duration and had come consecutively, with no pauses between them. It was the sign that a vessel was approaching from the Black Sea and encroaching upon their territory. But for someone to land on their shores deliberately would be an act of war. A war that they would undoubtedly lose. There were only two possibilities: either this ship had lost its way, or its sailors had lost their minds. Which one, she would not waste time wondering.

With the slap of a hand, she dug her heels into her horse's side. Raising the reins, she pushed her body forwards into its withers. The animal knew the command well. Within two strides it was galloping, its rear legs sweeping back and forth in unison as its hooves skimmed the earth. Hippolyte's hair flew back and away from her face with the force of the wind.

"Your zoster?" Penthesilea called to the Queen as she quickened her pace and galloped alongside her. "We must prepare to fight. We must prepare for war."

Fighting was always at the front of Penthesilea's mind. The kill. The glory. It was true there had been competition between the pair. The desire to shine brightest in their father's eyes. But out of all her sisters and the women she fought with, there was no one that Hippolyte would rather have at her side in battle. No one as fearless when faced with the gleam of a thousand swords against her. No one whose hand or mind were quicker. Her axe, her bow, her spear, whatever the weapon, if it were wielded by Penthesilea it would not falter or miss. She was the warrior of all warriors.

"I have the zoster here," Hippolyte replied.

The horse maintained its speed as the Queen leant to one side, slipping her hand into the satchel that was strapped fast to the saddle. From out of this bag, she pulled a large belt and, with only one hand now on the reins, she fixed around her waist.

The leather zoster which held her sword and knives was reinforced with bronze and gold plaques that shone with a soft lustre, reflecting all the light that fell on them. Etched into it were patterns so intricate and delicate it was obvious to all who saw it that it was the work of the gods. Despite its metal plates, it was supple between her fingers, and it had moulded to her body over the years. It had been a present from her father, Ares, on the day she had been crowned Queen of the Amazons. His acknowledgement of her strength and leadership of the women. It had cemented her position as ruler and served as a physical reminder of the ichor that ran through her veins. In every battle since receiving it, she had worn the zoster without fail. Now, she sometimes felt her women fought for the belt as keenly as they fought for her. For it represented a truth: that each of them was blessed by Ares, and through his gift, their fates remained secure.

Hippolyte spoke to her three sisters, who now rode alongside her, Antiope and Penthesilea to her left, her youngest sister, Melanippe, to the right.

"Signal the women to stay their hands until told otherwise. This may yet be a misunderstanding. I do not wish for bloodshed unless it is necessary."

"They have come unbidden to Themiscyra. They must pay the price."

Eagerness for battle rang out in Penthesilea's voice.

"They will if it is deserved. We do not condemn simple mistakes, though. There may well be an innocent explanation for this."

"I should ride ahead to the citadel to see that the children are safe," Melanippe said.

She was by far the youngest, barely old enough to fight when Hippolyte had been crowned Queen. Her hair was the fairest of them all but her skin the darkest. Her almond eyes, while the same shape as her sister's, were uniquely wide. She possessed a youthfulness, almost an innocence. This was the first time that Melanippe had joined them in battle since the birth of her twin daughters the previous spring. She had been eager to return to the field, to feel the weight of a sword in her hand again, to feel the crushing of a breastbone beneath her blade. Hippolyte had welcomed her back to the fray but could now see the pressure this absence from home had placed on her, which was only heightened by the current threat.

"Plenty of women remain in Themiscyra. Nearly half our number. They will protect them. You will stay with me. I wish for all the daughters of Ares to ride in together."

"As you wish, my Queen."

Melanippe dipped her head slightly. There would be no further discussion of the matter. The Queen had spoken.

No more conversation followed. No words passed their lips other than to spur their steeds on. The distant, sweeping sounds of the sea were drowned out by the hammering of the horses' hooves, the heaving of the riders' chests barely muffling the drumming of their hearts. The light on the steppes flashed only once more. The women up there on the hill would have noted that the army had changed its speed and would know their signal had been received. They would be arming themselves now, preparing for whatever was to come.

Led by the Queen, the warriors took a weaving path up the steppes. It was not the fastest route back, but it allowed them sight of the sea below, and what they lost in time they would gain in knowledge of these intruders. As it came into view, Hippolyte pulled on the reins of her mare, easing it to a slow canter before drawing to a halt. Her heart pounded as she checked the zoster around her waist and observed the scene below.

The water was choppy, with frothy white-capped waves that were broken up by the wind before sinking back into the swell, ready to rise again. Above them scudded dark clouds that threatened a storm. Experience told Hippolyte they would pass the mountains before the rain came. Normally the Queen might lose herself in such a view, the perfect backdrop against which to ponder future battle tactics. But today her gaze held fast on the ship.

Amazon women rarely travelled by sea. Their horses could take them any place they wished to go, often faster than what would appear to be a short trip by sea, and without the fear that Poseidon, or some other jealous god, might turn his wrath in their direction and impede their journey. As such, Hippolyte did not have an intricate knowledge of sea-going vessels, could not expatiate upon them in the way she might upon horses or weapons or how to erect a bivouac of leather pelts that could withstand any weather on any terrain. Still, she knew enough to know that what she was looking at was a trireme. And a trireme was a ship of war.

With three rows of oars and brass plates that shone a burnished orange in the muted evening sun, the percussion of the ship's mainsail slapping back and forth in the wind fought for dominance over the squalls of seagulls and the crashing of the waves. Hippolyte felt each slap of the fabric as if it were a hand against her skin. This was no lost vessel, no merchant ship blown off course by a storm. These were rich men. Powerful men. And powerful people knew exactly where Themiscyra was.

They had dropped anchor a fair way from the shore, perhaps suspecting the sharp coral and rocks that hid beneath the surface close to land. Perhaps they had chosen the distance knowing that they were beyond the reach of the women's venom-tipped arrows. The specifics didn't matter. They were too close by at least a hundred miles.

The Queen strained her eyes, trying to see more. At such a distance she could make out no details to identify the vessel's origin, but she knew around two hundred men could fit aboard such a ship. Perhaps three hundred. It was a fact that caused her confusion, rather than distress.

In some battles, such a number might suffice for victory, yet what were three hundred men against the two-thousand women of the Amazon army who could kill them all with a single salvo of arrows before they set one foot upon the sand. And if it came to it, they would. But surely the intruders knew this. Perhaps, if they had come as a fleet of a hundred such vessels, outnumbering the Amazons ten or twenty to one, they might have stood a chance. But one ship? What could possibly be the purpose of that, unless every person aboard wished for a swift death?

"There! Do you see it? They are coming ashore."

Just as Penthesilea spoke, the Queen's eyes fell upon another vessel in the water. It had been dropped on the far side of the trireme and was only now coming into view. It was a small smudge, a dark shadow among the waves, little more than a blot beside the trireme, though recognisable still as a rowing boat.

"That cannot hold more than a dozen men at most," Hippolyte said, her horse fighting against her as she held it steady. Had she dropped the reins, it would likely have run straight to its stable. She watched as the small vessel drew nearer. Only a dozen men on board, perhaps, but from the speed at which they were moving, oars ploughing through the water, they were strong.

"What can they be thinking?" Penthesilea asked. "This cannot be an attack. Can it?"

"We rule nothing out," Hippolyte replied. "Keep your arrows at hand. It will not be long now. Men have come."

CHAPTER 3

*S*unlight danced on the waves in the evening air. The two parties arrived on the beach at much the same time. Hippolyte and her army barrelled over the dunes flattening the saltwort, the horses snorting from the pace at which they had been forced to go.

The rowing boat had maintained a strong speed to the shore, and a chant from the men aboard now reached the women's ears. They were close enough now that the Queen could count the individual figures. Ten men. That was all. Clad in armour, weapons in their hands. Ten more than had ever set foot on their land before.

Three hundred of her women were already waiting, women who had not been needed at the last battle or who had stayed behind to tend to the children, although many would admit it was not their preferred way of spending their time. The days and nights were long, and the cries of young children did not set a heart pounding the way the cries of war did. *This* was their duty, to safeguard the future of them all. These women were ripe for a fight. Primed. Prepared. Hippolyte could see it in the way they gripped their weapons. She could see it, raw and smouldering in their eyes. They were itching to spill blood. Their arrows and spears were raised, their armour fastened, their steeds straining at the bit. One exchanged a glance with the Queen and dropped her chin. *The children are safe,* the look said. Hippolyte responded with a single nod. *They will stay that way.*

The other women fell into line without a word. Five deep and four hundred abreast, they formed an unassailable wall of warriors, through which none would pass. Hippolyte's horse snorted, the young mare foaming at the mouth, its breath forming clouds in the air. With her shoulders back and her bow in her hand, the Queen rode to the front, her sisters close behind. Any man who faced a daughter of Ares, let alone all four, knew their end would be swift.

All eyes were locked on the Queen, awaiting her command. She galloped the length of the assembled women, allowing the mare's head to flick back as it reared up, before turning in a tight circle and riding back the way she had come, kicking sand into the air. Within the salty sea air swirled the nuanced scents of plants found only in Pontus. The tang of chokecherry and wood sorrel. The sweetness of pine and hornbeam. Aromas she would recall no matter how long she had been parted from them, just as she would recognise the slopes of the steppes or the vastness of the sky. This was her land, given to her by the God of War, and she would defend it with her life.

Before the watchful eyes of her women and the men on the boat, she drew to a halt in line with the vessel and parallel to the shore, where the sand changed from dark to light and only the thinnest layer of water moved over her horse's hooves. It was now mere metres away. The men were no longer chanting.

"Hold your arrows."

. She projected her voice, but not for the benefit of her women, who would know not to attack until she gave the order. They had trained since birth, held spears in their hands while most their age had been playing with toys. And they would require no urging to fulfil the destiny for which they had been born. She projected her words so that the men in the approaching vessel could be under no illusion as to who was in charge. One word from her, and arrows would rain down on them. A hail of metal and wood from which the only escape would be death.

She turned to face the sea. The men had jumped into the water and were wading towards her, waist deep in the surf. All of them were of impressive stature, but it was the one at the front who drew her gaze. His shoulders were almost as broad as the boat they had rowed ashore in, his arms as thick as a horse's neck. Salt-water spray glistened like the stars in his wavy hair, which fell past his shoulders, and his face was framed by a tightly curled beard. If his figure was imposing, his cloak was even more so. From his shoulders hung the skin of a lion.

"Heracles."

Hippolyte had never set eyes on the demi-god before, but his reputation preceded him. As, she assumed, did hers.

"Queen Hippolyte," he responded.

The Queen stiffened. So, he did know who she was, which meant his arrival was no accident. Penthesilea was right. They had come for war. Hippolyte enunciated her next words very clearly.

"Given that you know who it is that you address, I would advise you to step no further. You will not find anything here, other than a swift end."

Heracles the demi-god. Heracles the son of Zeus. Is this where his story would end, at the hands of an Amazon Queen?

His lips pursed, and though he did not step closer, he did not appear concerned by her words. Simply contemplative. His men, however, had concern writ large across their features. Some were dark haired and dark skinned, some fairer and with skin bordering on chalk white. They had been hand-picked to join him on this expedition, no doubt for their skills with a blade. Every one of them bore scars upon his arms and torso. Some of the lines were faded, almost lost in the ripple of muscles, but others were fresher, pink and angry. All of them had seen fights before. They did not cower, but their eyes showed hesitation. They knew that this might be their last fight.

There was another man among the remaining nine who drew her attention almost as keenly as Heracles. He was the next largest, the sinews in his arms and neck bulging, and other than Heracles himself, was the only one viewing the scene with anything other than trepidation. His blond hair seemed almost to glow from within, and rather than scanning the lines of warriors as his companions did, his eyes were locked on her. When she noticed and caught him watching her, she could have sworn those same eyes glimmered, and his cheeks flushed pink.

"Believe me, I mean you no disrespect."

Heracles spoke, and her attention returned to him.

"I realise what I have done, arriving here unannounced, but this is the only place where I will find what I seek."

His eyes momentarily dropped to her belt. It was the minutest of actions, no doubt imperceptible to any without her level of observation but conveyed the reason for his presence.

Without breaking her gaze, Hippolyte rested one hand on the central, bronze plate of her zoster.

"I have not come seeking bloodshed," he said, palms raised in a gesture of peace. "Perhaps we could have a conversation."

"I believe we are conversing. Are we not?"

"I was hoping for a little more privacy, as welcoming as this reception is."

His eyes twinkled, and the corners of his mouth twisted up into the slightest of smiles, but it did not fix in place. Instead, he dipped his head.

"There are matters I would like to discuss discreetly with you."

How would this scene develop should she refuse his request? She quickly considered every possible outcome. Each move she made at the height of battle was instinctive, but she had never confused instinct with haste. Every action had a consequence, and with each strike of her blade, she knew exactly what the outcome would be and the next move she would make. How many arrows remained in her quiver. How many strides her horse would need to reach her next opponent. She knew where her nearest and furthest women were. Each action had its repercussions for her and those around her. Repercussions that could stretch out in time and space, affecting them all for seconds or for years. And this situation was no different.

From somewhere behind her, a horse whinnied, impatient. But it would have to wait and so would Heracles. For though her mind was settled on what she should do, she wished to delay him. To draw the moment out. To prove who had the upper hand. Yes, she could end him now. A single gesture, imperceptible to him and his men, would see her sister, Penthesilea, send an arrow straight through his sternum. The rest would fall in moments, dead before they even knew they were under attack. And with that, she could leave the bodies to the sea's tender mercies. Job done. It was an option. It was, she thought, the one her women would expect her to choose.

She could sense the tension behind her. Would she make the order to attack? She was well within her rights to do so, and none of the women would think any less of her; the men, after all, were trespassing. But that was not the queen she wished to be, the leader she aspired to or Ares had chosen.

Penthesilea moved her horse closer to her sister's, her fingers still firmly gripping her arrow and her eyes fixed on the target before her.

"I do not trust him," she whispered to her sister. "He is a killer."

"We are all killers here," Hippolyte reminded her. "And it is not what we are but why that matters."

She could feel her sister's frustration charging the air, as if she were Zeus himself.

"You cannot let him walk upon our sands. Surely you will not?"

"I can, and will, do what I believe is right," Hippolyte said, without emotion.

Her eyes once again moved away from Heracles and this time fell upon the trireme. The ship swayed back and forth, clinking and creaking with the rhythm of the waves. One ship. Three hundred men. They could end it all so quickly. But how many more would follow? A vessel that impressive had great funds behind it. Thebes, perhaps? Or Corinth? Either way, if blood was spilled that evening, she knew it would not be the last, and their homeland, their sanctuary, might suffer a war that lasted generations. In spite of their warrior heritage, her mother had fought to keep these lands free from the blood of war. That would not change under her rule.

"My women will take your boat," she said finally. "If you step on this sand, it is by my permission only and it will be by my permission that you will be allowed to leave."

"I understand," Heracles replied and nodded to his men at the same moment Hippolyte signalled to her women.

As the men, still waist deep in water, moved away from the small vessel, four women rode into the waves, which broke into white froth against their horses' legs. Only one dismounted, passing her reins across to another, then wading deeper, carrying a rope which she swiftly tied to the boat. The other women kept their arrows trained on the men, who had now edged closer to Heracles, their eyes constantly moving as they tried to anticipate from which way a missile might come. Only the blond-haired one seemed fearless. His eyes were rooted on the Queen, in a look of complete fascination. It was not the first time she had drawn such gazes and she paid it no heed.

As the woman dragged the boat up onto the sand, Hippolyte nodded to Heracles.

"You will follow me. Your men will go with my women."

"As you wish."

"And one wrong move will be your last."

What followed next took place so quickly that even later she could barely recall how it had happened. Penthesilea's arrow had not moved a hair's breadth, while Melanippe and Antiope had now shifted back, giving orders to the women behind them. Hippolyte did not think her attention had wavered for as much as a heartbeat and believed that her vision had encompassed all that she needed to see. But the scream that rang out told her otherwise.

One of her women, seemingly appearing from out of

nowhere, was on her knees in the water, mouth open and arms flailing, mere feet from Heracles' men. She picked herself up, hair dripping wet, eyes white with shock.

"He has come to kidnap you, my Queen. I heard it myself. Heracles has come to kidnap our queen!"

CHAPTER 4

Two dozen arrows were loosed, a hailstorm of copper and snake's venom. She knew they would not miss, and with one strike, the venom would permeate the blood and immediately render Heracles paralysed and dead within the minute. They shot through the air, like a swarm of locusts ready to devour whatever they landed upon. While his men dived for cover beneath the waves, Heracles had only to twist his body and wrap his cloak around himself. The lethal projectiles bounced harmlessly into the water. Hippolyte's gaze never left him as she pulled an arrow from her own quiver and shot it directly at his heart, only for it to fare as all the others had. Heracles stood tall scanning the sea. Not a single arrow had pierced his garb, let alone the man it covered.

"He wears the Nemean Lion skin!" Antiope's explanation came at the very same moment as the realisation dawned on the Queen. "No blade or arrow will pierce it."

The Nemean Lion. Many years ago, she had heard tell of Heracles' disposal of the beast which had plagued the men and women of Nemea in the Argolis. But she had not thought the task was truly possible.

To wear such a hide, he must have torn it from the flesh of the lion itself. Yet no mortal weapon could penetrate the skin which covered the creature—not even one cast by an Amazon. For it to be covering this man meant that he'd had not only the strength but the cunning, too. But how he had managed to kill the animal, unfathomable as it might be, mattered not to her. She would rip the skin from his body and plough the spear through his heart if she had to.

"Enough of this. I will wrap my hands around his throat and kill him that way," Penthesilea responded, bounding from her horse in a single leap. Hippolyte reached for her spear and jumped to the sand to join her sister. With Penthesilea by her side, she raced into the sea, but Heracles seemed not to notice. Instead, he turned a circle in the water, smashing the waves with his hands, oblivious to the warriors crashing towards him, spears ready to run him through.

"Show yourself!" he screamed. Veins, angry and thick, pulsed across his forehead and down his neck, as the sodden lion skin dripped with water. "Show yourself!"

Hippolyte paused, confused by his actions. His attention was no longer on her or her zoster. It seemed nowhere and everywhere at once. His eyes darted from side to side, an angry snarl upon his lips. From all the tales the Queen had heard of the hero, she had expected a man of reason, level-headed. Someone with the intelligence and inventiveness necessary to remove the impenetrable skin of the Nemean Lion. But the ravings of this man suggested he had lost his grasp on reality.

"I know you are here! I know that this is your doing!"

For a second, his eyes met those of Hippolyte, and yet he didn't lunge at her or her zoster. Rather, his violent movements had slowed, and still turning in a circle, he offered his impervious back to her.

Was it an act? Surely it must be. Some ruse to feign insanity and throw them off guard. But his men were not raising their spears to fight. If anything, they seemed fearful, concerned for their leader although they made no move to help him. They barely stirred at all.

"Stop now," Hippolyte shouted into the wind. "Stop or we will burn your ship and your men to ashes!"

At these words, over a thousand lights appeared behind her. A cascade of bright, fluttering orange that stretched from one end of the beach to the other. Arrows had been lit and were ready to fly to both vessels, simultaneously. Her order would be obeyed, without hesitation.

The hero, Heracles, stopped, stunned at the sight, almost as if he had forgotten the women were even present.

Hippolyte spoke again.

"This is your last chance, Heracles. Turn around now, or every one of your men will die."

To emphasise her point, she trained an arrow on his blond-haired companion, whose eyes widened. He was one of the youngest of the group. And a fool if he thought they could best the Amazons. But she felt no pity. She had killed men younger than him.

Soaked to the skin, Heracles took a step forward, but Hippolyte pulled tighter on her bowstring. He stopped and then genuflected. His flushed face turned white and sweat beaded on his forehead. It took several moments before he regained his composure enough to speak.

"I apologise, my Queen. Sincerely. What you saw ... I come only for the zoster. Please let me take it and none shall come to harm. Not my warriors or yours. I do not wish for bloodshed."

"You declared war when you set your anchor in our waters. When you defiled our lands."

"Perhaps that is so, but that does not change the fact that my sole purpose is to obtain the belt."

He enunciated his words with such force that spittle mingled with the sea spray. His eyes, once good natured, had turned black.

"I do not trust your intent," she replied.

A snarl escaped his lips.

"You cannot believe that I am here to take you. If I had wanted you dead, I would have reached your shores by now. I would have come here with a thousand men. Surely you can see that? This is her doing. She is the one casting doubt in your mind before I have even spoken my piece."

The Queen frowned, confused by his choice of words.

"*She?* Am I supposed to know to which woman you refer?"

"The woman who told you I was here to take you. The one who screamed. Find her. Find that woman. It will prove everything."

Hippolyte now stepped to within mere feet of Heracles, pulling her elbow back and increasing the tension in her bow so much that it quivered in her hand. A lesser archer would not have had the strength to hold it at such a point, yet for her it was as natural as breathing, the tension in the string at one with the muscles in her arms.

"You are giving orders to me, on my lands that you have desecrated?" Hippolyte's voice was calm, belying her anger. "You do not order a Queen."

"I am not ordering you; I am asking you. Find that woman. The one who said I had come to steal you. Find her and you will see that I only come in peace. I come only for the zoster." And then, after a pause, perhaps because the word was not one he spoke often and therefore took more time to compose, added, "Please."

Behind them, the arrows were still lit. The flaming tips flickering orange, illuminating the women's eyes as if they were wolves circling prey. Penthesilea stood in the water behind the Queen, while her other two sisters remained mounted on the sands. This could easily be a ploy. A way to delay her, to give them time. Perhaps there were another hundred ships on their way. It was not beyond the realms of possibility.

But even as these thoughts formed, she found herself absorbed by the glimmer that shone deep within his eyes. Anger? Hope? Desperation? There were women on guard across the steppes with a view out over all of Anatolia and the length of the coast. They would signal if there were other ships drawing close. And with their arrows already poised, they would not be so foolish as to let anyone leave the triremes again.

"Bring her," she said to her sister.

Penthesilea stiffened. Her eyes conveying her distrust of the men. The fact that she had managed to stay her hand for this long was close to a miracle, and even when she turned from her, Hippolyte could feel the burn of her sister's glare. But Penthesilea would never contest her Queen's will in public and hesitated only momentarily before returning to the women.

"Who was it? Who heard the men speak? Come here now."

Stepping closer still to Heracles, Hippolyte cast her gaze up and down the row of her warriors, whilst keeping him in vision. She saw her women's focus waver as they, too, loosened their gaze on the warrior as they waited to see who might step forward. A moment passed, then another. A tense silence surrounded them as they all waited with anticipation. Still nothing, bar the chorus of the cicadas and the crash of waves.

Hippolyte shifted her stance, bringing the tip of her arrow up against Heracles' neck, whilst simultaneously addressing her people.

"Step forward. I need to know who spoke. There will be no reprimand for keeping your Queen safe. You know that."

Every horse remained in its place, every woman waiting.

"I assume your women do not normally disobey your orders, Queen Hippolyte?"

She pushed the arrow tip deeper against his neck. She could feel the force of the lion skin pushing back against it. She would not reach his flesh, she knew, but her intention was clear.

"My women obey my every word."

"I do not doubt that. So, where is she?"

Unease ran through the Queen. Had one of his men taken the woman? That was the only explanation, yet none of the nine young men had moved. Perhaps another had lain hidden in the boat or swum ashore, unnoticed?

"Please, Queen Hippolyte," he continued. "She has come to torment me, as she has done my whole life through."

"Who? Of whom do you speak?"

Her legs were growing numb in the cold water. One way or another, she would need to end this soon.

"It is Hera. Please, my Queen, let me explain."

CHAPTER 5

*T*hey marched the men up from the beach to the city walls, the women on horseback, the men struggling to keep pace on the soft grass in their sodden sandals. To their credit, they did not utter a word of complaint, although it was possible that this had more to do with the arrows trained on them than with any stoicism on their part.

The city was built on the highest of the steppes, with far-reaching views from the towers, placed at intervals overlooking the sea to the north and land to the east, west and south. The sand-coloured limestone citadel walls were lower than most she had encountered on her travels, but there was little need for protection. Before today, no one beside her women and her father had even set foot inside them. The idea of an enemy making it close enough to breach them was simply unthinkable.

Nothing compared to arriving home after a battle, even the relief of reaching Pontus' steppes. A sense of achievement and well-being filled them when they finally entered their city and breathed in the air of home, heard the laughter of the women and felt the heat of the forges and the rugged stones beneath their feet that had been set down by her mother and the Amazons before her. There were no battles here. No fights or bloodletting. This was home.

As they rode through the north gate, Hippolyte dismounted and passed off her horse to one of the stable women.

"It is this way," she began, but before she could take a further step, she found her path blocked by Penthesilea who was looking daggers at her.

"Hippolyte!"

Her voice was a low hiss but threatening, her glare unfaltering. The Queen ran her tongue over her teeth, casting her eye over the men behind them, several of whom were now shivering violently. She knew there was no escaping her sister. If she did not deal with her doubts now, then her wrath would simmer, and her temper might fray and bring war down on them all.

"We should have left them on the shore. We could have listened to them on the steppes. Why here? By the love of Aphrodite and the honour of our father, why would you allow them into our home?"

Hippolyte took a moment before replying. Losing her temper with Penthesilea only ever made matters worse, a lesson she had learnt as a child.

"Think rationally, Sister. He will not dare lie to us here. He will not risk starting a fight when we have him surrounded on all sides. And if we want to end him, we need to remove that lion skin first, which will be far easier done when he has been plied with wine and made comfortable and relaxed in the home of women. Do you not think?"

She watched as these thoughts settled in her sister's mind. Finally, Penthesilea drew in a long breath through her nose.

"This is wrong. You are defiling our home. And I do not trust them."

"Neither do I, Sister. Neither do I."

Although she prided herself on being above such petty matters, Hippolyte found herself wondering what Heracles and his men made of her home. The buildings certainly lacked the grandeur of those she so frequently passed on her travels. They did not entertain guests and had not succumbed to the Hellenic notion that opulence was something to be admired. As a result, the layout of the citadel had been dictated, as everything else in their lives, by practicality. There were no cyclopean palaces with grand colonnades and open atria. No large archways or imposing gates, although their arena was sizable, and their largest hall could hold every woman in the citadel. But for the most part, their buildings were small, plain structures built from the densely packed yellow-grey stones that were found in abundance near the cliffs. The alleyways that ran between them were wide enough for two horses to pass, going to or from the stables in the centre of the city, where the armoury was also located.

However, simplicity of style did not mean that they were without their luxuries, and food was not the only commodity they possessed in abundance. The women had more than their fair share of gemstones and jewels, given in payment for their services and worn with pride. Stone or copper bathtubs could be found in almost all the homes, together with a plethora of oils and flowers to scent the water. But these were not a sign of vanity or frivolity. Like everything in Themiscyra, they had a purpose. The oil from a yarrow root would ease the inflammation of swollen joints. Tension and stiff muscles could be ameliorated with juniper and helichrysum, and even the aroma of clove oil could lessen pain, although not as effectively as when applied topically. The oils and herbs available in the bathrooms of Themiscyra would have put any great palace to shame. Not that she was intending to offer Heracles a soak in one of her tubs.

They silently weaved their way up the stone paths of the city. The laughter of children would normally be commonplace, but this evening there was none at all. With each step they took, the inhabitants disappeared into their homes and workshops. From the way they were gazing all around them and their slower pace, Hippolyte could tell that Heracles and his men wanted to stop and look more closely or ask questions. But they were not here to observe or learn about their way of life. They were here so she could decide what to do with them, and they slowly continued on their way towards the central building.

Palace was the word she had most often heard in respect of the residences of kings and queens, but that term did not seem appropriate here. There were no marble floors, and the cobblestone walls were no different from those of the stables. They ate from platters no grander than those used in homes near the gates of the citadel. Besides, palaces were inhabited and controlled by kings. The queens who resided in them were nothing more than puppets. Worse than that, even. Their sole purpose was to provide an heir for the king. They did not rule. They did not lead. They were not queens in the mould of Hippolyte.

"Are you sure you want to do this, Sister?" Penthesilea whispered as they reached the Palace steps. "It is not too late. We can end them here and now. The gods will grant us mercy. They came to us."

"This way will be best," Hippolyte said, gently brushing her sister's hand with the tips of her fingers, before turning to Heracles. She lifted her chin, commanding the attention of the men as she spoke.

"You understand that when you leave here it will be in a spirit of goodwill or else not at all," she said to him.

"I am confident it will be the former," he replied, with not a hint of a smile on his face.

The Queen and her sisters led the men through the many corridors, their footsteps echoing on the slate floors. The aroma of roasting meat suddenly floated around them and stomachs growled in response.

A feast would have been prepared for their return from battle. When their bodies had been cleansed and their injuries tended, they would indulge in the spoils of the hunts that had taken place in their absence. Deer, wild boar, rabbits. Flesh so tender, it would fall from the bone; the fat, crisp and juicy. Enough flavour to ensure that when they closed their eyes, their senses were as satisfied as their stomachs.

But Heracles' appearance had put paid to their usual practices, and tonight would, no doubt, be a more subdued affair than normal. Still, the clattering of pots and pans came from the kitchens, and Hippolyte hoped that there would soon be something to eat. They had taken the men into their home; they would need to feed them, too.

By tradition, Greek men and women gathered in separate rooms, where they could talk of matters of interest to their sex. Typically, the women would use these spaces to weave and practise their instruments and discuss issues away from the ears of the men, who in their turn would discuss things that they considered too crude or of no consequence to the women.

But Hippolyte and her women were not Greek; they were Amazon. Every inch of the city and the lands around it, from the seashore and the crumbling cliff faces to the lush grasslands and rivers beyond, was a sanctuary for women. Every action taken and decision made was for their benefit and security. As such, the Queen led the men through the innermost parts of the citadel and into one of its courtyards, with perfect confidence.

It was the smallest of three courtyards and offered no view. The lack of natural light made it feel somewhat inhospitable. Shadows overlapped shadows and kept the area cool, while a wind funnelled in, scattering the leaves from the few spindly trees that grew there in pots, bringing with it an undertone of manure from the stables. It was a space rarely used except, perhaps, by young girls who awoke in the night with the desire to practise their sword skills without the need to go far from their chambers.

"Please, take a seat," Hippolyte said, indicating the grey-stone benches around the edge of the space.

The men did as instructed, and when each of them was seated, the sisters did likewise. There were other women standing by in adjacent corridors, who would be in place to defend their Queen before any man had time to finish drawing his sword. It was not that Hippolyte did not have faith in the power of xenia, the undisputed tradition that a guest should never do harm to their host, but it paid to be sure.

"So, you have our undivided attention," she said, leaning forwards. "Tell me why you think the Goddess Hera is so intent on your demise that she would come to Pontus and masquerade as one of my women to bring it about?"

Heracles hesitated for a moment before pushing back his shoulders, not so much to appear arrogant, but just enough to lend weight to the words that he was about to speak.

"I am the son of Zeus," he said.

The Queen stifled a smile.

"You are hardly the only one to hold that title," she replied. "From what I have heard, your father has quite the eye for mortal women."

A small smile tilted the corner of Heracles' mouth.

"Yes, it is true. My father's gaze often strays from Olympus and, unfortunately, his wife. And while the blood that flows in my veins has benefited me in ways most men could only dream of, I have endured and continue to endure that which few others could withstand. Because of her."

It was clear he had deliberately avoided saying her name, as if it would be as ashes upon his tongue.

"You are not the only bastard child of Zeus. Why has she chosen you as the target of her wrath? You must have provoked her anger in some way."

Heracles scowled.

"If I have, then it took place in my mother's womb, for since the day of my birth, and even before that, she has never ceased in her attempt to rob me of my life. When she failed to prevent my birth, she sent vipers into my crib."

Hippolyte felt her eyebrows rise.

"How did you survive?"

"The same way I have withstood everything she has thrown at me. By sheer strength and courage. But every attempt that I have foiled has only seen her become more determined than ever. And when she knew she could not beat me by hurting me, she sought out other, crueller ways to destroy me. For it is not in our own deaths that we face the worst torment a man can know. It is in the deaths of those we love."

He paused again. The air had changed. A glacial chill had descended on them.

"She killed your children?"

It was Melanippe who spoke. Her voice was more delicate

than the Queen's, more lilting and higher in pitch and, most likely, more compassionate, too. Heracles tilted his head and frowned a little, as if he had forgotten she was there. Or that any others were there at all.

"I only wish that were so. But what she did was worse. She clouded my mind so that I could not even have told you my own name, far less those of my wife and child. In my insanity, I believed they were monsters, set on the destruction of my family. And so I did what any father would do. I believed I was protecting them."

His eyes were glazed with tears as silence descended upon the courtyard. Hippolyte was a hardened woman who had brought about more deaths in her life than an army of hoplites. Yet this was beyond anything she could fathom. She swallowed hard, before she spoke.

"You killed your wife and children?"

The dip of his chin was all the answer she needed.

"Strangled them with my bare hands, as if they were nothing more than serpents. By the time the madness had subsided, they were lifeless on the ground at my feet and there was nothing I could do. I have been seeking redemption ever since."

"Can one?" Penthesilea asked, from beside the Queen. "Can one gain redemption for killing a loved one?"

From anyone else, this might have sounded like an insult. A comment spoken purely to anger the warrior. But Hippolyte knew her sister's mind as well as she knew her own and understood that the words had come from a place of genuine curiosity. Thankfully, if Heracles had been offended by the question, he did not show it.

"I visited the Oracle of Delphi. I knelt before the Pythia and breathed in her incense. I wept on her floor. Wept more tears than I knew a man could hold. It was she who told me what I must do to gain the gods' forgiveness. It was she who said that it was King Eurystheus who could grant me purification, absolving me of my sins, and that I could only gain this in service to him. All my labours, all that I have endured, have been at his whim."

"And he is the one who sent you here?"

For the first time, Heracles seemed lost for words. Seeing his discomfort, Hippolyte signalled to one of the women, who brought a jug of water and a cup which she handed to him. His eyes met hers as he gestured his thanks with a dip of his head.

"His daughter, Admete, has one desire: to possess that zoster which you wear, and I have been sent to retrieve it."

He placed his cup on the seat beside him and locked eyes with her. The only other time she fixed her gaze so intently on a man was on the battlefield, just before she relieved him of his life. In that moment, she knew every thought that stirred behind those condemned eyes: what he was thinking; how he was praying to every god he could name that by some miracle he might be spared the fatal blow, even as he knew, in his heart of hearts, that he would not be. But here, now, with her sisters beside her and Heracles' men waiting with bated breaths, she sensed it was he who was reading her and not the other way around.

"Queen Hippolyte, we are both warriors. We understand that in any battle we must endure losses in order to be victorious. I ask this because I have no other choice."

The Queen felt her chest tighten with compassion. They were both demi-gods and ichor ran in their veins, but that was where any similarity ended. She had grown up the pride of her father, with gifts bestowed on her to the point of indulgence, but here was a man wracked with pain and loneliness.

"This daughter of Eurystheus, Admete, what does she want with my zoster? Is she a warrior?"

Heracles' laugh was so sudden that Melanippe jumped beside her.

"No. She's just a spoiled princess, who I think believes that if she owns the prized possession of the Amazon Queen, then she will be imbued with her strength and fortitude, not to mention her respect. And I am happy to let her imagine that. My part will be over by the time that she realises she is still the same, snivelling, little girl that she always was without it, and I will be one step closer to my purification. That is the only reason I wish for the belt. I hope you believe me. I have no personal desire for it, just as I have no desire to hurt you or any of your women."

As a new hush fell, Hippolyte studied Heracles, taking her time to scrutinise the knots in his brow and the lines on his sun-weathered face. It was not just a matter of whether or not she believed him, the zoster had been gifted to her by Ares. What would it mean if she gave it away?

"And if I say no?" she asked, although she already knew the answer.

"I cannot leave Themiscyra without that belt," Heracles said, plainly and without emotion. "And I cannot be killed while I wear this skin, which I have no intention of removing, whatever the situation."

He was not a man who skirted around the issue at hand, and she admired that, even though she was still undecided on how to react. Her choices were limited, but there were still options. As Queen, it was her job to find them.

"In that case," she said, rising to her feet. "Consider this a gift, from the Queen of the Amazons, to her first—and I hope only—guest here in Themiscyra."

As her fingers found the buckle on her belt, she watched as Heracles buried his head in his hands, and a sound akin to muffled weeping was heard. She removed the zoster, immediately sensing its absence against her stomach. She pushed the sensation away and presented the belt to Heracles.

His eyes lingered on the metal plates. His lips opened, although no words fell from them. Something unique had happened in that courtyard. An exchange like no other before had taken place, and it was the blond-haired man beside Heracles who acknowledged this.

With a coy smile on his lips, he said, "This is reason to celebrate."

CHAPTER 6

The Amazons found no pleasure overindulging in wine. The throbbing head and clouded thoughts that afflicted them after such revelries dulled their instincts and weakened their resolve. Instead, when struck with the desire for deeper relaxation, they threw a selection of leaves and seeds on the fire where they would pop and fizz in the flames. The rich and pungent fumes they emitted swirled in mists so intoxicating that the women's minds expanded beyond all comprehension. They would see an entire world in the reflection of a raindrop or hear a melody, harmonised at counterpoint, from a single, unpitched note. They would dance until the morning rays bleached the moon from the sky and their feet were black with ash from the cold embers. They would sing and sway and cast all memories of their losses in battle and all the bloodshed aside. And afterwards, they would sleep, not rising again until late into the next day, clear-headed and ready to train. But antics such as these, which lowered their inhibitions, were not called for that night. Instead, they moved from the courtyard to one of the dining halls and settled for a feast of venison.

QUEENS OF THEMISCYRA | 45

"This feels all wrong. We are giving them our food and acting as if they were our guests, when they have stolen from us." Penthesilea said, eyeing the men with distrust.

Hippolyte had known this moment would come, that Penthesilea would question her decision to gift Heracles the belt. Antiope and Melanippe might have also disagreed with her action—every woman in Themiscyra could have disagreed —but it would only ever be Penthesilea who voiced her dissent. And no matter how fearless the Queen was when chasing down warriors with spears, the same could not be said of her on those occasions when she was forced to face her sister's wrath. She had tried to avoid her all evening, but she knew this conversation was coming, and now, as a lyre was plucked melodically to the hammering of a drum, she had given up and stood still long enough for Penthesilea to corner her and demand her attention.

"They have stolen nothing. I gave him the zoster, as you are aware."

"It was as good as stolen," Penthesilea said again. "A gift from our father, and you gave it to him because he threatened to kill you, otherwise."

"You would rather I let him follow through on such a threat?"

"You think he would have stood a chance?" Penthesilea hissed in anger into her sister's ear. "There is not a man on Earth who can strike you or me, if we care to defend ourselves."

She had been the same since she was a child. Tempestuous. Impulsive. But also, truthful. In all her battles, the only wounds that she had ever suffered had been to her pride—when Antiope had fired off a shot before her, or Melanippe's horse had scattered dust in the eyes of her mount—and incidents like this were few and far between. Hippolyte could count them on a single hand.

"What you have said is true," she replied, softly. "And no mortal man can defeat us, but he is not a man. He is a demi-god. And his father is Zeus."

"And our father is Ares."

"The zoster is merely an object," Hippolyte continued, ignoring Penthesilea's interruption. "It was a gift, yes, and a treasured one indeed, but it wields no power of its own. It is nothing without us behind it. And xenia is sacred, Sister. A guest cannot harm their host without enticing the wrath of Zeus himself, as you know. We are safer with them in our home than anywhere else, and tomorrow they will be on their way, and our lives will return to normal."

"The sooner they are gone, the better."

Silence followed as Penthesilea took another large gulp from her cup. Hippolyte cast her gaze across the room, where large wooden tables had been laid with silver platters piled high with venison. Ten guests added little to their numbers, but the effect their presence was having on her women was evident. They were not deceived by the wiles of men nor were they impressed or intimidated by them. But contrary to rumour, the Amazons had no hatred of men in general. Every year they took to the beds of the Gargareans and enjoyed nights filled with laughter and copulation. Some of her women had formed bonds with these men—based not merely on how readily they gave them daughters but also on their conversation and the enjoyment they found in each other's bodies—and would spend their time with the same man, year after year. Others preferred to experience different men. Different bodies. This arrangement was older than memory and the women trusted the Gargareans. Any male child born as a result of this coupling would be returned to the Gargareans, to be raised as a fighter. The girls would become Amazons like their mothers, the greatest warriors on Earth.

But these guests were not Gargarean and had created an air of uncertainty and distrust that they undoubtedly deserved. As such, the women's conversations were guarded and the laughter that usually echoed so freely through the hall was muted.

Hippolyte's eyes fell on the man who had caught her attention on the shore, and her skin prickled as she noticed that, once again, he was looking at her. Without water flattening his hair, it was thicker than it had seemed before, but his stare was as penetrating as it had been.

"He has not taken his eyes off you all night," Penthesilea said, following the Queen's gaze. "I do not like it."

"You still fear he will try to kidnap me? I have told you already, we are safe with them here."

"I do not know what it is, but there is something about him that unnerves me. More than Heracles, even. Did you catch his name?"

"I do not believe I did."

"Then I shall go and find it out."

Penthesilea had barely taken three strides, when the young man rose to his feet. He moved effortlessly, gliding between the chairs and tables and then straight past Penthesilea. Without once looking away from Hippolyte, he strode right up to her and held out his hand.

It was a simple greeting that she had seen men use frequently during her travels. Several had attempted it with her —those who had not bowed in humble deference or simply retreated into themselves, desperately trying to hide the fear that overcame them when faced with the Amazon Queen. But she was not a man, and so she left his hand hovering in the space between them.

A hue of pink came to his cheeks as he lowered his hand.

"I wished to introduce myself. I am Theseus, son of King Aegeus of Athens. It is a great honour to meet you, Queen Hippolyte."

"So much of an honour that your friend threatened to shed blood on our shores."

It was Penthesilea who spoke, from behind him. Clearly, she would not allow her sister to be accosted in a such a manner, and Hippolyte felt a twinge of mirth at her sister's protectiveness. She needed no protection. None of them did. But it was the strength of this bond that kept them all safe on the battlefield. Theseus turned, observed Penthesilea briefly, then returned his attention to Hippolyte.

"I understand the manner in which Heracles expressed himself may have come across as impertinent. I apologise for my friend. And I am grateful that, in your wisdom, you have seen fit to come to a satisfactory agreement, which I know was his aim."

Once again, it was Penthesilea who answered. She had now moved to the side of Theseus, as if trying to form a barrier between the young man and the Queen.

"The arrangement is only satisfactory to you," she spat, "for it only serves you and your cousin. I struggle to see what this has done for us, other than giving us a smaller portion of meat to eat at dinner tonight."

A small smile twitched on Theseus' lips.

"I am sorry that you see it this way. Tell me, my Queen, do you feel the same as your warrior here?"

His attention was back on her again. In the soft light of the oil lamps, his deep, hazel eyes glinted with a restlessness like the stirring of the ocean, she thought. A desire to prove himself. That was it.

"I am more than a warrior, boy," Penthesilea snarled at the insult. "I am Penthesilea, daughter of Ares, God of War, Princess of the Amazons, and it will serve you well to remember that."

In spite of her harsh words, not to mention a reputation that Theseus would undoubtedly know about as well as that of the Queen, he paid Penthesilea no notice. His eyes remained locked on Hippolyte. His breathing was slow, his expression calm, as he awaited her answer.

"I suspect that only time will tell," she said.

Then she turned to Penthesilea and added, "Sister, perhaps you could see to it that our other guests are being taken care of. I would hate for them to think of us as poor hosts."

She could almost hear her sister's angry thoughts, and no doubt she would pay the price later, but she knew there would be no open disagreement now. Not in front of others, and particularly before strangers.

And so Penthesilea strode to where Heracles and the rest of his men were sitting at a long table. One of them was talking in an animated fashion, waving his hands high above his head, a fist clenched as if holding an imaginary dagger, his eyes wide. The women nearby looked on, unimpressed by whatever tale this man was regaling his friends with. She was not the only one who noticed this.

"It would appear that our hosts are not in awe of our tales of battle," Theseus said.

"Why would we need tales?" she asked. "Unlike your women, we are well-versed in warfare. Each woman at that table next to them has ended more lives than your entire party."

"I do not doubt it. I suspect it is you who should be telling us the stories."

"Without question."

The two of them remained silent for a moment. The man on Heracles' table was growing less passionate, although he had not yet abandoned his story entirely, now leaning forwards and making claws of his hands, as if portraying a giant beast.

"May I ask you a question?" Theseus enquired.

His eyes narrowed on her, although there was barely a crease on his youthful face.

"Possibly, although I may choose not to answer it."

"I understand."

He hesitated before speaking again.

"Do you find it difficult ruling alone?"

"You mean without a king?"

Laughter, laced with a contempt she made no effort to suppress, burst forth.

"That is not what I said."

"No, but it is certainly what you implied, with little subtlety."

"No, it was not implied, either. You have misconstrued my meaning."

His voice had hardened a fraction, and there was a terseness now that bordered on petulance and caused an unusual heat to rise in Hippolyte.

"I, the Queen, have misconstrued what you have said to me in my own home?"

"Yes. I am sorry, but you have."

Hippolyte could feel her back teeth grinding against one another. Xenia, she reminded herself, went both ways. A guest could not harm their host, but in the same manner, all visitors inside her home fell under her protection, and unless she wished to incur the wrath of Zeus, she would need to hold her temper. And yet Theseus showed not a hint of restraint in his speech. Rather, he seemed to be struggling to hold his emotions in check, to keep his anger at bay. Why he should display such indignation when it was he who had insulted her, was beyond comprehension.

"I did not mention a king," he spoke slowly. "It was you that brought that word into our discussion. I merely mentioned ruling alone. My father is a king, as I have already said. King of Athens. He too rules alone. It is hard for him at times, bearing all the responsibilities of a kingdom single-handedly."

"He has advisors, surely?" Hippolyte asked, bluntly.

"Yes, of course. Although I do not believe he always trusts their judgement."

"Then I struggle to believe it would be any different if he had a wife. After all, from what I know of your lands, if the king does not have confidence in a group of educated men, leaders in their fields, who have been appointed to guide him, I feel it is unlikely that he would act on the advice of a woman who has been placed by his side for the sole purpose of opening her legs and providing him with an heir. I'm assuming, of course, that she would not be trained in the strategy of war. Because you would never permit a woman of Athens to do that, would you? To train. To learn to fight. Your question was therefore point-less, no doubt intended to invoke some emotional response in me. If your father is lonely, Theseus, I suspect that this is of his own choosing."

The speed at which Hippolyte had found herself riled and spitting words like venom surprised her. Such a reaction was not uncommon in Penthesilea or Antiope, but she failed to recall an occasion when she herself had so readily succumbed to ill temper, especially as she'd been struggling to justify her previous indignation. Perhaps it was the stress of the day, for it had been an arduous one and that coming on top of leaving early the previous morning with little sleep after the battle. Given her obvious irritation, she expected Theseus to apologise or at least show a little deference or humility. But these attributes did not appear to be ones that Theseus possessed in abundance.

"So, I take it you are not ready to accept a marriage proposal this evening," he said.

For a moment, a stunned silence filled the air and all the other sounds of the room faded away. And then the Queen threw her head back and laughed but not as she had done earlier. There was no bitterness or resentment this time. What he had asked was truly hilarious. If nothing else, Theseus had a sense of humour. He had broken the tension that had momentarily shackled them and released it in a manner that brought her genuine amusement.

"What would I gain from marriage? I have no desire to extend my lands and we have everything we need right here. And I have even less desire to become a trophy for some egotistical king feeding his gout with wine and red meat while his men die in far off lands, or to be a home for his seed, while simultaneously being usurped by whores in my own bed."

"You have a poor view of kings."

"I have met many. I consider it a fair assessment."

Theseus pressed his lips together. How old was he? she wondered. The stubble on his chin was soft and downy and still patchy in places. His skin was not at all weathered. Twenty? Perhaps younger still. The confidence in his eyes gave her cause to wonder how many wars he had seen, if any. He shifted back, perching on the edge of one of the tables.

"But it would not need to be like that, do you not see?

Marriage can be a partnership. *We* could be a partnership. Imagine it. Two great leaders, both gifted by the gods. What a force we would be together. And imagine our children. They'd be warriors, the like of which the world has never known."

The energy that rose from him was infectious and the peridot hues that now shone in his eyes were almost mesmerising.

"I think you may have indulged in too much wine," she said. "You have lost your senses."

"My cup has been filled only with water, for I wished to keep a clear head. Tell me, Queen Hippolyte, will you think on it, at least? Would you consider becoming my wife? Hippolyte, Queen of Athens. It has a rather nice ring to it, would you not say?"

THE FOLLOWING MORNING, they returned to the shore. Four women carried the rowing boat across the beach to the water, the vessel propped on their shoulders as effortlessly as if it were a bound lamb. Behind them, eight of Heracles' men chewed on the bark of a ginger root, in an attempt to abate the sickness they had inflicted upon themselves with too much wine the night before. More than once, one of them lost his footing and slid on the sand, and Hippolyte watched the smirks of her women. Only Heracles and Theseus were clear-eyed and sure-footed. Heracles had even gone so far as to remove the lion's garb on the walk down to the water's edge. A grand gesture, indeed.

At the shore, the waves crashed, and the morning mist still lingered as the last of the dawn clouds fled towards the horizon.

"Thank you, again," Heracles said.

He stood ankle deep in the water. The Queen and her sisters had made the short journey riding bareback on their horses, which now stood in the same formation as they had the day before, her women at her sides, bows in their hands. This time, however, the arrows remained in their quivers.

"This gift will not be forgotten."

"And I wish you luck with your labours. May the gods be on your side."

"That would be helpful," Heracles chuckled, before offering a small half bow and retreating deeper into the water, where he helped his sluggish men to push their boat out. As they waded deep enough to climb aboard, Theseus remained, hanging back until enough distance had been placed between the boat and himself that he could no longer hear his companions' voices over the water. At this point, he approached the Queen. She did not move away or dismiss him. She wished to speak to him alone, as well as to hear what he had to say.

"Sisters, the women need to start their training for the day. We lost enough time yesterday. Please take them over to the plains."

The young women exchanged worried glances.

"I will be fine," she said with certainty. "Unless you do not trust my ability to handle myself with one young man?"

Nothing more was said. The three sisters dug their heels in and turned their mounts in such a tight circle that they carved trenches in the sand as they moved. They would not go far. Hippolyte knew that after all that had transpired the previous day, Penthesilea would no more let her sister out of her sight than she would turn her back on her when they sparred. The thought made her smile. Whatever rivalry plagued the sisters, it was far surpassed by their loyalty to one another.

"You will need to swim to catch up with your boat,"

Hippolyte said, looking down from her horse at Theseus.

"I can manage that easily. It would not be entirely untrue to say that water runs in my veins."

He grinned, and once again, Hippolyte found herself wondering about his age. Maybe only eighteen or nineteen? Old enough to consider himself a man, yet still oblivious of the burdens that fell on one who was truly accountable for their actions.

After a moment, he started speaking again.

"My proposal to you last night, I wish to give it context."

"Beyond your insanity?"

His laugh was gentle. Endearing, even.

"Perhaps some degree of insanity does indeed play a part. I will not deny that. The way I feel here, on this beach with you but unable to touch you, that alone is enough to drive a man to madness."

These were not words the Queen had expected to hear, but she did not stop him. It was not the first time a man had offered her his hand, and she doubted it would be the last. She remained silent and allowed Theseus to continue.

"What I told you about my father ruling on his own is true, but it was not always this way. Before I returned to him, he took a wife, Medea, and her wiles were nearly the death of us both. And because of her, I am fearful that the same fate may befall me. That I might be deceived. Athens is a new city, still finding its way. But it will not always be like that. One day it will be the greatest in all of Greece. Whoever marries me, it will be to their family's great benefit."

"Then you are lucky, for you will have the pick of every noble woman that Greece has to offer."

"But that is not what I want. I do not want my marriage to be based on a political or financial advantage for another person, family or state. I want a queen who will help me rule. Who can form strategies with me. Who will stand beside me. I want you, Hippolyte. I need you. There is no one else on Earth who would be a greater queen than you."

As Hippolyte looked down at the boy, she felt a tenderness towards him. Despite his youth and obvious rashness, he was right. There could never be a greater queen than her, for she was already the greatest.

"Your offer is endearing and flattering. And I hope that one day you will find the queen you seek," she said gently.

There was nothing more she could add.

Theseus took her refusal with grace, bowing low before rising again and placing his hand on the flank of her horse. His fingertips were only inches from her knee, and Hippolyte could almost feel the warmth flowing from him into her.

"I will come back for you, my Queen. And I know you will say yes to my proposal then," he said.

He did not wait for a response. Removing his hand from the horse, he fixed his hazel eyes on her one last time before turning and sprinting into the sea. Raising his arms above his head, he leapt into a dive and plunged beneath the surf. As he disappeared under the surface of the water, Hippolyte felt a surge of fear, for the waves had grown higher since the boat had rowed from the shore. A moment passed and still he had not emerged. Had he drowned? she wondered. Had his proposal been his undoing?

She urged her horse forwards into the shallows. And then, there in the distance, she saw him, much further out than she would have thought a man could swim in such a short time, already closing on the boat. Hippolyte found herself compelled to watch and wondered whether there might be truth about there being water in his veins after all.

PART II

CHAPTER 7

or the Amazons, time passed with a sense of certainty, reflected in the predictability of the changing seasons and the wax and wane of the moon, as sure as the flowering of buds in spring and the lengthening of the days, as Helios's sun garnered its strength for the approaching summer. The women were swept into the future just as the waters of a river are carried to the sea. And yet it was the unknown, the unpredictability of that journey, that was so alluring. One day the sea might be as calm as water in a cup, so still that a swallow's reflection could dance on the surface in perfect symmetry with the bird above. And the next, violent, white-crested waves could appear, rising like mountains and then crashing down again, as if spurred on by the wrath of the gods. And those same swallows would flock inland, hoping to find shelter.

Such were the lives of the Amazons. Sometimes weeks passed without a battle, or longer still. They would remain in Pontus, rehearsing drills on the steppes to perfect their sword skills, which they would demonstrate to each other in the arena of Themiscyra. They would salt their meats and train the children. They would mend their weapons and hammer new half-moon shields and breastplates, the copper emerging from the flames with the oil-slick colours of heat still swirling on their surface. They would strengthen their armour with further sheets of copper and bronze, the luxury of time allowing them to chisel patterns or motifs on the surfaces—the same ones that they would ink into their own skin, on their hands and forearms and biceps.

Some days, when the water was calm enough, they would take their boats into the shallows above the reefs, where the fish they caught could feed fifty of them and still leave flesh for curing. Then they would spend their evenings talking, laughing and reminiscing once more about the battles they had won and placing wagers on who would be the next narcissistic king to seek their services. And yet, alongside their screams of laughter were memories of other screams, those of pain and fear.

During the course of her reign, they had fought so many campaigns that the Queen could no longer keep a tally. Battles on green pastures, where bodies fell among the grass as flowers drowned in blood. Battles on arid plains, where not a scrap of grass grew, and the women tied cloths around their eyes to shield them from the sand, fighting blind and guiding themselves to the kill by the sounds of their enemies' laboured breathing and clumsy steps. They had fought battles that lasted mere hours and wars long enough for the moon to wax and wane above them. And they had lost women, many good women, who had been granted the most honourable death there was. For only death in battle was lauded by the Amazons.

Yet as well as death, there was new life, and within the walls of Themiscyra the cries of new-borns were heard each year and the noise of the children as they grew stronger and more vibrant. From dawn to dusk, their training grounds were full of young girls wielding their first wooden swords and riding bareback on horses they had raised as foals. They tamed birds, learnt to swim in the waters and brought down deer. Antiope was the strongest teacher among them. The one with the most patience to supervise their training, guide their hands and correct their postures so that they might kneel or stand on their horses without risk of falling.

One morning, a little over six years after Heracles' visit, it was Hippolyte who was watching the young girls practise mounting and dismounting in the fields. She had brought a small bowl of olives and had rested them on the stump beside her while she observed. In the mid-morning sun, the hum of insects and the sweet scents of mint leaf and lemon balm were all around. One of Antiope's daughters, Echephyle, had caught her attention. At nine years of age, her niece's riding ability was equal to many of those old enough to fight in battle, although her knife and bow work required attention. Even if these were to improve at the same rate as her other skills, she would not allow the girl to see action just yet. In battle, each Amazon had to hold her own, or she would die, and it was not a risk the Queen was ready to take. Four years more, and then she would be ready.

Echephyle was currently kneeling bareback on a mare, her balance not quite steady enough to make the transition to standing. Each time she tried, one of her feet would slip and she would slide off to the side, grabbing the horse's mane just above its withers and pulling herself back onto her knees. Hippolyte could recall how desperate the girl had been to ride, even before she could properly walk. As a toddler, she would often slip away from her nursemaids, only to be found later in the stables or watching the adults sparring. Was Echephyle a future leader? Hippolyte wondered. There was something about her. A tenacity and fierceness that stood out, even among her most dedicated peers. Would she be a future Queen to lead the Amazons?

It was not a thought Hippolyte ever dwelt on for long—were anything to happen to her, Penthesilea would take up the mantle, without question—but she could not help wondering from time to time. For, as she had said to her sister the night the men had arrived on their shores, they were not invincible, and Heracles was not the only demi-god eager to prove themselves a hero.

With her eyes still on Echephyle, Hippolyte picked an olive from the bowl and chewed it slowly, savouring its saltiness. When the sound came of footsteps approaching from behind, a heaviness came over her, and she refused to alter her gaze. Even when Penthesilea appeared at her side, she kept her attention on the girl.

"Why are you still here?" Penthesilea's voice was tense, frustrated. "Everyone is preparing to leave."

Everyone rarely meant quite that many. For the last week, the nomads had been arriving in Themiscyra, slowly at first and then in ever increasing numbers. They massed outside the walls of the citadel, ready to move out with the rest of the Amazon women when the day arrived.

It was not just those hoping to bear children who made the journey south to the Gargareans. There were those who had birthed boys who were now old enough and strong enough to make the journey to their fathers. Most sat between their mothers' legs, astride their horses, absorbing the last maternal warmth they would ever feel. Others would travel strapped to their mothers' backs.

There were also women, past the age of childbearing, who had formed relationships with the Gargarean men that continued long after their wombs had stopped being productive. And there were those who simply enjoyed the sense of occasion. The chance to ride out en masse and to sing and dance without an impending battle looming over them. Of course, there were many who stayed behind. Those with young children, yes, but also a select few to guard Themiscyra and protect the city if the need ever arose. Not that it ever had.

Hippolyte spat the olive stone into her hand before dropping it to the ground beside her.

"I will not be travelling with you this year."

"Why not?" Penthesilea's voice pitched higher.

"You know why."

Even without turning to look at her, Hippolyte could sense her sister stiffening. For a moment they stood in silence, watching Echephyle on her horse. Perhaps coming here this morning had not been the wisest of decisions, but given that every Amazon of childbearing age was preparing for her journey to the distant mountain ridge that lay between their lands and those of the Gargareans, there were few places in which she might seek refuge from the bitter truth.

"The gods will have their reasons, Sister," Penthesilea said softly. "You must believe in them."

"I do. I understand that. I accept it and I am at peace with it. But there is still no reason for me to travel with you. Not when I cannot bear a child."

There it was. She had said the words out loud. She was the Queen of the most powerful women on the Earth. Ichor of the gods flowed in her veins. On a battlefield, she was omnipotent.

She was undefeated. Every challenge that life had thrown at her she had met with a spear in her hand, ready to attack and conquer. Everything, until this.

"That is not true. You can bear children. You have borne a child," Penthesilea told her.

"One child. A boy. A decade ago, now."

"You have not lain with the right man. That is all. You should lie with Siranos. He has provided daughters for both Iole and Kepes. And two sons with other women, as well. Or there is Ouras. He has fathered daughters for Antiope and Melanippe."

"Last year I lay with them both. And a dozen other warriors of strong seed besides. I spent every night with a different man. It is not the seed that is the issue."

Silence swept in on a breeze, encircling the women and trapping them with their thoughts and the words they had spoken. As sisters, they usually conversed with such ease. After all, they had been together since before they could form memories. But no words or solace could be found.

"Sister, you need to go," Hippolyte said, shattering the silence like ice on a water trough. "I am at peace with this. This is the will of the gods. They will grant me a child, a daughter, when the time is right. And I will be ready and willing. But this is not the time."

"How do you know, if you will not come with us?"

"I know. Trust me. Please, Sister, do not press me on this."

"But what will you do? You cannot think to stay here all this time on your own."

"I will hardly be alone. I have plenty to keep me busy."

Penthesilea's faced remained creased with concern, and her voice dropped to a near whisper.

"We will be gone for two moons," she said. "We have never been apart for this long."

Hippolyte could not help but smile at her sister's childlike tone. This, from the fiercest of her warriors,

"Well, for two months, you get to be in charge. Think of it as training for the future."

She anticipated some enthusiasm with this realisation, yet Penthesilea remained solemn.

"That day will never come. I will always protect you with my own life. You know that."

"Go." Hippolyte drew her sister in for an embrace. "And enjoy yourself. You have gifts for the men? And offerings for the gods to give upon your arrival?"

"I have." They embraced again. "We will be back in two moons," she said.

"Ride safe, Sister."

Despite the departure of such a vast number from Themiscyra that day, there were still many women who remained. Alongside those who were too young, there were the nursing mothers, who had fallen pregnant during the last visit to the Gargareans. There were women who had not yet killed in battle —true virgins in the ways of the Amazons—and therefore not allowed to attend the annual gathering. Lastly, were the women still recovering from mishap in the more recent battles, whose bodies would not benefit from the long journey, and who thus remained behind to rest and recover and regain the strength in their muscles and the skills with their weapons that time away from training had taken from them.

The day after the exodus, Hippolyte stayed for a while, watching the young girls ride. After Echephyle failed to master the same move after several attempts, the Queen abandoned the role of passive observer and went up to the girl to offer guidance.

"You are trying to lift yourself from here," she said, tapping her knees. "You need to focus your strength here and here."

She tapped her stomach and toes. The young girl nodded silently, keen to absorb all the advice the Queen could offer her.

"And kick the horse into a canter. You should be one with your beast. If she is moving faster, you will move faster, too."

She slapped the mare's flank.

"Go. Let me see it."

While Echephyle failed on her next attempt, by the time the sun had begun its afternoon descent, she had mastered the skill not only at a canter but at a gallop, too.

A feeling of pride warmed the Queen as she left Echephyle to tend to her horse and headed back up to the citadel. Maybe this was her purpose in life. As a queen, she should be a mother to all her people. Perhaps that was why the gods had withheld a daughter from her for so long.

The next day, she followed the same loose schedule. She woke before dawn to watch the sun rise above the steppes, then headed down to help the girls with their drills. In the afternoon, she found herself addressing simple chores that often got neglected when the prospect of a fight took precedence.

A few days later, Hippolyte found herself in the armoury sharpening swords and restitching the leather quivers. It was true there were women who could do this for her, who were probably more skilled at such tasks than she was, but how could she lead people in all areas of their lives if she did not at least partake in some of their duties?

She slowly ran the whetstone along the edge of a sword, starting at the hilt. The low, familiar resonance was as comforting to her as the scent of leather and wax polish. Her hand swept down to the very tip, before she returned to the hilt and repeated the action, as the blade grew smoother and gleamed brighter with every stroke. It was more than a mere aesthetic improvement. A blunt blade cost both time and energy, which could mean death for the person wielding it. All her women took pride in this task, but today she took even more care than normal, labouring over each stroke, watching her reflection grow clearer as her hand moved along the blade. With her sword now gleaming, her image curved across its surface. She was just reaching for her dagger, to repeat the process, when the sound of approaching footsteps stopped her.

The woman who had sought her out went by the name of Glaukia. An older woman, who seemed at first rather plain, people were drawn to her by her eyes, their hue the most vivid of blues. At that moment, she was dressed for riding, in leather trousers, tunic and sturdy boots, the latter decorated with embroidered felt bearing coloured beads sewn along the scalloped edges. She wore no cap and had no weapons strapped to her belt, but her face had all the appearance of a woman going to war.

"What is it?" Hippolyte asked, standing as she spoke and picking up the sword she had just sharpened.

Glaukia hands were stained a deep purple. She must have been collecting the herbs which grew only on the higher peaks looking out across the Black Sea. She had come some distance to reach the Queen.

"There is another ship," she said.

"Another?"

"It has dropped anchor and is still a way off."

"Show me."

Hippolyte was already moving as they spoke. Her women were four days' ride away now. If an attack were imminent, it would be the young and the old who would be forced to defend the citadel. She grabbed her horse and followed Glaukia up the steppes towards the northern ridge, offering a clear view out to sea. When they reached the summit the old woman halted and pointed.

"Do you see it?" she asked. "And there is something else - a creature - and it is swimming to our shore."

CHAPTER 8

*S*hades of blue were interlaced with bands of brilliant white as the waves rolled back and forth, darkening then brightening as wisps of clouds bowled across the sky. Such perpetual motion would have made it difficult for the Queen to lock her sights on any object, but this one was moving, disappearing under the surface for some time before reappearing, each time closer and closer to the shore.

The vessel, she could see, was not the same as the one that had come before. It was smaller and had weighed anchor further from the shore than the trireme had. It was little more than a blot on the horizon.

"It could just be passing through. Ships do pass at that distance," Hippolyte said, searching for the other shape among the waves that had once again disappeared from view.

"That's what I originally thought," Glaukia replied. "But I first spotted it when I was gathering herbs yesterday, and when I returned today, it hadn't moved. Why would it remain in such a place? And what is that creature? I thought perhaps it might be a seal or a dolphin, but why would it be alone like that? Surely, if it were injured, it would make for deeper water?"

It was a question the Queen had no answer for and was about to say as much when it once again broke the surface of the water. Its body arched forwards, long arms sweeping up and over its head before it dived back down again. There was barely time to register that it had reappeared before it was gone again. Her heart raced.

"Was that a man?" Glaukia squinted. "What man moves like that?"

"We must hasten to the beach. Now."

As Hippolyte galloped, she nocked an arrow onto her bow. By the time they reached the sand dunes, there was no mistaking it was a man, and the only place from which he could have come was the ship. How could he have survived? Over the years, many a young girl had been tricked by the glassy calm of the waters on a fine day and waded out, forgetting the treacherous currents lurking beneath the surface, only to be knocked off her feet and dragged under. Yet this man swam as if he were a creature of the sea, unconcerned by currents or rips that carried people out to their death. But why?

"Should we shoot him now?"

Glaukia had her bow raised. Her hands were weathered, liver-spotted and deeply wrinkled, but her grasp was unwavering. More women had now joined them. Most were older warriors, too old to bear fruit from a trip to the Gargareans, but Hippolyte knew that whatever state their wombs might be in, their aim would be true. These women could fight.

"It is one man. We should find out what he has come for."

"He has invaded our lands. That is enough."

Soon the figure was in shallower water. Rising to his feet, he stood proud. His blond hair was darkened by the water. His stubble seemed to have grown denser since his last visit, and even from that distance, she thought she could see a glimmer of mischief in his eyes.

His face broke into a wide smile.

"Lower your weapons," Hippolyte said.

The women looked at her in disbelief, their bowstrings still taut, their arrows ready to fly from between their fingertips.

"Lower them," she said again, although she herself kept her arrow nocked.

She took a few steps forward, not so far as to reach the water, but close enough to separate her from the group. Theseus strode waist deep in the waves toward her, his torso glistening with beads of salt water. He had grown bigger, too, she thought. Taller, broader. He must have been younger than she had imagined when they had met before, for now he approached her a full-grown man.

"Do you not recall what happened the last time you set foot on these shores?" she asked, knowing he was within earshot.

Theseus' smile widened. It was not the same boyish grin he had once worn. There was a depth to it now. A maturity.

"I believe I proposed marriage and you turned me down."

"I was referring to the fact that I threatened to kill you all should you return."

His smile tightened a little.

"I seem to have forgotten that part. I came purely for the first part. Has it been long enough? Have you had time to consider what an extraordinary partnership we would make?"

Hippolyte did not know whether she should laugh at the man or shoot an arrow through him. Both options had their appeal.

"If that is why you have come, then you should turn around and swim back to your men."

He was only knee deep and mere metres away from her. He paused and rested his hands upon his knees. His chest rose and fell in long, laboured breaths that boarded on the theatrical.

"It is quite a long trip. I am not sure I would manage to swim all the way back without a little rest first."

"We have a fishing boat you can use. You can row, I assume?"

"And if I say that I do not wish to go, then what?"

There was so much confidence in his voice, so much arrogance it was laughable.

There was not a scrap of clothing on his body, and his thighs rippled, the contours of his muscles forming deep gullies for the water to run down. Hippolyte forced her eyes up to his face, where the smirk he was failing to suppress was enough for her to pull the string on her bow even more taut.

"If you do not leave, then you will find only humiliation on this beach."

"Is that so? Perhaps you should send your women away. I would hate for them to see you embarrassed."

Again, that same overconfidence. The way his shoulders lowered, his hand casually combing through his sodden hair. He might have been walking through an agora, inspecting ceramics or bartering down the price of wine.

"I am afraid you must have swallowed too much sea water. Even fully armed, you would not stand a chance. And here you stand without a scrap of clothing, let alone a weapon."

"Then it will be all the more humiliating for you when you are forced to yield."

Had Penthesilea been present for this deliberate provocation, her arrow would have already pierced his heart. But her sisters were not here. They would be enjoying their own entertainment—not entirely dissimilar in some ways.

Hippolyte's arrow flew through the air, but she had tempered its release, knowing it would not hit with deadly force, and Theseus, playing his part, clasped the arrow as it struck and fell back, disappearing beneath the surf. Hippolyte cast aside her bow and drew her dagger. Then, against her better judgement, she waded in. She immediately felt a pull on her legs from beneath the water and dug her heels deep into the sand, only for them to slide from under her. Using the momentum to her advantage, she allowed herself to fall and lifted her legs, clamping them around Theseus' waist. From there, she flipped her body over, pinning him to the ground. As the latest wave rolled back, it revealed Theseus trapped between her thighs as she sat astride him, her dagger at his throat. He let out a deep groan.

While the water lapped over them, he did not fight to topple her again, though she knew he could, his affinity with the water lending him an unnatural advantage, even in his current predicament. He did not move at all but remained motionless and naked between her thighs. The cold of the water felt like a cool balm against the heat of their flesh. Both of them were flushed and their pulses raced.

"I think it is time you sent the women away, don't you?" he said.

UNDER HIPPOLYTE'S ORDERS, the women returned to their tasks. She did not wait, did not care to seek out a chamber or a bed; she simply took Theseus there, in the water. This was what he had come for. She had seen it from that first glint in his eye as he waded toward her. And she would not disappoint. Her own exposed flesh rippled with muscles that lined her abdomen and thickened on her thighs. Very different from the frail, feeble bodies of the Grecian women.

For all that Theseus' body was now that of a man, his eyes widened as he cupped her breasts in his hands, a moan escaping his mouth before he hesitantly wrapped his lips around her nipple, as if this were his first time with a woman. Yet when he entered her, pushing himself as deep into her as he could, it was she who raised her voice in cries of pleasure.

Not until after their bodies had shuddered in climax did she return to the present. Foam rolled up toward them, then fell back into the deeper water ready to surge and break over them again. Each wave retreated with a gentle sucking sound, as if the sea were sighing.

Hippolyte stood, brushed the sand from her body and walked over to where she had thrown her blade.

"Water?" she offered, bringing her flask out to Theseus.

He rose, still as naked as he had been on his arrival, his eyes lingering on her.

"Thank you."

Taking the flask, he tipped it up to his lips, then drank until it was empty before handing it back to her.

"Your sisters, I take it, have gone to visit the Gargareans?"

Theseus sat down on the sand as Hippolyte failed to conceal her surprise.

"I am aware of your traditions."

"So, you were hoping to find Themiscyra abandoned? To pillage our unprotected lands?"

She searched his face for a reaction, but instead of the humiliation she expected to find there, Theseus looked hurt by the accusation.

"No. Hippolyte, believe me, I am not here to trick you. I was reliably informed you had not travelled with your women. I came for you and to reiterate my offer."

"Your offer of marriage?"

She struggled to maintain a serious look as she spoke. The anger, that had been close to boiling over, disappeared entirely, and once again, her head flew back in laughter.

"You cannot possibly want me as a wife! I am not like your Greek women. You do realise that. I am not placid, agreeable, reserved, content to spend my days lounging idly in the heat, eating grapes and figs and drinking more wine than is socially acceptable. That is not a life I have any desire for."

"Then it will not be the life you will lead. Nothing needs to change. You can live as you do here. Free to ride and fish—"

"And fight?"

"If you so wish."

His eyes drifted away from her to his ship, now only just visible in the glare of the sunlight.

"One day, Athens will be the capital of the most formidable kingdom Greece has ever known. Sparta, Corinth, Mycenae, all will pale in comparison to our strength, our numbers, our beauty. We will be the pinnacle of civilisation, art, education, politics. No other place will rival it."

He certainly now bore the physical shape of a man, but this still sounded like the same naïve boy she had first met, with his dreams of Athens' renown and of arriving at Themiscyra and convincing the Amazon Queen to become his wife. And yet she found herself drawn to him. Drawn to his lack of guile ... and his virility.

"If you are so confident in all of this, you do not need me by your side to make it happen. I am sure that whoever you choose as your queen will consider herself fortunate."

Hippolyte's clothes had now almost dried on her body.

There was no need for either of them to remain where they were any longer. But when she examined his face once more, she found his eyes wide and pleading.

"I need *you*," he said, like a petulant child, bewildered by her rejection.

The hurt expression remained on his face for a moment, and then, in a sudden movement, his hand shot out, grasping for the Queen herself. Leaping backwards, Hippolyte snatched the dagger from her belt and before he knew what was happening, the tip was pressing into his neck once again.

"It would pay to remember whom you address."

Her eyes bored into him. What was it about this man who had come to her shore? He did not fear what she might do to him, or rather he did not believe that this was to be his end. At the same time, his expression displayed the briefest flicker of remorse. With a dip of his chin, Theseus shuffled back in the sand, his eyes still fixed on hers.

"I apologise, truly, if I have offended you. But I will not apologise for coming here or for my motive. You must understand this, Hippolyte, my Queen. I have seen many things since you and I last met. I have visited places both wonderful and terrible. I have encountered the best and the worst of both gods and mortals, and I have changed. But despite all these experiences and how they have altered me, my feelings for you have stayed constant. My body has no purpose unless it is to stand beside yours. Please believe me, of all the women, of all the goddesses, there is no one else I would take as my queen. I would rather rule on my own, as my father now does, than endure life with someone other than you."

"Then perhaps that is what you should do."

"Or perhaps you should consider that my offer is genuine."

His lips parted in a sigh, and he turned his eyes to the

horizon as if searching for something beyond the realms of sight. Time had passed, more time than she had realised. The sky was streaked crimson and magenta and the sun was setting.

"I would prefer not to swim back to the ship at this hour," he said. "Who knows what manner of creature waits in hiding for darkness to fall?"

Hippolyte, too, was staring out to sea, disquiet churning through her.

"You can stay the night on the shore, then."

CHAPTER 9

That night, the Queen found herself unable to sleep, aware that, beyond the citadel walls, Theseus was sleeping outside in the moonlight. She had set her women to guard him from the lookout towers, with instructions to shoot should he advance from the beach to the dunes. While she trusted the women with her life, more than once she rose and went over to the window, to gaze out and search for his silhouette, only to force herself away before she glimpsed him.

It was her women he wanted, she repeatedly told herself. With the strength of the Amazons on Athens' side, his kingdom would be invincible. She could fathom no other purpose for his marriage proposal. But the Amazons would not be part of some dowry. And if he was expecting her to bear him a child, he would find himself bitterly disappointed. For if she were capable of such a thing, she would not have been here at all but away with her sisters. The next time she spoke to him, she would make it even clearer that his presence was unwelcome. There was no purpose to his loitering, other than to incur her wrath, which he may or may not live to regret.

When the light of dawn splintered across the skies of Pontus, she rode bareback to the shore where she found him in the shallows. A large fish with iridescent scales flapped helplessly in his hands.

"You have come in time for breakfast," Theseus told her, wading back up to the shoreline and gripping the fish by the gill so that it hung down by his thigh, still flapping, its mouth wide and gulping. "Shall we move to the dunes? It will be easier to prepare a fire there."

"You should have left by now."

"Are you aware that, in some cultures, the act we performed here last night would be enough for us to be considered married?"

Hippolyte laughed.

"In that case, you should know that I am married many times over."

She studied his face, expecting to see amusement, but instead, his features tightened.

"Hippolyte, do you not think it is the gods' gift to us that I was drawn to this land at the very time your sisters were absent? Do you not think it was fate that you were spared by Heracles?"

"Spared?"

A torrent of anger flowed through her veins, and she could not have kept the fury from her voice had she wished to, yet Theseus's eyes glittered. He was provoking her. Deliberately enraging her.

"Why did you come here, my Queen? You could have dispatched any woman to send me on my way. You alone returned."

"I came to ensure you left."

"I do not believe that is the truth. I believe you came because you want me. You feel this burning as fiercely as I do."

"The only thing that will burn is your ship."

She took a step toward him, drawing her sword. Her pulse drummed wildly as she raised her blade, yet he made no move to attack her or even to defend himself. Rather, he remained perfectly still. Only the fish moved at his side, though feebly now.

"Could we not skip this part? We both know how it will end."

His smile sat easy on his lips, and the fury she felt within her deepened.

"Is that so?"

Lunging at him, the Queen lifted her sword to the point beneath his neck where his collar bones met. With the slightest pressure, she drew it down in a vertical line that bisected his chest, stopping at his navel. Blood oozed from his skin, pooling into tiny beads like morning mist on a spider's web. Still, he remained unflinching.

"So, this is what you want? You want to die by my hand, without even defending yourself?" she spat.

He took a small step toward her, the pressure on the sword's tip increasing as he pressed himself against it. His breath came deep and laboured.

"No, that is not what I want. But I give you the choice, my Queen. You will always have that."

Time slowed as she recalled all the other men she had taken. The Gargareans who had fought her until their lips were bloody and their bodies bruised, and only then, as they continued to fight on through swollen eyes and broken fingers did she sometimes permit them to join her in her bed. And here was Theseus. Simply waiting. For what? For her to change her mind and push him to the sand and take him again as she had done the day before?

Once the thought had entered her mind, it took root.

Yes, that was what he wanted, and was it not what she wanted, too? As he had said, she might have sent any of her women down to send him on his way or dispose of him. Instead, she had come herself and come alone.

She dropped her sword and kicked him, sending him tumbling into the water's edge and watched him wince as the salt bit at the cut on his chest.

"Since you are here, it would seem a waste not to make some use of you," she said as she straddled him. "But do not disappoint me, or I will end you."

"I was born to serve you, my Queen. That I promise."

BY THE TIME they had satisfied themselves with each other's body, the sun had risen and was casting golden rays across their skin.

The Queen rose quickly to her feet, gathering her clothes as they drifted in and out on the gentle waves. The cut on Theseus' chest had stopped bleeding, a thin crust forming on the incision. Had he really doubted that she would kill him? If so, he was one of only a few men to have done so. And the first to have survived such a mistake.

Noticing her watching him, Theseus rose.

"Would it be impertinent to ask the Queen for some breakfast?" he said. "The fish I caught has been lost, I'm afraid, and I expect our activities will ensure that its companions will keep their distance for some time."

As he spoke, she found herself noting the curve of his

mouth and the way his tongue moved, adding a sheen to his lips.

"I did not bring any weapons with me to hunt and, in any case, I would hate to wander your lands unchaperoned."

"You should return to your ship."

"I will, of course, but perhaps one meal together? Would that be possible? Just a single meal. After all, I have been within the walls of your citadel before, and you know that, by Zeus' edict, I would never do you or any of your women harm."

"And you know that you do not have the strength to do that."

There was no humour in her voice, but Theseus smiled at her response as if she had made some coquettish remark.

"So, one meal together, then?"

Her horse ambled behind as Hippolyte and Theseus walked together over the dunes, through the long, brittle grasses and across the green plain that led up to the citadel. Here, the aroma gradually changed from the briny tang of the sea to the scent of damp, fertile earth, hinting at the lushness of Themiscyra.

His stride mirrored hers at every step, his arms swinging in the same rhythm as her own.

Wordlessly, they began the gradual ascent to the steps of her home. This was not a pace at which the Queen was accustomed to walk. The soles of her feet rolled slowly across the earth before rising again for each new step. Her knees lifted only slightly, her toes brushing the blades of grass beneath them. This was the walk of someone ignoring the passage of time, although whether she was delaying what was to come, or luxuriating in the present moment, she did not know.

No words passed between them, but their surroundings were full of noise. The chorus of birds, so numerous that a man could lose half a lifetime identifying their individual songs, and in the distance, the clang of hammer against metal. During the rainy season, the river Terme would roar as it raced to the sea; now it was little more than a gurgle.

Hippolyte's eyes remained looking forward, away from Theseus. She knew that to merely glance at him would cause her body to surge with emotions she seemed unable to control. By contrast, his gaze had never left her, as if he could read her mind and fathom what she really wanted if he only paid enough attention.

"The women, they built all of this?" he asked, speaking for the first time, as they entered the palace.

"Who else?" she asked. "We are only women here."

"You really do not have any men to attend to your needs?"

She chuckled.

"What needs do you think we might have that we would not be able to attend to ourselves?" she asked.

In the partial shadow on either side, she noted eyes turning in their direction. Only Glaukia approached them, her fingers gripping the knife at her side.

"My Queen," she said.

Hippolyte knew that the women would have seen her, this morning and the night before. They would have witnessed both the fighting and the copulation that followed. But they would speak to her of neither.

"Glaukia, please bring some food to my chamber," she said. "You can leave it outside the door."

She did not wait for the older woman's acknowledgement but pressed on, Theseus at her heels.

Silence cocooned the pair. The hallways seemed to have grown narrower, forcing their bodies closer together.

She chastised herself for these absurd thoughts. She had

taken plenty of men in her time, and even on the first occasion, with a Gargarean, she had remained more level-headed than she was now. Besides, she had already taken this man. But, she thought, it had been different. Yes, there had been enjoyment with the Gargareans, but the purpose of the act was always clear: to increase the population, to produce strong and capable offspring. This, by contrast, had served no purpose other than to satiate a hunger that was burning within her. An itch that had to be scratched the moment she had seen him dive through the waters and had returned with every step they took.

"Come," she said, as she took his hand for the first time and led him into her bedroom.

"Your chamber? Do you traditionally dine in there?"

His voice had changed. He was nervous, she realised and found comfort in the thought. Men were supposed to be fearful in her presence.

The warm, musty aroma of home was a stark contrast to the saltiness of Theseus' skin. Moving to him, she pressed her chest against his, inhaling deeply. Did he always smell so intensely of the sea? she wondered. Moving back again, she traced a finger across the light hair on his arm, still dusted with tiny salt crystals, and then across his chest to the line she had put there. She should have made it deeper, she thought. She should have ensured it would scar.

His skin was softer than that of the Gargareans, and no matter how his stubble had grown, he was still young compared to her. She could feel his pulse quickening to a relentless thud as she pressed her hand against him.

"I thought we were to dine?" he said, his eyes running up and down her body as she began to undress.

"The food will take some time. We need to find a way to occupy ourselves until it arrives."

Pushing him down on her bed, she took him once again.

CHAPTER 10

*T*he air in the room was thick with the scent of their tangled bodies. The tang of salt that had clung to him had become diluted and musky as his damp skin glistened in the silvery light. Dawn was once again upon them. The solo of the first blackbird had quickly become a chorus of trills and cadenzas. Furs from the bed were strewn across the floor, tossed aside in the heat of passion.

It would have been wiser to have slept, Hippolyte thought briefly as the crowing of a cockerel now broke through the mingled birdsong. She had tasks to do, chores that had been neglected from the day before, and women to attend to. Since entering the room, pausing only to take the meal brought to them, she had only left it to fetch more water and whatever food she could find to hand—a small bowl of peaches and a large pomegranate, red seeds bursting from within when pulled open.

Surely, she thought, this hunger for each other's bodies would eventually be satisfied? Surely, like flames that burnt with such strength that they consumed all that fed them, this passion, too, would suffocate and die? Surely, she would tire of the taste of his mouth and the curve of his neck? At some point, exhaustion would force them to rest. Whatever tasks awaited her, they would just have to be postponed. After all, she should be with her sisters and the other women, each of whom would now be performing the same act as she and Theseus had been engaged in all night, and much of the day before. One that, rather than growing predictable with every repetition, became more intense.

Now they had moved to the floor, insulated from the cold of the tiles by the discarded fur pelts. Her legs were wrapped around him and she pulled him inside her as deep as any man had penetrated before. But for all the majesty of his body, it was his face that she found irresistible, in the rare moments when she had been able to focus on him. No man with whom she had lain had ever made any attempt to learn what might bring her satisfaction. Until now. Until Theseus.

He had wanted to know what it was that she did to bring her body to climax, so that he might recreate it. Enhance it. And when he flipped her body over and pressed her to the floor, running his fingers up the inside of her thighs, she learnt that reproduction was not the main purpose of this act. In such moments, it was hard to deny that perhaps this union had, indeed, been ordained by the gods.

Beneath him, she could feel his thrusts begin to quicken. She pushed back against him, the motion now so familiar to her. She forced her hips up, arching her back until his convulsions were so intense he could no longer keep his seed within him. With a gasp, his body shook.

But Hippolyte wasn't finished with him and before he could relax or move, she quickly straddled him. When her own surge of ecstasy finally arrived, it came in waves that crashed within her one after another, shaking her body, limbs tensing and relaxing in involuntary spasms, her nails digging into his chest as she bit down so forcefully on her lip that she drew blood. As they subsided, she felt her heart pounding as fiercely as the first time she had spilt blood on the field of battle.

"I did not know that women could experience such passion," Theseus said, his eyes shining in awe.

"That does not surprise me," the Queen replied.

During the night, the oil lamps had guttered, and so Hippolyte had taken a tallow candle from a chest and lit that instead. The aroma was harsher, but she had little time to think or care of that in the moment. Time spent seeking oil would have meant less time with Theseus tending to her, and given how brief this encounter was to be, that was not something she was willing to sacrifice. Now, however, in the mugginess of the room, she regretted that decision. With the flame extinguished, the bitter wax had pooled on the stone, but the pungent scent lingered and tendrils of sooty smoke had marked the walls.

"You know that you have ruined me," he told her.

He lay on his back, staring up at the ceiling. His chest gently rose and fell, the delicate fuzz of hair upon it highlighted in the glow of morning.

"How can I leave this room, knowing that I will never experience pleasure like that outside it?"

"There is still time for more," the Queen said, rolling over and propping herself up on an elbow.

Her comment brought a laugh from Theseus.

"My sisters are not returning any time soon," she said, wishing to hear it again. "We can enjoy this a little while longer."

She ran a finger along his collar bone, then down over the ridge of the wound she had inflicted on him the previously. It would fade quickly, she thought again ... like memories of this encounter.

Lifting a hand, he covered his mouth to stifle a yawn. His skin displayed more scars than she had expected. They were not as great in number as those on the Gargareans, or on the majority of her women. But some of them were deep. Blades had cut through his flesh, not merely the skin. One began above his sternum, faded almost to silver, and she found her fingers drawing a line along it to his ribs.

"I may need a moment or two longer," he said, with a smile, taking her hand and turning it so that he might kiss her knuckles. "And some water, too? I can fetch it if you tell me where to go?"

Tension flickered in her. He registered it with a smile.

"I understand. Believe me, my Queen, I have not come here to invade your home. I am more than content to have invaded your bed. If it makes you happy, you could blindfold me while you are gone, so that I cannot look outside and see more than you wish me to."

Did he speak in jest? she wondered. His words might be construed as this, but there also seemed sincerity in them.

"It is fine. I will fetch us a jug."

She rose and moved to the doorway, her naked body reflecting the sunlight like newly polished bronze. Was it prideful to enjoy Theseus' gaze on her quite so much? Her body was magnificent; she knew this without question. Every day its strength increased. And never once had she taken the gift for granted.

Once outside the room, the Queen found the silence disconcerting. Another plate of food had been placed outside her door, but they had been unaware of its arrival, and now it was crawling with ants, bearing away as much of the fruit and meat as their little bodies could manage. She picked it up and moved through the corridors to the kitchens.

A bowl of hardboiled eggs had been set beside the stove, their mottled shells still warm to the touch. She took four, along with a handful of ripe purple plums, and placed them on a silver tray, beside a jug of water and two cups. But as she lifted it from the table, she paused. Was this how she wished to depict herself to Theseus? As a serving woman? She had no concerns about carrying food to her sisters, or any of the other women for that matter, but they had never considered her as anything other than their Queen. This man saw her as a future wife.

She looked at the food again and decided she was too hungry to bother with such nuances. A host always served their guest. That was one of the basic tenets of *xenia*. Although the service she had rendered Theseus had perhaps gone a little further than that dictated by the normal standards of hospitality.

When she returned to the room, he had returned to the bed. She poured cool water into one of the cups and handed it to him. He drank eagerly, then immediately took the jug himself, refilled the goblet and drained it a second time. His thirst sated, he placed the cup on the ground and took an egg, rolling the smooth oval between his palms until the shell resembled the tiles of a miniature mosaic, which he then peeled away, leaving only the flesh.

Hippolyte found herself watching him intently as he did this, noting the way the glossy white of the egg yielded under the pressure of his teeth and how he used the back of his hand to wipe his mouth. Such typically human actions, and yet there was something unusually fluid in his movements. She had already considered this more than once during the night and before that, when she had watched him swimming.

"You know I have been with many men?"

Her voice broke the silence. Theseus' hand paused, hovering above the bowl where the remaining three eggs and fruit sat. His eyes narrowed.

"I do, although I am not sure why you would bring this matter to my attention. Perhaps your aim is to flatter me? Perhaps you wish to tell me that which I already know, that my skills far surpass any you have experienced before."

There it was again, that cocksure smile, and Hippolyte found herself wanting to hold her hands against his cheeks. To frame his face and preserve that moment for just a second longer. There was actually something rather attractive about the arrogance of youth, which she had never fully appreciated. The infectious optimism that came with someone who had no responsibilities in life other than to gain a name for themselves.

"You are not like any other man," she said, slowly. "I know of your father, King Aegeus, but what of your mother? Was she a mortal?"

He pressed his lips together.

"She was. She is."

"Then you are mortal also."

She could not hide the surprise in her voice. It was a question that had been playing on her mind since she had seen him swimming to the shore amidst the crashing waves and against the lethal currents. It had not seemed a feat that a mere human could have undertaken and survived. But if both his parents were mortal, then he must be simply blessed by the gods, rather than being kin to them.

He made to speak but paused and instead selected a plum

from the bowl. His teeth pierced the skin and he pulled away a piece of its flesh and chewed it slowly.

"May I?" he asked, gesturing toward the window. "I will understand if you do not wish me to look out over the citadel."

"I think I can allow you to see it," she said, "given what else you have cast your eyes over this last day. I believe that if the gods or my women were to find me at fault, I have already committed those sins."

She expected a return of his smile, the boyish grin she had already grown to like. Or perhaps even a witty retort. But instead, he pushed himself off the bed and crossed the room to the window. It seemed that his movement created a draught, and the absence of his body next to her resulted in a chill that she had not anticipated. She reached down and lifted one of the furs from the ground, pulling the pelt up around her knees.

Theseus was standing at the window, looking out across the steppes, his silhouette a black void cut from the world beyond her chamber. From this point, he could see it all, the rolling green of the steppes and the vast waters of the sea beyond.

"My parentage," Theseus began, "is unlike that of any man who walks the earth."

CHAPTER 11

$\mathcal{T}$heseus continued to stand at the window. The same pale, silvery sun which illuminated his outline was bringing forth the scents of the warming Earth. Those of lavender, honeysuckles and rosehips swam around them. Hints of herbs, of thyme and rosemary that grew in the gardens, mingled with the pungent undertones from the stables. The aromas in Themiscyra were slightly different every day, their character formed not just by the warmth of the sun or which flowers were in season but also by the direction of the breeze and the moisture that had fallen in the night or risen from the earth as dew.

Under normal circumstances Hippolyte could predict the weather for that day by its smell alone. She could tell if a storm was approaching from beyond the horizon or if the clear skies would last until nightfall. Yet this morning, the scent of Theseus overwhelmed her. It was on her skin and seemed to have permeated every part of the room around her. She had never been aware of anything like this with the men she normally encountered and didn't want to let go of it now

He finished the plum, licking the last of the sweet juice from his lips and then each of his fingers, before finally turning back to Hippolyte.

"You know of my father?"

"I don't take much interest in the Kings of the lands, but yes I am aware of him by name."

"I understand," Theseus said.

After another, brief glance out of the window he crossed back to the bed and lowered himself down beside her but ensured a gap remained between them. He didn't want to be deflected from his story. As difficult as she found this, she restrained herself.

From outside, the clamour of the day was building. The whinny of the horses, the chatter and noise of women about their work. A call. A whistle. He seemed momentarily distracted but then his posture altered, and Hippolyte knew he was ready to tell his story.

"I was not raised in Athens," he began, "but Troezen. I assume you have heard of it?"

Hippolyte nodded.

"Vaguely. It is not a place we have been called to."

"My father had taken a very young wife, who proved unable to give him an heir. Understandably, this tormented him, as it would any king, so he married again, this time hopeful that a child, a son, would soon be born to his house. But alas, this second wife died of a fever, leaving him once again childless. By this time, he was not a young man anymore, and he knew it was only a matter of time before his rivals would decide to challenge him for the crown. And so, he visited the Oracle, in Delphi."

Delphi was a place that Hippolyte had heard of many times. The Delphic temples of Apollo were said to be the greatest in

Greece and the lushness of the land and the abundance of fruit trees the envy of the world. Of course, the men who said such things had never set foot in Pontus.

"My father gave his offering to Apollo," he continued. "It was more than generous, befitting a man of his standing. But the Pythia gave him only a riddle in response."

"A riddle?"

"She told him 'The bulging mouth of the wineskin, O best of men, Loose not until thou hast reached the heights of Athens, lest you die of grief'." The way that Theseus had recited it suggested he had heard it many times before.

Hippolyte ruminated over these words. It was impossible to deny that they were certainly cryptic.

"He was, as you can imagine, distraught at this. Was it a warning, an instruction, an insult even?" Theseus continued. "Condescension from the Oracle was the last thing he expected, especially as a man of such judicious habits. He had thought that the Pythia would offer him salvation, tell him how he might produce an heir.

"Considering his journey wasted and all hope lost, he took his time returning to Athens, and stopped to visit a friend on the way. One who was wise in the ways of the Pythia, King Pittheus."

"Of Troezen," Hippolyte added.

Despite her insistence that she did not follow politics, she was not entirely ignorant of the world, and in her line of business, an ear to the ground was essential if she and her women were to be ready when a call to action came.

"Indeed, of Troezen."

Theseus paused.

"Well, King Pittheus was also unable, or unwilling, to decipher the Oracle's words. By way of consolation the King laid on a lavish meal with the finest wines. My father would not usually drink to excess, as I am sure you can imagine for a man of his position. But these were not normal circumstances. He was suffering. Lost. And so he consumed far more wine than food and with his inhibitions lowered, he found himself in the bed of King Pittheus' daughter, Aethra. My mother."

Hippolyte continued to listen attentively, but this last statement had planted a seed of disappointment in her. Given the story so far, she struggled to see how Theseus' lineage differed from that of thousands across the world, and a pregnancy resulting from a night of drunken recklessness was hardly the makings of a hero.

"My mother conceived that night," he said, then paused again. "Although she cannot say for certain whether it is Aegeus or Poseidon who is my father."

"Poseidon?"

"Yes. When my father was finished with my mother, he fell into a deep slumber, more a stupor, I suppose. She, in contrast, found herself unable to sleep, and inexplicably drawn from her chamber, she left the Palace and its grounds and wandered down to the shore. It was there that he saw her and seduced her."

"Poseidon?"

"The God of the Sea. She walked into the water and lay with him there while the waves raged around them, on the very same night that she had lain with Aegeus—with the man the world knows as my father. My mother and Poseidon stayed together until the first rays of sunlight splintered the horizon, their bodies entwined, before he disappeared. There is no way of knowing whose blood runs in my veins. No way to be certain. Though there is little doubt, as you have seen yourself, that I have an affinity with water. One that seems beyond the talent of a mortal."

For the first time since he had begun to speak, he looked at the Queen, his eyes holding hers as he awaited her reaction. He had told her the truth, and now he wanted to see how she valued that. He knew the story of his conception was one she had not heard before. Gods with mortals, of course that was almost commonplace. But this ... the quandary in which he found himself was most certainly intriguing.

"Does your father, King Aegeus that is? Does he know of this?"

Theseus smiled, although he did not convey the cynicism she had anticipated.

"I am my father's son. I brought him tokens that he had placed in safekeeping for me to retrieve and return to him when I was capable. I rid him of his witch of a wife, Medea, the vile sorcerous who murdered her own sons and would have killed me, too, if my father had not been blessed with a keen eye. And I will rule Athens when he is gone. I am his son."

There was a finality to his words. A self-assuredness that Hippolyte had seen before, in her own father. And in the gods. She wondered if Theseus had shared this story with other women he had taken to bed. It was certainly a tale that would hold their attention, and yet there was something about the unease with which he had spoken. The way he had refused to look at her. The pauses, as if to consider his words, until his final, confident declaration. No, she did not believe that he had told many others, if any. She felt something had changed between them—like the moment a tide reaches its highest point and must draw back. The hairs on her arms prickled and she opened her mouth to speak, but before a word could leave her lips, Theseus spoke again.

"I know it may be impertinent, but I would like some fresh air, although perhaps away from the water. A wander around your garden, perhaps, before we return to your bed."

The Queen sucked in her cheeks.

"What makes you think I will let you return here?" she asked.

There was no hiding his smile now, as deep a smirk as he had yet dared show her.

"It is nearly two moons until your sisters return. Is it not?"

CHAPTER 12

*W*hatever duties and tasks she had intended to complete during her sisters' absence, they were quickly forgotten. The Queen now woke and slept not in accordance with her circadian rhythm, but as dictated by her whims. Some nights, sleep was neglected entirely, and it would be as if her body and his had fused together, sweat pouring down their spines as she carved half-moon crevices in his skin with her nails. Other times, the urge would strike early in the morning, as she observed the pale light glimmering on his skin, and accompanied by the chorus of larks, she would find her hands wandering across his body, urging him to wake and to tend to her again.

But there was more than just sex.

Every day, they fought. With no weapons of his own, she allowed him the use of hers. Arrows, blades, whatever his taste that day. His strength was admirable. He was a man who suited the brute power best wielded through an axe or a club. His skill at times was clumsy and his mind easily distracted. A single suggestive look could be enough to beguile him and give her all the opportunity she needed to disarm him. Had they faced one another in the heat of battle, with death as the final outcome, she suspected his lack of focus would be his undoing.

"If we were to fight in the sea, I would most certainly win," he told her.

"And have you experienced many battles at sea?" she asked.

They had also spent time out riding together, another skill in which Theseus lacked finesse. Given his height, he could mount a horse easily enough, but riding it, he would bounce and jolt around. The natural elegance of the creature departed with this mass of a man astride it. His form, which cut through water so gracefully, became ungainly and misshapen the instant he sat upon a horse. Hippolyte found herself obliged to offer him a different steed each time they rode, for fear the same one would get used to such a heavy hand. Thankfully, with practice, he improved to the point where she no longer feared for her animals' spines when they journeyed.

Some days, they travelled out to the river, taking the paths on the edge of the marshes, where the herons would stand with their long legs, whittling out grubs and insects from the mud. Others, they returned to the sea and Hippolyte would watch as Theseus dived beneath the waves, reappearing with his hair plastered across his face and water weaving down his cheeks. Occasionally she joined him, paddling until the water reached her knees but always armed and always alert.

More and more, she found her mind wandering to thoughts of her sisters and of Penthesilea, in particular. She knew she would disapprove of this arrangement. It would not be the Queen's use of Theseus per se that would anger her, for she had been known to take other men besides the Gargareans, just for pleasure. But Penthesilea would resent and be wary of his presence in Themiscyra.

As the weeks passed, he became known to the women who had remained there, and he knew many of them by name, too, although he never addressed them directly. At least in that sense he showed wisdom. He would dip his head slightly, acknowledging their presence but avoiding eye contact as he and the Queen walked together through the citadel, and acted as if he were deaf to the whispers that followed them.

A little over half a moon into his sojourn, they found themselves strolling through a garden just beyond the walls. Hippolyte did not concern herself with horticulture in general, being more interested in horses and weapons, but that did not mean she underestimated the value of the plants that grew on their land. They, too, were gifts from the gods, to strengthen and aid them. And while flora of many varieties and uses grew throughout Themiscyra, it was in this small area of land, situated southwest of the citadel and thus protected from the harsh winds that blew off the sea, that some of the women—mainly those who dealt with the injured—had cultivated crops of the most useful specimens. Between battles and training, they pruned leaves and plucked weeds. They snapped off dried flower heads and gathered seedpods, storing them and then sprinkling their contents back on the earth when the seasons changed, or grinding them for tonics to ease pain or swelling. Such was the dedication of the Amazons, that on the hottest days of the year, when the sun would blaze like a furnace on their backs, they would gather water from the river and douse the plants until the soil turned the deep, dark brown of a walnut shell and worms came wriggling to the surface.

In return, the garden provided them with an abundant harvest. The berry from the elder tree could be used to produce a syrup for coughs, or else dried and smoked for the purpose of relaxation. Sweet woodruff was stored with their clothes to repel inspects and moths that might otherwise settle there. The women could prepare a sleeping draft from valerian root, and the leaf from lemon verbena might ease the inflammation around a wound or reduce a fever brought on by infection. As much as the Queen would have liked to believe there was no problem that could not be solved with her sword or her sister's bow, she knew that was not the truth, and on more than one occasion she herself had been a grateful recipient of the garden's bounty. However, she had never looked upon it with such awe as Theseus did as they weaved between the beds.

"And what is this?" he asked, pinching the stem of a pink flower, its densely packed petals surrounding the delicate yellow stamens within its centre.

"That is a peony."

Hippolyte found herself laughing. This was not the sort of question she was accustomed to. A woman might ask her how to feather an arrow so that it could slice through the air with barely a sound or how to ride a horse without holding its reins, so that she could stand and fire a bow. Theseus seemed not to know the rules that attended her role as Queen, and this brought with it a new sense of freedom.

"What do you use it for?" he asked.

"It can provide a draft that will ease pain."

"And this?"

"That is aloe. The sap eases burnt skin," she added, anticipating his next question.

"And that one?"

"That is valerian."

He nodded, as if he had just been checking she knew. His eyes roved from one plant to the next, always asking their names and correlating uses. For over an hour, he was entertained in such a manner, before they bathed together in the fresh, running water of the river, then returned to feast in the citadel.

"Why is your ship still here?" Hippolyte asked one afternoon.

They had ridden out to one of the higher steppes and were lying together in the grass. The sweet smell of pine needles and burning cedar swirled around them.

"They cannot believe you are still alive."

Theseus rolled over onto his stomach and took her hands in his.

"I told them that I would return within two full moons. If I have not returned by then, they will leave."

"Two moons."

This was the length of time her sisters would be gone. When Theseus had arrived on her shore, that had seemed a long way off. Now, nearly half that time had already passed.

"Is it too much to hope that you have considered my proposal?" he asked, sitting up to view her more clearly. "You have had time with me. You understand my thinking. You can see that I am a man of my word, and Hippolyte, I know now more than ever that *you* are destined to be my queen."

Every time he returned to this theme, she thought of him as a young boy who could not understand why he was not allowed to go and fight alongside his father or brothers. As a child playing with a wooden sword, unable to swing it accurately yet still pleading for a sharper blade. The circumstances of his conception might have been unusual, but during these moments, all she saw was the brazen arrogance of a Grecian prince. The assumption that he could have whatever he desired. But she was not his for the asking.

"This time together ..." Hippolyte said, considering her words carefully as she spoke, "... is something I am unlikely to forget. Perhaps next year, when my sisters leave again, you could return? You could still take a wife, but we could enjoy each other's company whenever the opportunity arose for us."

She pressed her hand against his chest. To her, this seemed the most alluring of possibilities. She could never be queen in a place such as Athens, yet it was true: she and Theseus had formed a bond, the likes of which she had never experienced with any man or woman. It was a meeting of minds and bodies, of wits and almost of strength. But however appealing the idea was to her, Theseus did not share her sentiment. He pushed her hand away from him.

"Is that the type of man you think I am? The type of king that I would be? That I could take a woman as my wife and behave in such a manner? Do you really think so little of me?"

With that, he was on his feet, lifting their waterskin from the ground. Confused, Hippolyte rose, too.

"I do not understand why you have taken such offence. Is it not what most kings do? Keep their queens for their children and their concubines for their bed?"

"You consider yourself a concubine now?"

"No, I simply consider myself free of your deluded sense of decency."

"So now I am deluded."

Theseus had turned red in the face, his temper glowing in his eyes. "And next you will consider yourself above love, too, I suppose."

It was not the first time he had uttered the word, although until now it had been spoken only in jest, or in the moment before he climaxed, so focused on their bodies that his mind failed to conceive the weight of the words rolling from his tongue.

"I love you, Hippolyte," he said. "You must know that. With all my heart, I love you."

"Theseus, please. You embarrass yourself."

"Because I have fallen in love with you?"

"I do not have a place for that kind of love in my life."

His fists were balled at his sides, his jaw tight with tension.

"I do not believe you. I see you when you are sleeping, with a smile on your lips. Ares' blood may flow in your veins, but so does Otrera's. You are half human, as am I, and you are capable of love."

"You are telling me what I am capable of?"

Hippolyte rose to her feet. She had been wearing a small dagger strapped to her thigh, out of habit but also to catch rabbits or to cut away small branches. This was the first time she had reached for it in earnest.

"You should watch your tongue if you wish to leave here with it. Or at all, for that matter.

"You would stop me from leaving?"

"I believe I told you when you first came here that if you stepped on my shores again it would be the last time."

They were moving in circles now. Hippolyte's weight shifted onto her back foot as she locked her eyes on him.

"It is a little late to be recalling that promise, is it not?"

"I believe I decide what happens on my own land, not you."

They had sparred daily since his arrival, but always as a dance. A prelude to what would follow.

Now, Hippolyte felt the desire to hurt him.

On her first lunge, the dagger sliced a diagonal line across his chest, deeper than the first wound she had inflicted on him. At the sight of blood, her appetite was whetted. She leapt forward again, but this time he was ready. His fist landed squarely in her stomach, knocking the air from her lungs. He followed this blow with another, to her arm, sending her dagger flying.

"You forget that I know your every move," he goaded her.

He was displaying what she knew to be a false sense of security. Yes, they'd practised the same drills repeatedly, not because she needed to, or lacked the inventiveness to fight differently, but because it was part of their choreography. A flurry of footwork and spins in which they both ended as victor. This was a very different situation.

Most women would have fallen to their knees after receiving such a blow; even an Amazon woman might have struggled. But she was Hippolyte. With no one to aid her, she reached up, grabbed his hair and pulled hard, at the same time striking him behind his knees so that they buckled, toppling him. She twisted away from him in a cartwheel, grabbing her dagger as her hands hit the ground, then spinning back toward him before he had even seen where she had gone. She pushed the blade just far enough into his back that he knew she could have killed him at that moment. His body slackened. He raised his arms above his head and turned slowly to face her.

"How could I ever love another woman after you?" he asked, breathlessly.

That night, she told him it was to be their last. Rumours of the Queen and her concubine were rife and if her sisters were to return earlier than expected, they would not allow him to live. The thought of his death stung her more keenly than she cared to admit.

"Will you have a drink with me?" he asked, as they sat together, naked, in the dim light of an oil lamp. "If tonight is to be our last together, will you indulge me in this tradition?"

Wine was something she had resisted in his presence. Wine,

herbs, anything that would lower her inhibitions. Yet he gazed upon her with such pleading.

"Just a single cup ... and with water, please? I believe I saw some barrels over by the stables."

"Those were a gift from the King of Phrygia. Years ago, now. I do not even know if it can still be drunk."

"Old is better. Wine grows richer with age," he replied. "Let me go and bring a barrel back here. I promise, one cup only. A proper farewell to my Queen. That is all I seek."

In the light of the lamp, his hair shone like fire. Besides her own, his was the only body she had come to know so well. She knew the lines along his jaw and the tautness across his collar bone. She knew the position of each and every one of his scars.

"One small cup, then, and with plenty of water added. I will fetch the barrel."

"You stay here, my Queen. I will fetch it. You will be expending more energy on my return," he said, kissing her firmly on the mouth before he left.

When he returned, wine in hand, he kissed her softly, before raising his cup in a toast.

"To us," he said.

BLACKNESS FILLED HER MIND. There was an absence of coherent thought, a deep-rooted numbness. An impenetrable swirl of nothingness. And then her eyes flickered open. It was only a blink, yet it was almost enough for the light to blind her. A deep throbbing cut behind her eyes. The Queen lifted a hand and pressed her fingers gently against her forehead, only for the sensation to change from searing agony to unfathomable dizziness. The feeling rolled back and forth through her skull, as if she had taken a tumble from her horse and landed on hard ground. But it had been years since that had happened to her, and even as a child, she had known how to land to protect herself.

The ache spread downwards. Her muscles were unresponsive. A thickness was building in her throat. What had happened? What was causing her to feel this way? Her mind was as sluggish as her body, as she tried to push herself up to a sitting position, only to tumble back and strike her head on a hard surface. Was she sick? Did she have a fever? Never in her life had she or any of her sisters suffered from such an affliction, but some of her women had. Those whose cuts had become so infected and swollen with puss that it had addled their minds. Was that it? She could sense no broken bones or open wounds. She could not recall an accident which might have caused such an injury. And the pain seemed to emanate from a place behind her eyes, in the centre of her brain.

Gritting her teeth, she pushed herself up again and managed to sit. She tried to channel her thoughts into a simple stream that she could follow.

Where had she been before this? She tried to recall. With her sisters, perhaps? No, they were absent. But not at war. They were with the Gargareans. That was it. They had gone, and she had stayed behind. The relief she felt at being able to recollect this one fact was short-lived. She had been in bed. She had been with Theseus. The wine. She must have drunk too much. But how? She remembered taking only two sips, and then— and then nothing more. She screwed up her eyes, as if this would help her think straight, but nothing more came to mind. It was as if the time between then and now had evaporated, all memories wiped clean.

It was only as Hippolyte rubbed the bridge of her nose, that she noted the difference in her surroundings. Grey, stone walls had been replaced by wooden planks. Her soft, horsehair mattress by a wooden bunk. The smell of damp pervaded the air, heavy and briny. And the rocking motion, she noticed as she tried to move again, was not restricted to her, but afflicted the entire room.

She was on a ship.

She was on his ship.

He had taken her.

PART III

CHAPTER 13

The first day of their three-day trek back home was always the most challenging and treacherous. They rode over steep, rugged mountains along tracks where the horses were forced to travel in single file, barely a foot between them and a fall to certain death. Even with beasts as sure-footed as theirs, hooves often slipped on the stones. Some faltered and refused to move, their riders needing to slap their heels against their sides to keep them going forwards. One young woman fell from her steed and, by the grace of the gods, managed to catch hold of the edge of the ledge and pull herself to safety, her life saved by the strength in her arms.

After that, the women did not talk again until they had made it through the pass.

Toward the end of the second day, they reached flatter land, where they camped, feasting on the meat the Gargareans had presented them with—along with metals and leathers—as parting gifts. That night, their tiredness was overwhelming, and there was little to be heard in the way of songs or chatter.

By the next morning, all that had changed.

They packed up early, laughter already reverberating around them. The sky was immense, an endless expanse, decorated with clouds that drifted like great listless beasts of the sky. There was barely a flicker of wind to ameliorate the dry heat. They had departed for the Gargareans in the spring, but summer had arrived now, browning the grass and narrowing the rivers to streams. But nothing, not even the most arid land or scorching heat, could lessen the women's elation.

With the perilous terrain behind them, they were finally free to talk and laugh as they travelled. And once the laughter had started it was near impossible to stop.

There were so many stories to exchange. So many juicy titbits of gossip to pass on. Many of the protagonists of these tales were very happy to shed more light on even the most salacious rumours circulating about them. Chatter and whoops of delight continued to reach Penthesilea's ears as she rode at a stately pace out in front, for there was no need to rush. The happier the women were, the more fiercely they would fight to protect their way of life when the time came. Her mother had taught her that years ago, and it was the truism by which Hippolyte ruled.

Their trip had been fruitful, if for no other reason than to let off steam. When the women had left Themiscyra, they had been tired and battle-worn, never able to fully relax in case duty called. The winter months had been tough on their bodies as they spent their days training, perfecting their skills as if each sparring session were being observed by Ares himself. The endless pressure had crept into their minds, warping their thoughts and wrapping its cold fingers around their spines. They had not recognised how bad it had become, until it was released. That could certainly be said of Penthesilea, who only now appreciated the strain she had been under.

For the first two weeks of their trip, she had taken her leadership of the Amazons with a gravity that bordered on obsession. She had not indulged in the herbs that the men had offered or in the burning of the aphrodisiacal seeds they had brought as gifts. She kept watch at night more often than she needed to and slept in a small tent, alone, her axe beside her. She had positioned herself as Hippolyte would have, as absolute protector of her women, a regent queen who would be ready at all times should they need her. But gradually, she started to relax, joining in contests with those men who wished to challenge her, for she needed to feel the heat of a striking blade in her grip.

After a few days of sparring, she took a man to her bed. He was one of the older ones, his body more scar than skin, the hair on his chest rolled into tight corkscrews of white and grey. Afterwards, she had joined her women at one of the fires, watching the colours form in the flames as the scented smoke wove spirals through the air and their minds. With the narcotic fumes, came a final loosening of the tethers and responsibilities which she felt to her sister, which had bound her so tightly when she had taken up her temporary role as leader. From that moment, she was at one with the others.

She had spent the remainder of the days fighting with the men, allowing the fights to lead wherever she fancied. The previous night's challenge had been her favourite of the entire trip. Three young Gargareans had decided to tackle her together. Finding her unarmed but knowing her reputation, they had approached her with swords and shields raised, thinking that their advantage in numbers and with weapons would be sufficient to best the daughter of Ares. They had believed that taking her down—even outnumbering her as they were—would cement their reputations amongst the others.

Older, more experienced men, looking on, shook their heads in scepticism of their mission. Penthesilea herself had felt a twinge of sympathy for these young studs. In the blink of an eye, she had seized the closest sword and turned the tables before even one of them had managed to lunge at her. She had drawn blood. And that was just where the fun had started.

She had used them all that night, and what they had lacked in skill, they made up for in stamina and enthusiasm. Even now, the images of their three bodies entangled with hers and each other's, brought a smile to her lips.

"It is another daughter. I know it is. Every child that Oraras has given me has been a girl."

Melanippe's voice startled Penthesilea from her thoughts. How long she had been lost in her reverie, she could not say, but her sister, who had until then been riding halfway along the convoy, was now parallel to her.

"It will be a girl. I am certain," she repeated.

With her mind now in the moment, Penthesilea felt the need to temper her sister's expectations.

"You cannot know for certain. You may not even be with child."

Melanippe offered her a scornful look.

"I am. It is from the first night. I know this, in the same way I knew I was not on our last visit. I know my body just as you know yours. The gods have seen fit to repay my patience."

Her smile tightened as she surveyed Penthesilea's features for a tell-tale sign that she, too, might be pregnant. Her absence at the beginning of the trip had reduced the chances, though it was certainly still possible. Given Antiope's fertility and her history of conceiving on every previous visit to the Gargareans, it would be reasonable to assume that she was in the same condition as Melanippe professed to be. It would also not be unreasonable to believe that, this year, Hippolyte would be the only one of them not carrying.

Penthesilea inwardly cursed the Queen for deciding not to come with them and prove that her childlessness was not due to some bodily inadequacy. Not that she would be anything other than overjoyed for her sisters. The more of them who were carrying, the more there would be to carry on their parents' names.

"What do you think she has spent her time doing?" Melanippe asked, apparently aware from Penthesilea's expression that she was thinking about the Queen. "I suspect she has been so bored that she has lined up a battle for us on our return."

"Or else she has been off on her own and won it already," Penthesilea replied.

"I feel sorry for the poor women who remained with her. She has probably had them scrubbing the armour and sharpening the swords and a dozen other chores in our absence. I do not envy them."

A faint smile rose on Penthesilea's lips. It was true, Hippolyte had an eye for detail. An obsession, one might say. But she could not hold this against her. This was one of the many things that made her a great queen. But greater than Penthesilea would have been, had Ares chosen her instead? It was difficult to know.

That next night was to be their last under canvas, and when they rose in the morning, the atmosphere had changed. Pregnant or not, they were returning to their true calling. As enjoyable as their time away had been, having gone so long only sparring, tedium had started to set in. For all that Melanippe had spoken in jest when she had suggested Hippolyte would have their next battle waiting for them, Penthesilea suspected that she might, indeed, be correct, for any boredom they had experienced would have been multiplied for the Queen.

They approached Pontus from the southeast, their numbers now significantly reduced. Upon arrival in Anatolia, the nomadic women had separated from the group. Some preferred the warmer climes and had remained further south. Others, by contrast, would travel further north, as far as the boarders of Thrace, where the mountains and higher altitudes made for brisker weather. The remainder of the women rode steadily on with Penthesilea.

As the plains and forests of home came into view, the horses began to strain against their harnesses. Most of the women, the Princess included, dropped their reins altogether. The horses knew their way.

The citadel came into view.

"I am heading to the river to bathe and give thanks," Antiope said, having turned her palomino gelding in a circle so that it stood in front of Penthesilea and Melanippe. "Many of the women are coming with me. Do you wish to join us?"

The cool, running waters of the Terme bubbled with shallow pools suitable for bathing and for the horses to drink from. Several women, Penthesilea included, preferred to clean themselves there rather than wait for the heated water of a bath, but she shook her head at the offer, all the same.

"I should ride on and see our sister," she said. "No doubt she will have plenty to inform us of. I may make my way back, later."

Antiope nodded and turned to Melanippe for her answer, but before she could speak, the women's attention was distracted. Three horses were thundering towards them, three women on horseback but with no weapons they could see.

A response, unlike anything she had ever felt before, stirred in the Princess. Deep. Guttural. Primal. She immediately spurred her horse into action. Galloping at full pelt, she reached the women, breathless.

"What is it?" she demanded, as her horse skidded to a stop. "What is wrong?"

The women were ashen, their gaze searching beyond the Princess, scouring those behind her. It was the eldest, Glaukia, who spoke.

"The Queen?" she said. "Is she not with you?"

Penthesilea's face fell, as she shook her head in concern.

"The Queen stayed here, at Themiscyra. You know that. She decided against the trip this year."

Confusion was etched on the women's faces. Penthesilea could not interpret this. How was it possible they did not know that Hippolyte had stayed with them? It made no sense.

As she stared at them, each one refusing to meet her eyes, Glaukia whispered, "The Queen, she is gone."

CHAPTER 14

*S*he had gone to war. That was the first thought that ran through Penthesilea's mind. The Queen had gone to war, just as she and Melanippe had joked about, earlier in the day. It would not be the first time she had left with only a small army. Yes, a large one was intimidating, but so was the sight of a dozen women slaying a hundred men without suffering so much as a scratch. Penthesilea felt a twinge of envy. Those had been some of her favourite battles.

She was ready to ask how long ago they had left—she already had some weapons on her, and it would take but a moment to grab a fresh horse and retrieve her axe. But the words froze on her lips. These women were showing no hint of the pride that came when their Queen was away, spreading their fame. Their eyes were narrow, their foreheads creased with more than just age. The manes of their horses rippled as a wind curled in from over the sea.

The others had now caught up with her.

"What has happened?" someone called out.

Whispers ran through the throng. A cloud drifted in front of the sun, turning the azure sea a dirty grey.

Penthesilea's eyes were trained on Glaukia. She was one of their oldest and, when mellowed by the fumes of the seeds, would gladly regale the rest of them with tales of Otrera and Ares and the early days of the founding of the Amazons. She was known for both her agility and her frivolity and had broken more than one bone attempting tricks on horseback that she had not performed for years. Yet the woman who stood before them now displayed nothing but anxiety.

"There is something else," she said, quietly, glancing behind Penthesilea and her sisters to the waiting women, who had now fallen silent, hoping to catch a whisper of what was being said.

"What is it?" Penthesilea replied, in equally hushed tones. "What else is there we should know?"

The woman swallowed. Her hand trembled and she looked as pale as if she had taken a blade to the belly and was losing blood. This was not a response an Amazon would show, even if confronting death.

The woman was afraid.

"What has happened?" the Princess asked, this time more firmly. "What has happened to my sister?"

The old warrior took a deep breath and looked up to the sky, as if offering a silent prayer to Ares himself, before she spoke.

"The Queen had a man. A man who stayed with her here, in Themiscyra. And now they have both gone."

～

HOURS HAD PASSED. The horses had been brushed down and fed. In the time it had taken the women to reach the city walls, the winds had brought rain that pelted down so heavily, it bounced around the women's ankles as if the earth itself were retaliating against the heavens. No women had gone to the river.

Penthesilea paced the stone floor, mindlessly rotating an arrow between her fingers.

"I do not understand. You say she kept him with her. She ..."

It choked her to say the word.

"... *wanted* him here."

"I would say she enjoyed his company," Glaukia replied.

"In more than just a carnal sense?"

The old woman nodded.

"They were barely apart. And never at night. Ask any of the women. We all saw them together, fighting, riding, laughing."

This last one Penthesilea had the most difficulty understanding.

"Do you think it is possible that she has left with him?" Melanippe asked. "That she has abandoned the Amazons?"

Unable to bear their despairing looks any longer, Penthesilea turned and walked over to the window. The moon was high but had been transformed into a shapeless smudge behind the thin clouds. There were seven of them present, herself, her sisters and four others—the same three who had ridden with the news of the Queen's disappearance, plus one more. Glaukia and Eumache were the eldest, with their white hair in braids, worn tight to the scalp. The younger pair were Derione, who had been injured in battle prior to the trip to the Gargareans, and Andromache, whose skill as a wet nurse made her more valuable here than elsewhere.

Even though she had her back turned to them, Penthesilea

could feel their eyes boring into her, waiting for her reply. But what answer could she give them? She would never have dreamt that her sister might abandon her people and the honour bestowed upon her by Ares himself. But then, she could never have imagined that she would welcome a man into their home with open arms.

She turned back to Andromache. "You say he came with the offer of marriage?"

The woman nodded.

"Bold as brass. And not just once. That was the reason for his arrival, or so he said. I overheard him mention this several times. He had no shame declaring his purpose."

"And she did not rebuke him?"

"She did," Derione replied, forcefully. "Each time. She said she would never leave her home. That she would never choose to be the wife of a king, when she was a queen in her own right."

Some relief came with these words. Several sighs filled the air. Penthesilea could well imagine her sister saying this. It was as if the room itself had been allowed to breathe.

But the relief was short-lived.

"Then he must have taken her against her will," Antiope said.

"How? She would have struggled. One man alone could not have taken her against her will," Melanippe countered.

"While he was here, his ship remained moored someway out at sea," Derione offered, by way of explanation. "And one of our small fishing boats has gone, too."

"When was this?"

"About a moon ago."

Silence hovered. Was this not a piece of news they might have thought to share with her earlier? At least they could be certain how she had left, which only served to reinforce the notion that this had not been by choice. Given any say in the matter Hippolyte would only ever have left on horseback.

"How many sets of footsteps were on the beach?" the Princess asked. "If it is only one, then we will know for definite that he has taken her."

Do not let it be two sets of footprints, was the thought that ran through her mind. *Do not let it be that she has left us by choice.*

It was clear from their faces that her sisters were thinking along the same lines.

"We did not realise she was missing until late in the day," Derione said. "By that time the tide had swept in and washed away any signs in the sand. Any footsteps that might have been there had gone."

Disappointment filled the sisters, as heavy as rocks in their bellies.

There was no Queen anymore. She was gone.

"Why did you not come and find us immediately, to tell us this?"

The Queen had been gone for an entire moon. Who knew where Theseus might have taken her by now?

The women hesitated. Finally, it was Glaukia who spoke.

"We thought … We thought that perhaps she had gone to join you. Ridden out at night and none of us had seen her."

"Or that she had gone by choice."

Andromache bowed her head, chagrined by her own words.

Afraid that she might make an end of them there and then, Penthesilea turned away to her sisters.

"I will take a small group at first light," she said.

"A small group?" Antiope responded. "We need our full force. Every woman. We will make this prince pay for the abduction of our queen."

"If she was abducted."

"You heard what Derione said. Hippolyte refused his marriage proposals. She cannot have wished to go with him."

"She refused him in public. We cannot ignore the fact that she allowed a man within the walls of Themiscyra. If we attack en masse, only to find she left us by choice, we will have waged war for no reason. Others will then come to Athens' defence once they learn that we are in the wrong. We will be risking our home."

She knew it was not the response her sisters expected her to offer, and as she drew in a long, laboured breath, they exchanged a look that spoke volumes. She knew, without doubt, what they were thinking.

"I have no wish to seek glory for myself," Penthesilea said. "I am thinking only of Hippolyte. Of what is safest for my queen. Our queen."

She knew from their expressions that they remained unconvinced. They assumed her plan was to tear through Athens alone, to save her sister single-handed and receive all the glory. And while it was true that such a thought had, indeed, visited her mind briefly, she had dismissed it just as quickly.

"Then what?" Antiope asked, still unconvinced. "If we find out that she has been taken, what do we do then?"

"Then we will do what the Amazons do best," Penthesilea replied. "We will go to war. And Theseus will die."

CHAPTER 15

*T*he journey was more arduous than she had anticipated. From the moment they descended the steppes of Pontus, the rain assailed them. Drops as big as pebbles blurred the path before them and the landscape beyond, making it impossible to establish in which direction to ride. The sky, swollen and grey, pressed down on them with a weight that seemed to slow their minds, too, while the water filled their boots and soaked through their caps, sending rivulets of water down their faces.

"Princess, we cannot keep moving like this. The horses will fall," came a voice from behind, only just audible over the noise of the storm.

"We have fought in worse than this," Penthesilea shouted back, just as a bolt of lightning flashed in the distance, momentarily illuminating the sky.

"Please, Princess," called Cletes, "we cannot save her if we do not make it as far as Athens."

Penthesilea twisted in the saddle and tried to determine their location. They had been travelling west when they had left at dawn, but now the clouds were so dense, it was impossible to locate the position of the sun, let alone the sea, to guide them.

"We cannot camp here," she said, eventually. "Keep your eyes out for somewhere we can shelter. A rock face or a copse."

She heard the women murmuring behind her, muffled by the rain. Kicking deep into her horse's flanks, she pushed on.

The rain had still not abated when they reached a sandstone cave cut into a rock face with a small overhang that offered the horses a little protection. From the ashes on the cave floor, it was evident that it had been used for shelter before now, by farmers, perhaps, or possibly by their own nomadic women. The thought did not fill her with comfort. She had hoped to be further on the journey by now, past the Sea of Marmara and into Thrace. As long as the rain hammered down on them like this, she knew she had no choice but to wait for it to pass. She hoped that perhaps by the morning the clouds would have emptied themselves, but as night fell and then Selene's silver moon came and went, the rain persisted. Penthesilea and her women remained trapped within the confines of the cave, their clothing failing to dry in the damp, musty air. There was none of the usual banter of a normal expedition. This was anything but normal. Outside, the whinnying of the horses grew more intense as they expressed their own craving for food and warmth.

Five women had joined her on this rescue expedition: Klonie, Polemusa, Thermodosa, Derione, and Cletes. The first four she had picked not only for their skill in battle but for their looks, too. They were entirely different from one another in appearance, yet equally alluring, in a way that would appeal to the wandering gaze of any man fortunate enough to come across them. The swell of their breasts, the curve of their hips, all impossible for any red-blooded man to ignore, and necessary for Penthesilea's plan. Even if their beauty failed, their arms would not. They were each of them proven killers. Smart and ruthless. Efficient and deadly. All except Cletes.

She would not have been Penthesilea's first choice, although also very beautiful—her dark eyes, mahogany hair and eyelashes long enough to cause a breeze would be certain to bewitch any eyes that fell on her—their recent trip to the Gargareans had been Cletes' first, after only making her maiden kill in battle less than a year earlier. But she had begged Penthesilea to let her join them, having assigned herself the role of page to the princess. It was she who had brought food to Penthesilea on those first nights with the Gargareans, when the princess had felt it necessary to stay out in the cold, on guard, and who had rubbed down her horse after every long journey. And when Penthesilea had still refused her request to join them on the trip to Athens, Cletes had ridden after them anyway, dressed in her embroidered robes, hope and optimism flowing from her very pores. Given all that she had done for her, Penthesilea did not have the heart to send the girl away. And so, five women became six, riding together towards Athens.

She had decreed that Melanippe and Antiope should remain at home, a decision that was met with great animosity, particularly from Antiope. This time, she had not shrunk from complaining, accusing Penthesilea outright of seeking glory, of wishing to make her name as renowned as that of Hippolyte. After all, should something happen to the Queen then she, Penthesilea, would be next in line. Her words had been laden with venom. Penthesilea, she said, had been placed second by her father. Not quite worthy of his zoster, and for that reason, she should be the one to stay in Themiscyra and Antiope the one to lead the women to Athens. She was almost as good a shot as Penthesilea, she argued, and certainly a greater warrior than anything the Athenians could muster.

But Penthesilea threw her argument back at her. With Hippolyte gone, she was the one who ruled, and she would be the one to ride to Athens not, as her sisters believed, for the glory or so that her name would be sung in halls and taverns and not for her name to be recorded in history. She would go because she could not sit idly by and wait for news. Because the absence of her sister and not knowing what had befallen her had tied her stomach in knots, ones spiked with blades which were tearing at her insides.

In all her life, she had never succumbed to illness as so many did. No sickness of the gut or malady that caused her temperature to rise. This was as close to that as she had ever come, and it would only pass when Hippolyte was riding beside her once more. And *if* Theseus had abducted the Queen, as she believed he had, then his death was imminent. She would fight until Athens crumbled. But until she heard this from Hippolyte's own lips, however flighty and impetuous Antiope might think her, she would not declare a war in which she risked the lives of their women, without her sister's authority and not while there was a chance that she was still alive.

By the next morning the sky had finally and mercifully cleared, and sunlight shimmered unbroken on the sodden earth.

"We will travel close to the coast," Penthesilea told them as they attached their saddlebags. "The ground will be drenched and precarious. Be gentle with your horses, we cannot risk lameness."

She knew the route well enough. They had travelled from

Anatolia into Greece countless times. Sometimes their visits had lasted mere days, on other occasions for weeks on end, when king after king would call for their aid, fearful of losing their lands but unable to summon enough strength from their own resources to crush their invaders. They had turned green grass red, had decimated armies who had thought themselves invincible until they had seen the half-moon shields of the Amazons glint on the horizon. They had been called to swing their swords and fire their arrows in so many wars there that Penthesilea would need a week to recall them all.

But this was different. Every time they had ridden here before, to Macedonia or Thessaly or beyond, they had known who it was they were going to fight or at the very least, who they were going to fight for. This time, all was uncertainty.

They did not speak as they rode, pushing the horses into a gallop only when the terrain was flat, even and dry enough to permit it. Occasionally, one of the women would point out a spring or stream where they could stop to drink, but other than this, even Cletes remained silent.

As they rode in the thinner, cooler air, past the vast expanse of Mount Parnassus, the sky was a bright blue and the lush greens of cypress trees and cedars rose high above them. Orchards flourished on the mountainside and grape vines were so prolific that they almost obscured the houses, the fruit bowing the trellises they were tied to. The mountain was sacred to Dionysus, son of Zeus and God of Wine and Ecstasy. Given the abundance of fruit, it was easy to see why.

"There is a place a few hours south of Boetia," Penthesilea told the women as they slowed to traverse rockier landscape. "We have a friend there. We will be able to rest for the night. Eat and change our clothes."

"Change our clothes?" Klonie asked.

"We cannot travel to Athens like this. It will arouse too much suspicion."

Trousers and tunics were the standard wear of the Amazons. Leather caps fitted close to the head were worn while riding and in battle, occasionally adjusted to fit a metal helmet, should the severity of the fight require it. She had assumed the need to change their attire would have been clear to her women, as obvious as leaving the horses and spears where no man would find them. They could hardly go riding into Athens declaring their warrior status for all to see. But their cheeks paled, and Klonie gripped her bow tightly.

"But our weapons?" she asked.

Penthesilea inhaled sharply.

"We can take whatever we can strap to our bodies under our robes. As many daggers as you are comfortable wearing, provided they remain invisible. We cannot arouse suspicion. The rest of our weapons will stay in Boetia, with Cletes."

The young girl opened her mouth ready to object, then clamped it tightly shut again. The Princess had spoken. Unlike Penthesilea's sisters, Cletes did not question her rule. The other women exchanged furtive glances of apprehension that Penthesilea did not dignify with a response. They did not need weapons. She had seen Klonie snap a man's neck between her knees on the battlefield, Polemusa break a jaw with the swing of an elbow. The damage that one of them could inflict with a single dagger was easily comparable to that which a fully armed Athenian soldier might achieve. Their weapons, like Hippolyte's zoster, were simply a source of comfort, not their power. The comparison sent a shudder running down her spine. After all, Heracles' desire for that zoster was what had first brought Theseus to their shores.

They arrived at their resting point, south-west of Thebes,

two days later than she had hoped, the sky already ablaze with stars. Great constellations draped themselves across the firmament like mighty rivers, their countless tributaries glinting bright white against the endless indigo expanse. Sometimes, Penthesilea could lose herself in the thousands of stories they depicted, held in perpetual stasis by the will of the gods. Like that of Cassiopeia, the beautiful queen bound for all eternity to her chair in the sky.

While undeniably attractive, the boastful Queen Cassiopeia had claimed herself to be even more lovely than the nereids, the sea nymphs who accompanied Poseidon and aided sailors in their travels. The God of the Sea was protective of these maidens and had taken great umbrage at her remarks, sending the horrifying sea monster, Cetus, to ravage her kingdom. In a desperate attempt to pacify the beast, Cassiopeia had tied her daughter, Andromeda, to a rock in the sea, for Cetus to feast upon. The story told how Andromeda was saved. The hero Perseus, armed with a gorgon's head, had swept in on the winged horse, Pegasus, and rescued her from certain death. Unforgiven, Cassiopeia was tied to her chair and cast out to the stars, condemned to sit and watch the world revolve beneath her for all time.

"You will not be rash, will you?"

Penthesilea drew her eyes away from the sky. Cletes had spoken from the other side of their campfire. Twists of smoke wove their way upwards, darkening the air between them. The other women, on the Princess's orders, were sleeping, yet Cletes was awake, remaining with Penthesilea, as if it were her calling to do so.

"I know I cannot ask anything of a princess, but if I could, I would ask you not to be rash. Not to try to kill him on your own."

"I would have left you in Pontus if I had have known you would start speaking like my sisters."

"Your sisters say the things they do because they love you. I speak—"

She stopped short, as if Penthesilea might not want to hear what she was about to say.

Silence ensued until a crackle from the fire sent tiny amber sparks up into the air, rousing them from their separate thoughts.

"You should sleep now," Penthesilea told her.

When morning arrived, they dressed themselves in Athenian clothes they had purchased in a nearby town, fussing with the fabric that fluttered between their legs.

"This cannot be right," Polemusa insisted. "There is too much fabric here. How is one to run in a such a garment?"

"One does *not* run in such a garment," Penthesilea replied, attempting to conceal how she, too, was struggling.

Given the length of the journey still ahead of them, they continued on horseback. The women grumbled incessantly about their clothing, and gasps of frustration rang out every time a sharp wind whipped the fabric about them. Penthesilea herself remained silent, despite the discomfort she was enduring from the thin leather sandals on her feet. Boots were infinitely more practical for riding.

At mid-morning, they found a small area shrouded by trees, where they stopped and dismounted. The horses immediately dropped their heads to eat.

"This is where we leave you," Penthesilea told Cletes.

"Be safe, my princess," she replied.

Penthesilea could see a question glinting in her eyes. The need for a reassurance she could not provide. Turning, she tethered her horse to a nearby tree before recommencing the journey, without further word.

Now on foot, the remaining five women passed over rocky terrain and through verdant fields filled with olive trees, their gnarled trunks opening into crowns of iridescent leaves. Goatherds kept their animals beneath makeshift tents, within poorly built wooden fences that seemed no match for a determined beast, or else left them to wander amid the shade of the groves. The women made no eye contact as they walked and kept veils over their heads and across their faces, leaving only their eyes exposed.

"People are staring at us," Polemusa whispered, as they passed a family feasting on flatbread and olive oil. As the women drew closer, the family fell silent, and even after they had passed the hush lingered, though Penthesilea paid it no heed.

"Possibly it is their land," she said. "It does not matter, either way."

The closer they came to Athens, the more fertile the farmland and vineyards grew. Row after row of twisting vines cut across the landscape, interspersed with wheat, the golden yellow a stark contrast to the bold green.

At first, the air smelt of cultivation, of ploughed earth and pollen, of freshly pressed oils and burning cedar wood. Gradually, though, those scents faded and were replaced by the fetid odours of urban life, both human and animal, an unmistakeable rankness. And yet, even amidst the stench, when they reached the citadel walls, the women had no choice but to stop and stare, momentarily awestruck by what lay before them.

They had reached Athens.

CHAPTER 16

The fortifications were unlike anything Penthesilea had seen before. A deep dry moat had been cut into the earth in front of the first wall, which stood at the height of two men. This smaller structure was constructed parallel to the main citadel walls with their towers and battlements roofed with terracotta tiles that looked like burnt earth in the glaring sun. The narrowest of windows punctured the dense stone—wide enough for an arrow to be shot from but not shot into, unless the bow were held by an Amazon, she thought. Her arrows could fly through those with ease. If anything, they were a fixed target to aim at.

The wall wove around the mountainside, its yellow bricks encircling a city of which she could glimpse only the smallest part, that which was visible through the enormous gates. There were several such entry points positioned all along the walls, she knew. They had come from the north, the easiest approach to Athens, although they might need to reconsider this route when they left.

"Come, we should accompany these people. It will arouse

less suspicion," Penthesilea said, gesturing towards a group of around fifteen. Most of them were men, but half a dozen women dawdled behind, their pace slower as they exchanged gossip, whilst playing deaf to the wittering of those in front. With a nod of Penthesilea's head, the Amazons sidled up beside them and slipped seamlessly into step with the party as they crossed the moat.

There was so much to gaze upon. Too much for her eyes and ears to take in all at once, although, thankfully, her sense of smell had grown inured to the stench that only a short time ago had made her want to retch. The vast number of buildings and people struck her first. Hoplites—the Athenian soldiers—were easily identifiable, with their sculpted bronze breastplates and polished helmets, the gleaming metal imprinted with their crest. As Penthesilea passed them, she and the rest of her women slowed a little, each taking note of the same things: the number of guards, the weapons they carried and the places in which the wall might be scaled. The soldiers held spears and xiphe which would prove useful weapons once the men had been relieved of them. But not yet, Penthesilea reminded herself. Not until it was necessary.

The topography allowed only glimpses of the citadel. Unlike the steppes in Pontus, where the ground rose and fell gently, as if moved into position by the very breath of the Earth, the hills and valleys here felt as if they had been forced into place with hammer and axe, all jagged peaks, great rocky ledges and steep inclines, littered with yet more people and buildings. Temples sat on the summits of the hills. The Acropolis, shrouded in the smoke of incense and teeming with crowds, was visible even from their low elevation.

The women shifted closer together, as if preparing for an enemy attack.

"Are those temples?" Derione asked, in a hushed voice, only now noticing them. "And, if so, why do they need to be so large?"

"Because they are Greek. They revel in the ostentatious. It is like shouting a prayer and expecting it to be heard more readily."

Her voice was thick with cynicism, as she attempted to disguise the awe with which she herself was viewing these edifices and other buildings. Even the wall itself.

They continued to move with the group of men and women towards the agora. Athens was known for its trade and the marketplace would be at the heart of it, a place in which people could bargain for honey, lamps, silver jewellery and a thousand other things they might need or just want. She had seen plenty of agorae before, although usually in a state of disarray after a battle. However, whatever expectations she might have had, they soon paled into insignificance as they turned a corner.

"Where has this all come from?" Klonie asked.

This was it. The heart of Athens. A market so bustling and busy that even the goats failed to lie still in their pens. The aroma of not only olives but the deeper, richer, fragrances of rosewood, cinnamon, iris, cistus, myrtle and hyacinth, wove in invisible coils, perfuming the atmosphere around them. Perfectly spherical peppercorns, dark grey and flushed pink, filled small wooden bowls. Salted fish were displayed on tables, their colours graduating from deep red to a crystalline white. There were stalls selling leather, in pelts or cut and shaped into items such as sandals, and others offering fabric, wood, papyrus and more. The list was endless. People flitted from one to another, some with obvious urgency, others at a leisurely pace.

It was mesmerising. So much so that perhaps Queen

Hippolyte might have chosen to live here. The question had barely formed in Penthesilea's mind before she shook it away again. Beneath the attractive surface, less appetising aspects were all too apparent. Dung and rats were almost ankle deep in places, and drawn by the effluent running in the gutters, flies and mosquitoes buzzed around the lips and eyes of people and animals alike. Drunkards lay in the heat of the sun, snoring, some in pools of their own vomit, while children raced over their bodies as if they were nothing more than corpses. No, Hippolyte would not relish a life here. She was certain of it.

Several pairs of eyes were now fixed on the women, and she realised they had separated from the group with which they had arrived. At least she had not brought Cletes with her, she thought, for then they would definitely have something to stare at. Paying them no heed, she continued to survey the agora.

Under another canopy, a dozen men and women were packed together, their arms bound behind them, dark and light skinned and of varying ages. The Princess's eyes were drawn to a woman with her back to her. Her dark hair was of the same shade and thickness as Hippolyte's, a little shorter perhaps, but nevertheless, weaved in a plait that her sister could easily have worn. Was it possible that this was what Theseus had planned? To kidnap the Queen and see her humiliated as she was sold to the highest bidder?

Penthesilea's pulse raced. Her feet slid on the ground as she approached, the dung and mud oozing into her sandals and around her feet, but she did not even notice.

"Sister?"

The woman turned. Her dark eyes, lined with kohl, were almond in shape. Her jaw was square, her nose long and her brow low. There were no similarities.

"My apologies," she said and slowly backed away.

As they picked their way through the stalls, uncertainty churned within her. A sensation which felt akin to milk souring was ripening in her gut, as if she were heading into a battle with no idea from which direction an attack might come. She knew that her women felt it too. Even if it were somehow a straightforward thing to remove Hippolyte from the Palace, they would not manage to escape a place as busy as this without casualties.

They had fallen, quite accidentally, into a formation in which they regularly fought, moving slowly, their eyes constantly scanning around them, their hands gripping the waistbands of their robes, where their daggers were hidden.

The noises were distracting. Men shouting, trying to sell their wares, children screaming and crying. Dogs barking. Horses nickering.

"Garnets! Sapphires! Rubies!"

A hawker was calling to each person who approached, and seeing the group aimed his call at them.

"Garnets, the biggest you'll ever see!"

"Where shall we go?" Derione whispered.

A drumming had started beneath Penthesilea's ribcage and a rush of adrenaline was surging through her veins. She was scouring the horizon, still unsure which way to turn, when a hand reached out and grabbed her by the wrist.

Instinctively, the Princess snatched the dagger from her waist, spun around and pressed it against the hawker's throat. The remaining Amazons immediately fell into position around them, blocking them from the eyes of passers-by.

"You dared touch me?"

The hawker tried to pull back from the blade. Although acting automatically, she had managed to angle it with precision, so as to not draw blood, yet with enough pressure to constrict his windpipe and cause considerable discomfort.

"My mistake," he rasped. "I am sorry. Forgive me. Forgive me. Please, forgive me."

She loosened the pressure just a fraction and he fell back, gasping for air, tears glistening in his eyes as they darted from side to side. Even though the knife remained in the Princess's hand he looked past her, as if the worst was yet to come. When nothing else occurred, he slumped to his knees.

"You are on your own," he said, with a mixture of disbelief and horror.

The realisation struck Penthesilea a full heartbeat before Derione spoke.

"That is why all those people were staring," she said. "We have no man with us. All the other women here are accompanied by men."

Was that really the case? Penthesilea shifted her stance slightly to look around. Now that her attention had been drawn to the fact, it was so obvious. Of course, women in a city such as this were not allowed to be independent, and a chaperone would be required if one wished to wander the streets of Athens. She had already known this, yet somehow it had slipped from her mind. Or perhaps it was simply that when she had been in such places before, the rules had never applied to her, so she had paid them no heed. The situation now, however, was quite different.

"Prince Theseus, where does he reside?" she asked, her dagger once more at the man's throat.

He jerked his head up towards the Acropolis. Sitting at the same elevation as the Parthenon was a lower building, flat-roofed and with wide verandas. It was a sensible position for a palace, the Princess considered. If an attack were to come, its occupants would be out of harm's way, though even from here, she could see places by which they might scale the walls, if the time came for them to launch an attack.

Her sisters' words came back to her along with Cletes' hopeful request. This was not to be a storming. Not a fight in which she was to prove her worth as a warrior. If she was to enter, it would have to be with the willing acquiescence of those within.

A thought suddenly struck her, like a blunt arrow to the chest. With a smile on her face, she turned to the hawker.

"Pack up your gems," she told him. "You are coming with us."

CHAPTER 17

"*Who* are you?" stammered the man. His eyes were deep set and hooded. His bushy brows, presumably once black, were now grey and met in the middle. That he was not a native of Athens, Penthesilea had already established, from both his skin tone and his accent, but that would be to their advantage.

"Wrap this shawl over your head," she ordered, ignoring his question. "I do not want you to be recognised."

There was no longer any need for weapons. If he objected, he would meet a swift and bloodless end.

"Why? Why are you doing this? Who are you?"

"I am Penthesilea," she said. "Daughter of Ares. Sister of Queen Hippolyte."

"You are the Amazon Princess?"

Any colour that had remained in his cheeks now disappeared, and the trembling in his hands had migrated to his knees, forcing him to rest against his handcart in order to maintain his balance. Although he had previously looked fairly robust, he now looked quite helpless, frail even. The Princess allowed herself a degree of satisfaction at this. It was one thing to be feared with an axe in her hand, but another entirely to produce the same effect with words alone.

"Must I ask you again or do I need to use force?" she said,

He hurriedly began to pack up his things. As he did so, he glanced around, seemingly for a means of escape or a method of drawing attention to his plight. He seemed to think he could somehow race away from his captors without it ending in his death?

"There is nothing you can do," Klonie said, softly. Even menacing sentences, when spoken by her, had a lyrical lilt to them. "Either you do as she says, or you will not survive. Any one of us can end you in an instant."

He nodded his understanding as his shoulders slumped with the dawning of the truth. Even so, Penthesilea felt no guilt. A man who had accrued such a wealth of gemstones was no fool. And to make an enemy of an Amazon would be the height of stupidity.

With his bags filled, he stood up as straight as his shaking frame would allow and looked at the Princess.

"What do you want of me, now?" he asked.

The strength of his gaze was admirable, particularly from one who, judging by the smoothness of his palms, had likely never seen conflict in his life. Penthesilea felt an iota of respect for him

"Now you walk with us," she said, "to the Palace."

Time and again, Penthesilea found her eyes drawn to the stupendous edifices they passed. What did the gods think of such displays? she wondered. It was no secret that both Poseidon and Athena had competed for patronage of the city, each presenting the old King Cecrops with gifts that would help his land flourish beyond his dreams. Slamming his trident on the ground, Poseidon had spilt the earth open, and from it had come his gift: a spring of salt water, which formed an inland sea.

By contrast, Athena, under the watchful gaze of Cecrops, had planted a seed, which grew before his eyes into a lustrous olive tree, bursting with fruit. He immediately saw all its possibilities. Fruit could be used for oils, to burn in their dark nights or eaten, while they sat under the shade the leaves provided. It would give them wood that could be burnt or carved into weapons. It was an easy decision for Cecrops to make and the temples to Athena now stood proud. Penthesilea's father, the god Ares, by contrast, had never professed a desire for such recognition and was content for his daughters to show their dedication to him though the spoils of hunting trips and waging war.

From the rounded bellies of many of the Athenians, their offerings were still being well-received. The citadel was wealthy. Prospering. But if that were the case, why would Theseus have taken Hippolyte when he could have had his choice of women for a bride?

"Let your hands fall naturally," Penthesilea said to her women as they approached the steps to the Palace entrance.

"Clasping our daggers is natural," Klonie replied.

The Princess understood Klonie's concern. Discretion was not their forte. Hiding their intentions went against what any king would ask of them. They were Amazons. They rode into battle with spears raised and bows at the ready, their heritage pumping through their veins. Every man they had ever faced knew exactly who they were. Until today.

They reached the steps. The polished marble was slippery beneath their feet, slickened further by the mud that covered their sandals from the long walk and the slurry of the agora.

The veils which covered their hair and draped across their shoulders were little more than a thin gossamer, yet for Penthesilea it was claustrophobic, restrictive and, at times, suffocating. If they were to fight here, they would do so barefoot and in close contact, she decided. That way they could use the lack of friction of the floor and their opponents' weight to their advantage. They would need to place women around the citadel walls, too, and decide which gate to enter through and barricade the others so that no one could escape. A full-scale attack would be required if Athens were to fall.

The higher they climbed, the denser the crowds of people wishing to gain an audience with the King became. Those hoping to kneel on the floor of the throne room, where he might look down on them and, with mock interest, feign an understanding of their plight. Perhaps King Aegeus was different. Maybe he truly listened to his subjects. She thought it unlikely. She had seen enough to believe such audiences were nothing more than the affectations of tyrants. She had seen first-hand what happened when a king was given a *suggestion* he did not agree with. And just as the gem hawker had grown rich by his wiles, so did kings hold onto their power.

Time seemed to slow as they inched forwards through the throng, but patience was a skill her women possessed in abundance, honed during the long summer months, stalking a lone roe deer over miles by foot and perfected on endless dark winter nights, when they would keep watch for the slightest glimpse of an intruder on their lands. Penthesilea could see the women studying their surroundings, as did she, making a mental note if and how each person was armed, and the most efficient way they could be dealt with.

Over two-dozen hoplites guarded the entrance. The sight of the guards, with their plumed helmets and their formal cuirasses, pleased her. The presence of so many meant it more likely that royalty was present within the Palace rather than travelling. And if Theseus had taken Hippolyte, he would not have left her, knowing that she would try to escape at the first opportunity that arose.

Besides the hoplites, there was a man on his knees, the bottom of his sandals worn through so that the calloused and bleeding flesh of his feet was visible. An aroma of husbandry emanated from him. The oily scent of lanolin and goats.

"It is the third time this has happened. Please, let me speak to the King. I require a review with the Polis."

"The King will tell you to make offerings at the temples."

"I have done that! Please. Please. I am allowed another audience. The King will grant me that."

While the argument continued, Penthesilea scrutinised the hoplite with whom the man spoke, noting with interest how his weight was shifted to one side, causing his tunic to fall at a slight angle. He was taller than the other guards, almost Gargarean in size, but he had sustained an injury to his left side, and now it was slightly weakened. He was there for the purpose of intimidation rather than force. Knowledge of this fact could be vital if it came to a fight.

With the hawker still trembling next to her, she slid a little to the side to garner a better view from which she could study the other men who stood in the path between her and her sister.

The guard closest to the Palace door was smaller and slighter than the first one. His eyes were constantly moving, not only to observe those nearest to him but also those further away. He had a sharp ear, too, his attention moving quickly from one sound to another. When his gaze landed on her, their eyes met briefly before she lowered hers and shuffled back closer to the hawker. This felt strange. Men usually knew she had come to kill them. Having the time to read their strengths and weaknesses was not something she normally experienced.

"What are you here for?"

It took her a moment to realise that the first guard was now looking at her and her women. The man with the bleeding soles had moved on. Awaiting his next audience, he stood by the Palace walls. It was their turn. This, it appeared, was the only hurdle between her and her sister. Lowering her body into a deep bow, she glided forwards.

"I have women here," she said. "I am to present them to Prince Theseus."

The hoplite sniffed, recoiling with an air of deep repulsion.

"Why are you speaking to me?"

He turned to the hawker, whose trembling was now so pronounced that the gems in the bags he was holding were rattling. He opened his mouth, in a half gasp, before Penthesilea cut across him.

"My husband is a mute. He lost his tongue to bandits. It does not affect his ability to earn money, thankfully. No, as I have said, we have gifts, women, for the Prince."

The hawker snapped his mouth closed as the hoplite eyed her with suspicion.

"I did not know of this."

"They are a gift. From East Anatolia. A presentation to congratulate the Prince."

The guard remained stony-faced as he looked past her to study the four pairs of eyes that shone back at him through the slits in the women's veils.

"They have been requested by Queen Hippolyte as a gift to her future husband."

Was this not what Grecian men did, bartering and offering

women, as if they were cattle? She had seen it often enough. Women passed from man to man, the spoils of war, as transferable as gold or jewels, the only real difference being that the value of a human lessened with time and in old age, they became worthless rather than being considered valuable for their wisdom.

"We are to see Queen Hippolyte first," Penthesilea spoke again. "She can confirm this for you. You can take us to her now. We have come from Anatolia."

She added a little force to her final words. If they were keeping Hippolyte there, then they would know who she was and should not be surprised by the presence of women on their own who were able to speak their minds, even in the presence of their husbands.

With barely a twitch of his finger, the hoplite gestured to one of the guards behind him. A moment later he was gone and the new guard, pointing with his hand, indicated that Penthesilea and her women were to wait by the Palace entrance, next to the reeking goatherd.

"What now?" Polemusa asked when they were out of the hoplite's earshot.

"Now we wait."

"And if they do not allow us to see Hippolyte?"

Penthesilea drew in a deep breath.

"We are asking as a courtesy, that is all. If my sister is in this building, I will not leave until I have spoken with her."

Beside them the goatherd wheezed. He was covered in dust, no doubt from his animals which he probably kept in small pens but would bring into his home on the colder, wetter nights. There had been girls born in Themiscyra in such conditions, who wheezed from the day of their birth. They tended to prefer the nomadic life, away from large herds, and usually kept poultry, but they still had a place in Pontus and with the Amazons.

Penthesilea found herself wondering how long it would take them to find Hippolyte. The Palace was grand, but surely not so massive that a brisk walk wouldn't cover it all. Perhaps she had been wrong to assume Theseus had brought her sister here. Perhaps her refusal of his marriage proposal had seen him devise a more terrible punishment. She did not fear for her sister's life, but then she had not feared she would be abducted, either. When the guard reappeared in the doorway, he beckoned them inside.

"You can present your women to the Polis," he said, "who will decide if they are to be gifted, as you request."

"The Polis is for men, but my husband cannot speak to them."

"There will be no need for words. It is easy enough to see what is on offer here."

The guard lifted a hand towards Polemusa, as if to grab her and shackle her the way they had seen the slaves in the agora. The women stiffened, each one fighting the urge to kill him there and then.

"No," Penthesilea replied, stepping between them before his hand could graze her skin. "That is not what we requested."

A sneer twisted the hoplite's lips, his narrowed eyes gazing past Penthesilea and lingering on Polemusa a moment longer before he addressed the Princess once again with a look of deepest scorn. Repulsion seemed to almost ooze from his pores.

"You seem to forget your place, woman."

"And you seem to forget that the woman you are harbouring here is the Amazon Queen."

It was so fast, so instant, that only the Amazons knew it was coming. While the hawker watched dumbfounded, the guard had no time to adjust his look of disdain to one of incredulity before the women had surrounded him, shielding him from the sight of his comrades outside. Within the space of a moment, Penthesilea's hands had reached up, grabbed his head and twisted it, breaking his neck in one swift movement, causing a snap to ring out and echo from the high ceiling above them. The knees of the hawker buckled, but Penthesilea caught him before he hit the ground.

"Do not give us away, or you will meet the same end. Now, where would the women of the house be?"

He stuttered and gasped to the point of hyperventilation.

"If you cannot tell me anything, you are no longer of use to me."

His stuttering continued for a moment longer.

"The gynaeceum ... The women's room ... It will be near the centre of the building, so that they cannot see outside."

She held his gaze for a heartbeat, trying to read any deception there. Then, with a satisfied nod, she patted him on the shoulder.

"There, I knew you would have a use."

She turned to her women.

"Keep him with you. Find a place to put the body where it won't soon be discovered, then hide yourselves. If anyone finds you, deal with them without attracting attention."

The women nodded. Penthesilea did not wait to see the satisfaction she knew would glint in their eyes at the prospect of a killing. Instead, she headed inwards, to find her sister.

CHAPTER 18

*W*aves rattled against the sides of the ship as she tried again to clear her dazed mind from the effects of the drugged wine. She kept falling in and out of consciousness, one moment hearing the singing of men, the next the slap, slap, slap of oars on water.

She brushed her hand down her body, only to be startled by the feel of the fabric. Soft, smooth silk. The garment was unlike any she had worn before. As she shifted unsteadily to her feet, drapes of the material fell to the ground and over her bare feet, tracing the lines of her figure. Where had this come from? She collapsed back onto the bed.

Slowly images formed in her mind. Disjointed, fractured scenes in random order, accompanied by sounds that did not fit them. It was as if her memory had been broken, like an amphora dropped on a stone floor, only to be pieced back together again so that the images no longer sat flush, side by side. Her home. The horses. Making love to Theseus in her chamber.

Then, with a churning that caused bile to rise to the back of her throat, she knew what he had done. She had been naked when he had fetched her the drink. When he had drugged her. And this garment, this gown, fit so her perfectly, it could only have been tailored for her alone. Of course it had. This had been his plan all along. Theseus had always intended to kidnap her.

She tried to stand again, but stumbled, the effects of the herbs still evident.

"Theseus! Theseus! Come and face me, you coward!"

Two more attempts to stand and she was on her feet, hammering her fists against the door of her cabin with such force that they started to bruise. The wood had been nailed together and, she suspected, was reinforced on the other side. Either that or she was even weaker than she feared. It was as if she were experiencing a detachment between body and mind. She must concentrate.

"Father! Father!" The words *help me* formed on her tongue before she swallowed them back down again. She had never asked him for help before and she wouldn't start now. She had offered him sacrifices, yes, but that was not the same thing.

Her throat felt raw. As if the tender flesh had been gritted with sand. The sudden hunger that gripped her offered a further indication of just how long she had been on this ship.

Inching back to the bed, she noticed a flask of water, hanging on a nail. She opened the bottle and greedily drank mouthful after mouthful, gulping it down. Only when she paused for breath and tasted the earthy bitterness, did she consider what she had just done. Her head hit the bed before she could even retch.

~

A PLATE of food had been placed on the floorboards by the next time she woke. Salted meats, dried fruit and biscuits. Standard fare for those travelling. Theseus had told her that his men had enough food to last them while he was with her, and now they had an extra mouth to feed. One they had no doubt catered for.

She surveyed the marks on the heels of her hands and, more painful, those that were left by the ropes that bound her wrists. She tugged, knowing she would find no slackness there. She had been tricked again. Shame coursed through her, sourer than any poison. She had been enslaved by a man, and it had taken place in her own homeland. Humiliation mingled with the valerian potion that had curdled inside her.

A ship this size would have a crew of over fifty men, all of them, of course, loyal to Theseus and ready to follow his every command. Had she been on land, dealing with that number would have provided only moderate exercise, barely a challenge. But at sea? If she tried to take command by killing Theseus, he would best her. This was his domain. His father was Poseidon, God of the Sea. She needed to be on land. Then Theseus would get what he deserved.

She picked up the plate with some difficulty, then went back to the bed and sniffed the food, then touched it with just the tip of her tongue, searching for that tell-tale sign of valerian. Yet even when she was fairly certain the food had not been doctored, she did not eat. Something else had caught her attention.

The hard, jerking motions of the ship had been replaced by a gentle swaying. A rhythmic rolling that rocked her back and forth. And along with the sound of lapping water came another. Footsteps. She stiffened as they grew louder. Closer. Echoed by the pounding of her heart. When they stopped directly outside her door, she lifted her bound wrist and pointed her elbows as her only weapon.

The second the door opened, she flew into action. With her elbows still raised, she slammed her full body weight into Theseus. But he had come prepared. He hammered his shield into her, smashing her back against the timber planks of the walls with such force that she felt them crack. Pain shot through her arms as she dropped back down onto the bunk.

"Careful, my love. If you damage the ship, we may never make it back to Athens."

"How could you do this to me!"

"I knew you would not come of your own accord. Your sense of loyalty runs too deep. It clouds your vision. But this is for the best, my love. You will see. You are free now. Free to rule with me."

"Free? You have captured me! Bound me!"

"A precaution, that is all. I knew you would need time to adjust and see this is for the opportunity that it is. We shall rule Athens together."

"That is not what I want!"

"Is it not?"

He was bolder, more self-assured now that she was away from her homeland. It was understandable. In Pontus he had been outnumbered. Now the tables were turned. It was also the first time she had seen him dressed in armour. Naked upon his arrival, he had worn only what she had offered him—trousers or, more often, a simple tunic. But now he was every bit the warrior.

Knowing he would not go to all this trouble only to see her harmed, she shifted back, allowing herself the indulgence of studying her enemy. Beaten bronze was moulded to the lines of his torso, and smaller pieces had been formed into curved plates that sat upon his shoulders and around his biceps. Only a little flesh was exposed, but there were places she could penetrate. She would need to get her hands free first and subtly, without him noticing.

With a sigh, Theseus took a seat on the wooden slats next to her. How man could create something to sleep on that was less comfortable than rock, was beyond her, yet these shipbuilders had excelled at the skill.

"Hippolyte, please listen. It is just the two of us here. You do not need to put up a front anymore or be concerned that one of your women might overhear you."

"You have stolen me."

He frowned, as if in disbelief, before shaking his head.

"No, my love. I have made it so that we can be together."

He put his hand against her cheek to draw her towards him, but she refused to move and kept her eyes averted as her fingers worked steadily at loosening the knots. When he realised she would not respond, he dropped his hand in defeat.

"Hippolyte, my love, I did not bring you here to fight with you. I did it because I saw the truth in your eyes, every time we kissed. I felt it in your body every time we were together. I knew that you wanted us to be together, too."

"You stole me!" she spat.

Her words had no impact on him whatsoever. It was as if he were deaf to her voice and the things she was saying to him. Without warning, he dropped to his knees.

"I need you. I need you as my queen. Please, Hippolyte, you love me, the way that I love you. I know you do. Surely you see this is the only way for us? We could not be together in Themiscyra. I have a kingdom. The greatest kingdom in the world."

"You are not even the King! You are a boy with delusions of grandeur."

She had gained enough movement in her wrists to twist them. Another minute more, and she would have both hands free to throttle him.

"No, I am the future King of Athens, and I will be the greatest king on Earth. And you will rule beside me."

He rose and kissed the smooth patch of exposed skin on her chest. She was aware that his own skin was smoother than it had been before and his manly aroma was masked with oils and soaps.

"No," she said, leaning towards him. "You can't do this. You need to turn the ship around and take me back to Pontus."

"I will not do that."

"I will make you."

"I would like to see that."

A smile rose on his lips, yet it had barely formed when she smashed her elbow across his jaw. The strike took him by surprise, and he fell backwards and landed on the floor, just as the ship surged and caused her to topple, too.

"You will not get away with this," she said, rising at the same time as him and aiming a knee at his groin. But he caught her ankle before she could make contact and tipped her backwards, slamming her down on the wooden planking.

"There is no man alive who can tame you, save me. Do you not see that?"

In a flash, her ankles were around his neck and she launched herself sideways, flipping him back down.

"I do not need a man," she panted, ready to strike again.

She kicked out with her feet, just as he rose, connecting with his chest and knocking him backwards once more. But before she could land the fatal blow, he was upright and ready for her. The erratic motion of the floor beneath her made it hard for her to find her rhythm.

As she backed away from him, desperately asking herself what her next action should be, her hands lighted on the discarded rope of her bindings. With a leap and a scream, she had it around his throat and was pulling it tight with every ounce of strength left in her arms. For a second, his cheeks reddened, and his eyes started to bulge. Then the ship bucked, and he was free again.

Every time she struck out at him he was ready with a counter and, if anything, seemed invigorated by her continued resistance and while his body was protected by armour, hers was still struggling with the effects of the drugs and lack of food.

"This is what you want," he said, his hands on his knees and blood trickling from a cut above his eyebrow. "You want a man who can control you. Who can best you."

"There is not a man on this planet who can do that," she spat, tasting the ferrous tang of iron on her lips.

The plate that the food had been on was smashed into fragments. Reaching down, she grabbed a shard, but as she went to straighten up, she felt the tip of a blade under her breast and the skin between her ribs yielding.

"I am your King," Theseus hissed into her ear. "And I will follow you to the ends of the Earth. You know that. Perhaps your love for me is not as fierce as mine is for you, but it will be. I promise you. It will be. And if you think it will not, then end me."

And with that, he stepped back and the pressure on her chest was relieved. A gasp flew from her lungs. He was standing away from her now, his knife held out between them, the hilt facing Hippolyte. The seas were suddenly silent and there was not a hint of motion. The noises of the sailors up on deck were a mere murmur beneath the sound of their laboured breathing.

Even their first fight, in the shallows with the waves lapping at their feet, had not felt as intense as this. No fight she had ever engaged in had felt like this.

"Take it," Theseus said, holding the knife out further to her. "If you cannot love me, then end me. Do it now. For I would rather succumb to you, like this, than live my life without you. It is your decision, my Queen. What will it be?"

Her eyes locked on his. He deserved to feel a knife in his heart, and she deserved to watch him die. So why was she not moving? Why did the thought of killing him cause her own body such torment?

"You see," he said, dropping the knife and stepping forwards to take her hands. "You love me, too."

CHAPTER 19

*T*he same smooth marble that had so unnerved Penthesilea on the steps leading up to the Palace, lined the floors within it, too. Those who lived here clearly had not considered the implications if it came to a fight, either because fighting was something they rarely considered or because the notion that one might reach the inside of a royal palace, was inconceivable. The distinct scent of resin and wax, no doubt used on the ornate frescos that covered the walls, caught in her throat. Freshly painted, bold blues and ochres decorated the corridors as far as her eyes could see. Her gaze was drawn to a seascape, in which waves crashed against a cliff and a bird flew above. An owl, she noted as she drew closer. Athena's bird for Athena's kingdom. She left the picture to continue her search.

The evening sun reflected off the stone floor. The Princess kept to the shadows, her fingers never far from her concealed weapons. Following the hawker's advice, she moved ever inward, her footsteps making no more noise than a drop of rain falling on sand. She stood motionless beside each doorway, her back pressed against the cold wall, listening. She often heard deep male voices coming from within the rooms, sometimes with intermittent laughter, sometimes hushed, as if confidences were being exchanged. But no woman's voice. No Hippolyte.

More than once, she was forced to dart into an alcove or dash behind a curtain as servers scurried past, burdened with silver platters and amphorae, but each time her concern was short-lived; the servants' eyes remained firmly fixed ahead.

She had just avoided one such encounter, when the sound of laughter echoed along the corridor from the next room. It was high pitched, like the tittering of gossips. Hippolyte would never giggle in such a manner. But it was a woman's voice, for certain, and the first that the Princess had heard inside the Palace.

Sliding along the wall to the next doorway, she waited and listened. It was not beyond the realms of possibility that this was a private chamber and that a man was in there with the woman, or women, causing such merriment. But after another moment, she heard a woman's voice again, speaking this time, and two more female voices followed quickly after.

Penthesilea looked around poised for whatever might happen next. Shadows cut across every inch of the floor. There was no natural light, just the flickering candles, and the sounds of the agora could no longer be heard. She had reached the innermost area of the Palace. Rather than a door, a heavy tapestry hung across the entrance to the room. She would have to step inside, or else wait in the hope of hearing her sister's voice. She didn't have the time for that, she decided. Tensing, as if preparing to swing her axe, Penthesilea pushed aside the fabric.

The sunlight came as a surprise, causing her to squint, for

although the room was fully enclosed within the Palace, an opening in the roof flooded the area with daylight. Tapestries adorned the walls, but some were also in the process of completion, with multitudes of threads lying in tendrils across looms. Plants and flowers, seemingly chosen for their brightly coloured petals and aromatic scents rather than any nutritional value, grew in large terracotta pots which encircled the stone fountain around which half the women were sitting, perched on the edge, their feet dangling in the water.

"Come in. Sit. Amalthea was telling us about her wedding night."

Penthesilea realised that she was the one being addressed and stepped further into the room. The attention of the women had now turned to her. They were looking and speaking as if her presence had been expected. Or at least, not unexpected. And yet, she could not move or offer a reply, for her eyes were fixed on the far end of the room and the woman seated on a couch there, her eyes trained downwards. She wore an air of boredom, as if her body were there in the room with the women and their gossip, but her mind was somewhere very different.

The sweet air had suddenly turned sickly. Had she passed this person in the agora, or even outside in the corridor, she would not have recognised her, the way her hair fell in gentle coils, glistening with oil and adorned with flowers and the soft, draped fabric of her robe fitted her so perfectly. Penthesilea's heart quickened, beating so fast it felt like the buzzing of a hummingbird's wing as she stepped towards her sister.

"Hippolyte," she whispered.

The Queen lifted her head, and a small gasp floated from her lips.

"Leave us!" she announced, standing.

The other women looked up from their gossip, startled.

"Our husbands—" one of them began, but she was not given a chance to finish.

"I said, leave us!" Hippolyte repeated, in a tone even Penthesilea would not have disputed.

Hurriedly, the women rose to their feet.

"We are not to be disturbed," Hippolyte told them as they filed towards the door. "Take your leave for the day."

The women shot side-long glances and curious scowls at Penthesilea as they disappeared through the curtain and out of sight.

The instant they were alone, Penthesilea raced to her sister, holding her in the longest, tightest embrace she had ever given. She finally broke away, tears of relief in her eyes.

"Tell me you did not leave of your own free will, Sister."

Her heart continued to race as she waited for the answer, beating so hard and so fast it felt as if the wrong word might sever it clean in two. In all the battles she had fought, never had she felt such nervous tension as she did now.

"I did not. I told him I would not leave with him, but he put something in my drink, a sleeping draught derived from the valerian root, I believe."

"I knew that must have been the case."

Relief flooded through Penthesilea. It was as if she had been waiting for this moment to be able to truly breathe again. The tension had wrapped itself so tightly around her lungs that every inhalation without her sister caused her more and more pain. She had not gone willingly. She had been taken. That any of the women had doubted this for even a moment should, in Penthesilea's mind, result in punishment. Yet she still had questions of her own.

"What about Themiscyra? Is it true you allowed him into our city?"

The dip of the Queen's head was the only confirmation she needed, and her heart, which she had thought had been healed by her sister's previous words, now splintered and fractured into a thousand pieces

"Why would you do such a thing?"

"I cannot say."

Deep creases formed in the Queen's brow, as if she was unsure of what she was recalling, like a dream whose once-sharp edges vanished on waking.

"It felt so natural. Heracles and his men had already been inside the citadel."

"When they threatened to kill you."

"I understand how you feel, but I cannot explain it. Sister, please, I know you will not be able to forgive me for this. I cannot forgive myself. I never will. I was not acting rationally. Something about him made me behave that way."

A cold shiver ran down Penthesilea's spine. It was not the first time one of their women had reported that a man had made them act irrationally, although she could not recall it ever happening to any of the those in Themiscyra. The claims came from the nomads, who roamed the land, free to meet with men whenever they chose. There was a suspicion that some lived with their men, too, at least in the colder months. It was possible they even raised their children together. It was never spoken of. But this was different. She needed to know the truth.

"You love him?"

The Queen hesitated before answering.

"From what I know of love, I believe I may."

Penthesilea was distraught. How could it be? Hippolyte was the strongest and the most fearless of them all. Their Queen.

They knew that their mother had loved Ares, but that was different. Ares was a god. She had always believed that she and her sisters were immune to such folly. They loved each other. They loved their lands and their women. Wasn't that enough? What more could one man possibly bring?

"Does he love you?"

"Yes, very much, I believe. In his own way."

Why could she not read her sister? She had once known her every thought, sometimes before Hippolyte had even processed them herself. But now, she could not for the life of her fathom the workings of her sister's mind.

A breeze rustled the leaves of the foliage. It was a mere infatuation, Penthesilea wished to say. Or worse. Was it beyond the realms of possibility that she was still under the influence of some drug? Her sister's body might be strong, but perhaps her mind was still addled by a concoction of Athenian herbs. Yes, Penthesilea thought, that had to be the answer. But before she could say as much, Hippolyte spoke again.

"There are no bonds holding me here, Sister," she said, softly, bursting Penthesilea's bubble of hope. "I believe he could be a match for me."

Penthesilea struggled to make sense of the this.

"A match? What does that mean?"

"It means he challenges me. He does not coddle me."

"Why would you need to be coddled? You are Queen of the Amazons. You could have killed him a dozen times over by now."

"No. He is like us."

Whatever she was about to say next, she did not wish to be overheard. Her voice dropped to a whisper, barely audible.

"He has ichor in his veins. He is the son of Poseidon."

This was the first thing she had said that had given Penthesilea pause. The love she had spoken of was ridiculous, no, catastrophic, but this ... this added weight to her theory. Weren't the gods known for their cunning and deviousness when it came to the seduction of women? And Poseidon was rumoured to be the worst of them all. She had heard enough.

"You need to leave here, right now. You will be safe; I promise you."

She reached out for her hand, but Hippolyte took a step back.

"Hippolyte?"

The Princess's tone was low, almost threatening, yet the Queen merely pressed her lips together.

"There is more," she said.

Penthesilea found a heat rising in her that was nearly unbearable as she waited for whatever fresh torment her sister was about to inflict upon her.

Hippolyte raised her hands to cover her stomach. It was such a simple action, and the words she spoke next were superfluous.

"I am with child."

The heat was replaced with a sudden chill. Penthesilea felt as though her very spine had turned to ice. Time seemed to have frozen, too, as the same words repeated over and over again in her mind. *I am with child.* This was what Hippolyte had wanted. What she deserved. But surely not like this. A myriad of responses formed in her mind, only for each to wither before it reached her lips.

"Are you certain it is his?"

"I am."

Penthesilea turned her back on her sister. Her carefully concealed knife had somehow found its way into her hand as she paced around the central fountain. After two laps, she was certain; her sister's mind might have been taken over by some madness she called love, but she would protect her niece.

"Your daughter is an Amazon," she said, arriving back in front of Hippolyte. "More than that. She is an Amazon princess. She must be raised as such."

"Assuming I have a daughter. If I have a son ..."

Her words drifted away. Penthesilea had no time to entertain such a ridiculous notion.

"She will be a girl. The gods will give you a daughter to carry on your name."

Hippolyte shook her head.

"We cannot know that for sure. If this child is a boy, then he will be a king and heir to Athens."

"What are Athenians? Painters. Poets. Your child will be a warrior. The descendent of the God of War himself."

"But if it is born a boy, we cannot bring him up as such. That is not what we do."

"Then we will send him to the Gargareans, as with all our sons."

She was becoming even more exasperated. Why was this conversation even necessary?

"They know that I did not lie with any of them this year," Hippolyte continued. "They will realise he is not theirs."

"What difference would that make? They would be honoured to raise your child, especially if, as you say, his father is the offspring of a god."

"It may not be that simple."

"Then it is a bridge we will cross when we come to it."

She had never had the patience of her sister—of any of her siblings—and felt justified in wanting to scream at her. It was only the risk of the women waiting somewhere outside might hear that was preventing it.

"Penthesilea, you must consider that if this child is a boy, then Theseus will kill anyone who stands between him and his heir."

"So what? You stay here? You abandon us, your women?"

"The gods brought him to my shore. I have to believe that this is their plan. And I do. You will make a far better queen than I ever was."

"That is not true."

"Yes, it is. We knew this before Ares offered me his zoster but have never talked about it. You are a mighty warrior, with the truest arrows that have ever been."

"And what does that signify? If that was all it took to be a queen, Ares would have made me the leader. He did not. He chose you."

Hippolyte rose to her feet. The pregnancy was not yet visible on her body, though her cheeks were flushed deep pink.

"If it is a girl, I will return her to you. Theseus will understand. He will know that she must be raised as an Amazon."

"And if the child is a boy, you will leave him here and come back to us? Boy or girl, you will return home?"

Hippolyte crossed the room to where Penthesilea now stood and pressed her hands against her sister's cheeks.

"This will not be the last time you see me, Sister, I promise you that."

There were no more words to say. The pain in Penthesilea's chest felt as if she had plunged her own knife into it and torn her heart clean out of the cavity. Breaking away from their embrace, she turned and walked silently to the door, pulling aside the heavy fabric. She cared not if anyone heard her heavy footsteps as she made her way back through the corridors to where her women and the hawker hid in the shadows. When she reached them, another dead guard lay alongside the first and the hawker's chiton was stained with vomit.

"We are leaving," she said, striding straight past them without so much as a second glance.

"What about the Queen?" Polemusa asked.

"She has made her choice," she replied.

CHAPTER 20

As the sound of Penthesilea's footsteps faded, Hippolyte sobbed, and for all her courage, it was not the first time she had shed tears since being taken from her home. She had wept that night on the ship after she had not been able to take Theseus' life, as she had intended. He had exposed the limitations of her abilities as a warrior, and this was how she knew her words to Penthesilea had been the truth. Her sister would make a far greater queen, for she would never hesitate to make a kill.

When she had disembarked in Athens, all those weeks ago, she had been searching for a way of escape, for any weapon she could use. But his men had been told to keep their distance from her and their weapons hidden. What was more, Theseus, for all the love he professed, had continued to drug her with valerian. She had been awake, though in a constant state of confusion. She could walk, and talk to some degree, but it had been as if the connection between her thoughts and her actions had been severed. Every movement took more concentration and every word had to be searched for.

During those first days in Athens, she had accepted only pure water and fruit in an attempt to prevent him drugging her, yet he still managed it. Could it have somehow been in the air? Had she been given the opportunity to kill Theseus when he came to her, she would have done, she thought. But she knew in her heart of hearts that she was lying to herself. She would not be able to do it. And he knew this, too.

When he brought her before his father, he might have been introducing a wild beast to him for all the welcome she received.

"This is who you have chosen?" Aegeus had said. "An oirapata?" *A slaughterer of men.*

How was it possible for him to see her in that light, she wondered, when she did not even have control of her limbs or speech. She drooled and dribbled and was asleep more than awake.

Any moment, she thought, her sister would arrive and sever their heads from their bodies in front of her. Any moment Penthesilea would come and complete the task she herself had been too weak to undertake, one she yearned for and feared in equal measures. But at that time, she had not yet realised she was with child.

The day after the meeting with Aegeus, Theseus came to see her with an apple in his hand. He took a bite, before offering it to her.

"See," he said. "Perfectly safe."

Hippolyte eyed the fruit suspiciously. Its crisp red skin and white flesh dripped with juice, and though her every instinct told her to either refuse it or throw it at him, her stomach growled and hunger gnawed at her, from so many days of resistance. She grabbed it and retreated, devouring it like a starved dog. When she was finished, she glowered at him.

"You cannot keep me here."

"I do not wish to. I would much prefer that you stay willingly. I want you to consider this your home and lead with me, as we spoke of in Themiscyra."

"And that is why you are keeping me a prisoner, like this? You wish me to rule from behind high walls, my mind addled, never to see the land I am queen of?"

"I will show you what it is I want of you. And you will like it. I promise."

"When?"

"As soon as my father leaves. He has been invited to Salamis. I am encouraging him to extend his stay there and allow you some space to become accustomed to our ways."

She sniffed, now wishing she had taken time to savour the apple, for in her rush to satisfy her hunger, she had barely tasted its sweetness.

"And when will he leave?"

"They are preparing the ships now."

The arrangements for Aegeus' departure took four more days, during which Theseus spent most of his time locked in with Hippolyte, bringing her fresh fruit and wine each time he arrived. The fruit she ate, the wine she knocked over or, on more than one occasion, threw at him.

They were only halfway through the second moon of the women's trip to the Gargareans. It would still be sometime before Penthesilea came for her and ended Theseus, she thought. Yet this made her almost as sick as the idea of staying here. For, now, they fought each day, and each fight ended in the same manner, with their bodies entwined and their lips feeding off one another in a frenzy.

That morning, his smile was wide as he took her hands and

said, "Come. I have a gift for you. One I am certain you will love."

He had been right. Although she still struggled to move freely in a chiton and was uncomfortable with the way it exposed so much of her skin, she felt so at ease walking beside him through the colonnades of the Palace and down to the temples of the Acropolis. Perhaps it was the contrast with the lack of daylight she had experienced for so long. The fresh air seemed to revive her skin and reanimate her spirit. She felt a lightness and a sense of freedom she could not recall having before. Here, there were no problems to solve, save her own. No people needed or depended on her.

They continued, descending until they had passed through the walls of the citadel and onto the farmland that surrounded it.

"Where are you taking me?" she asked.

"You will see."

Next, they took a narrow path through a vineyard, where small grapes bubbled on the vines and the large green leaves were already ripe enough to be picked and softened in brine for eating.

"Theseus?"

Rather than speaking he tugged her hand. And there, at the end of the path, they came to a clearing and a boyish smile came to his lips.

"I knew you could not be content here without your horses, but I did not know what you would prefer to ride. I will be honest, though, your particular method of riding should be reserved for when my father is away. Still, I wished you to have a steed that you would be proud of."

She was rendered mute by the sight before her. Horses. And so many of them. It was not simply the number that overwhelmed her but the variety. Her eyes were drawn to a grey mare, small in stature, like those she had ridden a thousand times before. Behind the mare stood a stallion. Every inch of his coat was jet black, and his mane and tail shone as if they had been dipped in oil. There were bays and piebalds, as well as palominos whose pale coats shone like moonlight.

"Where? How?" she asked.

"Some have been gifted to my father over the years, not that he even remembers, and I sent out an appeal before I came to you in Themiscyra. I sensed the first time we met that your horse was of great importance to you and I wanted there to be one here that you would feel proud to ride if you were ever to see Athens as your home, the way I hope you will."

He had done all this before he had even taken her, Hippolyte thought, and a fresh resentment took root within her. This was what he had planned, before she had taken him to her bed. But even as these thoughts flashed through her mind, she found it difficult to remain angry. Stepping forwards, she placed a hand on one of the bays. It snorted and she felt its hot, steamy breath.

The clearing was not large enough for so many beasts, and several had already begun to paw at the ground. Some of the men holding them looked concerned.

"Do not worry yourself. My Queen knows what she is doing," Theseus shouted.

It was the first time he had called her this, at least in Athens, and it felt so natural. She was his Queen, and this acknowledgement, along with the wonderful horses in front of her, filled her heart.

She moved between them, examining their coats and running her hand down their legs and over their backs. Several backed away. Others came toward her, although they were skittish, with the exception of one. One grey mare remained perfectly still, her eyes locked on Hippolyte. Small and nimble, she would be the perfect creature on which to go into battle, assuming she could be ridden. But yes, Hippolyte felt she could ride this mare. In fact, she was certain of it. She could see a darkness, a desperation in her eyes. She was telling her that they were the same. She yearned for the freedom to gallop and feel the wind on her body.

"It's just you and me," Hippolyte whispered, as she stretched out her hand to the animal, her words so faint they were lost on the breeze as soon as they had formed. "You and I don't fit in here, do we? I think that's a good thing."

She took another step forwards and then one more. Soon she was within an arm's length. The horse's ears went back, yet this sign of annoyance merely amused her.

"No, you don't mean that. I know you don't."

One more step, and her palm was so close, she could feel the mare's breath. The other sounds of the day, of animals and people, all faded away.

"I think we were meant to find each other here, don't you?"

At that moment, the mare pressed her nose into Hippolyte, not against her hand, but lower, beneath her chest, and with such tenderness it was as if she were comforting a new-born foal. They stayed like this as the rhythm of their breathing steadied and synchronised. And then not just two but three heartbeats joined as one. Tears streamed down Hippolyte's cheeks. It was all the confirmation she needed, for she had suspected it these last two days, and now she knew she was not alone in sensing it. As the mare lifted her head, Hippolyte pressed her face into her coat, absorbing her scent, her affection, her everything.

That night, she told Theseus what the mare had confirmed

for her. That she was with child.

He fell to the ground, tears in his eyes, and buried his head in her lap.

"This is the gods' gift. My son. My beautiful wife and now my beautiful son."

That was the moment she tried to hold in her memory as Penthesilea turned her back on her and left Athens.

This will not be the last time you see me, Sister, I promise you that. That was what she had told her sister. And it was the truth. If she bore a girl, then she would return to Themiscyra with her daughter. If it was a boy, she would return alone, abandoning both her son and Theseus.

The sun had set without ceremony or splendour, quietly withdrawing its presence and leaving only a greyness which, together with the quiet of the gynaeceum, was overwhelming her. Theseus would not visit her yet. Not with his father present. For while he had promised that she would live her life with the same freedom in Athens as she had enjoyed among her own people, he was not yet king. And as Prince, he had his duties and had been busy, visiting farmlands and acting as an emissary. She was not even sure that evening if he had returned to the city yet.

And so, it was without a second's thought that she pushed aside the tapestry and headed outside.

Had she known where she was going or was she just randomly walking? If the former, she would never admit it, either to herself or to Theseus. She stepped into a chamber bearing a large fresco of a garden scene, complete with pillars and trees. A scent of fortified wine and honey mingled with the burning oils of the lamps. And there, at the window, hands by his side as he gazed out on the whole of his kingdom, was King Aegeus.

CHAPTER 21

The old man's eyes appeared lost in the dark vista outside. His tightly curled grey hair and beard were trimmed to equal length. It was immediately clear he was different from many of the other kings she had met. Men who ate and drank to excess and surrounded themselves with sycophants. No, King Aegeus was a quiet man. Contemplative. The Palace was a statement rather than a stage. It was easy to see that Theseus had been honest when he'd spoken of his father's vision for Athens to become a hub of art and the centre of civilisation.

She had made no sound as she entered, and yet he turned to face her.

"Oirapata."

It was only the second time he had addressed her, and still he used the same term: *Slaughterer of men*. Whether it was uttered in disdain or disgust, she could not be certain. Probably a mixture of both.

"Are you lost? The andron is a room reserved for the men of

the household. Are your own gynaeceum and chambers not sufficient?"

She studied him, surprised that he had not immediately demanded that she leave or called the guards to remove her. Perhaps he knew that none of them would be a match for her.

"I am afraid I am unaccustomed to limits being placed on a woman's location."

"It is something you must get used to, if you are to stay here."

"I doubt that. You are not naive enough to believe that Theseus brought me here with the intention of transforming me. I think that if he hopes to change anything, it would be you and Athens itself, rather than me."

"Is that so?" he scoffed.

Despite the presence of a servant, he took an earthenware amphora from a table at his side and poured himself a small cup of wine, which he then cut with water.

"I will take a cup, too," Hippolyte said, with a step toward him. "Although I would like mine with a little more water."

He studied her face, as if searching for a trace of humour. Upon finding none, he collected another cup from the ledge behind him.

Even at night-time, the view across Athens was mesmerising, the umbra of night only intruded upon by the gentle glow of candles and lanterns. The rhythmic slapping of the waves against the cliffs seemed to be keeping time for the harmony of the soft chanting of the priestesses and the song of the cicadas.

Aegeus poured the wine although, against Hippolyte wishes, he filled the cup with nearly as much as his own, barely leaving room for a splash of water.

He held it out but made no move to take it to her. A small smile played on her lips as she walked toward him. She wrapped her fingers around the vessel; as she took it from him she noticed how firm his grip was. Steady hands also, without so much as a slight tremble.

"Queen Hippolyte," he said, raising his own cup and taking another sip of his wine. "I have heard many rumours about you and your people over the years."

"I suspect there are many making their way across our lands. Is that not the nature of those vile things? Tell me, which have come your way?"

"That you murder your children if they are born male. That you murder your lovers after they have served their purpose."

"They can serve their purpose more than once, you know," she replied, with a smirk.

"Is that so?"

His eyes simmered in a familiar way. How was it possible that she could see Theseus in them, she wondered, when the blood of Poseidon so clearly ran in his veins? Could Theseus somehow be son to them both? The evidence certainly suggested it.

The King and Queen continued to stand facing one another. Hippolyte could do this quite comfortably for several hours, without so much as an ache in her thighs, but this stance had its own connotations. People who stood were waiting for something, more often than not, a dismissal. And she was not going to be discharged. So, without invitation, she strode across the andron, took a seat and awaited Aegeus' response. It did not take long to come.

"And what about your breasts?" he said, having strolled over and taken a seat opposite her.

"My breasts?"

She arched an eyebrow.

"I have heard that some of your women mutilate themselves. Remove a breast so that they might wield a bow with greater efficiency. Shoot an arrow with better precision."

Hippolyte was not oblivious to these stories. The idea that they killed their new-born sons was something she had heard before, but this one was new to her. She couldn't help but laugh.

"I am sorry to disappoint you."

"So it is not true?"

"I suspect this is a tale dreamt up by men who wished to insinuate there was some abhorrent reason for our skills."

"And you do not kill those sons born to you?"

There was no malice and little judgement in his words. He was asking as if he were a scholar, attempting to glean as much information as he could about his latest acquisition. It was almost endearing, she felt and, once again, reminded her of Theseus.

"No, we do not cut off our breasts, and we do not kill our sons. We take them to their fathers."

"You wish only for daughters?"

"Women are our way of life. Women are the most fearless of warriors."

For the first time, a smile flickered on the old man's lips.

"Do not let my son hear you say that."

"My husband knows my opinion quite well."

"Yes, your husband ..."

His eyes drifted off, as if this bond was not something he was yet ready to accept. There had been no ceremony, no visit to the temple to have the gods bless their union, but was the child in her womb not all the confirmation she needed of their approval? Was the very fact that he had swum to her shore, unaided and uninjured, not a sign that the gods wished them to be reunited?

Clearing his throat, Aegeus turned his eyes back to Hippolyte.

"I assume you know that Theseus has told me that you are already with child?"

"I do."

"So, you must be aware that he would, of course, prefer a son. An heir to the Kingdom when it is his. Would you resent that?"

It was a question she had already asked herself, even before her sister's arrival and almost every hour that had passed since. A daughter would mean returning to her women and the continuation of her name through the Amazons. A son would mean something very different. She could return to Themiscyra, but then what?

"I trust in what the gods will decide," she said and, once again, Aegeus smiled.

"You answer wisely. I imagine you were a worthy queen to your people."

"I imagine I will be a worthy one to yours, too."

Then, without waiting for further conversation, and certainly not for dismissal, she rose from her seat and placed her cup on the table.

"Goodnight, King Aegeus. We will do this again, I believe."

WHEN THE DAY FINALLY ARRIVED, it brought with it a pain she had longed for over many years. The pressure surging through her body. The tearing of her muscles. She did not scream, as she knew some women did, but rather closed her eyes and breathed in the moment. With each tightening of her abdomen, she inhaled the scents of the oils that had been soaked into towels and pressed against her head, but she took none of the herbs offered to her. None of the remedies that the women of Athens relied upon to birth their children. This was the last moment in which she and her baby would truly be as one. And she wanted to feel it all.

When the child broke free from her womb and entered the world, its cry filled the air like a melody. It felt as if her heart had been divided into two and could never be whole unless that child was beside her.

Tears stung her eyes, as she reached down between her legs and lifted the baby to her chest.

"A son," she whispered, raising her eyes to Theseus. "We have a son."

PART IV

CHAPTER 22

After departing Athens, Penthesilea did not return immediately to Themiscyra. For two nights, she and her women camped out in the northern hills of Attica, from where there was an excellent view of the citadel. There had been a mistake, she tried to convince herself. Hippolyte had been coerced into staying and she would leave the moment she was free to do so. She had heard rumours of a witch in the Athenian Palace, one that hailed from Corcyra and used not only potions and herbs but wielded the power of the occult. Could Hippolyte be under her spell?

This thought caused a rush of nausea. She should not have left her. But what else could she have done? Fight her? No, she should have found Theseus and killed him.

She had not spoken to her women of what had been said, and they knew better than to ask. They patiently waited, with the buzz of mosquitoes thwarting their sleep each night, as she sought answers. The witch, she quickly learnt from a local, was none other than Aegeus' former wife, who had been driven out of Athens by Theseus. So she was no longer there, and Aegeus, mortified by her trickery, would banish any others he believed to follow her vile practices. There was no darkness in Athens, they told her, and Theseus was a good man. A man who loved his new wife and lavished gifts on her.

These words made her sick to the pit of her stomach, and yet she knew the truth of them. She had seen this clearly in her sister's eyes and the resolution with which she had said she would stay until she had birthed the child. There were no spells holding her there, just the ridiculous notion of love.

Only when she told the other women to return to Themiscyra without her, did Cletes speak up.

"I will stay with you," she said immediately.

"I do not need company."

"But you should not be alone. You should have protection."

The Princess frowned. Cletes was a good fighter, but she was not so experienced in battle as the others. If it came to a fight it would be more likely Penthesilea who came to her aid, and they all knew this.

"What do we tell Antiope and Melanippe?" Cletes asked, realising the folly of her offer. "Your sisters. What do we say to them?"

"Tell them that I will return in due course."

"And Queen Hippolyte? What do we say of her?"

Polemusa spoke this time. Her voice was tense and wary. It was the question that had constantly been on their minds. Penthesilea knew they were entitled to an answer, yet each time she attempted to offer one, her throat closed up, strangling whatever words she might have used.

This was part of her reluctance to return, for what could she possibly say? Antiope and Melanippe would assume she had played some part in Hippolyte's decision, but even if they did not, how could she tell them that the Queen had chosen the love of a man over love for her people? How could she say that their sister would return only after birthing a child that might be raised by a foreign king in a foreign land?

"Tell them she will remain in Athens for the time being," she said, turning her face away from them as she spoke. "I will let them know more on my return."

During the following week, Penthesilea remained on those hills alone, waiting for a sign that she knew in her heart would not come, and fighting the guilt that raged constantly within her. Guilt that she had not been able to convince her sister to return home. Guilt that she had not insisted she come to the Gargareans with them. Guilt that she had not killed Theseus and Heracles and every one of those men when they had first arrived on their shores.

Even with her standing and lineage, Penthesilea was not immune to emotion. A good warrior should be capable of feeling remorse. Perhaps for the death of a young woman cut down before she had barely begun to live; or the killing of a seasoned warrior that she might have better protected. But they and the gods would have been proud of such a death, and every Amazon wished to eventually meet her end this way. This served as consolation.

As she stared out into the darkness, beyond which she knew flickered the perpetual lights of Athens and its temples, Penthesilea vividly recalled a young woman, Myrine, who had suffered from an affliction of the lungs. From the day of her birth, each breath was a struggle, and the cough that wracked her tiny frame turned her face puce. Viscous white mucus collected on her lips and tongue. They had thought she would not survive her first winter, given the difficulty that she found in suckling and gaining weight, and yet she did, and the second, and the third. The strength her body lacked was made up for tenfold by her mind. She learnt to ride, with a perseverance that could only have come from the gods themselves. The women had crafted her a bow, smaller than the youngest girl would train with, so that even with her weaker arms she learnt to carry and fire it. She was not agile, nor was she strong, but she was tenacious and headstrong and determined to prove herself worthy of the name Amazon. Year after year, she continued in such fashion until she could leap fences on her horse and fire arrows to strike a distant target. The women genuinely believed that she could take her place among them. That she would make her first kill in battle and be crowned a true Amazon. That was the year that the fever struck.

It came overnight, starting mildly enough, a slight rise in temperature that brought beads of sweat to her forehead. By morning, her body was soaked in sweat which drenched the thin mattress on which she lay. Wails of such anguish came from those frail lungs that the birds rose from their roosts. Her skin turned translucent, a web of blue veins shining beneath it like tributaries.

That same morning, while the young girl writhed in her bed, they were called to battle in Southern Anatolia. Penthesilea had not wanted to visit her and say goodbye. She had been desperate to believe that Myrine would achieve yet another of the miraculous recoveries she had managed so often over the years. Yet the Princess was not naive and knew that she would be gone by the time they returned. She could not wait until then.

As she entered the room, the girl had opened her eyes.

"Take me," she croaked. "Make me an Amazon."

Penthesilea had knelt on the stone floor and combed her fingers through hair so sodden with sweat it was as if she had been bathing.

"You are an Amazon."

"Not like this. Take me. Please. Do this for me."

Penthesilea did not ask for Hippolyte's permission. She rode out that day with Myrine sitting in front of her, so weak that she could barely keep her grip on the horse's mane. More than once, Penthesilea considered the absurdity of what she was doing and began to steer the gelding back to Pontus. But each time, Myrine cried out and pleaded with her not to. She needed this. She needed to become an Amazon.

When they reached the battlefield, Penthesilea braced her body against Myrine's and wound her fingers around hers, so that they gripped the bow together. When she pulled back the arrow and shot at the approaching soldier, they were as one.

At that moment, even amidst the squalor of the killing, Penthesilea saw a light shine from the young girl, her very essence lifted by the gods, elevated into realms which most women could only dream of. She would have her victor's death.

Penthesilea understood what had to happen next. She leapt from the horse, leaving Myrine alone with her bow, and swung her axe through the air, indiscriminately slicing through spines and necks. The battle was swift, as so many were. The few men who saw sense and tried to flee on foot were run down and slaughtered or else felled by arrows they did not see coming. When the dust had settled, only Amazons remained alive. But Penthesilea did not look to the living. She looked that day for the dead.

Myrine lay on the ground facing the sky, a mortal wound across her chest but a smile upon her lips, and the Princess knelt in the dust and wept tears of joy. They buried her the next day, along with her bow, for she had died a true Amazon.

Penthesilea often thought of that young girl, with a flash of pride at what she had given her. But now, alone upon the hills of Attica, her sense of achievement turned to guilt. What if she had not taken Myrine with her? What if the fever had passed as so many had done before? What more might she have achieved? And now, with Hippolyte. Perhaps she should have argued more vehemently, said that it was the wish of Ares, their father, the God himself, that she remained their Queen?

Where would they be if those things had happened?

Then one morning, nearly a month after she had first set up camp in Attica, the Princess awoke and sensed there was something new in the air. And when she sat up, she saw before her a doe, standing beneath a cypress tree. Perhaps if it had been a hawthorn or a cedar, she might have thought nothing more of it, but both the deer and the cypress were symbols of the Goddess Artemis. She had prayed to her often, as Goddess of the Hunt, but that was not her only role, for she was also the Goddess of Childbirth. As she gazed upon the animal, standing there unafraid, she knew what this symbolised: Artemis would watch over Hippolyte. The Queen would be safe under the eye of the Goddess.

Penthesilea dipped her head in deference to both the Goddess and her creature, and by the time she had raised it again, the doe was gone.

Packing up her belongings in haste, she rode for Pontus. As her horse's hooves pounded beneath her, she realised a truth she had never expected to acknowledge.

She, Penthesilea, was now the Queen of the Amazons.

CHAPTER 23

*M*usic drifted up from one of the temples. No doubt preparations were underway for a festival, although which one she could not say for certain. Come nightfall, a thousand candles would be lit and drums would beat out rhythms that would shake the citadel walls and echo across the far mountains, while men would dance in the light of the moon.

Had Hippolyte been with the Amazons, she would have known exactly what food the women needed to prepare and would have been overseeing the selection of the sacrifices and the planning of the celebrations. Yet here she only offered occasional guidance, more often than not leaving the tasks to the priestesses who had, after all, dedicated their lives in service to the gods. That was their calling, not hers. What her vocation was now, that was hard to identify.

More than once, she had tried to leave Athens behind her. The first time had been several months after her son, Hippolytus, had been born.

She had fed him one last time from her own breast, waiting until he had fallen into a deep slumber before she laid him down in his crib and kissed his forehead for the final time.

"Grow strong."

These were the last words she planned to speak to him, and though her voice was only a whisper, he heard it, opened his eyes wide and looked at her. This was her undoing. Doubt started to encircle her like bindweed, suffocating her intentions. Was this really the right thing to do? she wondered, as he stared unblinkingly at her. He was still so young, and though Theseus was a doting father, it was always she who he cried for at night. Summoning all her courage, she pushed past the pain and stepped away from him. Almost immediately his lower lip began to tremble. She continued to back away, allowing a wet nurse to cross in front of her.

"I will tend to him, my Highness," said the woman, but Hippolyte barely registered the words as she turned and fled down the hallway towards the Palace entrance, Hippolytus' cries echoing behind her.

Her limbs dragged, as if she were wading through deep water and being pulled backwards by an invisible current. She descended the steps towards the agora, where the noise of laughter and the chanting and prayers coming from the Temple of Nike should have been sufficient to drown out her son's wailing. Yet above this and even with the sound of the wind shaking the leaves on the trees, she could still hear him. When she reached the city walls the pain in her chest grew so acute, it was as if her heart were being torn from beneath her ribs. No, she decided, this is not the right time to leave him. He was too small. He still needed her. But soon, soon, she would return to the Amazons.

The night before her next attempt to leave, Theseus came to their bed later than normal having spent the evening discussing important matters with his father's closest advisors. When he rolled over beside Hippolyte, he groaned loudly, the pungent smell of wine on his breath.

"You have drunk too much, again," she told him, choosing to kiss his forehead, as opposed to his lips.

"A man in my position would never do such a thing," was his reply as he moved to kiss her on the lips. She blocked him with her hand and laughed at a pitch that made the Prince wince in discomfort.

"Your current state seems to suggest otherwise."

Drinking wine in excess was not an uncommon habit among Athenians, she had learnt, although, in general, it was usually found in lesser men. It was a foible of Theseus' that did not please her, but she had grown used to it, nonetheless. Theseus was not drinking to forget or numb his mind like those men she saw outside the tavern. He did not become raucous or aggressive. He simply had the habit of getting swept up in the moment, losing track of both time and of the quantity of alcohol he had imbibed.

"Perhaps I am coming down with a sickness?" he said, when he awoke the next morning. Pinching the bridge of his nose he squeezed his eyes tightly shut. "I think it is best if I stay here a while longer. You do not mind, do you, my love?" He then rolled over and away from her before she could even reply.

She had not planned on saying goodbye to any of them and Theseus' drinking was not a reason for leaving, but parting with him in such a manner seemed fitting. She needed to see Hippolytus once more, though.

She had anticipated watching him from a distance and then

slipping silently away. This was a good age to leave him, she told herself. He was young enough that he would barely remember her. That was the way it happened with all their male offspring. And yet, as she gazed upon him through a gap in the curtain, playing with a nursemaid who squeezed his chubby legs and tickled him until he laughed, she felt it again. That tangible tether. The bond that throbbed with pain at just the thought of separation. How would she cope without him? How would she focus on her role as Queen if her mind, not to mention her heart, remained here in Athens? She would not. That had been the truth of it.

It was not only Hippolytus who ruled her heart. For all his flaws, her relationship with her husband had flourished. It burnt with the same intensity as when they had fought each other on the beach in Pontus, but was more than merely physical now. They shared a deep friendship. A kindred understanding. Never had she spent so much time with any one person, other than her sisters. When he was away, she found herself missing his presence, his warmth, his touch and conversation, and when he returned, they were only parted when his duty as Prince rendered it unavoidable.

Not long after Hippolytus' fifth birthday, they spent the morning riding together. Theseus had recently been away for over a full moon cycle, travelling as his father's emissary, spreading awareness of the glory of Athens and presenting works of Athenian art to other kings, much to their obvious delight ... and envy.

On his return, he lavished Hippolyte with gifts including, once again, a new selection of horses to pick from. It had become a tradition, to mark the anniversary of her arrival.

"I have decided not to bother with stallions anymore," he told her, as they walked hand in hand down to the field where the horses had been gathered for her inspection. "Are you aware that in the last five years you have never picked one?"

"Is that so?"

"You know it is."

It had never been a conscious decision of hers, but the horses she chose always bore a striking resemblance to those she used to ride, out on the steppes. Small, nimble, quick to turn, and always with spirit in their eyes.

"I do not know why you continue to do this. I have no need of more horses. There is barely enough time to ride the ones I already have."

"I do this"—Theseus squeezed her hand—"because it makes your eyes shine as if they had alighted on the greatest wonder the world has to offer, which means more to me than if I were able to gaze upon the true form of a god."

He lifted his hand to her cheek and kissed her tenderly on the lips. After all this time, they had still not grown tired of one another. She was not ignorant enough to believe he did not take other women to his bed when he was away from Athens, but when he was in the city, it was only ever her company he sought. When he broke away from the kiss, it was with a familiar glint in his eye that told her they would soon retire and not emerge again for several hours.

"And if you do not have time enough to do the things you love, then we must find you some. Perhaps if you would let the nurses help a little more with Hippolytus?"

She had not intended her look to come across quite as challenging as her husband obviously took it to be and responded to it with laughter.

"The fierce Amazon Queen, undefeated warrior and feared throughout the world is outdone by a five-year-old."

It sounded absurd, but it was the truth, and she found

herself laughing, too. For Hippolytus had bested her in every way, from that first moment when he had lain, slick with blood and helpless against her breast, his unblinking eyes looking up at her.

Now, though, he was of an age when she could converse with him, could revel in his company and the innocence with which he viewed the world.

"You know, if you were any other mother, I would worry that your doting on him would make him soft," Theseus said, as they continued to walk.

"You wish me to be harder on him?"

"You can teach him to fight and still be gentle, as you are well aware."

Hippolyte knew of what he spoke. Only that morning she had taken their son to practise with wooden swords, the way she taught the Amazon girls. The slick Palace floors were less than an ideal surface on which to train, but at least they were away from the prying eyes that followed him whenever he left the palace. He held himself with confidence, blocking her gentle strikes, but there was something missing. Amazon girls watched their mothers train and spar and hone their skills on horseback. They saw arrows flying, and real weapons used, every day of their lives. They wanted to be pushed harder and further until their muscles ached so badly, they could fall asleep on their feet. They tended horses twice their height, reaching to brush their coats and cleaning out their hooves as soon as their chubby fingers would allow. They bruised and shattered bones, knowing that if they wished to be as strong and fast and fearless as they dreamed of, then they would have to break the shackles of their own perceived limitations.

Yet Hippolyte did not want her son to endure such pain or

even temporary failure. She wanted to keep him close. Protected.

"You would rather I adopted more Spartan methods of training, my love?" she asked, knowing the question would irk her husband. He gritted his teeth in feigned annoyance.

"Careful, or I shall return these horses whence they came."

CHAPTER 24

The young horses skipped and danced. Long legged and spritely, they kicked out every few steps before stopping abruptly and turning their necks from side to side, as if observing their surroundings for the first time. Theseus and Hippolyte stood together, hand in hand, her watching the animals, judging their temperament from the way they interacted with each other. Theseus looked only at her.

Unlike the previous occasions on which he gifted her a new horse, Hippolyte's eyes were drawn to a colt. Youthful and sturdy, he nipped at the others as if they were part of his herd. His shaggy mane had a wave to it, like summer hay drying in a field, and his bright eyes glinted in the sun.

"Him," she said to her husband, pointing. "That's the one."

Theseus cocked his head quizzically at the young horse and then turned back to his wife.

"This is because of what I said about you only choosing mares, is it not?"

"It is not. He reminds me of someone."

His coat was almost the exact shade as Theseus' hair and

the arrogance with which he conducted himself reminded her of the young man who had swum to her shores all those years ago.

"I think it must be the way I saw him attempt to mount a mare who was well above his status," she said, coyly.

"Is that right? You know I am to be King. Not a man to be ridiculed for my wife's amusement."

"And you know that, long before I met you, I was already a queen and could quite easily return to that life if I find myself dissatisfied with any aspect of this one. My husband included."

Once, he would have heard these words as a threat. Especially when she was pregnant. If the child had been a girl, then the only thing to hold her in Athens would have been him. Back then, they had both doubted that his love alone would have been sufficient to keep her from returning with her daughter to her sisters and Themiscyra. But things were different now. They were a family. This was Hippolytus' home, which he shared with the people he loved most, and Themiscyra could never be that to him. So, while her son remained here, so would she, with a husband who doted on her. There were certainly worse ways of living.

"Then I shall have him brought to the stables," Theseus said.

"After I ride him, you mean?"

He was not yet fully broken; she could see that before she had even approached him. Those who had already tried to tame him had done so with force and bad temper and this had left him skittish at even the slightest sudden movement. She gently coaxed him towards her, encouraging his trust with both her voice and the calm movements of her body. His muscles never relaxed, the tension rippling through them the entire time. Yet she was patient, never coercing, never rushing, her afternoon plans with her husband now forgotten.

Eventually, Theseus returned to the Palace, leaving Hippolyte alone with the animal. Now able to touch him, with each stroke of her hand, she felt the tension leave his body ... and hers. In rare moments like this, she felt like a young girl again, not much older even than Hippolytus, out on the steppes and eager for that first taste of battle and that first kill with which she could claim her Amazon birth right. It took her back to a time before her father had named her as future Queen, before she had laboured under the weight of responsibility for all her women. To a life when it felt as if she had all the time she desired to be at one with the earth.

She cast her gaze beyond the horse, almost expecting to see her sisters there, breaking in their own new steeds. Then, focusing again on the young animal and speaking softly to him she parted her robe and mounted him.

The small crowd that had gathered, murmured in shock and awe at the sight. Perhaps it was a terrifying reminder of who their future Queen really was. She still relished those moments when the people of Athens saw her riding bareback around their citadel, her chiton tucked beneath her, legs parted, skin on display. Many jaws dropped. Some men stared, while others looked hurriedly away, as if she were a gorgon and a simple glance in their direction would turn them to stone. Today her ride would be a brief one. The colt was more receptive to her than she had anticipated, yet still jittery as they passed those watching them. After riding to the stables, she dismounted and promised him she would return the next day.

At the Palace, Hippolytus ran to her. She bent down and caught him, lifting him up and spinning him around before placing him on her hip.

"We saw you, Mother! Pappouli and I saw you! Can I come with you next time? Can I go riding?"

"You saw me?"

"Pappouli took me."

The Queen looked towards Aegeus, who was now approaching. His beige robe descended to ankle length; his leather sandals were adorned with gold beadwork that matched the laurel wreath on his head. His skin was darker, more weather-beaten and liver-spotted than it had been when she first arrived, yet his eyes remained as bright.

"He did, did he?" she said, with a smile at her father-in-law

"There was quite a scene outside the citadel. My guards were concerned that something was amiss. Of course, I told them it was likely nothing but the Oirapata, causing her usual trouble in my Kingdom."

He smirked as he spoke these words. Over the years, the term had come to be one of affection between them, for even before Hippolytus had arrived the two had found common ground: leadership of their people and sacrifices to their gods. The differences between the Athenians and the Amazons were insurmountable, but the difference between good men and good women, Hippolyte had learnt, were not nearly so different. And Aegeus was undoubtedly a good man.

"Look, Mother! Look what Pappouli has given me!"

Hippolytus lifted his hand and showed Hippolyte what he was holding. A small intricately made terracotta doll with articulated arms and legs and a tall, pointed helmet. Its hair was carved as a long plait that fell all the way down its back and was painted the darkest of browns.

"It is the great Amazon Queen, Penthesilea," Hippolytus said. "She is the greatest warrior alive. Look, her arrows cannot miss."

He moved the arms around, making whooshing noises as if arrows were flying from an invisible bow.

"I saw it for sale in the agora. It seemed fitting, don't you think?" Aegeus said.

Hippolyte glowered.

"Queen Penthesilea?" she said, twisting her lips and casting a scathing look his way. "*She* is the greatest warrior alive?"

"That was what the vendor said. In his defence, the gentleman was not from these parts," Aegeus added with haste and humour.

"Well, let us ensure he does not return."

Hippolyte laughed, before looking at the doll again. She was not certain what her sister would have thought of the likeness. The facial features were far harder than hers, the brow deep set and the face frozen in a scowl. After this cursory glance, she spoke to her son.

"Shall I take you to your bath and tell you a story about Penthesilea, the greatest Amazon Queen and aunt to the future King in Athens?"

"Really?"

"Really."

She caught Aegeus' eye once more before she left, the light twinkling so brightly it was as if he were lit from within. Love for family did that, she realised.

Later, after she had kissed her son goodnight, Theseus found her in a bath scented with oils where he joined her, fully clothed and kissed every exposed inch of her body.

"I could live as long as Zeus himself, and I would never tire of your body," he said, lifting her out of the tub and lying her on a bed of soft towels. They made love on the marble floor, beneath the eyes of the painted men and women who covered the walls of the bathroom. When they finished, Theseus returned to the bath to wash the sweat and grime from his skin, while Hippolyte, once dressed, joined her father-in-law in the andron.

These meetings had become their habit when there were no guests present. On days when the King entertained, the Queen was obliged to hold court in the gynaeceum, although, surprisingly, she found she no longer resented this segregation. After all, having the company of only women was what she had grown up with.

"I had to prise that toy out of Hippolytus' hand," she told Aegeus when she arrived in the andron. "He fell asleep holding it."

The old man smiled.

"Then I consider my gift a success."

"Although you are not yet forgiven for your *greatest warrior* comment."

"Ah, but it was not my observation."

A half-smile played across his face, yet she could see a heaviness in his eyes. He was a man who was not afraid to show his emotions, though they rarely varied. He was placid and had a gentle disposition, a very different creature from the boisterous, bullying temperament of the many Greek kings she had met. In fact, his character was far more temperate than even her husband's. Another factor that strengthened the theory of Theseus' linage.

Aegeus rose from his seat and poured her a cup of wine. Unlike the very first time, he left it only one-third full, before topping it up with water, knowing her preference. She took the cup graciously, waiting until he had taken his seat before speaking again.

"Theseus will join us shortly. He says he has something to tell us," said the King.

"Is that so?"

Aegeus nodded slowly but added nothing more. Was there something she should already know? she wondered. A war on the horizon, perhaps? If that were the case, she could help. Strategise with him. It would not be the first time they had done so. But before she could ask, the King spoke again.

"You have never asked your sisters to visit you here, or at least, I assume you have not. I would have been honoured to receive them, had they called upon us."

This remark was totally unexpected and caused Hippolyte's mind to jump back to when Penthesilea had stolen into the Palace to free her and take her home. She often thought of this, especially the moment when she had turned and walked away. The last time she had seen her. Several hours later, two guards had been found with their necks snapped and, sitting beside them, babbling as he wept, an old gem merchant. They believed it impossible that a man so frail could have bested two hoplites and when they questioned him it seemed he had lost his mind. All he could do was cry and mumble something about not wanting to have his tongue cut out.

No trial was ever held and the old man was eventually set free, leading Hippolyte to believe that Aegeus thought her responsible. But he had never referred to it. To accuse Hippolyte would also be to blame Theseus for bringing her there in first place, she assumed, and this was something he would not countenance. It had become as if the incident had never happened.

"I have had no word from my sisters," she said, her thoughts returning to the present.

"You are sad about this?"

"I miss them, but they have their own, very different, lives to lead. And what grief this causes me is more than compensated for by Hippolytus' love for me. And Theseus'. And yours," she added.

The old man smiled, as if she had given the correct answer, although it was short lived and drifted from his lips almost as quickly as it had formed.

"You cannot know how happy it makes me to hear you say this. I always believed that if you birthed a son you would return to Themiscyra. And yet here you remain, year after year. But I worry."

"Worry? About what?"

He offered a short, sad chuckle.

"I worry that, should you leave, it would break this old heart of mine. Just a little, mind you. I am made of tough stuff. But certainly, yes, I would be very sad if you were to go."

"You have sacrificed much to be here with us," Aegeus continued. "While this is the normal way of royal marriages, it is not for your kind. The gods sent you to us. I am certain of that. We have been blessed."

The old King's voice seemed to have a tremor in it. Was he sick, perhaps? Was that the cause of this introspection? She opened her mouth to ask after his health, then changed her mind and remained silent.

After his declaration, the conversation turned to more mundane topics. Motions and proposals the Polis had discussed that day, new experts that he was employing to help ensure a constant flow of water up to the citadel. How many new boats they planned to build and which countries were currently at war with one another.

But the toll of his years seemed evident in his voice. She had not detected this before. This was new. As was the fact that he had taken Hippolytus out of the Palace to watch her ride. Spending time with his grandson was a pleasure that he indulged whenever time would allow, but certainly not on days when the Polis met. Something was playing on his mind that he was not yet ready to share with her.

By the time Theseus joined them, they were already on their third cup of wine.

Dressed in a full-length robe, he passed by Hippolyte, kissing her gently on the head. He smelt of the lavender oil that had scented their bath only a short time earlier, and she lifted her face to offer him a smile, one that acknowledged what they had done and what they would do again later that night. But he did not return it, instead, he nodded to a waiting servant to prepare him a cup of wine.

"That is enough," he said, after very little had been poured.

Hippolyte felt a twist of unease in her stomach. Her husband usually drank more fully than this.

"Will you not sit, my love?" she asked, as he continued to hover between her and his father. Aegeus, too, was shifting in his seat. Was the same problem affecting them both? And if that was the case, why did she not know of it?

"I am grateful that you are both here," he said, then drained his cup.

Hippolyte chuckled.

"Theseus, we always meet here when we can. Why are you acting so peculiarly?"

She kept a smile on her lips, but neither her husband nor her father-in-law reciprocated. Rather, Theseus stiffened his back and cleared his throat.

"I have something I must tell you," he said. "My darling Hippolyte, you are aware that we Athenians have many traditions of which we are proud. You have come into our world and graced it so flawlessly that I could not ask for more. The men and women of Athens revere you. You have given them a prince, who will one day rule over the greatest kingdom ever to exist. But there are things you have not yet been witness to."

Hippolyte froze at the solemnity of his voice. She struggled to think what he might be referring to. War? Death? She was not a woman to be thrown into despair by such things; surely her husband knew this? Yet when she looked and saw the gravity in his expression, the unease within her deepened. Unable to remain seated any longer, she rose from her chair, her eyes meeting his square on.

"Theseus, what is it? What do you need to tell me?"

Moments passed. Aegeus was studying his clasped hands, while Theseus' nostrils flattened against the side of his nose as he drew in a deep breath.

"Tell me, my Queen, what do you know of the Minotaur?"

CHAPTER 25

*E*very man and woman in Greece, Anatolia and beyond had heard of the Minotaur. Those same parents who frightened their children with tales of the mutilated barbarian women of Pontus would no doubt alternate such stories with ones of the monstrous creature, half-bull, half-man that spent its days stalking a maze of tunnels deep below the Palace of King Minos. Some of these had drifted to Pontus and they told of its huge horns, thick fur, vile breath and insatiable appetite for human flesh.

Hippolyte had thought that perhaps King Minos would call for the Amazon women to rid them of this beast, yet it had not happened. Being home to such a terrifying creature no doubt brought with it an awe, even a respect, that perhaps Minos was reluctant to relinquish.

It was said that when King Minos refused to sacrifice his prize animal, a great white bull, to Poseidon, the vengeful god bewitched his wife, Pasiphae, into falling in love with the beast. If the stories were true—and Hippolyte had no reason to doubt them—the minotaur was the result of a union between

Pasiphae and the great white bull. Since its birth the creature had resided in an elaborate labyrinth as a reminder of Minos' defiance.

"Yes, I know of the Minotaur," Hippolyte said in response to her husband's question.

"Of course you do."

Theseus now looked at his father, as if searching for a sign as to how much he should say, or perhaps he hoped Aegeus would take up the account. Tension rippled between them as Hippolyte waited expectantly, unsure what Crete and King Minos' burden could have to do with them in Athens. After all, it had been King Minos who had tried to trick Poseidon by sacrificing a stock bull, rather than the great white bull that had been sent to him. And Pasiphae who had birthed that great animal's child after she had become besotted with it. King Minos had brought this upon himself and his kingdom. How did this involve them? She could see no link, until Aegeus revealed how they were so devastatingly implicated.

"Do you know why Athens is such a great city?" the old man asked her.

He looked at her intently, and for a moment she thought he truly wished her to answer him, but then the moment was gone and he was speaking again before she had time to consider a reply.

"It is a great city, because I have built it from what I have learnt," he said. "I am no longer afraid to erase my mistakes and do better. I no longer believe that my opinion is the only valid one, or that I will always know best how to farm or build a temple or even pour a cup of wine."

He lifted his cup and a servant standing silently in the corner of the room stepped forwards to refill it. The old man drank deeply, allowing the fluid to rest on his tongue for a moment before swallowing. Hippolyte's eyes moved between the King and her husband. The tension that Theseus had brought with him into the room had now gripped her.

Aegeus lowered his cup.

"I know that I am ignorant about many things, but not everything. It is true that wisdom comes with age, but so do mistakes, and I have made many of those, my young Oirapata."

She remained silent. Occasionally, after guests had departed, she had seen him fall into a state of melancholy, retreating inwards and distancing himself a little from the world. But she had never before heard him speak like this.

"There have been dark times in my life, Oirapata. Many dark times, before Theseus found me. I am certain he must have told you of them. But not, perhaps, about this one, involving the Minotaur."

Hippolyte shook her head, not wishing to speak and disturb the flow of his words.

Aegeus nodded.

"As is the case with many young men born to greatness, I was arrogant. And arrogance always displays its most ugly side when it feels it has something to prove. You have seen Theseus with his dear friend Heracles, so I am sure you can testify to that."

Hippolyte mulled over the comment. Had Theseus acted as if he had something to prove when she had first met him with Heracles? Not on the beach, perhaps, but later, in the citadel, most certainly. After all, he had returned home with the Amazon Queen, had he not? She smiled slightly to show Aegeus that she understood, and he should continue with his tale.

"There was one young man around whom my competitive nature and arrogance reached new heights, and that was King

Minos' son, Androgeus. He was younger than me, by nearly fifteen years, so for the greater part of our lives, I had always beaten him at any challenge that arose. I know it is hard to believe it now, but I was quite the athlete in my youth. Then, one year, I returned to Crete, and he had grown. I had aged—I was older then than Theseus is now—and my body no longer had the physical prowess it once boasted. I am not ashamed to admit such a thing now. But I was ashamed then. Androgeus, however, had become a pillar of strength and beauty. His hair was blond, so light in places you might have believed that he, too, was an offspring of Poseidon's bull, but he was good natured with it. Humorous. Charming. A doting son and a beloved elder brother.

"I had returned for the Panathenaic games, as I always did, and Androgeus suggested we might perhaps gain more from spectating than from participating. We could sit with his family, the King, his sisters and mother. We could drink wine and relax. That was what he said, and that was something my arrogance could not brook. I insisted we compete, convinced that he was simply fearful of me showing him up."

There was a pause as Aegeus, visibly repulsed by the memory, snorted in disgust.

"I thought he was casting about for an excuse. Even at my age, I believed I would outdo him. But it quickly became apparent that things had changed. Androgeus beat me at every challenge set. At running, he was faster. At discus he was stronger. It did not matter what I chose; whatever event it might be, he bested me. He was crowned the winner, to my deepest humiliation. Which is why I then offered him one last challenge, not in the eye of the public but in private, that would determine for certain if he was the greater warrior. I told him we should kill the great white bull."

A cold chill swept in, rippling the heavy curtains, as Hippolyte tried to hide the dismay and disgust she felt at this revelation.

"Oh, I know what you are thinking," Aegeus said, with a bitter chuckle. "You were thinking the gods would be angered. That they would seek revenge on us for killing their sacred creature. But that was the very purpose for which the creature had been gifted to him. *Not* killing the bull was the reason that Pasiphae had her way with it.

"I suspect my thinking was twofold, each tine of the fork equal in its selfishness. I could gain favour with Poseidon for doing his original will and finally killing the bull, and since I planned to sweep in and finish the creature before Androgeus could, I would prove that I was still the greatest and strongest of the two of us.

"Perhaps I could offer the fatal blow while Androgeus battled the bull's horns. I was not really sure of my plan if the truth be told, only that I should redeem my honour. But it was over so quickly; it was as if the bull knew what we had come to do. It charged along the ground, head down, like a bolt of lightning, and ploughed a horn straight into Androgeus' stomach. The King's son hung there like a broken puppet, arms splayed, legs drooping down. The moment had come for me to lunge and kill the beast; even with Androgeus in such a state, I knew what I should do. But I could not. I was a coward. He had bested me in all the games, and if he could not defeat the bull, then how on earth could I? Like the recreant I was, I ran back to Minos, begging forgiveness for my deed. Forgiveness for the death of his beautiful young son."

As he finished, his eyes lingered on Theseus, and it was plain to see where his thoughts had wandered. As the old man brushed away a tear, Hippolyte thought back over what she had heard of the incident. She remembered only vaguely some rumours regarding the death of King Minos' son, though she could not recall how far back that was. However, the look on Aegeus' face told her that, for him, it was as if it had taken place yesterday.

"And now," Aegeus continued, "it is my people who must suffer. Every nine years I am obliged to send fourteen Athenians—seven young men and seven young women—to feed their monster, the Minotaur. You know, there is such a passage of time between the offerings, that I almost allow myself to forget. No, that is not right, not to forget, to hope, rather. To hope that they will find another way to subdue it. Or kill it. A way that does not require me to pick out Athens' finest and have their lives end so brutally. But this is to be the third time that my people have to pay the price of my arrogance."

When he turned back to face Hippolyte, the flames from the oils lamp reflected in the sheen of moisture across his eyes.

"That is why I am sometimes this way, Oirapata. That is why you have, on occasion, seen me descend into the cavern of my own darkest thoughts. It is the least I deserve."

At that moment, if she had been the type of person to do such a thing, Hippolyte thought she might have embraced the old man, like a daughter would. She wondered if Theseus might do so. But he did not move. Instead, he inhaled deeply, his shoulders dropping a fraction, as if his father's confession had somehow alleviated the tension he'd been feeling.

"And that is why I needed to speak to you both today," he said, causing Aegeus to look up suddenly. "Because I have decided that I am going to end this now. I am going as one of the seven men on the ship to Crete with the other sacrifices.

I intend to kill the Minotaur."

CHAPTER 26

*T*he air seemed to freeze around them. The curtains no longer fluttered and the lamps glowed without so much as a flicker. From outside, came the distant bleating of goats and the sound of hymns being sung in the temples, but Hippolyte could not draw her eyes away from Aegeus. Angry words for her husband were ready on her tongue, but her mouth remained closed. She would not speak until she knew that she and the King were in agreement.

"No!" he said. "I will not allow it. I forbid it."

Hippolyte breathed a sigh of relief that Aegeus felt the same way as she did, but she knew her husband well enough to be aware that their approval would be desired but not required. At least the King was on her side.

"I need to do this, Father. Surely you understand. You said it yourself, it is a cycle of pointless deaths."

"So, you would add yours to the numbers? No, it cannot happen."

Aegeus was on his feet now and striding towards his son.

"I did not wait so long for you to come to me, only to have you die because of one of my mistakes."

"I have no intention of dying. I will kill the beast and then I will return to you, again. Hippolyte, tell him. Tell my father I am capable of doing this."

"Tell him this notion is ridiculous, Oirapata. Tell my son he has lost his mind."

Both men looked at her expectantly. Was he capable of killing the monster? He was the strongest warrior Athens had to offer, of that there was no doubt. But was he as strong as this beast? Was he even as strong as her? The only time he had bested her was when her body had been under the influence of valerian root and she had been struggling with the unfamiliar motion of a ship at sea, in Theseus' domain. The Minotaur, by contrast, would be in its own home and surrounded by objects, sights and smells that it alone knew and could use to its advantage. What was the probability that one man, even her husband, would win against such odds?

But then a spark of an idea lit within her. Perhaps he would not need to.

"Let me come with you," she said.

"What?"

"Seven young men and seven young women," she said. "I don't believe I am too old to be accepted. Think about it. What chance would the beast stand against the two of us? You, the Prince of Athens and its finest warrior and me, an Amazon Queen." She turned to Aegeus. "I am certain that we could achieve it, together. Then Athens would be free of this burden for good."

She watched the idea taking shape behind the old man's eyes, the pain and the possibility swimming together in his thoughts. This would work; she was convinced of it. But even before he could offer an answer, Theseus spoke.

"You think I cannot defeat this beast alone? You think me in need of a nursemaid like a snivelling child? You have so little faith in me?" His temper and petulance flared as never before.

"Theseus, listen to her, I beg of you. The idea is not without merit."

Aegeus spoke softly, but his words, too, fell on deaf ears.

"This is *my* destiny. This is *my* father's legacy, and I must be the one to put things right. She is mother to the heir of Athens, and her place is in the Palace, looking after him."

Hippolyte felt a pounding in her chest, a rhythmic drumming beneath her ribs, like when she had ridden into battle. Heat rose to her cheeks.

"My place?" She could feel herself growing in stature. How could she have shrunk so much in her time here and not even noticed the way her shoulders had started to curve inwards? She straightened her back and stood as if she were about to nock an arrow. Never had she been spoken across like this. She would take this from no man and certainly not from her husband. "My place"—she spat—"is that of an Amazon Queen."

For the first time she could recall, Theseus paled, as if he had forgotten that the creature he had brought into his home was not a kitten to be petted and tamed, but a wild animal, a tiger, with powerful jaws and claws, and that the only reason she had not yet ripped his head from his shoulders was because she had not yet chosen to. But it was too late. Hippolyte the Amazon had been released.

"My place is where I wish it to be. I have beheaded men by the hundreds, put arrows through the hearts of hundreds more. I am here, in Athens, with you, my husband, because I choose to be. And if I were to leave and kill the Minotaur then that, equally, would be my choice. You seem to have forgotten who you took as a wife, *Prince* Theseus."

He stood there, seething with anger. She had reprimanded him as if he were a naughty child.

"Please, my children, I can see you are both upset. Understandably so."

Aegeus stepped between them, placing a hand on each of their shoulders.

"Theseus, you must understand how ridiculous this is. You are risking your life. In fact, it would be almost certain death. Hippolyte only wants to keep you safe."

"I do not need a woman to keep me safe! This is not a discussion. I came here tonight to inform you both of what I intended to do, *not* seek your permission. The ship sails in the morning, and I will be on it." He turned to Hippolyte. "I have issues that I wish to discuss with my father now. Perhaps you should retire to the gynaeceum or your chamber. I care not which. Your presence here is no longer required or welcome."

Her anger was transformed into disbelief. She studied his face, searching for an indication that his harsh tone was only in jest. But there was nothing other than cold disdain. She was preparing a riposte, her tongue ready to slice through him, when Aegeus squeezed her arm.

"Perhaps it would be for the best if I talk to Theseus alone, my Daughter."

His eyes looked weary and heavy. Old. Hippolyte thought of her own father. How he would never suffer such a trivial encumbrance as age. Her heart filled with affection for her father-in-law. She nodded to him, and not daring to glance at Theseus for fear that she might not be able to contain herself, she swept out. Whatever the outcome, his comments tonight would not be easily forgiven, she promised herself.

The air outside the room was fresher. With anger still flowing through her, she did not wish to retire to bed. Instead, in spite of the connotation, she returned to the gynaeceum, with its looms and tapestries and everything else she detested about being a female in this place. But at least there was wine there.

How dare he? How dare he tell her what she could and could not do?

She paced around the room. She should go. She should leave right now and return to Themiscyra. That would show him where her place was. And yet just the thought of this caused her anguish. For it could no longer be in Pontus but somewhere she had never anticipated. It was with Hippolytus, her son. That was where she wanted to always remain. Slapping one of the tapestries as she went, she strode out of the gynaeceum.

Hippolytus was sleeping soundly, although he must have woken at some point, for he had removed the terracotta doll from the table at the side of his bed and was now holding it to his chest. How could she ever leave him? Not until he was King, she thought. Not until he was married and had his own child, perhaps. Maybe then he would know how deeply her love for him ran.

She leant down and brushed the hair from his eyes, breathing in his scent, before taking a seat by his feet. There she sat, listening to his slow, shallow breathing, attempting to conceive of a life without him in it. It was impossible. Those days, before Theseus and Athens, felt as if they were part of someone else's life. A splendid life, full of adventures that could be recounted around a fire to eager ears. But these were now stories from which she was almost entirely absent. They were of someone else's battles, someone else's brave deeds.

Still watching the rise and fall of his chest, Hippolyte's anger subsided, her emotions soothed by this small figure, so blissfully unaware. And then, when her neck began to ache and she could no longer contain her yawns, she kissed him gently on his soft pale skin and retired to her own chamber.

Sleep did not come, not that she had invited it, sitting upright as she was, waiting for Theseus to join her. Would he not come to her that night? Surely he would. He always did at some point, even when he and Aegeus entertained until the first splinters of dawn came over the horizon. She continued to sit in the inky blackness, alone. Only when a faint light showed at the edges of the curtains, did he appear in the doorway.

"I am leaving."

He stood there, his shadow stretching towards her, though he himself made no attempt to move.

"Already?" Hippolyte did not know at what point she had fallen asleep, but her neck ached as she righted herself. "Do we not get to discuss this further?"

"There is nothing to say. The ship leaves in a few hours, and I will be on it. I must prepare."

He paused. There had been a bitterness in his voice but this must have been because of the situation, surely, for why would it be aimed at her?

"Theseus, please. Will you not at least consider what I said?"

"I must ask something of you," he said, ignoring her question, "if you do not find it beneath your station, that is."

She had seen so many men behave like this. They were usually the weak ones, who attempted to hide their fear by belittling those around them. She normally killed them on the spot. But since this was her husband, she broke with tradition and, instead, spoke as gently as she could.

"What is it I can do for you, my husband?"

Theseus sniffed.

"My father has not taken the news well. I would appreciate it if you could mind him in my absence."

She waited to see if there was more he wished to say. Of course, she would look out for Aegeus, and not simply because Theseus asked. She thought back to when he had referred to her as his daughter. It was a fondness he had not expressed in words before, yet one they had reciprocated for many years.

"You know I will."

"Thank you. And Hippolytus too? You will look after him while I am away?"

"Given that he is my son, and I already do this whether you are present or not, I do not consider that too much of an inconvenience," she said. Her attempt at gentle humour had morphed into sarcasm.

If he was not going to apologise in words for how he had spoken to her the previous evening, then surely a physical acknowledgement would come soon. She waited, wondering whether she should rise and move to him, but she decided instead to remain on the bed. The scowl on his face said it all.

"I will be seeing you soon, Queen Hippolyte."

And with that, he turned on his heel and left.

CHAPTER 27

The sound of footsteps came and went, echoing along the hallway outside Hippolyte's chamber. Every time someone drew near, her hopes would rise a little, her breath quickening. Perhaps he had changed his mind, had thought better of his foolish obsession with the Minotaur, or else he had returned for her, so that they might fight this battle side by side. Would he not at least return to wrap his arms around her and kiss her in proper farewell, the way he had always done before leaving on one of his voyages? Surely an argument could not erase the love between them so completely? But he did not come, and soon a new silence fell upon the Palace, one that told her the black-sailed ship had departed, along with the fourteen Athenians on their way to their deaths, her husband among them. His tenacity was a characteristic she had always found endearing, but now, it seemed little more than petulance.

"Where has Father gone?" Hippolytus asked, as she brought a breakfast of grapes and figs to his room. "He said goodbye to me this morning and told me he was going to kill a monster. When will he return?"

The terracotta doll was tangled in his bedsheet, seemingly forgotten after only a day. Hippolyte pulled it out and placed it on his bedside table.

"Father said he will return the greatest hero of all. Even greater than Heracles," Hippolytus continued.

"Is that so?"

Now ignoring both the doll and the food, he jumped from his bed and picked up a small wooden sword and swung it through the air, as if he were battling the very same beast his father was soon to face.

Hippolyte looked at it with a sense of disappointment. It was made of birch. A wood light in both colour and weight, too flimsy to be of any real use in training, little more than a toy for farmers' children. More than once, she had spoken with Theseus and his father about this. And there were so few people in the Palace who were capable of teaching Hippolytus properly, and then they would most likely always hold back for fear of hurting the future King. But the least they could do was furnish him with appropriate training weapons. She sighed. She would remove it from his room while he slept and replace it with something more suitable.

"Here, place your front foot further forward," she said, abandoning all hope of finishing her breakfast. "And bend your knees. Yes, that's right. Like that. Now swing your sword at me, but stop before you hit me. You need to control it first. As you would your own arm and hands."

He swung at his mother, only to strike her squarely on the shoulder. A look of shock flashed across his face, but she merely smiled.

"What did I say about control? Go again, my love."

They played like this for some time, Hippolyte teaching him the different ways to hold and then swing a sword and how to move his legs to maintain a perfect balance. She occasionally allowed him to hit her, failing to block his strike and pretending to buckle under his attack, to his glee, until the desire for food finally became too acute for the child to ignore.

"I wish to ride, Mother. Can we go now?" he asked, chewing as he spoke.

"Of course we can, my love," she said. "But first I must speak to your Pappouli."

"I will come too!"

Hippolytus stood, bread in hand.

"I will show him how I have learnt to slay monsters with my sword."

"Not this time," she said, pulling him to her chest and pressing her lips against the crown of his head. "But I will not be long."

As much as she wished to push the last image of her husband from her mind, she could not forget his request to watch over the King. Aegeus would need her, and she would be there for him.

The King and the members of his Council conducted business in the megaron, a large open room, with pillars of cyclopean proportions, tiled seats and a flat central area where Aegeus would stand to make himself heard. It was not a place for women—unless feasts or such events were being held there —and though Hippolyte had tried to rectify this situation soon after her arrival in Athens, patriarchy remained at its strongest in this part of the Palace.

"The men find you too much of a distraction," Theseus and Aegeus had both told her, after she attended one morning to listen to them engage in weak, desultory debate on how to strengthen their defences and build their armies. Given her expertise on such matters, she had begun to voice her opinion and chaos ensued. While some men shouted, desperate to drown her out, many cowered, convinced that this Oirapata had come to do as her epithet suggested and end them all. Others were too stunned to speak or move.

"If they are so discomforted by a single woman, fully clothed, then I suspect the issue is more with them than with me," she had replied.

"It is not as simple as that," Aegeus had tried to explain. "I have gathered them here from throughout Greece to guide my construction of Athens. Bithys' family hails from Pella and he is not the only one. I do not wish to upset them."

There was no need for him to say more. Hippolyte had been called to Pella to end a war there, and had swiftly done so, leaving no fighting man alive. No doubt these old men recalled those attacks, which made the fear with which they observed her all the more understandable.

"The only way you are going to make them see that I do not want their heads, is to let me sit with them," she argued, but Theseus and Aegeus were both in firm agreement. Now, the only time she entered the room was to remove Hippolytus when he had run off in search of his grandfather. And even in those brief moments, she relished the looks she received, the confusion in their faces. She knew they were wondering how it could be that she appeared like any other women in Athens: motherly, caring, doting even, whilst beneath her exterior lurked a savage killer. An Oirapata.

That morning she knew her son had not made his way there but still entered the vast room, her head held high. She was not there to try and speak again, just to meet Aegeus' eye and assess his state of health. But as she stepped from the corridor into the echoing chamber, it was not his voice that she heard.

An elderly man was standing in the centre of the room, waving his hands and declaiming on the subject of crops, while the others looked on, entranced. Hippolyte stepped further in, looking around for the King. Even with the sea of grey beards and white chitons, she knew she would spot him in an instant, and yet he was not there. As more and more men became aware of her presence, the nervous movements began. They shuffled in their seats and glanced at each other anxiously, until even the speaker had been reduced to a barely audible mumble. She had not intended to address the Polis, but now that she had their attention, there seem to be little else she could do.

"I seek an audience with the King," she said.

The speaker, now shaking, cleared his throat.

"The King is unwell. He was unable to attend today. He asked me to ... to ..."

His already pale skin turned a shade whiter.

"Do you intend on staying?" he asked, in a trembling voice.

Hippolyte smiled as serenely as she could, although she could not hide the twinkle in her eye.

"Not today," she replied. "It is the King I wish to speak to. Though perhaps, soon, I will sit with you all."

She turned slowly, hearing a collective sigh of relief from behind her. In all her years in Athens she could barely recall Aegeus excusing himself from matters concerning the city. Even last winter, when a cough had sunk deep into his lungs and he was unable to manage more than two or three words without doubling over in pain, he had sat at the back of the hall, sipping a syrup.

Hippolyte headed straight to the andron, only to find it empty but for a servant, who was attempting to sweep dust into a pile only to have it rise and fall again two feet from where he was standing.

"Where is the King?"

"I have not seen him, your Highness," he replied, gripping the broom tightly as he spoke. "It is the meeting of the Polis today, is it not? He should be there."

"He is not."

The man shrank back, as if she were about to blame him for the King's absence. But she did not wait to speak further.

There were countless places throughout the Palace and the Acropolis where Aegeus could go to seek solitude, and yet she knew in her heart exactly where she would find him: on the southern veranda, with its view out across the port and the seas beyond. It would have been from there that he would have watched Theseus' ship sail away, and it was to this place that she went to find him.

A cool breeze billowed the fabric of his robe, although the old man seemed not to notice as he stared out across the water. The clouds were white and fluffy, the sky blue, the wind gentle. There was nothing foreboding in the scene.

"He has gone?" she asked, quietly.

The King did not move at the sound of her voice, his gaze remaining fixed on the waves. Several ships appeared as smudges on the horizon. Was it possible that her husband was aboard one of them?

"How long will it take him to reach Crete?" she asked, trying again to gain her father-in-law's attention. Finally, as if trying to decipher the source of the sound, he turned to face her.

In the hours since she had last seen him, he had aged a decade. His eyes were sunken, as if set in great grey hollows. His thin lips were dry and deep lines were etched into his already wrinkled face.

"I think the reason I enjoy my grandson's company so much, is that I never knew Theseus at his age. You are aware, I suppose, of how he came to be here? How I left him with his mother until he was old enough and strong enough to fulfil his destiny?"

He had not answered either of her questions, though she knew she did not need to ask again. Instead, she nodded, allowing him a moment with his thoughts.

"I wonder now if that was a mistake," he mused. "He is a good boy, my Theseus, as you know, but this desire to prove himself ... I sometimes worry how far he will take it. I wonder if this yearning to demonstrate his strength comes from not having had me there to guide him as a child. Not being able to learn from my mistakes. Perhaps I am to blame."

Hippolyte moved to stand next to him. His feeling of guilt resonated with her. She had experienced similar pain and doubts when her women had lost mothers, daughters, sisters, friends in battle and she knew that once blame had settled, it sent out roots so strong that no mere words could stop them. So instead, she chose silence.

For a while, the two of them stayed like that, motionless, both of them thinking about a person they loved and what might await him when he finally disembarked. Perhaps he could find someone to aid him in his task. Perhaps the inevitable could somehow be avoided if he could find a way to escape the labyrinth in which the Minotaur lived.

"You have been such a gift of life to me, Hippolyte."

Aegeus broke the silence quite suddenly.

"I want you to know that if anything were to happen to me, or to my son, this will always be your home."

"He is strong," she replied, only to immediately realise how trite and patronising this must sound.

Still, the old man smiled.

"I cannot bear to be in this world without him, Oirapata. I cannot. I know he has his faults, but who among us does not? We have made an arrangement, so that I do not have to live in Athens without him."

Anxiety fluttered in Hippolyte's breast at these words.

"Your Highness, please, you should not be thinking this way."

"We have made an arrangement," he repeated. "I know it may seem morbid, especially to one such as you, my Daughter, but I have had my life. If the gods choose to take him from me, then it will be my time to go, as well."

She was immediately struck by the significance of this revelation. Her son was next in line to the throne. If both Theseus and Aegeus were gone, the wolves would come knocking. Would Athens be strong enough to defend them both? And would her women be willing to fight for her son after she had left them for so long?

Before she could explore these thoughts, Aegeus spoke again.

"I asked him to ensure the sails are changed," he said. "You should know this, too, so that you are prepared. If his ship returns with white sails, it will mean he has succeeded, that he has been victorious, and my son, the hero, will be returning to us, alive. And if the sails are black …"

His words drifted into the air and evaporated. Hippolyte took his hand.

"If they are black, then I will be right beside you, and we will get through this together."

CHAPTER 28

$\mathcal{E}$stimating time and predicting events were skills Hippolyte had mastered as an Amazon. She could look at a clear sky and know beyond doubt if it would remain that way long enough for them to complete their outside chores or whether the rain would come sweeping in off the mountains. When thunder clouds appeared, she knew if they would break above them or would wait until they had reached the sea before bursting. She knew how long it would take her women to win a battle from first sight of an enemy warrior and, more often than not, know how long it would be until that same weak king called upon the Amazons again for help. And yet now, it was as though time itself had forgotten how to behave.

Some days moved so slowly it was as if the threads that dragged them towards nightfall had become tangled and unable to move. She and Aegeus would lose hours together on the southern veranda, watching wavelets form or the sun move millimetre by millimetre across the sky. At other times, they sped by so quickly, it seemed as though dawn had barely broken before they were lighting the lamps and she was once more ushering Hippolytus to bed. Yet, throughout all the uncertainty, one thought was unchanging. Theseus.

Questions went endlessly through her mind. Had he reached Crete? If the winds were strong, and they encountered no obstacles, the journey could be completed in less than half a moon cycle. Would the sacrifices be offered to the Minotaur the moment they arrived or might there by a period of grace to allow the young people a few last pleasures? A chance to eat and drink and feel the heat of the sun on their faces and the sand between their toes before they were fed to the beast. Would they be offered up all at once or one by one, dragging out the agony for those who waited their turn?

At one point, Aegeus had muttered something about games being held in honour of Androgeus, but they were just words he whispered into the wind, as he had taken to doing more and more with each day that passed. However deep her own anguish might be, Hippolyte did not want to add to the King's by questioning him.

"Theseus saved me," Aegeus said, in one of his more lucid moments. "Did he ever tell you that? Did he tell you of my wife, Medea? She tried to have him killed. No doubt she would have done the same to me, too. But he saw through her. He saw her for the witch she was. Without him, I might never have met my grandson. Or seen my city thrive."

"And you and your son will continue to see it thrive for many years to come," Hippolyte replied. "And you will live to watch Hippolytus grow into a strong brave man, just like his father and grandfather."

He had taken to standing on the cliffs each morning from the moment the sun glinted on the horizon, his eyes searching for a hint of approaching sails. Ships came and went, some days in their dozens, but not the one he was hoping for. Not Theseus'. Nothing but waiting.

After a week, she joined him there and they waited together, sometimes standing and holding hands, sometimes seated. In either case, rarely speaking. As the sun came into full view, and there was still no sign of the ship, Hippolyte would feel the first flutter of relief. No news seemed infinitely better than bad. Yet she knew the day was far from over. They would remain there for hours. Only when the sun reached its zenith and the turn of the tide ensured no more ships would make it to harbour before nightfall, would she see the tension that gripped every inch of the old man drain from his body. *Not today*, were their unspoken words, at which point Aegeus would stand up, offer her a short nod to indicate he had business to attend to.

With no husband to occupy her time, she spent the remainder of each day almost entirely with Hippolytus, keeping him busy so that he did not dwell on his father's absence or catch wind of the insidious gossip regarding his inevitable demise. It was time she treasured. She saw him develop in ways she had never done before and she came as close to training him in the Amazon tradition as was possible in such a far-removed location. But all the hours they spent together, practising with bow and sword, left him tired, sometimes so exhausted he fell asleep against her as he picked at his dinner, and she had to carry him to his bed, leaving her alone once more with her thoughts. Thoughts of her family, both there and far away.

Over the years, she had garnered what information she could of the Amazons, from the markets and the women in the gynaeceum, not to mention snippets she picked up outside the Polis, before the men noticed her and muttered their distrust.

Penthesilea had led a battle in Dascylium and won. Penthesilea had aided the King in Sardis and decimated her opponents. Queen Penthesilea. Queen Penthesilea. Queen Penthesilea.

It sometimes felt as if that was the way it had always been or, at least, was meant to be, but she felt no animosity. She had found a different way of life in her new home and, with it, satisfaction in what she was doing.

Nearly a full moon cycle since Theseus had left, Hippolyte learnt from her servants' trips to the agora that a sickness had struck the people, one that came with a heavy fever. Four farmers had left widows behind in the past few days. A potter's wife had died, leaving him with seven children to care for, including a new-born that was not expected to survive. Hearing of such long, lingering illnesses and deaths only made her appreciate the way of the Amazons more. No sickness had ever afflicted her nor did she expect it to. But whatever protection she might have been granted through her upbringing and the blood of her father, it was not extended to her son.

One day, she noticed that Hippolytus was struggling to lift his sword as he trained with her in the courtyard. It was true she had recently replaced the light birch weapon with a small bronze one, which was weightier, but he had lifted it and managed to swing it cleanly several times in the days previous. Yet that morning, he could barely raise it from the tiles. By the afternoon, his forehead and neck were gleaming with sweat, and the next morning his bedsheets were soaked to the point of translucency. All that day, he refused to eat, sipping at water only when she insisted. He remained in his bed, listless and lethargic.

By the time night fell, the fever had taken hold in earnest. His skin was flushed and clammy, bright red in places and stark white in others and, most worryingly, emitting an aroma of sour milk. For hours she tried to reduce his temperature, but he was still burning up.

"This is too warm," she snapped at the servant who had brought a bowl of scented water and a cloth to place on his brow. "I need cool water."

"We have none, my Queen," the servant replied, bending so low to the ground she was almost kneeling as she backed away.

"Find some!" Hippolyte ordered.

Never had she felt so helpless. Over a hundred had now succumbed to the disease, men and women of all ages and children, whose previous health had been no different to that of Hippolytus. But her son was not just any child. He was a future king. He had to live.

It was not unheard of for Amazons to come down with fevers, but they were almost always caused by an infected wound, not something that floated in on the air, as this one had. She felt her pulse rise as she contemplated a future without him. She would not lose him. She refused to.

When morning arrived, there was still no improvement, but the sickness had spread to his mind, too.

"Father! Father!"

Hippolytus writhed on his bed, his eyes rolling back and forth. His dark complexion had turned pallid and the sour smell had strengthened. Hippolyte snatched away the flannel from his head and replaced it with a cooler one.

"I am here, my love. I am here," she repeated, combing her hands through his soaked hair. "I am here."

She stayed all that day, neglecting food or drink for herself, watching her son alternate between raging hot flushes and chills that seeped into his core. His cries sometimes became whimpers, sad and pitiful. At other times he spoke, but it made very little sense. He called for his favourite horse. He cried for his father or grandfather but most of all, for his mother.

"I am here, Hippolytus. I am right by your side," Hippolyte reassured him, her mind fighting off an exhaustion the like of which she had never experienced. It was not as if her body or her mind had not been tired before. She had endured more physical trials than any warrior could imagine, had suffered the loss of friends, had been taken unwillingly from her home, but seeing her son like this, teetering on the edge of a precipice, was draining the very life from her.

Night brought a darkness so complete that not even the stars shone above the citadel. Hippolytus' fretful movements had slowed. There was no more writhing of twisted limbs, just the occasional feeble groan. Was the end near?

Still holding his hand, Hippolyte finally fell asleep across the bed.

The next thing she knew, she was abruptly awoken from whatever dream or nightmare she had been in.

"Mother. Mother. I am hungry."

The fog of sleep shrouded her eyes and mind for a moment. Her right arm was numb from sleeping so long at a peculiar angle. This was odd. Even after all these years, she usually slept lightly, ready to rise in an instant and reach for a weapon. Her muscles protested as she sat up to stretch out the knots in her neck.

"Mother, did you hear me? I said I'm hungry."

Hippolyte blinked and turned to her son. His skin was still pale and damp but there was a light in his eyes that she had not seen for two long days. She pressed a hand against his forehead and found its temperature a near perfect match of her own. Relief flooded through her as she pulled him to her chest and kissed him over and over.

"Does that mean I can have some food?" he said, wriggling out of her grip.

"Yes, of course you can, my darling."

She turned to issue orders to the servant, only to find there was not one present. A spark of anger flared. What if something had happened? What if she had needed someone in the night? But then she remembered. Had she not asked to be left alone with her son? Yes, and they had obviously followed her instruction.

"I will fetch something for you straight away," she said, kissing him again, before rising to her feet.

Only a few steps out of the room, she caught a passing servant.

"We require food," she ordered, ravenous herself from days spent without food. "Please, bring it immediately."

"Yes, your Highness."

"Make sure there is plenty. And that it is fresh. Today's harvest."

She was about to turn back when the sight of the first rays of sunlight stretching across the marble floor, reminded her of Aegeus. He had been to see them the previous night, had stood in the doorway and enquired about Hippolytus' health, just as he had done the day before. A pang of guilt struck her. Had she been aware that her son's fever had broken in the night, she would have risen to join the King that morning and watch with him again for Theseus' return. He tended to linger on the cliffs these days, even after he had seen that his son's ship was not approaching. With a little luck, he would still be there, and she could tell him of his grandson's recovery as soon as they had eaten.

Out on the cliffs, the dry earth crunched beneath her feet. The landscape was rugged and stark in comparison to that of

Pontus, and yet there was a beauty in it, in the way the rocks glimmered in the sunlight and the plants grew despite the sparse soil. She continued to climb, aware of the state of her clothes from the days spent tending Hippolytus, but she knew Aegeus would not judge her.

Disappointment struck when she passed out of the citadel and found no silhouette up on the cliff. She was too late, she assumed. He must have already returned to the Palace to eat. As that thought crossed her mind, it was immediately followed by another. If that was the case, then surely she would have met him on the path. There was only one route up to the vantage point he used, the same well-trodden track she was now standing on. Unease churned within her as she continued onwards.

When she arrived, the sun had cleared the horizon, its rays turning the clouds a deep magenta, their stately progress mirrored in the still sea.

And there, in the centre of it all. A ship ... with black sails.

CHAPTER 29

*T*he air rushed from her lungs and a searing pain gripped like a vice around her ribs. Every breath caused her to gasp.

Black sails. Theseus was dead. Her husband was gone forever. Her son had no father. And Aegeus? A new agony struck her.

"Aegeus! Aegeus!"

She twisted around on the spot, as if she could somehow have missed seeing him and he would suddenly appear, and yet she knew that would not happen. After a moment's hesitation, she raced to the very edge of the cliff, and the air fled from her lungs for a second time.

His blue robes were spread out, like the petals of a rare flower growing on the grey rocks below, floating then sinking as the waves rolled over his crumpled body, then retreated.

"Aegeus!" she screamed.

The spume rose once again, and his body lurched to the side. This had to be caused by more than just the movement of the waves. Was there reason for hope? He could still be alive. He had to be. She would not lose them both.

"Aegeus!" she screamed again.

The quickest way to reach him was directly downwards, Hippolyte knew. She tied her chiton around her waist and lowered herself over the edge and onto the cliff face. Her clothing billowed in the wind, as if it were a sail, forcing her in directions she did not want to go, while the spray from below showered her and made it impossible for her feet to find any purchase on the wet rocks. Glancing down, she saw that his body had shifted slightly towards the cliff. Had he tried to crawl there, perhaps? He was still face down, but she could not lose hope.

Breathless and teary-eyed, she hoisted herself back up and peered down again, looking for another route. While there was still the slightest chance of saving him, she had to keep trying. But how? Not this way. Not risking her own life, too.

Pulling the robe back over her body, she raced away from the cliff. In her mind, she heard the clang of metal and the thunder of hooves, but this was not a battle. It was a fight for all that remained of her son's family.

In all her years in Athens, she had never run like this. Her sandals cut into her feet, which had softened from all the years of pampered inactivity but she barely noticed. The sound of blood rushing in her ears was as loud as the waves she would soon be chasing.

She was not heading for the Palace, she had no need of guards. She was looking for a boat.

She heard more than one confused voice call to her, but she did not stop. Perhaps she could get there in time. Perhaps the gods would see fit to save him. That was all she could hope for.

As she reached the port, she dreaded to think how much

time had elapsed. She stopped, her eyes surveying the boats in front of her as she caught her breath, not wasting a precious second.

There were dozens of vessels of all sizes at anchor, bobbing up and down. Alongside the docks themselves were the larger ones, either being loaded or emptied—and behind them, she saw the ominous black sails, that told of her husband's death, drawing ever closer. But she could not think about Theseus. She would mourn him later. Now she needed to cling to the hope that Aegeus could be rescued.

Against a rising tide and with the state of the sea, a large boat would easily be smashed on the rocks. Her gaze fixed on a rowing boat, of the type used by children to practise their skills, or by the poorer fishermen, who struggled to catch enough for their family to get by each day. A small man, older and greyer than her father-in-law, was hunched over in it, tidying his nets. Hippolyte dashed through the water towards him.

"I need your boat," she said, pulling herself on board, ready to take it from him, if necessary.

The old man righted himself slowly and opened his mouth to speak, when his eyes widened in disbelief.

"Your Highness?"

"Your boat. I need it. And your oars.'

"Yes. Yes."

His head was bowed as he went to get off, but she could not rescue Aegeus on her own.

"You must row us," she said. "Over to the south side of the headland. To the cliffs directly below the Palace. You know them?"

He hesitated, the crumpled, leathery skin on his neck moving as he swallowed, but before she found herself obliged to issue a threat, he had started to fix the oars.

The old man's weather-beaten arms were sinewy, but he was struggling against the force of the wind and the tide. His action was becoming disjointed. How was it possible that he could move so slowly? Hippolyte wanted to scream, but instead, she simply barked out an order.

"Give them to me."

The man did not hesitate and handed the oars to her.

Using all the strength she possessed, she pushed against the waves, then lifted the blades again ready to plunge them down once more, in a steady pattern.

"Please ... please..." she muttered to any god that might hear her. "Let him live. Let him live."

She could now hear the whip and slap of the black sails approaching them, but she could not look upon them, could not bear to think about them. Not now. She had to get to Aegeus. With the increased speed her strength and technique provided, they moved swiftly around to the edge of the cliff.

"Here, take over and keep the boat steady."

She handed the oars back to the old man and pushed herself up to a standing position. The boat rocked beneath her feet, but the waves were rhythmic. It was no different to standing on a horse at full gallop, she told herself, and she could do that if Zeus himself raged above her, and with that, she found her balance. Her point of stillness in the tempest.

The waves broke into white foam as they hit the rock face and then washed back down again, but the water around her was dark and she had difficulty seeing through the undulating mass. Where was he? Her pulse was soaring again, but her feet were holding firm.

She suddenly saw something bright. Could that be his robe?

"There!" she shouted. "Row me over there!"

But it was no use. The old man had no more strength now than he had before and was struggling to keep the boat in position against the tide. She looked down again. Shadows swirled and blended, There was so much movement in the surge of the tide that it was impossible to tell where the water ended and the rocks began. Try as she might, she could not catch another glimpse of colour from above the surface. There might be a better chance from beneath. But as she placed a foot on the edge of the boat, a weathered hand grabbed her ankle.

Frozen in shock and confusion, Hippolyte twisted to face the man.

"How dare you?" she snarled.

"Please, your Highness, you cannot do it. This spot is known to me. My own son lost his life here. The water will drag you under before you can even draw your breath."

Never before could she recall being quite so taken aback.

"Release me, while you still have the ability to do so," she said with quiet menace.

The waves were rising higher around them, the incoming tide bringing a greater force of water with it, and the fisherman was struggling to remain seated. Yet despite this, he kept his grip on Hippolyte.

"You cannot save them. I promise you. Not here. Every man and woman of Athens knows it. Whoever it is you seek, if they are of Athenian blood, they will too."

Hippolyte cast her eyes back out over the water. The tide had risen so far and so quickly that she could no longer tell if this was even where Aegeus had fallen. Perhaps that was the problem. Perhaps she had chosen the wrong place to look.

She stepped down again, and the man released her.

"Give me those," she said, and snatched the oars back.

She spent that morning rowing around the cliff, screaming

Aegeus' name loud enough to drown out the screech of the gulls above her and the thunderous crash of water against the rocks. Yet not louder than the noises in her head. She could not go back to Athens. She could not return to the Palace. How could she tell Hippolytus that he had lost the two most important men in his life? That Athens, his home, had no ruler. That his youth would attract older, fitter, stronger men to take a crown that was rightly his and who would show him no mercy. She continued to row until the sun was high above them. Only then did the old man dare to speak again.

"I am sorry," was all he could say.

He was sorry. How little that meant.

When she reached land again, she cast her eye to the black sails of the ship now docked. Her lungs burnt anew. Although she had not admitted it to herself before, she realised that she had spent so much time futilely searching for Aegeus to keep her mind from a truth that she could not face and had not even allowed herself to think of again since that first moment.

Theseus was dead.

The man whose child she had birthed, who had loved her and prized her from the first moment he had set eyes upon her, was dead. And she must tell their son.

She trudged back to the Palace, her soaked body shivering, although whether from cold or the torment of her thoughts she could not tell. With each step, she felt as if she were leaving a part of herself behind, a fragment of her soul in each wet footprint, and soon it would be gone entirely.

When she arrived back, she was greeted with worried expressions and eyes that avoided her. Only hushed whispers, too quiet to be intelligible, reached her ears.

"A towel," she said to one of the servants, not looking at him, the cold now deep within her bones.

Only as she passed him did she realise he had not moved.

"Did you hear what I said? I need a towel."

"Yes, your Highness. At once," he said, and scuttled off.

Her first inclination was to head to Hippolytus and tell him the truth, but she could not. Not yet. Today he had risen with colour in his cheeks, seeking food, feeling well again. And now his world would be turned upside down. If she could delay that moment a little longer, she would; if anything, it was her duty to do so. So instead, she headed on through the Palace, almost numb to everything around her.

When she reached the megaron, she stopped. What would be the point of going inside? She would find neither of them there. The Polis were not gathered, and no voices echoed from within, yet something made her push the curtain aside and step into the room.

He was standing with his back to her, forming a silhouette whose edges were so bold and strong against the sun that he seemed more than a mere demi-god. Hippolyte felt her knees buckle. It was her imagination playing tricks on her, she thought, as she forced herself to remain upright. It was all in her mind. He could not be here. And yet, she knew that form as well as she knew her own.

"Theseus."

The word was barely audible as it drifted from her lips. Her eyes blurred with tears.

"Theseus, is that you? It cannot be."

Slowly, the man turned. He was dressed in stately fashion, in purple robes, a laurel wreath crowning his head. In that moment all her pain was washed away in a deluge of gratitude surging from every fibre within her.

"How? Your ship ... your father ... Theseus. Oh Theseus."

She ran towards him, her legs shaking unlike anything she

had ever experienced on the battlefield. Her heart thumped with the power of a mighty stallion. The gods had gifted her. They had returned her husband, and she would never let him go again. She opened her arms, ready to feel his embrace, when another sight caused her to pull sharply to a halt. Slightly behind him, stood a young woman with blonde hair and large eyes ringed with kohl. There were many such who came to the gynaeceum to drink her wine and gossip incessantly.

But this woman was holding onto his arm, holding onto her husband, and she moved closer to press herself against him.

"Theseus, who is this?"

He lifted his chin in a slow, considered move, before he tilted his head towards the woman.

"This is Phaedra, Princess of Crete," he said. "She is to be my wife."

CHAPTER 30

*S*he wanted to kill him. There were vases to both the left and right of her, gargantuan objects that served no purpose other than to display the scale of Athens' wealth. Even at their neck, the red clay was thicker than her thumb, but they would be easy enough to break with a strong kick of her heel. She could use a shard to slice his throat or his belly or plunge a thinner piece through his eye and let him bleed out in agony. She could take the fabric curtain from where it was draped casually behind him and wrap it around his throat so tightly that he would gasp for air while his eyes bulged. There was no rocking of a storm-swept ship to protect him here. Or she could simply use her bare hands. Snap his neck. Or beat him until his ribs cracked and pierced his lungs. There were endless options at her disposal. And yet she did none of these.

"Theseus, what is this?"

He moved to adjust his posture so that he blocked Hippolyte's path to the woman. This girl. This Phaedra.

"I do not have time for this." He rubbed his temple with the tips of his fingers, as if exorcising an ache that had just formed there. "I need to see my father. Wedding arrangements need to be made. He must be made aware."

Hippolyte studied his eyes. So many emotions rippled behind those dark pupils, including fear—of her, most likely —and distrust, too, but along with that, a new sense of pride and arrogance. Pride that he had returned when no one thought it possible. Arrogance to think he could play whatever game this was with her. Yet one was missing. Grief. Only now did his request to see his father register with her. He did not know.

"Aegeus is dead."

She said the words with as much compassion as she could muster.

Creases formed in his brow. Confusion. And when he spoke, he sounded exactly like Hippolytus on those occasions when he had been requested to do a task that he had never before performed and was perplexed and unable to piece together what was required of him.

"I do not understand," he said.

"Your sails, Theseus. They were black. And your father saw them. He threw himself off the cliff in grief. I am sorry. I tried to save him. I tried so hard to save him."

His legs visibly buckled. Silent tears streamed down his cheeks.

"I ... I ..." he stuttered, and the girl at his side grasped him a little tighter.

"I searched the water. I took a boat out ..." Hippolyte began, but it sounded pathetic now.

She had not dived beneath the waves to look for the body. Theseus would have done that, but then he would have had his other father to guide him.

"Why did you not change the sails?" she asked. "That was

the arrangement, was it not? Aegeus told me: white sails if you lived, black if you had died. How could you forget?"

He opened his mouth to speak, only to close it again. And then she noticed the manner in which his hand rested against his head. That cradling motion. She had seen him do it a hundred times before, and always for the same reason. A self-inflicted one. The anger that had only moments before subsided at the sight of his grief now returned, blazing hotter than ever.

"You were drunk," she spat. "You forgot to change your sails because you were drunk! Did you even think of him once, you selfish, arrogant—"

"You do not speak to a king like that," he interrupted.

"You are no king!"

From behind him came a whimper, like a puppy locked in a cage. Phaedra was standing to the side now, her arms crossed her chest defensively. His eyes went to one of the servants.

"Take her to her room. The one overlooking the temple."

"Theseus," she whispered.

"Do not worry, my love," he said, taking Phaedra's hand and kissing it. "I will be with you shortly. I must speak with Hippolyte first."

And when his eyes met hers, she could see even more guilt than grief.

The megaron was not the place to hold such an intimate conversation. The large space allowed their voices to resonate around them. But Theseus didn't suggest a more private venue, and Hippolyte was not going to ask. They waited as Phaedra's footsteps receded, the silence growing heavy like the pressure before a storm.

Her teeth ground together. She, it appeared, would have to be the first to speak.

"What is this, Theseus? Who is that girl?"

"As I said, her name is Phaedra. Daughter to King Minos. She is to be my wife."

She shook her head in disbelief.

"You have a wife. I am your wife."

Her response elicited a laugh so bitter, it should have burnt his tongue like acid.

"Is that what you are?" he replied. "For there has never been a ceremony to confirm it. No agreement has been made, no dowry passed from your family to mine. You have been a guest. That is all. And one who has outstayed her welcome."

Her jaw dropped. She could think of no deed she could have committed to merit such a response. Whatever it was had wounded his pride so deeply, that the damage to their relationship seemed irreparable. There was only one thing she could think of that might have elicited this reaction.

"This is because of what I said before you left. Am I right? Because I wanted to come to Crete with you. Because I wished to aid you on your quest."

"But I did not need your help, did I?" Theseus snapped. "I did it on my own. I killed the Minotaur. I did not need a woman's help to complete a hero's task."

"And so, this is your revenge on me? Please, help me to understand."

He let out a heavy sigh redolent with petulance.

"There is nothing for you to understand and our betrothal has become even more important now, with my father gone. Athens needs stability. It needs a queen who will not repeatedly threaten to leave. You think I am unaware of all those occasions you have contemplated it? I have had eyes on you since you first arrived here."

"You did not trust me?"

His next words punctured her heart more than anything he had said before.

"How could I ever trust you, Queen of the Oirapata?"

For so many years it had been used as a term of endearment for her, by Aegeus, and yet now the words were thrown at her, full of venom and intended solely to inflict pain.

"You loved me," she whispered. "You still do."

"I love Phaedra."

"How? You cannot even know the girl. And she is just a girl."

"A girl who will grow to be a magnificent woman and queen. What I do and whom I love has nothing to do with you."

She felt her knees crumbling beneath her and she reached out to him, but he let her fall.

"It has everything to do with me. I cannot believe this is true. I cannot believe you have fallen out of love with me. Please, Theseus."

"Your begging is repugnant to me. For someone who once used to be a warrior, I am surprised you are not disgusted at yourself."

Those were the words that she needed to hear, for he was right. She was disgusted at herself. She was disgusted that she had believed his lies and trickery and honeyed words of love. She was disgusted by this snivelling woman she had become. She was disgusted by this slothful life she had been so content to lead, away from her women and her sisters and the steppes. As she rose to her feet Theseus stepped away, sensing the shift.

"I will arrange for a ship for you immediately," he said, as if he were sending an emissary back to their king. "I will ensure you have safe passage back to your home."

Yes, she thought, because Athens would never be that again.

"A ship? I am an Amazon Queen and I will travel as such."

"As you wish."

She straightened her spine and pushed back her shoulders.

"Hippolytus and I will leave immediately. We have no tide to wait for. I will gather our things now and I would appreciate it if you could ready the horses."

This time it was Theseus who stiffened. The bubble of satisfaction that he had felt at her submission burst.

"Hippolytus is not leaving with you."

"Of course he is. He is my son."

"This is not negotiable, Hippolyte."

"On that, at least, we can agree."

A red fury flashed through her that tore at the bloodless wounds he had already inflicted. Bile burnt the back of her throat as she forced the words out between her teeth.

"You have a brought a new *queen* into my home. She is young enough to provide you with a dozen more sons. You cannot have it both ways, Theseus. Hippolytus comes with me."

Theseus bit back with just as much venom.

"Hippolytus is my son, and he will stay with me. You are an Amazon. You are not capable of raising a boy. You burn babies born male. It is a miracle he has been safe in your presence for as long as he has."

He spat these lies at her, and she knew the sole intention was to wound her. He knew exactly what happened to all the males they birthed. She had told him before he had stolen her from her family, and they had often talked about it since. She had expressed her happiness at being able to keep Hippolytus by her side as he grew, rather than sending him to the Gargareans as would have been the case if she were still with her people. Countless times she had thanked the gods for allowing her this privilege. He knew this and yet he still uttered those hateful words, to inflict the most pain he could. This, from a man who had professed his love for her. His endless, undying love.

Her voice cracked as she choked back the tears.

"You bastard. Every child born to us is raised with love. Raised to be a warrior."

"And it will be no different here. I shall ensure he is taught to fight and kill even more efficiently than any of you women."

She scoffed at his arrogance.

"As if you are even capable. I have seen you with a bow, remember? You might be able to swim like a fish, but you fire arrows like one, too."

His face hardened. Teeth bared, he stepped towards her, his hot breath so close that she could smell the stale wine that must be curdling in his stomach.

"Tell me then, great Queen, if we can still call you that, where will Hippolytus go? You truly believe he will be welcomed by the Gargareans? He is not one of theirs. He is nothing to them. If anything, his very presence would be a symbol that the Queen of the Amazons was dissatisfied with their seed."

"He is my son. He will have a home with me."

"In Themiscyra? The only man, raised among women? Truly? How do you think he would feel about that? Moreover, how do you think the women would feel about it? Each of them forced to hand over their sons and yet you stroll in, after years of absence, with Hippolytus? You think they will be grateful for his presence? You think they will trust him? He has my blood in his veins, remember? The blood of the man who stole you from them. Perhaps they will even think he is a spy. Perhaps they will wish to rid the world of him."

There was no containing the tears now, as they spilled down her cheeks and splashed onto the cold marble floor. How was it possible for one person to inflict such pain without the use of a weapon?

"You cannot keep him from me."

She spoke the words, but her voice wavered, for she knew the truth as well as he did.

Theseus, now knowing for certain that he had the upper hand, straightened his back and lifted his chin.

"I am King of Athens. You have no idea what I am capable of. Now gather your things quickly, unless you wish to learn what happens when someone defies King Theseus."

CHAPTER 31

*N*ever before had Hippolyte experienced such agony, both physical and mental. Her head throbbed and her eyes burned, but worst of all, her heart was broken. She somehow managed to pull herself together and walked through the servants who had gathered outside the megaron, looking neither to the left nor to the right. These people had waited on her for years. Some had looks of pity on their faces, while others seemed smug, as if enjoying another's downfall, particularly someone with so far to drop. Then there were those who were undoubtedly relieved that they would no longer share a roof with the Oirapata.

Gather your things, Theseus had told her. But which? If this home did not belong to her, then what of the items within it? If even her son, who she had grown in her belly and raised on her milk, could not be considered hers, then did anything else matter? When Theseus had abducted her, all her own weapons had remained in Themiscyra, but he had gifted her many replacements over the years. A bow, carved from bone and etched with images of women on horseback. Knives of varying length. Xiphe with garnet-encrusted handles. She had dozens to pick from, but in the end chose only the bow, three knives, a zoster of dark-stained leather and a quiver with four arrows. This was all she would need for the journey. Whatever memories had been attached to them were now little more than ashes in the embers of their relationship.

One of the daggers, however, had been given to her by Aegeus, the King, who had become like a father to her. How would he have reacted to Theseus bringing this Phaedra to the Palace? she wondered. Would his love have been as fickle as his son's? She doubted it, but then, before this day, she had not believed Theseus could be so cruel.

She attached the blade to the front of her zoster. It would be the first weapon she drew, should the need arise, and part of her hoped it would. Perhaps plunging a dagger into a man's heart would lessen the pain in her own, yet at the same time, she knew that even a thousand such deaths would never be enough.

With a small leather satchel crammed with provisions, she was ready to depart, but there was still one last thing to do. She had to say goodbye to her son.

The walls and floor of Hippolytus' chamber were illuminated in the early afternoon sun, which had brought into the Palace the aroma of warm earth. Only hours had passed since his fever had broken, and he had roused her with the desire for food, but it felt as if she had been dragged through enough emotions to fill days, if not weeks, in that time. Aegeus' body on the rocks. The fishing boat. Theseus and Phaedra. She stood there a very different woman to the one who had left the room that morning.

She watched him from the doorway. He was sitting on the floor with his back to her but seemed busy with something in front of him. He had always been such an active child, and she had needed to find ways to keep his mind and body occupied. As soon as he was able to crawl, he had wanted to walk and then run. If he was told to sit quietly, he would squirm and fidget, unable to stop himself from rebelling against the constraint. And here he was now, quietly muttering to himself about whichever toy he had decided to play with. She could watch him like this for hours, Hippolyte thought and then realised, with fresh despair, that she never again would.

She quickly stepped inside the room before she could start crying again, coughing to alert Hippolytus of her presence. He turned and his face immediately beamed with delight.

"Mother! Mother! Come and see! I have made an arrow. I cut the wood just the way you showed me."

Holding his hand out to her, she saw that it was true. His fingers clasped a stem from a cedar tree, which he had whittled at one end with his small knife to produce a point. It was rough and the piece of wood was far too misshapen to form an actual arrow from, but it was the first time she had seen him achieve such a thing unprompted. Tears that she had hoped not to shed in front of him, filled her eyes.

"Goodness,' she sniffed, swallowing hard. "With a tip that sharp, you could pierce the hide of boar. Maybe even the skin of the Nemean Lion."

His eyes lit up at this fulsome praise.

"Do you mean that?"

"You mother is a warrior. There is no one in the entire world who knows arrows better than I do. And that," she took it from him and turned it in her hand, "is perfect."

How could it have been that only a day ago she had feared for his life? Been terrified that the fever would not let go of him? Her reaction to a single illness in a child that had been so strong all his life had been absurd, now she considered it. She had been strong for him then, but nothing could have prepared her for this.

"Hippolytus," she said, sitting down on the floor next to him and patting her lap. "Come here. I have something to tell you."

Still holding the arrow, he moved to join her. He smelt so sweet. Of his own, youthful musk. Were all boys like this? she wondered. No, it was not possible. It was him and him only. A scent that would remain with her forever, like the fragrance on the steppes of Pontus after a heavy rain.

She closed her eyes, breathing him in and praying silently that she would find the strength she now needed.

"You mother has to leave you for a while," she said.

He frowned and his bottom lip protruded slightly.

"For how long?" he asked.

Of course he would ask questions. He always did and why would this be any different? Why did chickens roost at night but owls flew? Why did lightning strike before the thunder roared? He wished to know more, to know why, or how or when. But Hippolyte knew that this time, she had no answer for him.

"I cannot say," she said, stroking his hair. "But your father is here now and he will take care of you."

"And Pappouli, too."

Never had she faced anything like this before. Amazons lost their mothers, sometimes at his age, but the group was formed in such a way and with bonds so strong that some girls did not even know who their birth mother was until they were eight or nine years old, far less their grandmothers. They were all family.

"I am sorry, my darling. Pappouli has had to go somewhere, too."

"With you?"

"No, somewhere else."

"So why can I not go with you?"

Why? Why? Why? Guilt roiled through her. Was this her doing? If she had stayed silent before Theseus had departed for Crete and the Minotaur, had she possessed the faith that he could complete the quest on his own, then perhaps he would have not taken it upon himself to find a more *permanent* bride. But no, she would not allow herself to take the blame for his behaviour. The decision to abandon his family had been his and his alone. She could have controlled his actions no more than she could the direction of the wind or the radiance of the sun ... or the tears that now wove their way down her cheeks.

"You will be happy here, my love," she said, offering her son the only possible truth she could find. "You have your father, and he has all his wonderful adventures to tell you about. You know he defeated the Minotaur?"

The child's eyes widened.

"He did?" he gasped.

"He did. Your father is a hero."

She could have choked on these words that were spilling from her lips, but what choice did she have?

"He is here? He has returned?" Hippolytus asked.

"He has returned."

In an instant, the boy was on his feet ready to dash out of the door, dropping his arrow on the floor.

"Hippolytus, wait," she said, catching him by the hand.

The boy stopped, confused.

"Can you first hug your mother goodbye, please? Remember what I said? I must leave you for a while."

He stood there, torn between her request and his desire to

see his father and hear the tales of his heroism. Somewhat grudgingly, he turned and wrapped his arms around her neck.

She could no longer hold back the tears and let them roll freely down her cheeks. She couldn't bear to release him. She wanted to stay like this for ever, holding him, feeling his heart beating against hers. Feeling his warmth against her skin and hearing his breath in her ear.

"Mother, you are squeezing me too tight!"

He squirmed and wriggled, trying to free himself from her grasp. As his struggles increased, she knew she had to let him go. She dropped her arms and he spun around and raced to the door, to his father, without so much as a backwards glance.

"Hippolytus?" she called, for one last time.

He turned, his expression showing annoyance at these constant delays.

"Be strong. Be fearless. And remember ... your mother loves you."

She had barely finished speaking and he was gone, his footsteps fading into the depths of the Palace.

Lying abandoned on the floor was the thin stick of cedar, crudely whittled at one end to a blunt point. No, it would never have made an arrow, not even with her help.

She picked it up and slipped it into her quiver.

PART V

CHAPTER 32

The bags were so heavy they were forced to split them between two dozen horses. Some of the payment had been agreed in advance: the metals—brass and the copper—and the sacks of salt, too, but the king had been so impressed at the swiftness with which they had dealt with the situation, that he had lavished upon them everything he could spare: gems, necklaces, silver platters. And there was more besides: large quantities of earthenware, vases painted in orange and black, many of which they had been forced to refuse due to the sheer size and impracticality of carrying such objects. Several of the women had been handed personal gifts. Two of the younger ones now sported gold necklaces which fell awkwardly onto their chests—a fact which didn't stop them being worn with pride.

Penthesilea had suspected the battle would be straightforward enough. An army of only three-hundred men would not take long to dispatch, and so she had picked this particular night to bring younger girls, some of whom had never been to war before and whose virginity in battle remained intact. The older, more seasoned warriors had been given the instruction to intervene only if necessary, and where possible to let them do their part. And they had.

Arrows had flown through the air, crisscrossing and rising and falling like a murmuration, piercing one heart and then another. They whistled and struck and pierced and blinded. One man and then another fell, before they had even realised they were under attack. By the time they knew who it was they were facing, it was too late for them to flee. They were surrounded. They did not know that some of the women were only girls, as yet untested in battle, but it did not matter. They were Amazons. Every woman, young and old, who had fought that day, had killed and every one of them had lived to tell the tale.

"We must offer a great sacrifice to our father," Antiope said over her shoulder as she rode. "We must thank him for our prosperity. He will be proud of what we have achieved in his name, too."

She slowed until she was parallel with Penthesilea and spoke more softly.

"And he will be especially proud of you, for all you have accomplished as Queen."

Penthesilea kept her eyes forward as she rode, her axe held by her waist, its weight counterbalanced by her bow, quiver and knives.

"I have done only what has been required of me," she replied.

"Maybe that is true. Yet the number of women who have been anointed today has given us the largest army we have ever known. You have proven yourself to be a great queen. Greater, perhaps, that Hippolyte herself."

The fact was undeniable. Every year since Hippolyte's

departure, their numbers had grown, not merely through the good fortune of birth, but due to her and her sisters pushing the young girls to train faster and harder. She took them to battle, not when they believed they were ready, but when she knew they would have to prove themselves or die. And each time, her gamble paid off. In all those years, they had lost only a few and had become the strongest band of warriors she had ever known. Despite this, it was a natural instinct in Penthesilea to rebut all compliments and defend her sister's name as true Queen of the Amazons.

Rumours of Hippolyte had ebbed and flowed since she had left. When it was discovered that she had birthed a boy, many of the women had assumed she would return to them, Penthesilea included. She had laughed and felt a joy she would not have expected at the anticipation of handing back the crown, one she had never felt she truly deserved. But when Hippolyte had not returned, a bitter seed was sown within some of the women.

"She has abandoned us," Antiope said.

"You do not know what he has done to her," she replied, trying to reason with her sisters in private. "He stole her, remember. He drugged her and carried her away. There is nothing that is beneath that man."

"She must have stayed of her own accord. She was Queen of the Amazons. If she cannot overpower a single mortal prince, then she is not worthy of our father's name."

Penthesilea had no response to that. She had told them only selected parts of her conversation with the Queen that day in the gynaeceum. She had related how he had drugged her and stolen her away. How she had refused his offer of marriage just as the women had said she had done before. She had told them that Hippolyte was pregnant and would not risk the war that Theseus would bring down on them should she try to leave with his unborn child. She had said nothing of Hippolyte's love for him, though, instead reassuring them that she would return when she could. She would take up her place as Queen again.

Yet as the years went by, it became harder to defend these claims. There were no rumours of further pregnancies or children to hold her in Athens. Could it be that Theseus had threatened war if she left, even though he now had control over his child? That was the only explanation she could think of. Apart from one other factor. And she didn't dwell on it for long because of the anger it caused her. The fact that her sister, Hippolyte, had left them for love.

And so, as they rode over the rolling hillsides and the short verdant grasses that led back to their homeland, she was not quite so quick to rebuke Antiope as she might have been.

"Our father blessed us today," she answered, diplomatically. "I only hope that he will continue to do so."

They were travelling north. The battle had taken place close to the lands of the Gargareans, where the hills and valleys were steeper than those of Pontus. The yellow rocks crumbled beneath their horses' hooves and the trees were bent over so sharply from the prevailing winds, it was a wonder they stood at all. But the weather had been temperate, and the cloudless sky was illuminated with a moon so candescent it allowed them to travel on well past sunset. There was the temptation to keep going further still. Riding through the night would allow them to reach home by dawn, but the younger ones had earned their rest, and thus they camped out beneath the shimmering constellations, digging several small fire pits, deep enough to prevent any sudden gusts of wind from extinguishing the flames.

From somewhere in the distance, came the noise of hooves on rock. There would be farmers around here and families with herds of goats, but they would pay them no heed. Lighting a fire sent a clear signal: these women did not fear intruders. And so Penthesilea lay back and closed her eyes, letting the warm air wash over her.

It was difficult not to feel a sense of calm and happiness, listening to the young girls talk about their kills. About their arrows that had cut through both the wind and the enemy. About how some had feared the worst, only to find a strength they did not know they possessed. In fact, they were not young girls anymore. They were true Amazons, and the following year they would make the trip to the land of the Gargareans. The Queen smiled. She recalled so clearly the sense of power and elation that came with her first experience of battle. The pride that swelled in her with the realisation she was truly part of something greater. She would allow the women plenty of time to sleep. They could leave a little later in the morning. After all, there was nothing to hurry back for. They would need to hunt to prepare their sacrifices, but there would be time enough for that.

Still relaxing, she heard footsteps approaching, and she smiled again. She did not need to open her eyes to know who it was.

"Do you wish any food, my Queen?"

Penthesilea opened her eyes. Cletes had grown into a warrior whose skill had surpassed all her expectations. Talented with both sword and bow, she could loose two arrows mere moments apart and still hit targets some distance from one another with perfect accuracy. Her arms rippled with muscle as if carved by the hand of a god. Her long hair, worn in a single braid down her back and so dark it was almost black, was a vivid contrast to the azure of her eyes and the curvature of her pink lips. She knelt on the earth by the Queen, causing Penthesilea to raise herself up onto her elbows.

"Thank you for the offer, but I have eaten."

"Then a drink? I can fill your flask at the spring if you have not already done so."

"You already did that for me, remember? When we first made camp."

"Of course. How could I have forgotten?"

Cletes looked at her, a small smile playing on her lips. She traced a finger along the outside of Penthesilea's thigh.

"Then is there, perhaps, some other way I can be of service to you?"

The Queen looked around at her women and tried to distract herself from the heat that was building inside her. It would not be the first time she had taken Cletes to her bed. In fact, she had lost count of the number of times they found pleasure entwined together. It had first happened when they were staying with the Gargareans, where they had shared a tent and then the same men and then each other. An almost insatiable desire rose in them both upon touching each other's body. Returning to Pontus and without the option of men to couple with, they found satisfying each other equally gratifying, if not more so. And nothing could arouse Penthesilea's desire as much a good battle.

Cletes lowered herself down next to the Queen. Her warm breath on Penthesilea's neck only deepened the yearning within her. She was not the only one to have taken one of the women as a lover. It was far from unheard of, and yet something about this moment did not feel quite appropriate.

"I believe I will be greatly in need of your attentions when we return to Themiscyra," she said, with a look that could not be misinterpreted.

Cletes smiled and her eyes gleamed in the moonlight.

"You are certain there is nothing I can do for you now?"

The desire for her touch was becoming agonising. Penthesilea drew in a deep breath as Cletes slid her hand towards her inner thigh. Before she could reach any higher, the Queen grabbed her wrist and twisted it away. A yelp of surprise flew from Cletes' lips, which quickly turned up into a grin.

"As you wish," she said rising to her feet. "Tomorrow night in Themiscyra it shall be."

Then she stood and deliberately sashayed back to the other women, so that Penthesilea could see what she was missing. It would be a difficult and lonely night.

When the Queen awoke the next morning, Antiope was already moving about, packing up their gear and filling canteens.

"The young ones are still asleep," she said, offering her a piece of dried meat. "Do you wish me to wake them?"

Her instinct was to say no, let them sleep, but deep-purple clouds had drifted in during the night, threatening a storm. This side of the mountain was notorious for tremendous downpours, and it would be better to reach the other side as soon as possible.

"Yes, wake them. We need to make a start."

The previous air of festive celebration among the group of young women, had transformed now into more thoughtful reflection on such things as their areas of weakness and what they needed to work on. Whose help they needed to seek with sword fighting or horsemanship. This constant desire to better oneself, to improve as a fighter, as an Amazon, was at the heart of who they were, just as much as the battles were. There was a reason that they were unbeatable, and she was listening to it right behind her as she rode.

The sea came into view first. A silver sheet with barely a ripple on the surface. Then they were riding on the lusher grass of the steppes. Finally, a hill came into view and on its crown, their citadel. Themiscyra. Penthesilea slowed her horse and turned it in an arc to face her women.

"From now on, the rest of the day is yours," she called to them. "You are free to spend your time as you wish. You can sleep. You can train. We will sacrifice to Ares tonight, when you will offer up your gifts, but whether you hunt for them now or later is your decision."

She smiled to herself as she spoke these words, for she knew that none of her women, despite needing it, would choose sleep over hunting, particularly not when a sacrifice was required.

She would ride straight back to Themiscyra. Melanippe had waited there and would want a full account of all that had taken place.

"I think I shall hunt," Antiope shouted across to her as the women resumed cantering. "I will ensure none of them becomes overzealous after such a fortuitous battle. It will not serve us well to anger Artemis."

With a nod of approval from Penthesilea, the Princess steered herself south towards the forest, the majority of the women breaking off to follow her.

Penthesilea rolled her neck from side to side as she rode, feeling the satisfaction of the tension in her muscles easing as she stretched them out. Tonight, she would have a long soak to relieve the rest of her aches and prepare herself for Cletes' arrival. Or perhaps she could join her in the bath. They had experienced great pleasure like that in the past, and no doubt Cletes' muscles needed relaxing as much as her own.

Her mind was still wandering in this way, when she caught sight of a mounted figure, a short distance from the citadel. It was the steed that she noticed first. It was broader than the horses they rode. Taller, too. She had seen such animals before on their travels. They were often used to pull chariots in the ridiculous games men held to try and assert dominance over one another. They had owned one or two themselves, she recalled, received in payment for services rendered to one king or another. But none of such a remarkable colour, such a pale coat.

It was at this point that her eyes rose from horse to rider. It was a woman but she was not dressed in Amazon clothing or the garb of any of the nomads. There was no tight-fitting cap on her head, no leather boots or trousers on her legs. And yet, even in her Grecian attire, she sat astride her horse the way an Amazon would, straddling it. And there was something about how she held herself and her confidence. With a sudden thumping of her heart, a gasp flew from Penthesilea's lips.

Hippolyte had returned.

CHAPTER 33

The three sisters, Penthesilea, Antiope and Melanippe, had gathered together outside the citadel. Melanippe's voice was a hushed whisper, no louder than the sigh of the breeze that gently moved the trees around them. The sun had sunk low onto the horizon, its last rays illuminating the frayed edges of the clouds above it a dusky pink, while the sea glimmered serenely, barely a white crest to be seen. Everything appeared so peaceful. Yet Penthesilea had learnt long ago that this could be deceptive.

"Has she still not spoken a word to you?" Melanippe asked her. "You are Queen now. Surely she has told you why she has chosen to come back to us."

Penthesilea shook her head, uncertain whether she could still refer to herself as such, even in her thoughts. The true Queen had returned, Ares' choice of leader. And yet the Hippolyte who was now within the walls of Themiscyra was not the person who had left them.

"She spent all day training," Antiope said. "All day. She was up before sunrise and refused to stop for a rest, even when her fingers bled."

"We need to give her time," Penthesilea replied, knowing the response her words would elicit before they had even left her mouth.

"How much time?" Antiope demanded. "Three days have already passed. Three days and she has told us nothing. What if she is laying a trap? What if she is keeping us idle here so that the Athenians may attack us? You know the nomads have been arriving to see her. With all our women gathered in one place, it would be the perfect opportunity to strike. She may just be biding her time until her lover arrives."

Eyes locked on her sister, Penthesilea pulled her dagger from its sheath and twisted it between her fingers, knowing that Antiope would heed the warning. It was not a threat, per se, more a reminder to consider carefully which words she chose to use next. The sisters had never fought one another in earnest. They were always at each other's sides, whether on the field of battle or in the daily running of the Kingdom. But things could always change.

"Hippolyte was Queen," she said slowly, enunciating each syllable in a way that made her feelings evident. "She is the rightful Queen, anointed by Ares, and would never put her women at risk."

"You do not know that. You do not know what she might do, anymore. It has been nearly six years. She must tell us why she has returned. If she will not speak, then we have no option but to assume and prepare for the worst."

"You are wrong!" Penthesilea shouted, no longer able to hide her wrath. "We have the option to trust her."

"Yes, and you are Queen now," Melanippe said, her quiet tone the antithesis of Antiope's. "But you are only one of thousands of women here, Penthesilea, and they are already becoming uneasy, even fearful of her presence. If you do not get an answer from her soon, you may face a revolt."

"That has never happened!" Penthesilea retorted, outraged that she could even suggest such a thing.

"No, and there had never been an Amazon queen who married an Athenian prince. Please, Sister, we do not say this to be cruel. We love Hippolyte with all our hearts, you know that. But you must find out why she has retuned, and what her intentions are. And you need to do it soon."

Twisting away from them, Penthesilea clenched her fist around the dagger. She was defeated. Outnumbered. She had been backed into a corner and they knew it. So that was it, then. Hippolyte must talk.

A SMALL LAMP had been placed in the corner of the room, its thin flame leaving an oily mark on the ceiling above. It provided barely enough light to see by, much less perform any useful tasks, and yet it was by this that Hippolyte sat on her bed, drawing a whetstone against the side of her blade, the scraping echoing off the bare stone walls around her. This was not a room she had been accustomed to sleeping in. It was one usually allocated to the pages. For a time Cletes had slept here, before she had found a permeant place in the Palace. Was this how she should view herself now? As nothing more than a servant?

"Antiope took your horse to the pastures with the others."

Penthesilea had carefully considered how to open the conversation before entering the room. This seemed as inoffensive a remark as she could begin with.

"I hope that was the right thing to do?"

Hippolyte nodded, still looking down. The noise of stone against metal was rhythmic, almost hypnotic. Scrape and clink. Scrape and clink.

Penthesilea had learnt that you could not force someone to speak, if they were unwilling to, without a threat you could make good on. And although her position did not call for her to take part in interrogations, confession and death often went hand in hand. Men would say anything if they thought it might spare their lives. Of course, Hippolyte's life was not at risk. Even if it had been, she seemed not to care.

Knowing she had a hard task ahead of her, Penthesilea picked up a small stool and moved it closer to her sister. She had hoped that mentioning her horse might bring about some reaction and start a simple, straightforward exchange of words, but that had not worked. She now had no choice but to say why she was there and pray that her honesty and directness would bring about a swift and peaceful resolution of the problem.

"Our sisters think you have come to betray us," she said. "That you are here as part of a trap."

Hippolyte's hands stopped and she finally looked up.

"You do not believe that, do you?" she asked.

No. Penthesilea wanted to say. *No. With all my heart, I do not.* But she knew that if this was the reply she gave, they would be no closer to learning the truth of her return.

"I struggle to know what to believe," she said, instead.

There was silence and Penthesilea hoped her sister was about to speak once more. Then Hippolyte bent over her work again, although her motion lacked its previous steady rhythm. Her hands were shaking.

"You told me you would return after your child was born. Boy or girl, you said you would come back to us."

"I believed I would," she replied, keeping her eyes down.

"So why did you not?"

Hippolyte refused to say more. The sound of metal against stone was starting to grate, now. Out of desperation, she reached across, grabbed Hippolyte's shoulders and shook her, once but forcefully.

"Please! I need you to talk to me. I need you to tell me something. The women are worried. Whatever it is, whatever has happened, we will help you. We will forgive you, if necessary. But please, please talk to me."

Her pulsed hammered. Her sister was weak. Not in body, but in spirit. She had not even responded to her outburst.

Beyond the room, footsteps pattered lightly. She might have known that Antiope and Melanippe would be listening in, wanting to ensure that the account she later gave them was accurate. But there would be no lying, no false claims that Hippolyte had provided her with an explanation or confession. Only the truth.

Penthesilea's hands squeezed a little tighter on her sister's shoulders. No shaking now. Just flesh against flesh.

"Please, Hippolyte. We need to know. The women need to know. Otherwise ... otherwise ..."

She allowed the unspoken consequences to drift in the silence between them. One moment passed and then another. There were no sounds now, inside or outside the room. *Do not make me say it,* Penthesilea prayed, as Hippolyte's eyes rose slowly to meet hers. Even in the dim candlelight, the sheen of tears on them was clear.

"Otherwise, I must leave Themiscyra?" Hippolyte asked. "Otherwise, you will make me leave?"

Penthesilea could only offer her more silence and yet this spoke volumes, its meaning as clear as if she had shouted from the top of the highest steppe. Sitting up straighter, Hippolyte drew in a long, deep breath, then placed her sword on her lap.

"I heard rumours in the Palace, when I first arrived, of the things he had done. The people he had killed. Not warriors. Not monsters. Just people. Most of the servants would shrink away from him. Lower their eyes as he passed. But they were little more than slaves. That is how they act, is it not? They fear their masters."

Penthesilea remained silent on the matter. As long as Hippolyte was talking, she did not wish to stem the flow.

"There were other rumours too, that he had taken a young girl, called Helen, when she was but a child. When he was a child, too, for that matter. I asked him about it. I asked about all the rumours. But that was all they were, he said. Slander. Two young children at play whose reputations jealous people had attempted to tarnish. And I believed him. With my whole heart, I believed him. Even after what he had done to me. Even after he had taken me."

Her voice drifted off, as did her gaze, to a place that Penthesilea could not see and could only imagine. Her fists were clenched at her sides.

"He showed me so much love, Sister. He did love me. I am certain. Why come back for a person after so many years if it were not for love? Why welcome them into your home? I knew he could be vengeful and petty, but I never believed he would wield his cruelty against me."

Hippolyte shivered as if a cold breeze had rolled in through the window, and yet the room was warm.

"I tried to save Aegeus, for him. And Hippolytus. My Hippolytus. I do not know what I will do without him. How could he do this to me?"

The lamp flickered as Penthesilea sat and listened. There

was still silence from the hallway, her sisters motionless. Her sister's story came in fits and starts, not a simple narrative but rather fragments of events, often told without any connection, at least none that Penthesilea could see. Yet she slowly started to draw lines between the pieces and bring them together to form a picture. An image of a man, his child and his wife. It was one of pain and betrayal and loss.

Penthesilea asked no questions, not about Theseus or Hippolytus or this new woman he had brought home. Only when Hippolyte pressed the heels of her hands to her forehead and asked two simple questions, did she feel so enraged that she knew she had to speak again.

"What did I do wrong?" she asked. "Why was I not enough?"

Penthesilea's fury was as hot and dangerous as smelted iron on skin, and she made no attempt to cool it.

"You? It was not *you* who was not enough. You were too much for him, Sister. Always too much. Too strong. Too powerful. Too smart. Too compassionate. Too brave. Too loving. He tried to knock these wonderful qualities out of you and bring you down to his level, but he could not succeed. He did not replace you because you were inadequate, my darling Sister, believe me. He replaced you because he knew you were more than he could ever live up to."

Hippolyte's jaw wobbled. Laid out for her like this, Penthesilea thought, she must now see the truth. Hippolyte was the Queen of the Amazons. Invincible in human terms. Fearless. How was it possible that any man could break her like this? A wave of appreciation for Cletes' devotion flowed through her. Never had she doubted her loyalty, and never, she hoped, had Cletes doubted hers.

"Sister. He has wronged you. In so many ways."

Hippolyte laughed, a sad, bitter chuckle.

"Even if that is the case, what is there I can do? He is King of Athens now, and he has my son."

Penthesilea turned her head to the doorway. She had no doubt that her sisters continued to listen outside and hoped that they would be in agreement with what she was about to propose.

"What do you want to do?" she asked, first.

Hippolyte's eyes went down to the weapon in her lap. She stroked a finger along the flat of the blade before lifting the sword and turning it over in her hand.

"I want him dead," she said quietly. "I want my son back and Theseus dead."

For the first time since Hippolyte's return, Penthesilea felt a genuine smile come to her lips and the familiar sensation of anticipation flow within her. She raised her voice just a fraction, to ensure her sisters could hear.

"In that case, I suggest we do what we do best. We go to war."

CHAPTER 34

*H*ippolyte reached forwards and kissed her sister on her cheek. Her old smile seemed to have returned.

"Go to war with Athens?" She gave a little laugh. "That is one fight I fear even we cannot win."

"We have won every battle we have ever fought. Why would this be any different?"

"For a hundred reasons. The size of their army. The arrangements and structures that surround and support them. The layout of the city streets, that every soldier has committed to memory. The defences that must be surmounted even to enter the citadel are greater than anything we have ever faced before."

"In that case, I shall relish the challenge."

It was clear to Penthesilea that Hippolyte considered her words to be little more than a sympathetic comment intended to raise her spirits. But as they looked at one another, she could see the realisation dawn in her sister's eyes. She had spoken in earnest.

"You are serious?" she asked. "You believe we can do this?"

"I know we can. You want Theseus dead. I want him destroyed for what he has done to you and to this family. I want him to suffer in ways he cannot conceive of. I want his walls to fall and his city to burn, and if you search your heart, I know you want this, too."

The words came in a deluge. This was what Penthesilea had desired more than anything, since the moment she knew Theseus had stolen her sister away.

"We can do this," she pressed on. "I swear on the gods, we can take Athens."

Her breath quivered in anticipation as Hippolyte's eyes glinted with something she remembered from all those years ago. She slowly dipped her chin. Was that a nod? Had she agreed? Hippolyte's movements were so tentative, she could not be sure. Then, she spoke again.

"If you truly believe we can win, then we should start preparing."

FROM THE MOMENT of Hippolyte's abduction, Penthesilea had dreamt of the moment she would attack Athens, kill Theseus and retrieve her sister. But this was even better, for this time she would watch as Hippolyte sent an arrow though his heart.

The call went out to summon the nomads back to Themiscyra, and messengers were sent far and wide to their allies to secure the warriors, horses and food required to mount an attack against Athens. In the normal course of events, scouts would go ahead to assess access to the citadel and locate its weakest points for entry, along with those areas where they would be likely to meet the most resistance. This information would ensure the battle was swift and efficient. But there was no need for this. They had Hippolyte.

"There are many gates into the citadel, but we will need to enter here."

She pointed to her sketch of the citadel. It was far from comprehensive, omitting many places she had not visited. From what Penthesilea had seen herself, she knew that the Palace offered a sweeping view of the lands below.

"There are high points throughout the citadel that we can use to our advantage. Here," she said, indicating to the west of the Acropolis, "the Areopagus should be the first place to take and establish our stronghold."

The other sisters nodded in agreement. As Hippolyte continued to speak, Penthesilea carefully scrutinised her sister. Her tone had altered since her return. She now approached each task with a detachment, as if the places she named had no meaning for her, rather than ones she had previously considered home. There was also a hesitance in her planning, deferring to Penthesilea when any major decision had to be made.

They recalled all the nomads and the Amazon women who had settled in Ephesus, to the west of Anatolia. They reached out to those who lived in auls, camps gathered on the steppes with large tents in their centres where they lit fires to ward off the winter frosts. They called on the Thracian tribes, with whom they had formed alliances over the years. Then, when all had promised their aid, they loaded their horses with enough supplies to last them. Half a moon had passed since Hippolyte had returned, and they were finally as prepared as they could be. Only one task remained.

They rode en masse past the dark choppy Sea of Marmara, to the rocky outcrop. Every woman, with the exception of those who remained with the children, was present. Even the older warriors, who suspected the looming battle would be their last, and the young, not yet blessed with the blood of a kill. Here, they offered up to Ares the most significant sacrifice possible: horses from their homeland, beautiful male beasts, loyal and strong. Gifts that were worthy of their father. Even with all the blood she had seen, Penthesilea had to force herself to watch as the light flickered out from the eyes of each stallion. But there was no waste here. Ares would reward their dutiful observance of sacrifice to him.

The scent of blood was thick and cloying as the last animal was led to the rock, a dark bay, which Hippolyte guided with a single rope around its neck. Kneeling on the ground at its feet, she whispered words that only she and the gods could hear, before plunging the knife upwards into his heart.

Afterwards, they danced until sunset, with spears in their hands, sending their prayers far and wide with their chanting and the stamping of their feet. Penthesilea had prayed like this countless times before. She had danced at festivals, celebrations and feasts to honour the gods for the bounty constantly bestowed upon them, but she had never done so with such urgency in her step. Never had she, again and again, stabbed her spear into the air with such force. She was lost in it all, in the voices rolling around her, deep, resonant and mesmerising. When the fires had dwindled to embers and the sun had disappeared below the horizon, they took to their beds, for tomorrow, they rode for Athens.

Shallow moonlight glowed around her as Penthesilea knelt in the shallows. The water here was colder than on the shores of Pontus, yet the icy sting on her skin was refreshing after the smouldering heat of the dance. Antiope was busy sending women off with orders to meet with leaders and kings between there and Athens, to ease their passage. Melanippe had gone to tend to an issue with supplies, but Penthesilea had chosen to stay close to Hippolyte.

Despite all these years away from Themiscyra, Hippolyte had lost none of her accuracy with a bow, nor skill with her spear and sword. She must have trained in Athens, Penthesilea assumed, perhaps with Theseus. Or perhaps it was simply her godly heritage. She did not wish to ask.

But while her body had remained firm and active, her mind had not. Penthesilea often glanced at her and found her eyes drifting away, her gaze lost somewhere beyond the horizon. She would lose track of her words, stopping and restarting sentences with an uncertainty Penthesilea had never seen before. The distrust that the women continued to show in her, despite all her help with this planned attack, meant that Penthesilea kept her near at all times, even going so far as to sleep in the same bed, which necessitated Cletes' absence, something she wished to rectify as soon as possible.

As they washed their hands, Hippolyte turned to look at her sister.

"I need to ask something of you. Something more," she said.

Penthesilea lifted her hands from the water and dried them on the seat of her trousers.

"You need not fear. This attack will succeed. We will take the citadel and we will reunite you with your son."

Hippolyte nodded but did not respond, instead pressing her hands tightly together before releasing them to fall back into the water.

"I am sorry," Penthesilea spoke again. "You wished to ask something of me. Please. I will listen to you."

Hippolyte lowered her gaze a fraction, and Penthesilea felt something tug at her heart. How was it possible that these eyes could convey such sadness? Were they not the same ones that had shone with laughter and joy, compassion and love? But a heart has the ability to change, to allow darkness to enter it. And at that moment, darkness dwelt so deeply in her, there seemed to be no light reflecting from her soul at all.

"I want him to die. I want Theseus dead, for what he has done to me, and for all the atrocities I am certain he has committed before I knew him and will continue to do so, if he is not stopped. I want him dead."

"I know, I understand that."

Penthesilea quickly closed her mouth again, remembering her promise to listen.

"You are certain that we can defeat him?" Hippolyte asked. "His army is great in numbers and his hoplites are well trained."

"We have destroyed great armies before. Ones with double, triple even ten times our numbers."

"This will be greater even than that."

"And the rewards that the women will reap will ensure that this war is never forgotten. The Amazons will be remembered forever as the greatest warriors ever to have lived."

Small waves continued to lap over their knees.

"I am worried that, when the moment comes, I may not be able to do it myself," Hippolyte said, finally. "I am worried that I will not be able to kill him."

Penthesilea took her sister by the shoulders and forced her to turn and face at her.

"You are the true Queen of the Amazons," Penthesilea said. "You will not fail to hit him, whether with sword or spear or arrow. He will die by your hand."

A half-smile lingered on Hippolyte's lips, but she shook her head.

"This is different. It is not a failure of my ability that I fear, but one of my resolve. If he speaks to me, his words will seep too deeply into my thoughts. I know it is wrong, and I do want him dead, but nevertheless, I still love him. He will make me doubt myself, I am sure of it."

"He might once have been able to do this to you, but we will be beside you. We will not let that happen."

Despite Penthesilea's confidence, Hippolyte shook her head again.

"I need you to promise that if the moment comes and you think I may be wavering, then you will do it for me. You will kill him."

To her own surprise, Penthesilea hesitated. She had dreamed of plunging a dagger into Theseus' heart, but what Hippolyte was asking was far more than just the death of the treacherous man she had considered her husband to be. Amazon women took pride in their accomplishments. Gloried in them. For Hippolyte to even consider the possibility of being unable to kill him, this concerned her. Perhaps her sisters were right. When all this was over, would she be fit to rule again as Queen? She shook away the thought.

"When you are there, at the height of battle, you will see things differently. You will find the strength."

"Perhaps. But perhaps he will find my weakness, first. Please, Sister. I cannot face Athens if I do not have your promise that if I tell you, or signal to you, that I am unable to do it, you will take that shot. Please. Do this for me."

Knowing there was only one answer she could give, Penthesilea nodded, although her words weighed heavy on her heart.

"If you cannot do it, then I will. I will kill him. But first, we must take Athens."

hey rode out in numbers and with a quantity of supplies as never before, the sweat of the heavily laden horses turning their coats dark and slick as their hooves pummelled the ground. North they went first, then west again, through Thrace. Hippolyte knew what a formidable sight awaited the Athenians when they galloped towards them, their patterned tunics glinting, quivers loaded and bows at the ready.

Children cried and men and women cowered or bolted for their homes, as they rode past settlements. No words were spoken, apart from the occasional order from one of the princesses or tribe leaders. The wind whistled over their tightly capped heads.

Hippolyte could see why Penthesilea was spoken of as the greatest Amazon Queen. It was clear just how proficient a leader she had become. The women hung on her every word, and each speech she delivered was more rousing and inspiring than the last. They rode together, not as individuals, but as one entity with a single goal.

And it could not be a coincidence that, under her leadership, the army had grown larger and stronger than ever before. So many of those young girls, who had struggled to nock an arrow or stand atop a stationary horse, were now riding out, tunics and trousers already stained with the blood of battle. Perhaps she was the better Queen. All evidence indicated as much.

Before departing from Thrace, they changed their horses for fresh ones, gifted to them by King Tyragetae. As much as they would have wished to move faster, time had to be spent with each of the tribal chiefs and kings whose land they rode through, talking tactics, agreeing repayments and spoils that would be presented to them on their return, after the citadel had been brought to its knees. They also had to negotiate for more supplies, should they be needed if the siege extended longer than anticipated.

"So, it is true?" Tyragetae had asked, the same question that had come from each of the leaders they had met.

"Theseus truly stole the Amazon Queen?"

Each time it came, Hippolyte felt herself squirm, as if her skin had shrunk and become too tight for her body. At least they had not been impertinent enough to ask if she had fallen in love with Theseus or whether the son she had borne him was a prize worthy of war and so she answered them honestly: Theseus had drugged her and he was not a worthy father for the child of an Amazon Queen.

The closer they came to Athens, the calmer Hippolyte felt. She would soon be fighting again, swinging her blade at the enemy and spilling blood on the stones. The thought of once again riding into battle brought her peace.

"We will leave as soon as the moon is it at its highest," Penthesilea told them as they camped in Attica, to the north of the city.

On Hippolyte's advice, they would enter through the Pirean Gate on the east side of the citadel. There were hills without buildings there, where they could make their strongholds. She only hoped her memory would not let them down. Had she known it would come to this, she would have insisted that she see more during her time there. She would have roamed daily, learning all the weakness of the city, all its shortcomings and vulnerabilities. But then, they were a lot of things she would have done differently.

If Theseus was expecting an attack—and she considered he would be a fool not to—then he would expect it to come from the north, the more obvious route, with several gates to choose from. He would expect to win by sheer force of numbers in a short bloody battle, rather than considering the topography of the land and the likelihood of a siege. She knew the way he worked, could anticipate how he would think. So, there had been some advantages to their relationship, after all. Yes, more men would be placed on those northern gates.

Penthesilea had asked her to make the pre-battle speech. To rouse her troops to fight for her the way she had done all those years before. For a moment, she had considered it, but this was not her army anymore. It was Penthesilea's. Not just because she had trained most of the women and lived with them, but because they trusted her.

"Perhaps I will speak to them later," she had said, softly. "When he is dead, they will trust me again."

She felt none of the pain she would have expected uttering these words, for it was the truth. Yet even as she spoke them, she thought it unlikely. How could they trust her when she did not yet trust herself? What would she do when Hippolytus was returned to her? Where would her true loyalties lie, when she was forced to decide the fate of her son? She knew the same question had been on her sisters' minds for as long as the battle had been planned. She had watched them swallow it down, again and again. She reasoned that they did not want to hear her answer any more than she was able to provide one.

And so, it was Penthesilea who stood before three thousand Amazon women, together with their Thracian, Scythian and Samaritan allies. And Hippolyte stood behind her with Antiope and Melanippe, an Amazon princess, if nothing more.

All watched in awed silence as Penthesilea lifted her eyes to the heavens, as if able to see Olympus and the other gods residing there, listening to her every word. She paused for a moment, before lowering her gaze back to the women.

"I do not need to tell you that not all of you here today will return to your homelands."

A murmur rippled through the women. Several older hands squeezed younger ones. There was no need for reassuring smiles. It was a rite. A privilege. The young ones were thirsty for it, and the older ones knew that, whatever happened, they would have played their part.

"This will not be an easy battle. And it will not come without loss. But we will be victorious. Athens and its king will fall. Those of you who do not survive will die heroes. And we will show them that we are all daughters of Ares!"

With that, she raised her spear to the sky and, a second later, three thousand more were lifted to join it, their tips shining in the moonlight, as a battle cry echoed through the sky. They were formidable. They were unbeatable.

They were the Amazons.

∼

WHEN THE TIME CAME, they left bivouacs along the roadside, to hold their supplies and as somewhere they could send the injured back to, while the rest continued to fight. A hundred warriors remained to protect them, although no Athenian it his right mind would attack them. He would be too busy trying to stay alive.

Clouds obscured the stars and moon that night, but the faint flickering of lights from the distant citadel guided them to their destination.

"Of course, they will put many guards around the Palace," Penthesilea said to Hippolyte, breaking the silence, as the lights on the hills grew brighter.

They had been riding slowly for some time now, barely a hair's breadth apart.

"The moment they see us coming, Theseus will immediately be surrounded by guards. It will take a small group of our best women to break through to him."

"And take Hippolytus," Hippolyte reminded her, with more sharpness than she had intended.

"And take Hippolytus. We will get your son, Hippolyte. I know why we are here."

After that, she found there was nothing more to say.

As the sky lightened and the night melted away, the city walls came into view. At first, they were nothing more than a silhouette, like a long black snake slicing across the hillside and over the horizon. But as they drew closer, everything came into focus: the cyclopean brick structures, the heavy gates and, at the apex of the hill, the Temple.

The guards outside the walls were silenced before they could utter a word, much less raise the alarm. As they approached the Pirean Gate, Penthesilea signalled for the women to stop and turned once more to her sister.

"You should begin this," she said. "You should send the first one out."

For a moment, Hippolyte considered refusing the request, just as she had refused to address the women, the night before. But this time it felt right, it was her place to do this.

And so it was that, with her breath held, she drew back a flaming arrow, raised her bow, and released the fiery missile high over the walls and into Athens.

War had begun.

CHAPTER 36

*P*enthesilea and Hippolyte led half of the army through the Pirean Gate, while the remaining half went with Melanippe and Antiope through the Acharnian Gate on opposite sides of the citadel. They flowed through the wall, a river breaking its banks, releasing a torrent of arrows and silencing every hoplite within range. Their horses snorted as they raced across the open space between the citadel wall and that of the Palace, the cobbled stones a far cry from the soft earth of the steppes. Hippolyte stayed low on her steed, her back level with the horse's flank, offering her opponents only the smallest amount of visible flesh to strike at, while allowing her to reach down and pull arrows from dead hoplites and fire them again and again.

By now, every man woman and child knew that Athens was under attack. Theseus would know it, too, and he would know exactly who had come for him.

"We must get to higher ground to gain the advantage," Hippolyte shouted as she led them to the Areopagus, the large rocky hill where they anticipated paying a sacrifice to their father.

It was a matter of trust now. Knowing each woman would do what was required of her. Antiope would be doing her part holding the gates for when they needed to leave while Melanippe had gone to the east side of the Acropolis and two of her strongest women, Dorymache and Antandre, were at the south as the Amazons surrounded the centre of the city, forcing the Athenians to spread themselves thin. Shrieks of panic filled the air. Shrieks which caused a glimmer of satisfaction to rise in Hippolyte. As she had hoped, the attack from the southernmost gate had caught them by surprise. All they would be able to do was defend and limit their loses as best they could.

The hoplites moved in tight formation, their shields held in such a way as to create a metal shell around their bodies, their glistening spears held upright, at the ready. Each collective footstep sounded like thunder and shook the ground. But their movements were necessarily slow and cumbersome by comparison with their enemy who was more decisive than Hippolyte had even seen them before. At this rate the battle would be over quickly. Under Theseus' arrogance, all that Aegeus had built was about to crumble.

One after another the hoplites fell. Their shields and armour forming a crust upon the earth. For her part, Hippolyte took everyone she could, never stopping to glimpse the eyes beneath the helmets, for fear that a familiar pair of eyes might stare back at her. Blood soaked her boots and sprayed her skin. And with each kill, a little part of her reformed. A part that had been lost within these very walls was returned to her.

"We will breach them and reach the palace before midday," Penthesilea called across the clangs of metal.

"They will not hold even that long," Hippolyte responded. Yet the words had barely left her lips when a new cry shot up into the air. One she had heard so infrequently that her mind could not process it. Even as fear flashed across her sister's face, she could not make sense of what she was hearing.

"Sister, they are attacking from behind!" Penthesilea's words met her ears, yet Hippolyte could make no sense of them. How could her women be under attack? "Come! We need to get higher!"

Spurred only by her sister's movements and words, Hippolyte kicked her horse into motion. Tugging on their beasts, they weaved their way through swinging swords and falling bodies, their animals' hooves stamping on flesh, armour and earth indiscriminately. There was no denying the change now. The air, that less than had hour ago had rippled with the excitement of their impeding victory, was now taut and fragile as if it could fracture at any second. And there, from the higher ground, she saw the reason why.

Thousands upon thousands of men poured through the gates of the outer wall. These were not hoplites, burdened with heavy armour and shields. These were peltast troops. Unencumbered men, with barely a scrap of armour on the bodies, raced towards the Amazons, raining down their spears in an unending torrent. The women were battling on both fronts. They had encountered such numbers before, but never when confined to such a small area. They needed room. Room for the horses to gallop and weave.

"I don't understand." Hippolyte cried as she watched on.

It was clear that Theseus had expected her attack, this many men could not have been concealed by accident. The drumming of feet and the clanging of weapons against shields formed a metronomic pulse that shook the ground and vibrated through the soles of the Amazons' boots. She needed to get back down there. She needed to fight, but no sooner had she dug her heels into the flanks of her horse, than a new terror caught her eye.

"What is that?"

"A ballista," Hippolyte answered her sister, with a new surge of pain and anger. Theseus had spoken of such an instrument before. One that would see him undefeatable in war. And she had dismissed it as nothing more than a boy's toy. How wrong she was.

Mounted on a wheeled chariot, iron tipped bolts the thickness and length of a man's arm were fired from the giant crossbow. And though they were not as fast to reload as a simple bow and arrow, they ripped through the Amazons. Undeterred by flesh, bone or armour, each bolt struck down half a dozen Amazons, scattering bodies and horses like leaves from an autumn tree.

"Sister! We cannot hold all our positions," Penthesilea shouted over her shoulder at she swung her axe horizontally in front of her body and brought down first one hoplite and then another. "Where do you wish to concentrate the attack?"

Confusion flooded through Hippolyte. Never before had she seen her women so outnumbered. They fought more effectively than any of the men, but there were simply so many of them. Theseus had called on all his forces to fire these new weapons. He had even liberated his slaves to fight and die for him. And all of this to keep her from her son.

She could hardly bear to acknowledge it, but there was no doubting it now: the Amazons were, for the first time, losing.

"I need to get to Theseus," she said. "There is only one way we can end this. If their King is dead, they will have to submit."

Penthesilea nodded.

"Show me the path you need clearing."

Still fighting off soldiers, Hippolyte glanced behind her.

"You and I shall cut through the agora," she said, pointing her arrow towards an area that was swarming with men. They would be outnumbered twenty to one, but she knew her sister would not refuse.

"Then let us do it."

They had fought in such a manner before, the two of them breaking away and forcing a path through the enemy. At such close quarters, Hippolyte would rely on her kopides, her small swords, that she would use too fast for her foes to counter. Every movement of the blades, each twist and turn, would bring about another Athenian death and another step further towards Theseus and Hippolytus. From behind her came the sound of Penthesilea's axe cleaving flesh and bone with the same relentless fluidity.

One by one, the hoplites before them fell. And not for the first time, Hippolyte found herself filled with sympathy and admiration for the men. They fought fiercely, knowing death was imminent, all to serve a king with the scruples of a bandit. *He was my husband*, she wanted to shout at them. *He promised me a lifetime of love, and this is how he treated me. He does not care about Athens or his people. He cares only for himself.* But there was no time for that. No time for anything other than the grunts and guttural screams that rattled from the hoplites as death greeted them at the end of her swords.

"There!" Hippolyte called, momentarily pointing her blade in the direction of the steps to the Palace. A hoplite thrust his spear at her, but before the tip could reach her she knocked it aside and kicked out, sending him tumbling back and making swift work of both him and the soldiers behind him.

No other women had made it this far into the citadel, and the soldiers here were more densely packed and heavily armed than anywhere else. A human blockade. A wall of beating hearts. Dread rolled through her, for she knew exactly what their presence meant.

"He knows I am coming for him."

"Then he knows you are going to kill him, too," Penthesilea replied. "You will do this. You will end it today."

They fought through the scorching heat of midday. Each step forward was achieved at the cost of a dozen more deaths. Streams of sweat poured off their skin. It was as if Helios were unwilling to descend from his peak. The golden rays reflected off the buildings, nearly blinding them as they turned, pivoted and lunged. They flung themselves against sword and shield and each time rose up to do the same again.

"We are nearly there," Hippolyte cried, reaching the final line of reinforcements. Behind them lay a path littered with Athenian bodies. However certain Theseus might have been that Hippolyte would come for him, the dwindling numbers of guards told her that he had been equally sure she would not make it this far. As she passed the threshold of the Palace only a handful of hoplites remained. Men she had seen every day for nearly six years.

"You know how this ends," she said, with as much kindness as she could muster.

"Oira—"

She cut the man's throat before a further syllable could escape it.

Inside, the Palace was cool and quiet. The noise of the battle below was muted here, deadened by distance, the thickness of the walls and the sound of her own heartbeat. The heat of her body bled away through the white marble tiles, and the dark shadows turned the sweat and blood on her skin icy cold.

"Where will he be?" Penthesilea asked. "Where do we go from here?"

Hippolyte pressed her lips together as her eyes scanned the corridors that had once been so familiar to her. The same colourful frescos graced the walls. The same tapestries hung from the same doorways. And yet this place felt more alien to her now than it ever had, even in those first days, when Aegeus had met her with distrust, and Theseus had laced her drinks with valerian root. She did not doubt that he would have been watching the progress of the battle from up here, cheering loudly as he witnessed the massacre of her women.

As this thought struck her, another came swift on its heels. There was one room that offered the best view.

"The andron," she said aloud and quickened her step.

The room had been Aegeus' domain, his sanctuary. Without warning, a maelstrom of grief and anger rushed through her. Theseus had murdered his own father. Not with blade or poison but with his selfish, self-absorbed arrogance. And when she killed him, it would be in revenge for the old man's death, just as much as it was justice for herself.

Her mouth became dry as she readied herself for what was to come. With the tip of her sword, she whipped the curtain aside and stepped inside, only to find the room empty.

The scent of wine hit her, momentarily flooding her with memories. Their late-night conversations. The stories they shared of the battles they had fought. The dreams they both had for Hippolytus. The old King picking him up, placing him on his lap and bouncing him there. She had laughed in this room. She had laughed and breathed and felt at perfect ease and comfort. And now she was preparing to shed blood in it.

"Hippolyte, they are not here. Where else might they be?"
Her sister's voice buzzed distantly behind her as she gazed on
the furnishings. Nothing had changed in her absence.
"Hippolyte!"

She snapped out of her reverie. If they were not here, then
where? She supposed it was possible they had retreated to the
throne room. Given the urgency of matters in the city, it would
be a large enough space for all his advisors to gather and
discuss strategies. Yes, that would make sense. She started to
lead the way through the corridors, only to draw swiftly to a
halt once again.

At first, she assumed the sounds she was hearing came from
outside, a distortion of the cries of battle. But these noises were
not that. They lingered, growing in intensity then fading again,
only to swell to an even greater pitch than before. Straining to
hear, she sheathed her sword, exchanging it for her bow and
arrow.

"That sounds like laughter," Penthesilea said. "Like someone's holding a feast."

No sooner had her sister spoken, than Hippolyte was
moving again, racing along the corridor, leaving rust-red footprints on the white marble and shedding dirt with every step. A
feast. A banquet. She could hear it now. The smell of roast meat
and wine and the tart tang of salted cheeses. The closer she
came to the hall, the more intense the noise became. There was
laughter and cheering. Were they already toasting victory? No,
surely even Theseus could not be so arrogant as to celebrate
while his men lost their lives for him.

As her feet slowed, she heard something else. Nausea
swelled in her stomach. It was a lyre. Music. Music in a time of
death. Never had her blood boiled so furiously or her pulse
pounded with such burning rage. These men were not afraid of

them. There were not hiding or cowering like men did when the arrival of the Amazons was imminent. Why not?

Supressing an unexpected tremor in her fingers, she nocked her arrow, her fingertips squeezing the shaft of her arrow. Yet as she stepped from the corridor and the light of the banquet hall hit her, she froze at the sight before her.

CHAPTER 37

*W*hen she had first arrived in Athens, the scale of the feasting had taken some time for Hippolyte to become accustomed to. The excesses to which they ate and drank, with so little regard for their bodies and even less for the waste of the earth's bounty, with which the gods had blessed them, simply disgusted her. Fish and meat, flaking from the bone, dried fruits, sweet sticky honey drizzled over crumbling breads. No expense was spared, not taste left unsatisfied. This was how the Athenians celebrated. And they did it often.

On one occasion, around the time of Hippolytus' second birthday, she had attempted to eat as they did, filling her plate with everything on offer, gorging beyond the point of enjoyment. Her body became bloated and her limbs grew sluggish, so much so that she wondered if Theseus had drugged her again. Yet, watching the others, she saw that she was not only one who was affected like this. With their distended bodies, no one could even dance properly anymore. And the effects did not end when the feasting did. The next day, she found herself groaning with discomfort, her belly swollen as if she were growing a second child there. After that, she had always shown restraint, regardless of the temptations on offer.

And yet what she saw before her today was greater than any feast she had ever attended in all her years there. For it was not a celebration of victory, she realised.

It was a wedding.

Theseus sat at the far end of the room, on a table set upon a dais. His hair was thickly oiled, curling down his shoulders in greasy tendrils as if he were a gorgon, and the purple tunic he wore was elaborately embroidered with gold thread. Upon his head sat a wreath of gold shaped into twisted leaves, set with a garnet the size of an arrowhead. Beside him, sat the young girl he had brought into their home. The young girl he had said he was going to make his wife.

The room fell silent, every pair of eyes on Hippolyte and her sister. Several women had their hands to their mouths, others were pushing their men towards the intruders. But they did nothing, other than grow paler by the second. She recognised them as members of the Polis. Men who had regarded her with disdain and distrust from the moment she had been dragged to this place. They looked upon her again now, as if she were a monster. But she knew the truth. It was their king who was the monster here, and as he himself had so recently proven in Crete; monsters could be killed.

Her mind took on a new clarity. She tipped her head to the side and spoke.

"It would appear that my invitation went astray."

Whimpers came from the table closest to her, from a woman whose hand was shaking so badly wine was slopping over the edge of her cup. The man beside her—from his age it was impossible to tell if he was her husband or father—straightened his back.

"You are not welcome here. You are defeated. You should leave now."

"My sister is speaking." Penthesilea's voice as sharp as the point of her arrow which she aimed at the speaker.

He instantly recoiled, his reserve of bravery already depleted. Still, it was a better display than that shown by the rest of the guests, who simply cowered in their seats.

Hippolyte waited a moment for the assembled company to reflect on her sister's words and then spoke again.

"I fail to see how I have been defeated," she said, increasing the tension on her bowstring, the weapon pointed directly at Theseus. "To me, it looks like there is an arrow trained upon your king. No one else in this room needs to die. All I want is my son. My son ... and my husband's head."

With a nod, Penthesilea stepped forwards and took up Hippolyte's place, aiming her own bow directly at Theseus, while her sister turned to examine the room. At least two hundred people were present, men and women, old and young, mostly Athenians, with a smattering of dignitaries from neighbouring kingdoms. There were also several children present, all dressed in their finery. But not her child.

She marched towards Theseus, who remained seated.

"Where is he?" she spat. "What have you done with him?"

It was his turn to tip his head, mimicking her.

"Am I supposed to know of whom you speak?"

"Where is Hippolytus?" she said, enunciating each syllable.

Still he played his game, wrinkling his brow in mock confusion, before widening his eyes.

"Oh. You mean my son. He is not here, as you can see."

His speech was unhurried. He was taking his time to savour the pleasure of ridiculing her.

Suddenly, from behind her, came the flap of fabric, so light it might have been nothing more than the fluttering of a bird's wing. Swivelling on the balls of her feet, she fired off an arrow before the other guests had even realised what was happening. A guard, previously concealed by a curtain, fell to the floor an arrow protruding from his eye socket, his sword clattering to the ground. Stepping forwards, she rolled his body over with a foot, pulled out the arrow and fixed it back in her bow, before addressing Theseus.

"Do not test me," she said, meeting his eye. "I will kill everyone in this room to get to my son."

The arrogant look on Theseus' face had shifted slightly. Beside him, his young bride was white with fear as she clutched her new husband's arm.

"This does not end well for you, Hippolyte. Leave now. Remove yourself from my wedding celebrations. I will spare what is left of your army, and I will send word of Hippolytus to you."

"I do not believe you. Every word you speak is a lie."

"You cannot escape here alive. Your women are dying out there. You know that. They will all fall."

"They will not fall until I have my son."

His eyebrow rose by a fraction.

"You would do that? You would offer up the life of every single Amazon for a child you did not even want?"

"I always wanted him!" she cried. "I am not playing games, Theseus. Tell me where he is now, or I will kill you. And when you are dead, I will kill each of your guests, and starting with this child you have taken as a bride. It will be a mercy killing. Better to free her now than condemn her to a life of misery with you."

He turned to Phaedra now, almost with surprise, as if he had forgotten she was there. Hippolyte's words floated in the air, like the motes of dust that glinted in the sunlight. He knew that she had seen him for what he was. A liar, a manipulator, a narcissist. But he had seen who she was, too, and he knew that every word she spoke was true.

Phaedra herself looked down and Hippolyte noted the way her hands shifted from the table to her belly. Could it be? she wondered. Already? As she thought of the child that might already be growing in the girl's belly, her mind raced from present to future. What would become of Hippolytus should this woman bear Theseus another son? What schemes might she hatch behind those blue eyes of hers? Certainly none that would be favourable to her child.

"I am done with this," she said and once more aimed her arrow at her husband.

Shaking off Phaedra's grasp, he rose to his feet and stepped out from his chair. His voice, barely a whisper, had none of its former arrogance.

"Please, Hippolyte, not like this. I will take you to Hippolytus."

"More hollow words and trickery?"

His skin had now developed a noticeable pallor.

"Please, Hippolyte. You have caused enough destruction. You can fire an arrow through my heart if that is what you think is just. But not here."

He looked at her, pleading with those eyes she had seen for the first time on the beach at Pontus. When he next moved his lips, no sound came from them, just the shadow of the word in the air. *Please,* he mouthed.

"Hippolyte!" Penthesilea's voice came sharply from behind her. A reminder of their promise. But she was not there yet. Not until she was with Hippolytus.

"Take me to my son," she said, resolve in her voice again.

"Of course. Just let these people be. Do not be the woman they think you are, *Oirapata*."

It was the second time that day she had been called such a thing in this Palace. Yet this time it was not with the malice the guard had used. Nor spat at her, the way Theseus had addressed her before banishing her from Athens. It was said with the same affection that Aegeus had used those times in the andron.

Hippolyte nodded, and Theseus made his way out from behind the table and toward the door. Hippolyte fell into step beside him while Penthesilea kept her bow at the ready.

"I heard what you did for my father," he said softly when they were in the corridor. "How you tried to save him. They told me later how you had rowed out and searched for him. I never thanked you for that. I am sorry."

The memory stirred her emotions afresh, yet she did not reply. She would not let her voice betray her.

"He loved you. He loved you very much," he continued.

Her head seemed to nod of its own accord, as if her body wanted to be with him, even if her mind did not.

"Sister," Penthesilea called to her.

"Wait by the door and make sure no one leaves," she said.

It would be so simple to kill him now, she thought, with his back to her, but then what? Ransack the Palace and the entire citadel for Hippolytus, in the hope that she would find him before her army was completely defeated, or someone killed him out of spite? Young children had certainly been killed for less. No, she would see this through. She would let Theseus think he had beaten her, and then she would relish his death all the more.

CHAPTER 38

*P*enthesilea had positioned herself so as to have a clear view of all the guests—most of whom were weeping pathetically and some of whom had fainted—and still be able to observe her sister and Theseus as they moved down the corridor. More soldiers would soon be on their way to the Palace, troops diverted from other duties to protect their king, yet Hippolyte seemed oblivious to the danger. Oblivious to everything, except Theseus.

Brutal men were not new to Penthesilea, and neither were arrogant kings, but the revulsion that swelled within her today was stronger and harder to bear than even her encounter with Heracles had been.

She wished she could give her sister as long as it would take to extract an answer about her son's whereabouts, for without doubt the Queen needed resolution, but Penthesilea had to think of her women. And what of Cletes? She had not seen anything of her since the battle had begun and those weapons had taken out so many of the Amazons. She immediately rejected the thought before they could distract her any further.

While her eyes remained trained on the wedding guests, she noted that Hippolyte had stopped walking. Any moment now, she would end this.

"This is far enough," she heard her sister say as she drew her dagger and held it to Theseus' throat. "Now tell me, where is Hippolytus?"

Theseus turned slowly but was looking down at the floor. He seemed to be stalling, Penthesilea thought, obviously hoping for help to reach him in time. Did he really think Hippolyte would fall for this? Her fingers twitched with the urge to send an arrow through his heart, but she resisted. Her sister would never forgive her for such an action if it lost her Hippolytus.

"He is not here," Theseus said, looking up. "I have sent him to Troezen."

"To Troezen?"

"To be raised by my mother."

Penthesilea breathed a sigh of relief. That was it. They had all the information they needed. They could return to their women now. She could find Cletes and they could leave. She was waiting to catch her sister's eye, to beckon her to leave, when three hoplites simultaneously rounded the corner. Young men with broad shoulders, each armed with a kopis, zig-zagged down the corridor. But for all their speed and agility they had not a fraction of hers or her skill. The arrow she fired sent the first toppling back. One of his comrades hurled his dagger straight at her head. His aim was good, and it might have worked with someone less capable, but for Penthesilea, a slight sidestep was all that was necessary for it to fly harmlessly past her and bury itself in the wall behind. Within an instant, she had fired off two more arrows, by the time the men hit the ground, her focus was back on her sister.

The blade of the dagger was still pressed against Theseus' neck, but he was gripping Hippolyte's shoulders and his mouth was moving close to her ear.

"Sister," Penthesilea called.

Theseus continued talking for a moment longer before he released Hippolyte and she in turn lowered the blade.

"Hippolyte," Penthesilea spoke. "This needs to happen *now*. We know where your son is. We can get him. We must go. Finish this, or allow me to."

As the sisters' eyes met, a single tear trickled down Hippolyte's cheek. She swallowed and dipped her chin by barely a hair's breadth.

Later, Penthesilea would recall this moment and that simple movement, many times. There had been a time before this war, before Theseus, when she could read every one of her sister's intentions without misinterpretation or doubt. Perhaps it was because she had been waiting for the signal with such anticipation that she saw something that was not there. Or maybe it had been there and was what Hippolyte had wanted at that instant.

But whatever the case, the second Penthesilea released her arrow, her sister's expression changed. The blood drained from her face and the whites of her eyes shone more brightly than polished marble. And as Penthesilea watched it fly, with perfect precision, towards Theseus, she knew it would not miss its target. At this range it would puncture his ribs and render him dead in seconds. She saw it all in her mind's eye and was certain it was what the gods wanted to happen.

Until it did not.

CHAPTER 39

*A*s a child, Hippolyte had dreamed of a warrior's death. Hers would come as the result of one of the greatest battles of all and a famous victory. Thousands would have watched on, awed by her skill and strength, although how the final blow would be dealt, precisely, she had never quite worked out. It was, after all, a child's fantasy, a moment she thought about only in terms of courage and power. The honourable end of a queen's reign.

Of death, she had been certain, but love, on the other hand, she had found harder to believe in. Whether it be romantic, passionate or one in whose name a war could be waged and armies brought low, the whole concept seemed absurd to her. She had ridiculed the idea of people who felt it, particularly on those occasions when they had been summoned to the aid of a king whose entire people had been sent to war because of it. Fighting for family, honour, wealth or territory, all those things made sense. But for the love of a single person when thousands of others walked the earth? Why anyone would choose to do that had always been a mystery to her.

But as she grew older, she started to recognise it. The emotion she felt for her women was undeniably love, even though it was a different feeling from how she felt for her sisters. The bonds forged between the Amazon women evolved over years, with a deep foundation of trust, which came from fighting beside one another and witnessing each other at their strongest and their most vulnerable. It was rational that she would love these women as well as her sisters, whose blood she shared and beliefs she valued as dearly as her own. But her love for Theseus was not rational. It had no roots in logical thought. It was raw and uncontrollable. This, she now saw, was the emotion which drove men to lose their minds and go to war, without the briefest consideration of the cost. And it became every bit as real to her as the blood that flowed in her veins.

Then Hippolytus had been born. The first time she had gazed into his deep blue eyes, she had felt a surge of tenderness so intense, it was as if her whole existence had been reshaped to make room for this tiny child. And love took on a whole new meaning.

"He is not here," Theseus said, looking up. "I have sent him to Troezen."

"To Troezen?"

"To be raised by my mother."

Relief flooded through her, knowing he was safe and that she could reach him.

Three guards burst into the corridor and she allowed herself barely a glance, knowing that Penthesilea would end them without a second's thought. But that single glance was all the distraction Theseus needed. In that instant, he grabbed her shoulders and put his mouth close to her ear. His hot breath damp against her skin.

"You cannot win," he hissed. "If you kill me the gods will decree that Hippolytus avenge me, as a son should, and he will come for you."

She shifted away from him, and studied his face. A hint of arrogance played on his lips.

"Sister," Penthesilea called from behind.

"Or maybe your sister kills me," Theseus continued, his voice barely a whisper so only Hippolyte could hear. "As his mother you might allow him to kill you to avenge me, but would she? He is nothing to her, he will come for her and she will cut him down. If I die, so will Hippolytus, sooner or later."

As he released her shoulders she knew at once that he spoke the truth.

"Hippolyte, this needs to happen *now*. We know where your son is. We can get him. We must go. Finish this, or allow me to."

She sensed the impatience in her sister's tone. And not merely impatience; unlike Hippolyte, Penthesilea somehow still had hope. Hope that they could save the women. Hope that the Amazons would remain strong after such a battle. But whether Penthesilea would admit the truth to herself or not, they were beaten.

She looked at her sister. A stray tear rolled down her cheek before falling toward the cold metal of the dagger in her hand. She lowered her head to look at it. Too late she realised how that movement might appear to her sister.

The arrow flew from Penthesilea's bow, its glistening point heading straight for Theseus.

She closed her eyes and images of her son as they played together with wooden swords and toy figures of Amazon queens filled her mind. The softness of his skin and that glint in his deep blue eyes. The sound of laugher and the pressure of his hand in hers. All were there, visible in her mind's eye as if her son were there beside her as she stepped in front of Theseus and claimed the arrow for herself.

CHAPTER 40

*N*ever had Penthesilea frozen in battle. Never had the screams of the injured, the stench of spilled guts or the sight of blood spewing from the maimed and dying been too much for her to endure. Never had she found herself not knowing where her next arrow would fly or which direction to swing her axe.

She had seen plenty of men freeze. Warriors, beasts of men, with oiled skin and glistening muscles, who came snarling at them, spears raised, only to find themselves rooted to the spot as, one by one, their friends fell beside them. Some did not even get that far. Often the mere sight of the Amazons hurtling towards them, the ground shaking from the force of their horses' hooves, would be enough to paralyse them with fear. It was always a matter of when, not if, these men would die.

There were rare occasions, though, when it had been an Amazon who had frozen. And not necessarily a younger one, less accustomed to the sights and sounds of the battlefield. Sometimes it would be an older woman, rendered immobile by the sight of a loved one—a daughter, perhaps—succumbing.

They knew, of course, that with battle came death, but they were, after all, only human. She could recall a dozen times when she had been forced to call out to a woman and shock her back to the present.

But not her. Never Penthesilea. She was a princess, a queen, a daughter of Ares.

Until now.

The sea of crimson spread quickly on the marble floor. She watched helplessly, powerless to change anything. She had seen the point of her arrowhead force itself through the metal of her sister's breast plate. She thought she heard every sound that followed. The puncturing of the skin, the cracking of bone, the piercing of the heart.

And yet, even as she saw the moment unfold, she could not believe what was happening. It was incomprehensible.

"She is gone."

Theseus's voice stirred her. Hippolyte had fallen backwards and, now kneeling, he had caught her and was cradling her body in his arms. Why on earth was he looking at her like that? she wondered, as he gently brushed aside the hair that had fallen across her eyes.

"Get away from her," Penthesilea snarled, finding her voice at last.

His head snapped up, yet he remained where he was, holding Hippolyte in a gentle embrace.

"I said get away from her!"

Still, he did not move. There were no tears in his eyes, but his skin had turned ashen. His brow was deeply lined and his cheeks seemed to have sunk in on themselves. He cast only the briefest glance at Penthesilea before returning his gaze to Hippolyte.

With a swiftness that spoke of her lineage, Penthesilea

slung her bow over her shoulder, removed her axe from her belt and hoisted it into the air. Her heart was pounding with such force that it almost blurred her thoughts.

"There is no one left here to save you, now," she rasped.

Her hands quivered, the motion magnified as it ran along the handle of the axe until the blade shook. Her weapons were always rock solid in her grasp, but this one wobbled as if it were held by a tavern drunk. It mattered not. She would be strong enough to mete out the punishment he deserved.

Her resolve again firm, she stepped towards him.

Immediately, his hands flew into the air.

"Think of Hippolytus!" he cried, with the same urgency in his voice she had heard from many a man who knew he was about to die. "Think of Hippolytus. If you kill me, he is as good as dead. Someone will kill him and claim the throne of Athens for himself."

"I care nothing for Athens nor for the boy. He is nothing to me."

The King looked shaken and words tumbled from his lips.

"I understand. But you cared for your sister, and he was her world. That is why she did not return to you. And that is why she sacrificed herself. Not to save me, but to save him. You must see that."

"Your slippery words do not work so easily on me, *King* Theseus."

One blow was all it would take. So why had she not done it? As she glanced around in confusion, her gaze fell on her sister. Her eyes remained open, glassy and unfocused, yet, regardless of how she shifted her position they remained focused on her. No light shone from within them anymore but somehow, their very gaze seemed to be judging her.

She felt the air thinning in her lungs and the taste of iron on her tongue as she twisted the axe in her hands. Those eyes. She had to close them and stop that accusing stare. Yet she could not move without giving Theseus the opportunity to strike her.

As if reading her mind, he shuffled backwards, slowly at first because of the weight of the body on his knees. Then, with an agility she had not anticipated, he jumped up and onto his feet, dropping Hippolyte. Her head landed with a crack on the marble floor.

"Queen Penthesilea, you have lost," he said, with a snarl. "Your women will have been defeated by now, and if you end my life, then yours will be over, too, one way or another. And wouldn't your sister be upset if you had risked all this for nothing? Poor Hippolyte, she did miss you so terribly."

"Do not speak of her! Do not say her name!"

Tears stung her eyes and the axe wobbled in her grip. What should she do? She had never met her nephew. Why would she feel any loss at his death? And yet she knew exactly. This was not any Amazon child; this was Hippolyte's son. Could she live with his blood on her hands, too?

She made her decision in a split second. She was, as Theseus had said, Queen now, and it was her duty to ensure her remaining women returned home. And Hippolyte, too.

Leaning down, Penthesilea pulled the arrow from her sister and threw it aside as she flung her over her shoulder. Her bow was tumbled to the floor in the process. She abandoned the weapon without a second thought; she would not be able to use it and maintain her balance while carrying her sister's body. She had her axe. That would have to be enough.

"Goodbye, Queen Penthesilea," Theseus said, offering her a mock bow. "Give my regards to your *great* warrior women."

Outside, the massacre had reached truly monstrous proportions. The Athenian numbers were so great, it was near impossible to make out where her women stood amongst them. Bodies, male, female and equine were piled on top of one another, as if a new layer of the earth had formed. One of two of their horses cantered about lost, with arrows in their thighs and flanks. Had any of her women survived? Everywhere she looked, she saw embroidered tunics, caked in blood and grime. The Amazons would not have retreated without an order to do so, and neither she nor Hippolyte had been there to give it. Perhaps, she thought, with a faint spark of hope, Antiope would have had the sense to withdraw, if only to save a few.

Several hoplites had noticed her descending the palace steps towards them, though none made a move to attack her. They had no need. They knew her only way out was past them. She jumped down, landing on the upturned shield of one soldier and the helmet of another, holding Hippolyte's body close to stop her swaying limbs from toppling her.

With hoplites swarming over the Areopagus and surrounding hills, she had to find another route out of the citadel. The Diochares Gate. That was where Melanippe had been holding. If she could reach it and find a horse, then she would be able to return home and give her sister the burial she deserved.

They came at her from every direction, jabbing spears and swinging swords. The extra weight on her shoulder altered her balance, and a solitary arrow cut at the fabric of her tunic. Anger and surprise heated her skin. It was as close to hitting her as any man had ever managed. Instinct and years of training took over, as she raised her axe above her head and in a single stroke parted two men's heads from their shoulders.

"I will kill you all, if that is what I have to do to leave this place," she yelled.

But still they came. The noise was deafening, the endless clashing of metal and the dull thud of flesh striking stone as men dropped face first to the ground.

Three hoplites approached, one from her left, one from her right and one from directly in front of her, meaning to trap her. Normally, they would have posed no threat to her, but exhaustion was finally needling at her.

"Perhaps we won't kill you straight away," one said. "I think we might have a little fun with you first."

Penthesilea adjusted her stance to better offset the weight on her shoulder. She would kill the one in front of her, first. The others would lunge, without thinking, when he went down. She readied herself to strike, but when they were only feet from her, their eyes widened. A moment later, they fell, one after another, in quick succession, each with an arrow to the chest.

"My Queen! This way, Melanippe holds the gate still!"

She stood lit by the dying sun, her face smeared with grime and blood, her eyes wild and wide, and yet never in all her life had Penthesilea seen a more beautiful woman.

"Cletes," she whispered.

CHAPTER 41

Time seemed to have stopped. Nothing could hurt her now. It was as if the two parts of her broken heart had met again and been stitched back together with invisible thread. Cletes was still alive and standing strong, her half-moon shield dented and battered but fixed firmly on her arm. Her bow still quivered from the arrows she had just released.

"Come! Quickly!

As she called to Penthesilea, her eyes flickered momentarily to the body draped over her shoulder and yet she said nothing, but rather beckoned her Queen towards her, whilst simultaneously unleashing further arrows at the hoplites who surrounded them.

Together, they fought their way to the gate, although the ferocity was diminishing. The soldiers' numbers were thinning, the men less willing to risk their lives now that they knew the victory was theirs. Some fired at the women from a distance, in a merely defensive action, others scurried hastily away, happy to allow them their freedom, if it meant their hearts continued beating for another day.

320 | HANNAH LYNN

For her part, Penthesilea slew only those she had to. She had failed to kill Theseus, so what did these men matter? There would be no glory in their death.

With Cletes beside her, they staggered and stumbled through alleys, past burning buildings and over broken stalls, her eyes scouring every nook and cranny. Time and again, she flinched as her eyes met those of dead Amazon women, staring up at her from the ground. Most had fallen with their weapons still in their hands, and all bore the deep lacerations and purple bruises from fighting for their lives. She could do nothing for them, not even cast a prayer.

Cletes had survived. There must be more, Penthesilea told herself. They could not be the only ones, but she could not bear to ask, even when the pace of combat slowed. Neither spoke, until the gate came into view. Melanippe was nowhere in sight, but the way was mostly clear, the last of the hoplites blocking their path falling beneath their blades.

"We need horses," Cletes said. "We can make our way to the camp at Attica. That is where the princesses told us to gather."

"My sisters are alive?"

Penthesilea's knees started to buckle at the news, but there was no time to rejoice. Any moment, Theseus could give the order for his men to leave the citadel and run them down.

"Here! There are horses here!"

Cletes raced ahead to an olive tree, where four Amazon colts struggled against the coarse ropes holding them.

"Take this one," she said, undoing a knot and flinging the rope over the animal's head.

With no time for due respect, Penthesilea threw Hippolyte's body across the horse, before leaping up behind it. The horses followed the steep path that zigzagged up the hillside and away from Athens.

The citadel walls grew smaller in the distance, and the sounds of the hoplites celebrating victory grew fainter. There would be feasting in Athens tonight. Not only for Theseus and his new bride, but for all those who had survived to see another day. The thought sickened the Queen to her core.

She found herself continually looking back, although what she expected to see, she knew not. Even the fastest soldiers would not be able to catch up with them now. Perhaps she was hoping that other women had somehow managed to escape, who would also be fleeing a battle for the first time since Ares had blessed them.

The ground was dry and brittle and crumbled beneath the horses' hooves, while above them, dense clouds blanketed the sky, a massive sheet of grey penetrated by only the thinnest shafts of light. It had seemed such a short distance from Attica to Athens on that adrenaline-fuelled ride there, on their way to kill Theseus. Now, even though the city was barely visible behind them, she felt no closer to their destination.

Penthesilea rode a short distance behind Cletes. Normally they would travel side by side or share a horse, but that place was already taken. So many times, words formed on the tip of her tongue, only to be swallowed. She wanted to give thanks to the gods for sparing Cletes' life and for the love that had seen her return to help her escape with Hippolyte in her arms. Yet it felt inappropriate, even insulting or selfish, to have this glimmer of joy, when so many had lost everything.

As they neared Attica, they slowed to a trot when their tents came into view and as they trudged wearily into camp, they were met with a scene they had witnessed so many times before, but never on this scale and never involving their own fighters. Hundreds and hundreds of injured Amazons lay in row after row before them, many knowing their end was surely near.

Penthesilea's eyes watered as the stench rose to meet them. It caught in the back of her throat and made her want to gag. Those who were fit enough were rushing around doing their best for the others but unable to tend all those who needed help and knowing that so much of what they did would be in vain, anyway. They usually rode away from such sights, leaving behind them the dead and dying of their defeated enemy, satisfied in the knowledge that they had caused such devastation. But never had she seen one of these camps filled with her own people.

"No! No!"

The cry came from the shadows of a nearby tent doorway, yet Penthesilea did not need to see the person to recognise the voice. A second later, Melanippe ran forwards, her hands clasped over her mouth.

"No. It cannot be possible. How? How on earth?"

As her sister reached her horse, Penthesilea allowed the Queen's body to fall into Melanippe's arms.

"How did this happen?"

The question kept repeating in her brain, yet she could make no sound in reply. A thick lump had lodged in her throat. Hippolyte was a daughter of Ares, a woman who had lived her life with such energy and determination that no man could ever have extinguished the spark of life in her. And no man had.

As hands supported her and helped her to the ground, the same inability to form a single cohesive thought hit her again, just as when she had faced Theseus. She allowed herself to be guided to where Melanippe wept over her dead sister's body, her head buried in her chest and her own tunic so deeply stained with blood that none of its patterns could be distinguished.

Time ebbed and flowed around them, and all Penthesilea could do was look on. Cletes' fingers were wound around hers, offering her what comfort she could. Any moment, Melanippe would see the hole in Hippolyte's chest and realise what arrow had caused it. She would blame Penthesilea then, and rightly so. And then ... and then only the gods knew what would happen.

"Where is Antiope?" Penthesilea said, at last, knowing she could manage these few words only once. "She should be here, too. Where is she?"

Melanippe lifted her head from Hippolyte's body, her eyes so bloodshot that there was no white left visible. She looked up at her sister for a moment, then lowered her head and shook it once, then started sobbing again.

Penthesilea fell to her knees.

"No! It cannot be! It is not possible! Not Antiope, too!"

The cries of the two women echoed on the hillsides around the camp. A small group of those still able to stand watched on from a respectful distance.

"There were so many soldiers," Melanippe stuttered. "We could see them swarming around her but we knew we would lose both gates if we went to help. She did everything she could. She took so many of them. But they surrounded her from every angle."

Images swirled in Penthesilea's mind. Antiope had been in situations like that before. How was it possible that these men had succeeded where all others had failed? Why would the gods have allowed this to happen? A raw and unfathomable fear gripped her.

"What do we do?" she asked. "What do we do now?"

CHAPTER 42

While Cletes and Melanippe focused on the injured, Penthesilea kept watch for any other women returning, riding out to help them as soon as any appeared on the horizon. And at first they did come, although only in trickles and usually in pairs, holding one another up as they limped towards camp. Some struggled to speak after the horrors they had endured, bruised and torn from head to toe. Few arrived unscathed and most were too badly injured to risk moving immediately to Pontus.

"We have allies in Macedonia. We could take them there. It would only be two or maybe three days' ride," Melanippe suggested.

"Which is two or three days more than they would survive," Penthesilea replied. "Besides, who would help us there? Many of their fighters rode to their death with us. No king will welcome us now."

"We cannot stay."

"We have to. Besides, we must wait for the others. There will be more."

She said the words with total confidence, ignoring the glances that she knew Cletes and Melanippe would be exchanging.

There simply had to be more survivors. They had been nearly three thousand strong and now, between those injured and those still standing, there were barely a few hundred remaining. Yes, there had to be more. Maybe some were hiding out in the ruins of the city, waiting for the moment when they were strong enough again to attempt to escape.

For four days and nights, Penthesilea waited. Night-time, she decided, would be when they would try to flee, under the cover of darkness and whilst there were fewer people about, so she was particularly hopeful and vigilant as each day dawned.

On the fifth night, Cletes came and sat close beside her and she smelt, once again, the aroma of pomegranates, long since absent in her life.

"Talk to me, my Queen."

Penthesilea flinched.

"Do not call me that."

"I called you my Queen when you led us before, as did every Amazon woman, and you are most definitely that now."

She stared into the flames of their small fire, built of only twigs and kindling. It crackled, sending tiny sparks up into the air. If only they had known what would eventually happen when Theseus had arrived on their shores with Heracles all those years ago. *Xenia* be damned, she would have slit his throat then and there. The wrath of the gods could have been no worse than this misery.

"I do not know what we are supposed to do," she said, quietly.

Cletes took her hand.

"We will rebuild. We will return to Themiscyra, and we will start again."

"What if we cannot?"

"We can."

"I do not think that I can."

They had been forced to bury their dead—excluding those they had had to leave in Athens, the princess included—there, in the Attican hills, even though all Amazon women deserved to be laid to rest in their homeland, among the gentle green slopes of the steppes, beneath the wings of eagles and the endless sky. But that had not been their fate, not even their Queen.

"The Queen will find Antiope and guide her to the under-world," someone had said, when they laid Hippolyte in the ground, along with items for her to use in the Underworld: a bow, a shield and her breast plate. At that moment, Penthesilea had thought of the zoster, the belt that Heracles had taken from Hippolyte. It, too, should have been with her. It had been a gift from her father and she should have had it for her journey to the underworld.

"Tell me what happened," Cletes said softly.

Penthesilea continued to stare into the flames. She was sitting so close that the heat was burning her skin and yet she cared not. Melanippe had seen the wound when they had bathed and dressed Hippolyte's body. She had avoided Penthe-silea's gaze and said nothing, perhaps because the manner of her death did not change the outcome. But the truth of what she had done still burnt within her.

"You already know what happened" she whispered.

Cletes nodded slowly.

"It was your arrow," she said. "Your arrow killed her."

"Not just my arrow. It was me. I am the one who killed her."

So saying, she attempted to wrest her hand free of Cletes' grip and stand up, but her lover held on, twisting Penthesilea around to face her. Was it really she who was half god and Cletes fully mortal? At that moment, her skin glowed so luminously in the firelight it was as if she were a gift from Helios himself, and it felt it must be the other way around.

"You must speak of this. You must let go of this burden you are carrying. Please, my Queen. I am afraid for you."

"Afraid for me?" she said, with an almost hysterical laugh. "Why in the name of the gods would you be afraid for me? I am the only one in this place who stands without an injury. Not so much as a scratch."

"Penthesilea, tell me!"

"All these women here you are trying so hard to save ... you know some of them will never walk again, let alone ride. We are just waiting here for them to die. If I were a real Queen, I would kill them in their sleep."

Her voice was raised now, and there were whispers coming from the camp behind her, and yet Cletes remained calm and composed, her eyes fixed on Penthesilea.

"Tell me what happened," she repeated, slowly. "Tell me how we can put this right for you."

The laugh came again, and it was bitter this time. "You cannot put this right. No one can. She chose to save Theseus and I killed her, with my arrow. The one intended for him."

It was the first time she had spoken these words out loud, but the pain in her chest did not ease, but rather intensified.

"It was meant to be Theseus. It was meant to be him," she sobbed, taking great gulping breaths.

Tears tumbled from her eyes and cascaded down her cheeks.

"Hush now. You are not to blame," Cletes said, pulling her

to her chest and rocking her gently, as if she were a small child who had done no more harm than break an amphora. "You are not to blame."

"Yes, I am. I should never have led us into this damned war. I encouraged her to seek vengeance when she clearly did not want to. I am to blame for everything."

And there it was, the truth that she had not allowed herself to speak. It was not merely that she had been responsible for Hippolyte sacrificing herself. *She* had promoted, almost insisted, on this war. How many times had she tried to dissuade her? How many times had she told her about the size of the Athenian army and all that supported it, not to mention Theseus' utter ruthlessness? But she had been too stubborn and too headstrong, too enamoured of their reputation to concede that the Amazons could ever be defeated.

"We can rebuild our numbers again. You helped us do it once. You will do it again," Cletes told her.

Penthesilea shook her head.

"It was different then. Look at who remains. Even if every woman here survives the return to Pontus, which they will not, how many do you think would be capable of riding to the Gargareans again, much less carry a daughter to be born fit and strong? We are done for. I have ruined everything. I have destroyed my father's legacy. My mother's legacy. My sister's. And Theseus still lives."

Yes, Theseus was still alive. Her body quivered with rage and she flexed her fingers, itching for a weapon.

"I should have killed him long ago," she said, then realised. "That is what I must do. I will go on my own."

She imagined his blood pooling on the marble floors. She would show no restraint. Offer him no honour in death. She would destroy him.

"You will not do that," Cletes said firmly, preventing her from rising.

"I will, I must."

"No. Think. Hippolyte meant for that arrow to strike her," she said more softly. "She allowed herself to be killed, because she knew that if Theseus died, then Hippolytus would be forced to avenge his murder. She knew he would come after you. Maybe not immediately, but eventually, most certainly. That is why she did it. To protect, you, her sister, and her son, too. So, consider that, if you want to protect her legacy."

Silence fell then and, in the hush, she realised that Cletes spoke only the truth and while Hippolytus meant nothing to her, he had been Hippolyte's world. So that was it. Theseus would escape unscathed, with not a scratch on his skin, while Hippolyte's body lay cold in the earth.

"It is not fair," she whispered. "This is not justice."

"I know, my love. I know."

As the fire burnt down to a soft amber glow, neither of the women moved to replenish it. Wrapped in Cletes' arms Penthesilea continued to cry softly, until there were no more tears left to shed.

"You must sleep, now," Cletes said as if Penthesilea were a child being bidden to sleep by a gentle parent. "You have barely rested since the battle ended. I will keep watch tonight. If any more women arrive, I will come and fetch you."

And with that, she planted a kiss on the top of her head, and like a child, Penthesilea obediently rose to her feet and retired to her tent.

No women came that night, nor the day that followed. And while they lost several more at the camp during that time, there were others who recovered to a point where they could stand and some even ride.

"We should head back to Themiscyra now," Melanippe said.

"Themiscyra is too large to defend," Penthesilea replied. "With our numbers so depleted, we cannot protect it and post lookouts across the land. We can send word to those there to gather the children and head south."

Hippolyte and Antiope's absence was being felt. With only two sisters remaining, there were not enough of them to have productive discussions. There was no one of rank to take a side and produce a majority when they had opposing views or explain or reinforce ideas or add a third counter argument they hadn't yet thought of. As such, it had been necessary to form a court, of sorts, bringing into their talks the strongest of the survivors. Klonie, Polemusa, Amina, and Dorymache were among them.

"There is security in those walls," Melanippe continued, unconvinced. "We know the city paths like the backs of our hands. If we are attacked, we can avoid and confuse the intruders as we move around."

"Or they could simply block the gates and starve us out."

Just as Penthesilea might have predicted, Melanippe shook her head in disagreement.

"That will not happen. Theseus has let us go. He could have sent his men to follow us and finish the job they started. He shows no indication of wishing to retaliate. We have relationships with allies to repair. It is vital that we remain in Themiscyra, where we can be found and called upon when we are ready to fight again.

"Come, Sister. You know as well as I do, that we have fought plenty of battles in the past that you could have won yourself, single-handedly. The Amazons will rise up in strength once more, if you let us."

Her words were almost an echo of what Cletes had said, but this time she took something different from them, a clear line of thought that told her exactly what she had to do.

CHAPTER 43

*G*uilt roiled through her as she guided her horse quietly away from the camp. The biting cold air stung, as the strength of a sea breeze ebbed and flowed, like the water itself. But perhaps it would help counteract the stench of her body and clothes. She had about her the smell of death and decay, from all those they had buried in the previous days. So many graves. Her hands were grimy and her nails were black, reflecting her mood.

She had taken over the watch from Enchesimargos, was almost as renowned for her skill with a spear as Penthesilea was for hers with an axe. She had once led women of her own, a nomad of the greatest renown. But in Athens, she had taken a spear to the shoulder of her throwing arm. In wrenching out his weapon, the hoplite had torn muscle from bone and dislocated the joint so badly that it was now useless. As she had fallen, one of her women had caught her and somehow managed to help her retreat to safety, where she had stemmed the flow of blood. It seemed a miracle to everyone that she had survived at all.

In the safety of the camp, Enchesimargos had slipped in and out of consciousness. When she finally became lucid, a darkness clouded her eyes and she spoke only in monosyllables. It was clear that she wished her rescuer had left her to die. For what was she now? Penthesilea might have pondered over the future that awaited this woman and those like her, but she had not even worked out what her own path should be, much less that of anyone else.

She waited until Enchesimargos had gone to her tent, then a little longer still, estimating how long it would take her to remove her weapons, lie down on the hard earth and fall asleep. She then slipped back to her own tent and retrieved her satchel from where she had left it, just inside the doorway.

She had promised to keep watch in those final hours between night and day when Selene's moon grew weak against the brightening of Helios's sun. She would raise the alarm if Theseus' men approached or if any more of their women returned. She had told Cletes that she would remain there until dawn arrived. But had no one realised that she and truth were no longer bedfellows, and her promises were worthless? Had she not sworn that their attack on Athens would be a great victory? Had she not promised that they would kill Theseus? Instead she had relegated the once mighty Amazons to the stuff of lore and legend.

As Penthesilea rode slowly away, barely a patch of unturned earth remained along the path her horse followed. They had planted much in that foreign soil, but there would be no harvest.

She passed first through Boeotia and then Mount Parnassus and on towards Thessaly. When hunger struck, she foraged for whatever she could find, berries mostly, sometimes catching a rabbit, which she would roast on a small fire, sharpening her axe while waiting for it to cook.

Melanippe would have woken to find her missing and known then that the women were hers alone to rule. She would have ordered them to pack up their belongings, fold their tents and follow her homewards. They would ride through Thrace and around the Black Sea to the lush steppes of Pontus. And while Penthesilea's heart yearned for that soft billowing grassland and those rushing rivers, she continued north.

Her plan was to ride as far away from Athens and Themiscyra as her horse would take her and then to lose her mind, and hopefully her life, in the heat of one last battle. She did not care whose side she fought on or what she fought for. Just that she fought. But the fight that found her, five days into her journey, did not come on a battlefield, but rather on a small farm, a few miles east of the coast, in Epirus.

The land there was verdant, and the crests of small hills lined up like ripples on water. The fields were planted not just with grapevines and olive trees, as had been the case of the land around Athens, but with citrus fruits: oranges, lemons and limes. The scent was fresh and heady.

She had just stopped to help herself to a handful of oranges for her journey when the screaming began. This was nothing new to her. She had been practically weaned on it. But there was something different about this. It was one voice, and it was a cry of desperation. Dropping the fruit, she leapt onto her horse and kicked her heels with such force that it reared up before racing off.

The whitewashed buildings of the farm were set behind a low wall. Nearby vines created a canopy so dense that no sunlight could penetrate it, and there was a fountain in the centre of a small courtyard, where the water came from a natural spring. To the right of the farmhouse, goats were bleating loudly in a paddock. A barn-like structure stood behind them. It was a peaceful setting, the type of place a recluse might find his longed-for seclusion, yet this was where the screaming had come from.

Dropping from her horse, she checked the position of her bow on her back, then took hold of her axe and trod quietly towards the house. She felt no pounding in her chest, just the determination that, whatever was happening inside those walls, she would end it.

She could now identify the noise as coming from a young person, a desperate one. As much as she prayed she was wrong, she knew what she was going to see when she stepped into the building. A girl, little more than a child, was pinned up against one of the whitewashed walls, held in place by two men, while a third stood in front of her. She writhed and screamed, kicking out as she tried to escape their grasp. But there was nowhere for her to go. She must have realised that, Penthesilea thought to herself, her mind momentarily distracted. And yet still she fought them.

Without further hesitation, Penthesilea raised her bow and pulled an arrow from her quiver as easily as one might shrug their shoulders. The arrow was nocked before she had even taken another breath, and simultaneously turning side on, she shot. The man in the centre, the one inflicting his body on the girl, fell first. He slumped to the ground as the screams reached a new crescendo. The second man turned around, he received an arrow straight the chest. The third managed to open his mouth, as if to say something, before he too fell.

Two more men came running from the back of the house, knives in their hands, shock and anger written across their faces. They jabbed at the air with their feeble weapons, still clinging to bags which jangled with what they had plainly just stolen. As her axe sliced through their bellies, silver and jewellery spilled onto the ground. These were not soldiers. They wore no breastplates, no protection at all, and their flabby flesh parted as though it were soft cheese.

With all five down, Penthesilea moved to retrieve her arrows from the first three. The young girl remained pressed against the wall despite the men now being dead.

"My sister," she wheezed, gasping for air. "The barn. A man ... he took my sister to the barn."

$\mathcal{A}$s the girl dropped to her knees, retching and weeping, Penthesilea twisted on her heel and sprinted out of the house. Her stride was long, and she sprang over the wall as easily as if it were a crack between flagstones.

The doors to the barn were open and the girl inside had already been forced to the ground, the man above her grunting as he thrust away at her. As she reached them, Penthesilea could smell wine on his breath, so strong it could have been seeping from his pores.

In one swift motion she brought her axe down on his neck and then swiftly sliced him open the length of his spine. Blood sprayed in the air as he toppled forwards, his entire weight falling on the girl's chest. There was no grunting now. No thrusting.

With one hard kick, Penthesilea pushed him off her. There was straw and dirt in her hair. Her lips were split and bleeding, and her right eye was swollen so badly, it was nearly closed.

"Aikaterini!"

The younger girl ran in and dropped to the stone floor next

to her sister, who pulled her into her arms and they clasped each other, sobbing.

Seeing them embracing like that brought an image to Penthesilea's mind. It was so similar. The pair on the ground. The tight embrace. The bloodied bodies. And yet these two were both alive.

It suddenly felt as if the humidity had increased and the air had thickened. The wheezing that had moments before afflicted the youngest girl had somehow transferred itself to her. She needed air. Cold air. In fact, she had to be on her horse again and galloping away from here. But as she turned to leave, a voice called her back.

"Please, wait," the girl called Aikaterini shouted, clambering to her feet. "Thank you. They would have ... they would have killed us too ... like our mother ... and brother."

The girl's voice shook so badly it was if the air were being stolen from her lungs each time she went to speak. After a moment, she tried again.

"Stay with us," she pleaded. "Please. There may be more. They may come back."

"They will not come back."

"We do not know that. There have been others before. But my father, he has always seen them off. Please!"

"Where is your father now?" Penthesilea asked. "Is there a man of the house to protect you?"

Hearing herself saying these words, as if a man could be their only source of protection, it made her want to vomit, but she could see from the paleness of the girls' skin, and the lack of callouses on their palms, that they were not the type to have wielded hoes or trowels, much less swords or spears. A farm like this, with silver accumulated in such large quantity, would likely mean their father would be planning on offering a good dowry for them one day, if he had not done so already, and passing them on to the next man in their lives. No, they would not know how to fight.

"Our father and brother have taken a trip to Dodona. They will not return for at least another week. Please, please stay with us. We are all alone now. We have money we can give you. Or silver, if you prefer. And food. Please. Please. Anything you ask. You can take anything you wish."

The girl was shaking. Her hands were tightly clasped together, her knuckles turning white, the younger sibling clung to her robes.

"You should be able to protect yourselves," Penthesilea said, and turned away.

She had taken only two steps when she was grabbed by the back of her tunic. Acting purely on reflex, she spun around, muscles flexing. The girl in front of her stood unblinking, her eyes wide and shining, as death stopped only millimetres away from her neck.

"Please," she croaked. "Please teach us how to do that."

Blood was pounding through her veins and a heat was burning up through her chest and along her arms, all the way to her fingertips. How was it possible for a country girl to be like this? So weak. So unable to defend herself. And yet she had not flinched at the sight of her axe.

"I am not a teacher," Penthesilea said, turning again.

But Aikaterini scrambled forwards, blocking her exit and clinging onto her clothing.

"Please, just teach us something. Anything. If they come back, we will not survive."

"Survival is not always the gift you believe it to be," she replied, yanking her tunic away.

The girl dropped to the ground, finally defeated.

Without her willing them to, Penthesilea's eyes returned to the younger child, who stared back, her own eyes unblinking, just as her sister's had been. She could sense a darkness that matched her own swirling within them.

"I am sorry. As I have already told you, I am no teacher."

Looking down, she strode out into the sunlight, plucking a lime from a tree as she went, before mounting her horse and riding on.

She travelled for half a day, barely noting the position of the sun, allowing the animal to choose their path almost as often as she did. For the first time since leaving Attica, her thoughts were not fixated on Hippolyte, and the images in her mind were not solely those of the arrow piercing her beloved sister. They had been joined by others, of Aikaterini and her little sister, the one who had fought those men with teeth and claw, as if she were a wild animal and who, upon being freed, had thought only of her sister. No matter how much Penthesilea tried to distract herself, her mind refused to be steered away from them. Their brother and mother were already dead. Those youngsters would have to deal with their bodies and those of the men who had attacked them.

If more returned, they certainly would not survive. It could be even worse than before, it that were possible; they would be made to pay for what she had done. The sound of a nearby stream caught her attention and, in one of her first conscious acts since leaving the farm, Penthesilea steered her horse towards it. She felt gratitude that this gift had come when her flask was nearly empty, and the sun was about to claim its highest point in the sky.

The stream was smaller than she had expected, more a brook, with a rocky bed that caused the water to foam white. Although narrow, it was fast moving and icy cold as she scooped up a handful and brought it to her mouth. Next to her, her horse pursed its lips and siphoned in all it needed to quench its thirst. They stayed there for a while, the babbling of the water and the birdsong above them almost sufficient to drown out her thoughts.

There was nothing special about those girls, she reminded herself. They were likely to be married off in the next few years and would produce more, exactly like them. Weak. Feeble. More young women who did not know how to wield a blade or defend themselves. And she could hardly teach them all. Save them all. Besides, most had no interest in fighting.

But these two sisters had wanted her help, and these two she could save.

She waited a short while longer, until her horse had taken another drink, then filled up her canteen and rode, for the first time in days, with a destination in mind.

AT THE FARM, it was as if time had stopped the moment she had left. Although the bodies of the men she had killed now buzzed with flies, they were in the same positions they had been in when she had ended their lives. The scent of death was ripening. Soon it would be a foetid backdrop to the smell of the farmland around them.

This time, Penthesilea saw the mother and brother who had been spoken of, tucked in a corner of the room. They were younger than she had expected, and the woman had cuts on her hands and across her arms, where she had tried to block the men's blades and protect her child. It had been an admirable death, Penthesilea thought.

Among all the bodies, though, she could see nothing of

Aikaterini and her sister. They had certainly made no attempt to clear up the mess or prepare the bodies for burial, although perhaps they did not know how. Deciding to check the barn, she was turning to leave when a small sound, no louder than the squeaking of a mouse, made her stop. It was coming from behind a wooden door, leading to a pantry, most likely.

She slowly stepped towards it. She could almost feel the fear radiating from behind it and the atmosphere beyond so tense, it was as if they were straining to keep the whole world still. She stepped forwards again, and the floor beneath her creaked.

When she pulled open the door, her heart nearly broke. The two girls were crouched as far back as possible. The youngest was sitting behind her sister, whimpering, with her arms wrapped around her knees as she rocked back and forth. Aikaterini jumped to her feet, a small blade in her hands that looked rusty and blunt. In the gloom of the cupboard, her pupils were so wide her eyes had no colour to them at all. Her hand trembled and the knife shook so wildly it was a miracle she was managing to hold onto it. When she saw it was Penthesilea, she dropped to her knees and buried her head in her hands.

"I will stay for one night, that is all," she said. "And if you do not listen to what I have to say, I will leave before that."

CHAPTER 45

*T*ime at the farmhouse slipped away faster than she could have imagined, and simply having a purpose kept her mind busy in a positive way.

That day, there was no training, after all. The younger girl, Calista, had to be coaxed from the cupboard. She might have been small, but she was feisty and dug her heels into the stone floor as if it were clay and gripped at the wooden shelves until splinters ripped her skin. She stank of urine and had soiled herself. She reminded Penthesilea of a puppy, the runt of the litter who had done nothing but lie listlessly by its mother's teat and refuse to eat. The one for whom the owner would decide that a dip in the river inside a hessian bag would be the kindest course of action.

Had a girl behaved like this back in Themiscyra, Penthesilea would have dragged her out and thrown her to the ground. She would then have forced her to clean up her mess, to apologise to those she had inconvenienced, and then Penthesilea would have been made to work harder than ever. The

344 | HANNAH LYNN

training of Amazon girls was tough, but that was so they never had to experience what Calista and Aikaterini had endured.

Aikaterini had crouched on the ground in front of her young sibling, murmuring sweet words of comfort to her, but still she refused to move. She stared out at the kitchen, shivering, the blood stains on the tiles a cruel reminder of what had happened there.

So, while Aikaterini continued to try and coax her sister from the pantry, Penthesilea used the time to remove the bodies from the house. The men she burnt. No coins on their eyes. No treasures to take with them to the underworld, to pay Charon to row them across the Styx. They deserved none of that. Rather, she left their bodies to sizzle and smoulder, filling the air with the acrid smell of charred meat.

The mother and the younger brother, they buried in an orchard of peaches and fig trees just before sunset, after Aikaterini had finally coaxed Calista from the cupboard. The canopy of leaves scattered the amber light into tiny shards, building a mosaic on the ground. The girls had collected some of their favourite things to go with them: a small mirror with a twisted-silver handle and a bone comb, carved with a delicate pattern of hares, for the mother. For the young boy, a toy horse, beautifully carved in wood for him by his father.

As the evening sun finally disappeared behind the rolling hills, she realised it was far too late for the girls to learn anything that day and, anyway, they were in no fit state, pale and limp with exhaustion. Aikaterini had, on her advice, filled a bowl with warm water and salt to bathe Calista's hands and draw the splinters, and she had found clean linen to dress the skin. Several small fragments of wood remained, buried deep in the soft pads of her hand, but she had removed the worst of it.

The girl then prepared them a small meal of goat's cheese and bread, which she did by the light of single lamp, placed low to the ground, to make their presence less obvious. It was a sensible decision, and Penthesilea wondered whether she had been taught such a thing or if it had been intuition.

Aikaterini had not cried again, she realised as she watched her fall asleep sitting upright, her arms still around her sister who was fighting her exhaustion and striving to stay awake. She had not panicked or retched at the sight of the dead men. She had not complained as she mopped blood from the ground or helped her sister change her soiled clothes. In another time and place, she would have made a fierce Amazon, Penthesilea thought, which immediately brought back the pain, and she stood, controlling the rage as best she could.

Outside, the night was as quiet as she had known it. No wind rustled the trees, and the tinkling of the fountain was the only accompaniment to her footsteps as she walked across the courtyard. She had tied her horse to a tree close to the barn, where it could feast on the same hay that had been left for the goats, but had since reflected that it would be better to keep it closer to the house. She had spotted few horses on her journey, and to lose him would cost her immeasurably.

"Don't eat too much while you are here," she whispered, as she worked the knot in the rope free. "I do not want you to become accustomed to this life."

The horse whinnied and nuzzled her, as if it knew what she was saying. Penthesilea felt a sad smile falter on her lips as she led it back towards the house.

"This is better," she said and tied him to a post directly in front of the door. With a final stroke down its broad cheek, she turned to the steps, only to find herself face to face with Aikaterini who was brandishing a knife.

"You said you would not go anywhere!"

"I was just moving my horse."

The weapon remained raised. Gently, Penthesilea wrapped her hand around the girl's forearm, close to the wrist, feeling the trembling of the fragile bones.

"I am not going anywhere," she whispered, taking the knife from her. "You are safe. You can sleep now. Go back indoors."

For all that Aikaterini had been keeping the tears at bay, sleep, when it finally came, brought with it nightmares. Listening to the girl's whimpers and moans, Penthesilea found herself wishing she had paid more attention to the preparation of the sleeping draught her women had concocted in Themiscyra. As things were, there was nothing she could do other than keep her promise. And stay.

"YOU WILL TEACH US NOW!"

Penthesilea was awoken by Aikaterini's strident voice, to find that morning had arrived, and she had slept well, considering she had spent the night in a chair next to the girls. The silence of the night had been replaced with a cacophony of sound. While the sea was too distant to be heard behind so many hills and trees, the goats were bleating loudly, demanding their morning feed, and chickens she had not seen the previous day had entered the house, their feet scraping at the stone floor.

Aikaterini, by contrast, looked even more tired if that were possible. Her skin was blotchy, and her lips cracked and bleeding, yet it was the furrow between her eyes that aged her by a decade.

"You are in no fit state for me to train you," Penthesilea said, stretching. "You will injure yourself."

"You promised!"

How was it possible for a girl to be so thin and frail and still stand? No visible muscle on her legs or chest. No strength in her arms. It seemed inconceivable that anyone could survive past infancy in such a state, and yet there she was, standing up to the Amazon Queen as none had dared to before and hoped to live. Not that she had any idea to whom she was speaking. Perhaps, Penthesilea thought, she should tell her. That might change matters.

"I am stronger than I look," Aikaterini insisted, noting her look. "I help on the farm. I milk the goats. I carry water. Please. You promised."

Down on the mattress, Calista was twisting and turning in the shallow tides of sleep. The bandages had come loose and her hands were still red.

"I know who you are," Aikaterini whispered.

"What do you mean?"

"You wear trousers. You ride a horse with a cloth on his back, and you shoot arrows better than any man. It was not hard to work it out. You are an Amazon."

Penthesilea twisted her lips together, an impulse to refute this rolling through her. Once more, she was filled with self-loathing. Never had she wished to deny who she was. Never had she even considered denying her heritage, her parentage, the calling that made her stand above all others. And yet here she was, hesitating to respond to this girl. It would be for their safety, she tried to convince herself. For Aikaterini and Calista. It was better they did not know who she was, given the enemies she had made.

"I am a warrior of sorts," she said. "But you are not. And I will not be able to teach you. You are too old to learn."

"How do you know you will not be able to teach me, if you do not try?" the girl responded.

CHAPTER 46

Despite Aikaterini's best efforts, the floor was still tacky with blood, so they moved outside. It also offered them greater room and fewer memories.

Penthesilea would have preferred to teach them how to make their own weapons first, the way the young Amazon girls did. After all, a poorly constructed knife that broke under pressure could cause more harm than good when trying to defend yourself. But there was not enough time. So, instead, she asked them to seek out anything they had. Knives for skinning rabbits or peeling vegetables. Those that their father used when sacrificing to the gods.

"You are aiming to kill," she told them. "You must think of nothing else. You must always be trying to cause your opponent as much harm as possible. Because that is what they will wish to do to you. Now, you are short and light and should be swift on your feet. You need to use that to your advantage. You aim here—" she pointed to the soft pouch of flesh under her jaw, nicely within their reach "—and here." She drew a line across the belly. "Soft areas only. You do not have enough strength to break ribs, and your weapons are not made for it. You should attack from the front if you can. It will be harder for you to cause sufficient damage from the back."

Calista sat on a nearby rock. The chickens that had invaded the house that morning were now gathered around her as she threw them seeds she was pulling from a sunflower head in her lap. She watched vacantly as they pecked at the ground by her feet. Her bottom lip slanted as she bit down on one side of it, exaggerating the lop-sidedness of her face that the swelling had caused. Periodically, she would cock her head towards the house as if she had heard a noise from inside. She would stay like that for a moment before returning to the birds, seemingly oblivious of Penthesilea and her sister,

By contrast, Aikaterini hung on every word Penthesilea said. Barely blinking, she absorbed every sentence as if it were a blessing from the gods. She mimicked every action of the Amazon, a miniature mirror image of the mighty warrior Queen. Her legs were black and bruised, the insides of her thighs scratched and red, yet she did not flinch. Did not complain.

"I can do better," she said, as Penthesilea knocked her arm aside as easily as if it were one of the sunflower stems. "Try me again."

The Amazon stepped back, noting that Calista had moved and was now staring absentmindedly up at an orange tree.

"You have done enough for now," Penthesilea told her. "Your body is not used to this. Your muscles will be sore tomorrow."

"It is only midday. I want to learn more. There is more I need to know."

"That may be so. But you also have your chores to do and if you wake tomorrow and your hands hurt so much they cannot even grip a broom, how will you protect yourself? Part of being a warrior is learning when you need to train and when you need to rest. And now, you need to rest."

More words teetered on the tip of the girl's tongue, before she pressed her lips tightly together and nodded.

That evening, her appetite seemed to have returned. She ate boiled eggs and goats' cheese and drank plenty of milk. Penthesilea looked on with satisfaction and a slight degree of pride. But this evaporated the moment she shifted her gaze to Calista, who was once again huddled on the mattress, which reeked of fresh urine.

"Do you think she will speak again?" Aikaterini asked, softly. "It has only been one day. She will speak again, won't she?"

False hope was something she had rarely been forced to give, so she tried to imagine instead the words that Cletes would offer in such a situation.

"Like you say, it has only been a day. She will need time. And the young are resilient. More resilient than adults."

Aikaterini nodded quickly, approving of her answer.

"Perhaps tomorrow she will train with us, too. I will ask her. She is strong, you know. Stronger than me. She will be good. You will see."

With a new spirit of optimism, Aikaterini rolled another egg, cracking the shell before peeling away the broken fragments. Yet Penthesilea knew she was about to burst her bubble of hope.

"I will stay with you a second night, but I will have to leave in the morning."

Aikaterini stopped peeling.

"But we need more help."

"I have given you help. More than anyone outside my family has ever received from me."

The egg rested in the palm of the girl's hand, the soft centre oozing slowly between her fingers.

"What if they come back?"

"They cannot return. I have killed them, remember?"

"But there may be others."

Her voice was panicked and high, the composure that she had shown while training had deserted her.

"And you know how to defend yourselves now. Trust me. You showed skill. And you have a determination to ensure that no man takes advantage of you again. Besides, your father will return in just a few days."

"Please ..." Her voice trembled, and tears that she had kept in check now welled in her eyes. "Please."

"You have my answer. You will fight for yourself and live, or you will not."

The harshness of her own tone took even Penthesilea by surprise. Aikaterini recoiled, her lower lip trembling. Dropping her egg on the plate, she fixed her gaze on the Queen, then got up from the table and joined her sister on the damp, urine-soaked bed.

That night, her own words echoed in Penthesilea's head, together with Aikaterini's look of betrayal. She could not face that again. So, once the pair had fallen into a fitful sleep, she gathered her things, slipped outside, mounted her horse and rode away—for good this time. A mantle of stars spanned the sky, illuminating it with the power of a thousand lamps. It was time she moved on. She had already stayed too long.

~

SHE SOUGHT out first one battle, then another. Any size and with any clan, tribe or king, it did not matter. The larger the fight, the better. She arrived fresh from one skirmish, the sweat still slick on her horse's coat, and joined the next, always choosing to fight with the weaker side. Her only condition was that she be outnumbered, and the greater the disadvantage, the better. It never stayed like that for long, though. It was just as it had always been, her arrows unstoppable, her axe unforgiving.

Death had to come on the battlefield. And yet it evaded her at every turn. It had to happen with her being honestly outmanoeuvred in the art of warfare, but how was that ever going to happen to a daughter of Ares? Even in Athens it had not been Theseus or any of his men who had managed to best Hippolyte. And who was left to rival her? Melanippe? She had her strengths, but her own superiority with axe and bow meant she would defeat her in any genuine duel. Besides, she knew her last remaining sister would never fight her. And so, she continued on.

With the changing of the seasons and the rise and fall of the tides, months and then years passed. She had changed horses and restitched her tunic and boots several times and had ridden further north than she had ever ventured before. She travelled to lands where the snow buried her mount to its knees, and the air was so cold it formed a cloud with every breath from horse and rider. She travelled to towns and cities beside lakes, with walls that looked impenetrable. To citadels defended by deep moats. And each time she fought she came away unscathed.

At some point, she realised she no longer cared which direction she was heading. She returned to her old habit of following clear skies, turning south or west, or whichever direction allowed her to evade the rain. She traversed mountain ridges, waded through rapids and tasted fruits both sweeter and sharper than she had ever eaten before.

To those who asked, she said she was from Thrace and had been a nomad all her life. Yes, she told them, she knew of the Amazons. They were legendary, but no, she was not one of them. Once someone suspected her true identity and addressed her as "Queen Penthesilea," but she had just laughed and changed the subject, before thanking him for his hospitality and continuing on her way. Year after year passed in such a manner but, no matter where she went, death avoided her.

It was another spring morning and the air was fresh as a familiarity washed over her. The grasses she passed had been growing steadily more verdant, rippling like waves across the sea. By contrast, the sea itself was calm and as flat as a plain, and seabirds sat on the water unmoving, as if frozen.

Deep down, she had always known it was coming. She had been travelling east for several weeks, watching as the sky expanded and the hills softened to a gentle roll. The horse she was riding was a dapple grey, given to her in payment for a battle fought and won on the borders of Macedonia. The king there had stood with his queen at his side, although Penthesilea had looked only at the man. The looseness of the woman's robes, and the flowers that garnished her hair, reminded her too much of that first time she had seen Hippolyte in Athens. He had offered various rewards for her efforts, including gold and gems and even men or women for her use, if she so wanted. But the metals and stones would have only weighed down her saddle bags, and she had no desire for any of the slaves, so she took only the horse.

He was larger than those she usually rode, his legs thick, almost cumbersome, but what he lacked in agility he made up for in strength and fearlessness. Not once, in the battles that she had fought upon him, did he rear or shy away, or even flinch at an oncoming spear. His pace, whether a canter or gallop, was steady and rhythmic, allowing her to twist and shoot arrows, knowing he would remain sure of foot. They had built a relationship that should have taken years to form but had somehow been there from the start, and he rode into battle just as she did: as if it were his very purpose in life. But she could not bring herself to name him. Not when she knew that one day, he too would leave her.

As the wind teased stray hairs from her cap, she gazed out from the steppes at the citadel beneath her. It was smaller than many she had visited on her travels, and even from this distance she could see the simplicity of the place. But it was her home. It was Themiscyra.

The quietness struck her from where she sat. Where was the clang of metal? The angry shouts of the women training? Where were the shrieks of children and the whinnies of the horses, so large in number that their aroma should hang thick in the air? Where were the Amazons?

Had they been attacked? she wondered, as she stared at the walls before turning her attention out to sea. There were no ships. No invading army, not now at least. And none of the kingdoms through which she had ridden had spoken of war in Pontus.

She dismounted and led her horse along the twisted stone path to Themiscyra, rubbing a hand against his neck as they went.

CHAPTER 47

They sat opposite each other in the dim light of three small lamps. Shadows seemed to gather in the corners of the room, which had once been lit by a dozen torches.

Melanippe was seated, her hair loose around her shoulders. Her face was lined with wrinkles, deep creases across her skin. She had been the youngest of the four sisters. The one who had possessed endless energy that, at the time, had seemed to portend eternal youth. If this was what she looked like, Penthesilea dreaded to imagine her own reflection. She had not seen it in a very long time. Perhaps it would be best if she avoided mirrors.

"You look tired," Melanippe said. "But strong. You have been fighting."

This was no question. The words hung between them in the musty air. Had Themiscyra always been so humid, Penthesilea wondered, feeling her back beginning to grow clammy. Perhaps it was the time spent in the north that was making her more susceptible to heat.

"I have fought a little," she responded.

Melanippe only nodded. Where was the young girl who spoke constantly? Penthesilea wanted to ask. The one who could fill any silence with her words. She had gone, she realised. In her place, a woman. A Queen. And an ageing one at that. The pauses in their conversation expanded.

"And what now?" Melanippe asked. "Are you planning on staying here? Planning on ruling again?"

Penthesilea swallowed. The heat that had drawn moisture from her skin now dried her thoughts, and her tongue along with them. She had known the question would come yet still felt unprepared. So instead, she did as she had grown accustomed to doing over the years and changed the subject.

"Have you visited the Gargareans recently?" she asked. "I could not hear the sound of any children when I approached."

A hard light shone in Melanippe's eyes; she knew exactly what game Penthesilea was playing. And yet she answered her question all the same

"I decided we should stay in Pontus. There would be too many risks on such a journey. Should we be attacked, our numbers are not great enough to defend ourselves. Besides, the Gargareans ..."

She allowed the sentence to fade out, and for a moment, Penthesilea wondered how it might have ended. Then, with sickening shame she realised. They did not want to meet with the Amazons anymore. Not after they had lost so many of their women, not to mention their queen and one of their princesses. Not after they had proven themselves weak.

"They think we have lost favour with Ares," Melanippe said, suddenly. "Do you think it is true? Because I have tried to make amends. I promise. I have tried."

In that moment the mask fell. The old woman in front of

her was still that same younger sibling, in need of Penthesilea's assurance. But she had none to give her. No way to ease the burden she shouldered.

"We are still alive," Penthesilea said, although bitterness laced her words more than she had intended. "Have you been sacrificing to him?"

"Of course. Have you not?"

Penthesilea turned her eyes towards one of the lamps. A draught was causing the flame to flicker.

"No," she said, looking back at her sister. "I have not. Not for some time."

She expected this confession to elicit a gasp of incomprehension and censure, but all she received was a simple nod of the head.

"Cletes is still here. She has a room in the north tower, facing the sea. I am certain she would like to see you ... before you leave again."

This was the first hint of animosity since her arrival, although now it had been set free, it could no longer be contained.

"We know what you have been doing, Sister. We know that you have been fighting on your own. And we know why. You believe you have a better chance of victory without us by your side."

Penthesilea's jaw dropped.

"That is not the reason!"

"Is it not? Why, then? You have good women here. Strong women, who fought by your side in Athens and left with their lives."

"I know that."

"Then why did you not call upon us. Upon me?"

There was a hardness to her sister's voice, when most

people would have expressed sadness, grief even. But she did not cry. She had nothing left to cry for.

"I ... I needed to be alone."

"For seven years?"

Melanippe rose, and her shadow loomed large on the wall behind her.

"I did not realise it had been so long," Penthesilea lied, with a feebleness she knew her sister would see straight through.

Of course she knew how long it had been. She had watched the seasons change, seen first the mountaintops turn white and then gradually the rest of the slopes until the ground beneath her feet had frozen, before it all retreated again, replaced with the kaleidoscope of spring colours. Yes, she knew that she had suffered from more than one frozen winter and scorching summer. But was it really that long since Hippolyte had died in her arms? How was it possible that so much time had passed, when she could still remember the light leaving her sister's eyes?

She straightened her back, preparing to stand.

"It is best that I go. I can see I have no place here."

But before she could rise, Melanippe had crossed the room and was towering over her.

"You have no place here because you chose not to have one," she spat. "Because you chose to leave your people when they needed you the most. You are the one who decided to do this, Penthesilea. No one else. Now, if you are going to leave, please do so. I have crops to think about and grain to store and more than just your ego to attend to."

Penthesilea left the citadel and headed north, to gaze upon the beach where Theseus had first arrived with Heracles. She found herself thinking the same thought she had turned over in her mind a thousand times before: how much death and suffering might have been saved if she had ended his life here, all that time ago?

The moon was a thin crescent and reflected perfectly on the surface of the sea. She could wade out into the water, she considered. Offer herself to Poseidon. But why? He would not want her, any more than her father or any of the other gods did. And so, she simply stood there.

The sea had begun to move a little, flurries of white foam distorting the image of the moon, when a voice cut through the darkness behind her.

"You have been out here for quite some time. Anyone might think you were waiting for someone."

Penthesilea closed her eyes and squeezed them tight, as if in doing so she might hold that moment in her mind forever. She had heard that voice in her sleep, calling to her across battlefields, only to find no one there the second she drew near. She had seen her, too, in those same fields, a flash of black hair between raised spears.

"Cletes," she said, softly.

"So, do you care to tell me who or what it is you are waiting for? For if it is a boat, you may find yourself out of luck. I believe they only stop here once every ten years or so."

She could not turn. Could not face looking at her. She could picture the small smile curving her lips as she waited for Penthesilea to reply to her joke. And in spite of herself, a single, gruff laugh forced its way from her throat.

"No. No boats for me," she said.

"Good, I am glad that at least some things have not changed."

In years past, they had shared so many silences. Lying together in their bivouacs, or outside, staring up at the night sky, watching the stars and moon slowly moving across the heavens. Cletes was someone Penthesilea could always speak to. Someone she knew would never judge her. And yet at that moment, she did feel judged.

She wished she could think of something to say, words to fill the void that yawned between them, but no sound came, bar the soft lapping of the waves as they rolled up onto the shore, then the gentle whisper as they receded back to lose themselves again.

"I know what you have been doing," Cletes said, stepping forward and taking her hand. "I know what you have been hoping to achieve. We have heard of the battles you have taken upon yourself."

"I have been fighting. That is what we do. That is what I was born to do."

"No, you have been trying to get yourself killed. You know, I heard one rumour that you went into battle without a breast-plate. Is that true?"

Penthesilea kept her eyes fixed on the moon. She had thought little of the rumours that reached Themiscyra when she had lived there. But now, the tales shared in whispers behind the citadel walls were about her.

"The breast plate was damaged. I did not have time to fix it," she said, offering an answer as close to the truth as she could. Cletes would not believe her, though. She knew that.

"You would never have allowed one of us to ride into battle in such a state. You have been reckless."

Penthesilea wished that she could refute this. Defend herself. Find her sharp tongue and insist that she did not know of what she was speaking. But she could not. Not with Cletes. She could find no other words, except the truth.

"I deserve to die, Cletes. I deserve to die for what I have

done. I cannot endure living like this, and yet death will not greet me. What do I do?"

The strength in her knees vanished, and she dropped to the ground. Cletes pressed her hand on her shoulder. All this time, and her scent had not changed. That sweet pomegranate, that deep muskiness of the earth. She would recognise it anywhere, she thought, as she drew in the deepest breath her lungs could hold. Perhaps this would be it. Perhaps the gods were granting her one last night with Cletes before they took her.

Cletes took her chin and lifted it, so that their eyes met. There was so much kindness there. Melanippe's gaze might have hardened during the years of her absence, but the light in Cletes burnt as bright as it always had.

"I think there is somewhere we can go," she said. "Someone we can see who could help you."

CHAPTER 48

*S*o many years had passed since Heracles had arrived on their shores that the details had faded in Penthesilea's mind. She remembered the most important facts, however. He had come into their home, he had taken Hippolyte's zoster, and he brought with him Theseus, the man who had destroyed them all. That was enough. But Cletes remembered the smaller, finer details of those days. Not only what Heracles had done, but what he had said. The reason for his arrival on their shores had been as part of his quest to seek purification and absolution for killing his wife and child. And it had been a king who had granted him this.

"It is a gift the gods bestow on the kings, to grant absolution for such acts. This could be your way out. Ask a king for purification. He will set you tasks, and once they are completed, you will be cleansed."

There was that smile again, which could so easily draw Penthesilea in, hungry to place her lips against it. But now, her thoughts were stirring. Was it truly possible that she could be absolved like this?

They sat on the beach, watching the dark silhouette of an eagle cross the moon, before Penthesilea's impatience got the better of her.

"I should go and talk this through with Melanippe. If what you say is possible, then I must leave as soon as I can."

Cletes rose slowly. She was barefoot, Penthesilea now noticed, and a new tattoo coiled up over the arch of her foot and towards her ankle.

"I understand your wish for answers," she said, softly, "but even if you do not need sleep, Melanippe does. Come, spend the night beside me. You can go to her at first light."

Seven years, and no one had laid so much as a finger on her body. Any softness Penthesilea had once possessed had disappeared and her skin had been ravaged by the elements. But Cletes looked upon her as she always had. As if she were a gift from the gods.

"You have been missed, my Queen."

"Don't—" Penthesilea began, but Cletes put a finger to her lips.

"You will leave again soon. We do not have time to waste with words."

SHE AWOKE AT DAWN. She had forgotten, on her travels, the strength with which the sun cut across the horizon in Pontus, and the manner in which the sky would transform from deep blue to burning umber in the space of a heartbeat. She had forgotten, too, how intense the song of the birds could be, as they fluttered in the rafters and made nests between the roof tiles. She had forgotten all of this because she had forced herself to do so. Because remembering had been unbearable. And now she would have to manage it all over again.

It was not only in her looks that Melanippe had changed. These days, she was up well before dawn, and after a brief time scouring the building, Penthesilea found her down at the stables. One of the horses was resting its foot in her hand, as she chipped clods of mud from its hoof with a small hook.

"Sister," Penthesilea said, leaning towards her. "May I talk with you?"

Melanippe's head remained down. The animal waited patiently, using its tail to flick flies from its back.

"I have to finish this first," she replied. "Two horses have become lame in the last few days alone."

Penthesilea stiffened at her coldness, although she knew she deserved nothing else.

"I understand." She stepped back, feeling her body shrinking a fraction.

Still bent over, Melanippe continued to chip away, before pausing and looking up at her sister.

"I suspect this will take some time," she said. "Perhaps, when I am done, we could eat breakfast together. If you are hungry, that is?"

"Yes," Penthesilea replied quickly. "I am."

MELANIPPE APPROACHED every task now with thoughtful deliberation, from the cleaning of the horses' hooves to the preparation of breakfast. The same consideration showed now, as she rested her chin against the knuckle of her forefinger and contemplated Penthesilea's question. The old Melanippe would have given her opinion immediately, good or bad, whereas now it was hard to even read her expression. This saddened Penthesilea, as she well remembered the same change had happened with Hippolyte, and how that had ultimately cost her sister her life.

Squeezing her eyes shut, she pushed away thoughts of one dead sister and tried to focus, instead, on the only one who still lived.

"So, do you think it is possible? Do you think there is a king who would do such a thing?"

Removing her chin from her knuckle, Melanippe clasped her hands together.

"King Priam," she said.

"King Priam? Of Troy?"

"The very same. He is Thracian, and Father always favoured him. Besides, his wife, Hecuba, hails from nearby Phrygia. If any king will help you, it would be him. But you need to consider the consequences of what he might ask you to do in return. Heracles was sent off to perform harrowing tasks, remember? The skin of the Nemean Lion, Hippolyte's zoster, not to mention passing into the underworld. Could you carry out such deeds?"

"I can face anything other than this guilt," she replied, honestly. "He can keep me in his house as a concubine, if it will absolve me of it."

For the first time since Penthesilea's return, a small smile passed across her sister's face, and in that instant, a youthful light returned to her eyes.

"This is what you should do, Sister. Perhaps what you should always have done."

Before last night, it had been so long since Penthesilea had held another person. So long since she had wrapped her arms around someone and felt the heat of their body. Melanippe pulled her in close, perhaps closer than they had ever embraced. Her hands pulled her in so tight, it was as if they were one. And when they broke away, Penthesilea felt the absence as keenly as if they were now seas apart.

"When will you go?" Melanippe asked.

"Tomorrow morning. I can reach Troy in three or four days and the sooner I arrive, the better."

"And will you take Cletes? We are short of women here, most of them have taken to the life of a nomad. They feel safer on the steppes than confined within the citadel. But I will need to make arrangements if she is to go with you."

Penthesilea shook her head. "No, I need to do this alone."

"I understand."

Penthesilea could not count the number of times she had ridden away from Themiscyra and looked over her shoulder to see the walls of the citadel retreating or lost in a heat haze or beyond a downpour. Yet never had she looked at it the way she did on the morning she departed for Troy. She felt this might be the last time she ever gazed upon those yellow bricks and stone, laid by her ancestors.

She could not imagine what trials King Priam might assign, if he agreed to her request, or if she was even capable of purification, but she knew she would have to succeed, or never return to Themiscyra.

CHAPTER 49

The city of Troy was located in northwest Anatolia. Despite its proximity to Pontus, it was not a place that Penthesilea had ever visited. There had been no need. The Amazons came to kings in need, who required protection and faced battles they feared they would lose without their help. King Priam was not such a one.

She had heard plenty of rumours of the citadel, whose fortifications made those of Athens seem paltry by comparison. She had heard tell of its vast walls with towering turrets, surrounding hectare upon hectare of land, where the citizens farmed and lived a life so full there was no reason for them ever to leave.

She had heard stories of the King, too, of his virility and humour. Although she could not recall the names of his daughters, she knew that Hecuba had birthed at least one son. She assumed the boy, Hector, if she recalled correctly, would be trained to become a formidable warrior.

She rode slowly, pondering on these matters and thinking about what acts he might assign her. Wondering how long her future would be pledged to this king of whom she knew so little.

On the fourth day, drizzle filled the air, growing heavier as she rode further west towards the coast, and by the time the city came into view, the sky was laden with black clouds. But this did nothing to diminish what stood before her.

Athens had taken her breath away and made her reconsider the wonders that man could achieve, but this ... this was a marvel worthy of the gods. It was no wonder her father had admired such a place.

The city was enclosed within walls of sandstone yellow, thirty feet high, topped with turrets and towers that pierced the low-hanging clouds. They bristled with armed guards at every point. Her journey should have seen her arrive from the eastern, land-locked side, yet she knew that the strongest defences would be on the west, by the shore, for if anyone were foolish enough to attack Troy, they would come not from Anatolia, but across the sea. And so she circled around, to ensure that she was seen. She wanted King Priam to know that she had arrived.

She had replaced her clothes in Themiscyra and now wore new boots, calf high and thick-soled; leather trousers and tunic with a bright geometric pattern freshly sewn on; and a hat which tapered to point. All undeniably Amazonian. She might have hidden her true self from the world for the last seven years, but now she wanted all to know who she was.

As she approached the massive gates, one swung open with a great clang and the grinding and grating of metal, not for her to enter but to allow Trojans out. The moment the gap was wide enough, guards raced through it and swarmed all around her horse, their spears raised and their shields up. When she was completely encircled, the gate clanked shut again. She noted this defensive action with interest. If this was how they handled one woman, who knew what they would do for an army?

"Who are you?"

The soldier who spoke held out his spear towards her. The tip quivered, the length of the weapon amplifying the tremor in his hand.

"This display would suggest that you are already aware of who I am," she replied.

The man jabbed his weapon towards her. It was a pointless action. Foolish, even, for no man would prod a snake if he did not wish to get bitten. But she would withhold her venom. For now, at least.

"Tell King Priam that Queen Penthesilea is here to speak with him."

The man's lips twisted, his Adam's apple rising and falling as the trembling of his spear increased. Keeping his eyes firmly on her, he turned his head to the side and nodded. A soldier behind him immediately backed away from the circle, leaving a gap which was instantly closed. A moment later the gate reopened a crack, just wide enough for him to slip inside. How long would it be before the message reached Priam? Penthesilea wondered. It might take the man an hour to cross the citadel on foot. The Palace was sure to be high up in the centre. She had no choice but to wait.

She shifted slightly in her saddle, to adjust the weight on her pelvis. The instant she moved, every spear sprang up again. Even in this tense situation, she found the scene comical.

Her horse, for its part, looked somewhat indifferent to the display.

"Would it help if I offered you my axe?" she asked.

She posed her question to the soldier who had spoken to her. He hesitated, obviously wondering if this were a trap. The additional adornments on his armour implied he had the authority to make decisions, and he also appeared to have a modicum of common sense. He pursed his lips. Was accepting an Amazon's offer to take her weapon more or less dangerous than letting her keep it?

"And your bow and arrows, too," he said, eventually.

She dropped the axe to the ground, where it landed with a thud, creating a depression in the sand.

"I will need that back when I leave," she said. *If* was the word that had been in her mind before she spoke. *If I leave.* And yet her tongue had wisely chosen *when,* instead. A young soldier rushed forwards. As he went to pick up the axe, his shoulders jolted, its weight surprising him. When he looked up at Penthesilea, the alarm in his eyes had been replaced by a new sense of fear.

"The bow next," ordered the first soldier.

With a small nod, Penthesilea reached over her shoulder, and her fingertips touched the warm wood they found there. Cletes had offered her this bow when she left Themiscyra. It was newly made, strengthened with bone and engraved with the images of deer and eagles. She had made it for her.

"We will hunt together with it, on the steppes," she had said, and Penthesilea had smiled, knowing that they might never get the chance to do such a thing.

"I will give you my quiver, but I must insist I keep the bow," she said. "Besides, the bow is useless without my arrows."

Distrust glowed in the man's eyes, but he nodded in agreement, and Penthesilea slipped the quiver from her belt and allowed it to fall to the ground.

Then there was nothing for them all to do but wait.

From her position on horseback, she regarded the seashore. Its length was immense, and though rocky outcrops rose boldly at either end, it comprised deep soft golden sand, with rounded pebbles scattered close to the water. A beach this long would be enough to land a thousand ships on, should anyone ever choose to attack. And for the invader, there would be much to gain, for without doubt Troy was in a most advantageous position. Trade routes passed through her from all of Anatolia to Greece. As such, it was unsurprising that such a stronghold was required. But it would need a thousand such ships to carry enough men to attempt to take the city, and no king in all of Greece, or beyond, possessed such numbers.

The gulls squalled overhead as she waited, and her mind slipped into its usual train of thought when she found herself surrounded by men with weapons. Where would she strike first? There was, after all, a chance that things could go badly and Priam would refuse to see her at all. He might have formed an alliance with Athens that she was unaware of. No matter how much she wished to die, she knew she would not be able to sit there and allow an arrow to strike her heart without putting up a fight. She would need to find a way to die as a warrior, if that was to be the gods' wish.

She would require weapons first, but they need not be her own. The men were foot soldiers, looking to their leader for orders, so she would take him out first. By that point, she would have reached either her quiver or her axe. After that, she would forge a path to the city wall. This would be a foolish tactic for the inexperienced, for those who did not know how to escape when penned in, but for her, it made perfect sense. It was the best way to control a stream of opponents if they could approach her from only one direction. She would pick them off, one by one, and when the time was right, she would make good her escape by horse. Priam would not send more soldiers after her, knowing how that would end. These men would be his sacrificial lambs.

Her mind was still moving through this scenario when the gate opened again, and the soldier stepped out.

His face was flushed, an indication of the speed with which he had moved.

"Let her in," he said. "The King will see her."

CHAPTER 50

*T*roy buzzed with life. Within its walls were acres of farmland, full of crops and animals, not a scrap of land going to waste. Golden wheat reflected the ochre of the stones, while goats grazed beneath the high canopy of twisted grapevines. Passionflowers burst with colour, and butterflies flitted between their vibrant petals.

This was a hidden oasis, worthy even of Themiscyra, and Penthesilea's senses were overwhelmed. Escorting her, in front and behind, the soldiers' feet drummed a steady beat on the ground. Further in, the strong sunlight reflected off every wall and door, elevating ordinarily dull material to the realm of precious metals.

She looked longingly as they passed a long trough, where animals drank, their fleshy tongues lapping impatiently at the water. That would be her next stop, if King Priam did not offer her refreshment upon arrival.

The deeper into the city they moved, the more condensed the buildings and people became. Men and women bustled along, arms jangling with copper bracelets as they carried their wares, while children ran about their legs, laughing. One group was taunting a stray kitten, dangling a piece of string in front of it. Hawkers shouted with booming voices and others urged animals along, just as they had in Athens, with chickens squawking underfoot and mice and rats scurrying out of sight, only to reappear a moment later. The air was rich with the aroma of roasted nuts and honeyed fruits. So much life. Such vibrancy.

As Penthesilea approached and passed, all human noise stopped and a hush descended. Men who had been dozing sat up, as if their daydreams had turned into nightmares. Mothers pulled their children behind their legs and clutched their babies close to their breasts. Even the animals sensed that something was not right. If this was a portent of the greeting Priam would offer her, then she shuddered to imagine what labours he would see fit to impose upon her.

When they reached the steps to the Palace, the soldiers at the front stopped and parted, indicating for her to walk up, alone.

Never had she approached a building of this grandeur on her own. The kingdoms that she had fought for during her solitude had been similar in size to Themiscyra, and her stays had been as brief as was required to take her fill of food and collect any bounty she wished.

When she reached the top, King Priam stood waiting for her. It was easy to see from his stature and the poise with which he held himself, that he had been a warrior himself and possibly still was, although he must be past his prime. His short curly hair had begun to turn grey, as had his beard. He was dressed in a simple chiton with red embroidery. From a fleeting glance below her at the Trojan men and women who had gathered, Penthesilea could see that his people revered him. He was loved. Respected. He was a true leader.

As she climbed the last two steps, his eyes were locked on hers. Not on the bow she had refused to surrender and not on his soldiers, indicating that they should be prepared to strike. Her stomach churned and her palms started to sweat, a reaction so unfamiliar that it took her a moment to understand what she was experiencing. Nerves, she realised. This was what it felt like to be nervous.

She halted on the final step, for there was nowhere left to go. Was she expected to bow at this point? she wondered. She had never done that before. She was Penthesilea. Daughter of Ares and once Queen of the Amazons. Who could possibly be worthy of her obeisance? And yet, she reminded herself, she had journeyed here for Priam's help, and if showing deference was what it took, then she would have to do it.

She was preparing to step back with one foot as she told her muscles to perform a movement as strange to her as the nerves that continued to rumble through her belly, when Priam spoke.

"Queen Penthesilea," he said, dipping his head. "It is a pleasure."

He beckoned her to join him, inviting her into his home as if she were an expected guest, an acquaintance of many years or a friend who had been absent for too long. As they walked, he spoke continuously, offering his apologies that he had not been at the gate to greet her himself, and for the hostility with which she had been met, for had he known of her arrival he would most certainly have prepared a proper welcome.

She followed him along corridors, and up a large staircase. Red and white mosaic tiles formed geometric patterns on the floors with similar motifs decorating the large arches through which they walked. The walls were plain, the red stones giving the impression of barrenness, which vanished when Priam led her into a courtyard.

Every shade of green shone there. Vines grew around trellises, and trees, twice her height, sprouted from immense pots. A table had been laid, with plates of food and a jug of wine, next to a large fountain. Its cool waters sparkled in the sunshine as dragonflies danced around it, occasionally resting on the side or flitting over to the buddleia or honeysuckle which also grew there.

"Please, you must be thirsty after your ride," Priam said to her.

A young girl in a blue chiton stepped forwards and offered her a cup of water on a silver platter. Penthesilea drank gratefully, before replacing the vessel on the platter, whereupon it was immediately refilled.

Smiling as graciously as she could, Penthesilea remained silent, her eyes moving across the frescos that covered the walls. Although they were somewhat lacking in detail, they more than made up for this with their warmth. The scenes were of men and women lounging together, eyes creased in smiles with food at their fingertips, as opposed to the usual images of battles or hunts.

The King had, so far, asked her no questions, seemingly content with the sound of his own voice, but as the courtyard appeared to be their final destination, Penthesilea knew she could not rely on his loquaciousness to hide the fact that she had questions of her own.

"I heard tell of the events in Athens," Priam said, taking a seat on a couch and gesturing for her to do the same. "I can only offer you my most sincere condolences."

Penthesilea nodded, her gaze involuntarily sliding to the floor. She did not know what to say, how much she should give away. Did purification warrant pure truth? she wondered. It seemed likely, but some facts were hers to reveal, and she did not want to sully Hippolyte's name by mentioning others.

Priam let out a long heavy sigh and Penthesilea noted how his lips were pressed together tightly as if, for the first time since her arrival, he was contemplating what he should say next. Then he nodded, gently, and spoke again.

"You know, your father has always blessed us graciously here."

"He always spoke fondly of Troy," she replied, echoing the words that Melanippe had spoken, even though she herself could not recall him saying any such thing. Slowly taking another sip of water, she prepared to speak.

"King Priam, you should know that I have come to you for a specific reason. I am here for redemption and purification for Hippolyte's death. For her murder. Committed by my own hand."

The whole story spilled from her as if it could no longer be contained. As she finished she brought the cup back to her lips, only to find her hand trembling so badly, she feared it might not be strong enough to even hold a feather in its grasp.

"I thank you for your candour, Queen Penthes—"

Whatever else he might have said, it was cut short by a shout from the corridor.

"Father, Father!"

A young boy raced into the courtyard. His cheeks were flushed, and his face shone with sweat, as he came to a halt.

"Father," he said once more, now with obvious relief that he had found him.

As his eyes shifted across to Penthesilea, his expression immediately changed.

"So it is true. She is here. Queen of the Amazons. Queen Penthesilea."

Mouth agape, he dropped to his knees. Laughing, King Priam stood and crossed the courtyard to pull him up by his shoulders. He slapped him lightly on the back, a hearty chuckle escaping his throat.

"Queen Penthesilea, may I introduce to you my eldest son, Hector. As you may have already gathered, he is quite in awe of you."

The boy was, in many ways, a miniature version of his father. They shared the same narrow-bridged nose and hazel eyes. But Hector was stockier than Priam. Despite only looking around ten years of age, he already stood only an inch shorter than the King. Beneath his thin robe, she could see from the width of his shoulders that he would grow to be a man to rival the Gargareans.

She rose from her seat, dipping her head slightly.

"Prince Hector," she said. "My pleasure."

Grinning in obvious disbelief, Hector appeared unable to tear his eyes from her, and it was only when Priam touched him lightly on the shoulder that he once more noticed his father's presence and a new level of excitement overtook him.

"Will you ask her, Father?" he said, bouncing on the balls of his feet. "Will you ask her?"

"Patience, Hector. The Queen has only just arrived. We have barely sat down."

"But you will ask her, won't you?"

There was clearly something afoot that Penthesilea was not privy to. The boy's enthusiasm was contagious and reminded her of Cletes.

"Is there something I should be made aware of?" she asked, realising that the sooner she attended to his request, the sooner

King Priam would be able to attend her own. "Do you wish to ask me something, Prince Hector?"

His cheeks flooded a new shade of crimson, as deep as the embroidery on his father's robes, and the confidence he had shown only moments earlier, ebbed away.

"We have something of a tradition when great warriors come to Troy," Priam said.

His eyes met Penthesilea's, twinkling in appreciation of her attention to the boy. She knew that all kings favoured their sons. They were an extension of themselves and were expected to preserve the legacy of their name. Yet this seemed to be something more. There was a special connection between them.

"And you are the greatest warrior to have ever visited," Hector declared breathlessly.

"Hector wishes to be warrior, maybe even a great hero one day, and would consider it a great honour if you might spar with him a little, Queen Penthesilea," Priam explained.

"You wish to be a fighter?" Penthesilea asked, standing as she spoke.

The boy nodded eagerly, his hair bobbing up and down.

"Maybe even as great as you."

"That would be a fine thing, indeed," she chuckled.

She watched as he swallowed, once and then again, and wondered what type of king or warrior such a boy would become. This positivity and energy were good but Penthesilea had always believed a child needed a strict, sometimes harsh, upbringing to grow strong. It needed to be tested. To face trials, like those her mother and father had set for her and her sisters when they trained. She struggled to see that Prince Hector would have faced anything remotely so challenging.

"I have an axe," the boy said, suddenly. "And arrows and a

sword, lots of swords, and you can choose whichever one you want me to use. I want you to teach me, I am a good listener and a fast learner. You can tell her, Father, can't you?" he said, turning to the King. "You can tell her how good I am at listening. And learning. I promise you won't be disappointed," he continued, addressing Penthesilea again.

The boy looked at her expectantly, eyebrows raised. She saw again that light in his eyes that reminded her so much of Cletes.

CHAPTER 51

"*I* do not train people," she said, trying to quash the memory of Aikaterini before it could rise to unsettle her. She had taught her and her sister barely enough to stay alive. Whether they had needed to use those skills and had been successful was not her concern.

"But in your citadel at Themiscyra, you must have trained with the women? You must have practised? Or else how did you get to be so good?"

"Being a good fighter does not mean I am a good teacher. Trust me. It is my sisters you need, not me."

Sister. That was what she should have said. A pang of sadness swept through her.

"But you are Queen Penthesilea."

He said this as if it was an explanation for everything, although his young shoulders slumped in disappointment and the flush of excitement was replaced with sallow regret. Tension was building in the courtyard. The gurgling of the water no longer sounded inviting, and the birdsong had turned shrill.

"King Priam, if you and I could finish our conversation?" Penthesilea said, unable to bear Hector's look of despair any longer.

The boy was looking up at his father now. She could see in his eye the soft sheen of tears he refused to allow himself.

"Hector, let me talk to Queen Penthesilea. You have said your part, but now there are things we must discuss."

The boy's eyes returned to her and she quickly lowered her gaze. He glanced back at his father once more and then turned on his heel and ran off the way he had come.

Raising his eyebrows, Priam let out a short sigh.

"He *is* actually quite a fighter," he said, with a smile. "He will be formidable when he has grown. It is hard to believe, but half the men in my army already run in fright from his sword."

She did, indeed, find this difficult to believe. The men must know what was expected of them. All the same, she smiled politely.

"King Priam," she began, "the reason I am here—"

"For purification. I understand. As I said before, I am sorry for what happened to your sister and for the part that you played."

Condolences were kind, but they were not what she needed

"Will you do it? Will you grant me purification?" she asked, leaving no room for ambiguity. "I know I will be beholden to you. I understand that. Whatever tasks you ask of me, I will be at your disposal. And any gifts you wish me to offer to you, any enemies you wish me to dispose of, whatever you require, I will do it for you. However long that may take."

And then, with no awkwardness at all, she dropped to her knees, head lowered, just as Hector had done before her. Yet rather than raising her up, as he had his son, the King roared a full-throated laugh.

"Dear Queen. Have you seen Troy? I am in need of nothing here, and I do not require you to kill anyone for me."

It was as if the fateful arrow had struck again, this time piercing her own sternum. King Eurystheus had required fame, notoriety, power. That was why he had sent Heracles to endure his labours. They had given him a reflected glory that he alone would never have attained. If King Priam wanted for nothing, then she was not needed. And if she was not needed, then why would he purify her?

The chill of the cool floor was seeping into her knees as the King held out his hand to her. His fingers were adorned with gold rings, studded with precious stones, counterparts to the thick gold bangles around his forearms and biceps.

Still Penthesilea hung her head, the weight of disappointment feeling like shackles pinning her to the ground.

"I was wrong to come here," she said, rising to her feet without his assistance. "I am sorry. I will leave."

The temperature in the courtyard seemed to have dropped and the air soured. A sudden dizziness blurred her vision as she hastened to the doorway. Yet she had barely managed two steps when Priam spoke again.

"You misunderstand me, my Queen. I said I did not need anything from you. But that does not mean I will not perform the purification ritual for you."

She stopped yet did not turn around.

"I do not understand. You want nothing from me? You will purify me of this deed for ... for nothing?" she said, slowly moving to face him again.

Even as she spoke the words, she was struck by the absurdity of what she was saying. No king performed acts like that from the goodness of his heart. After all, a man did not become a king through philanthropy. There would always be an ulterior motive or a catch. A twisted web of nuance which, once the bargain had been struck, entrapped the petitioner forever, with no more hope of escape than the maidens and youths who had served as sacrifices in the labyrinth beneath Minos' Palace.

She waited for King Priam to set out his conditions, as the blood pounded in her ears.

"There is nothing I need from you now. Nothing I require. Although, if the time ever came when Troy needed your help, if ever it seemed as though our walls were about to be breached, perhaps, then, you might come to our aid to fight against such a formidable foe."

Penthesilea remained silent. If he knew of what had happened in Athens, then he must be aware of how few of her women remained. The pause stretched out between them until she could endure it no more.

"That is all? That is all you ask of me?"

"That is all," he said, "except ..." and he stopped abruptly, in a manner that caused her stomach to tighten again. Here it was. Here came the inevitable blow she had been waiting for. But what could he say that produced such reticence? A smile curled at the corner of his mouth.

"... perhaps you might take an hour out of your time and make a young boy very happy?"

IT WOULD TAKE time to prepare for the ceremony, Priam told her. She could rest now, if she preferred, and see Hector the following day. But she shook her head. This absolution had come at so little a cost. To ride into battle and fight for Troy.

That was all she had to do. As long as there was breath in her lungs and strength in her legs she would continue to fight, and to do so for a king who was favoured by her father, was more honour than burden.

As so Priam led her through the winding corridors of the Palace, where the sounds of laughter drifted from behind many doors. It was impossible not to feel small in such a place as this, not to see your insignificance amongst such glory.

"This way, my Queen," he said. "The young Prince will be practising."

He led her down a set of steps and out into a wide space which was less courtyard, more small arena. It was open-roofed and the sunlight poured in. The ground was tiled, like elsewhere, but with slabs made of sand and stone, and the hot dust filled her nostrils. Around the edge, a variety of weapons, including daggers, spears and bows, were arranged against a wall.

"A father's indulgence, I'm afraid." Priam smiled. "Hector wants to learn to be a hero. And who am I to stand in the way of such a noble calling?"

"You came?" Hector shouted, bounding up to them.

He had changed from the robe he was wearing earlier and was dressed in a short tunic, exposing his long tanned legs.

"Does this mean you will show me how to fight? You will teach me?"

"I'm not sure what I can teach you in an afternoon, but it would be an honour to test your skills, young prince."

"I want to be the greatest warrior in all of Troy," he continued. "I will command the army and protect the city. Keep my wife and children safe."

"A wife, already," Penthesilea said with a half-smile that she shared with the King. "Let us see what we have here," she continued, moving past the Prince to examine the weapons. They were of excellent quality, the metals burnished and polished, the handles sanded smooth then inlaid with bone. What detail the frescos lacked, was more than made up for here. She ran her fingers along the flat of a sword, feeling the heat seep from her skin.

"You can use anything you want," Hector said, appearing beside her once again. "Father bought them all for me. You can even keep what you choose. It would be my honour. My gift to you."

Again, Penthesilea's eyes found Priam's.

"He has a good heart, your son."

"Very much so. He must have gained it from his mother."

She realised her exchanges with Hector had been the longest conversations she had ever had with a boy of his age. In fact, the only such one. This saddened her a little, as she thought of the nephew she had never met.

"Let me see how you attack, first," she said, lifting a shield from the wall. "Once I know where your skills lie, then we will look at what I may be able to teach you."

Unbridled joy poured from the young Prince as he chose his own sword, then shuffled back into the centre of the arena, keeping his eyes on Penthesilea the entire time.

"Now, your aim is to try and hit me."

The sound of clashing metal rang out, echoing off the walls and resonating in the weapons that hung from the wall, patiently waiting their turn.

Hector moved his feet constantly, landing strike after strike on Penthesilea's shield. There was no escaping the fact that the child was gifted. He moved instinctively, his feet dancing over the tiles, and used his sword as fluidly as if it were an extension of him. Time and again, his blade came down, striking with a force that reverberated along her shield arm. Each time his weapon ricocheted off, he quickly regained control, already prepared for the next strike.

By the time she called a halt, an audience of a dozen people had gathered. In the centre, beside Priam, was a young woman with flowing hair as black as a raven's wing, a child on her hip, while two more stood at her side, one clinging to her robe.

With a brief nod to Hector, Penthesilea motioned for him to lower his sword and left the boy to approach the onlookers.

"Queen Hecuba," she said, bowing.

Somehow it was easier to abase herself in this way before a woman.

"Queen Penthesilea. It is an honour to meet you. As you may be aware, there is a great deal of admiration for you within these walls."

Now they had stopped sparring, Penthesilea saw just how hard she had worked the young Prince. His arms gleamed with sweat, and his breath, which had been so focused and controlled, was now fast and laboured.

"He is exceptional" she said, in all honesty. "There are few I have ever seen who could fight like that at such an age."

The same sense of pride she had witnessed in Priam washed over Hecuba. The Queen of Troy reached out her hand and, obligingly, Hector came and took it.

"He is our pride. They are all our pride."

A brief moment passed before Penthesilea spoke again.

"King Priam," she said, with an intensity that conveyed the importance of what she was saying. "Is it possible? Have arrangements been made?"

He nodded.

"The temple has been prepared, but there is no rush if you require more time."

But Penthesilea had already waited long enough.

"I am ready," she said.

CHAPTER 52

*S*he had changed her clothes and was dressed in a simple robe of pale blue that Hecuba had given her and, thankfully, had assisted her to put on. It was only the second time Penthesilea had worn such attire. She would not allow herself to think of the first.

She had stood awkwardly as Hecuba fastened the material at her shoulder with a silver clasp and folded the pleats, so that they gathered around her waist and fell gently to her ankles.

"Your hair is beautiful like this," she said, having unplaited the braids, so it now held the same soft waves as her own. "You should wear it this way."

The woman possessed the same endearing quality she had seen in both Priam and Hector. What would it be like to live in a city with these people as your king and queen? she wondered. She could not imagine Hector growing into a man who would chop and change his wives, as Theseus had done. But then, if she had learnt anything of people, it was that you rarely knew what they were capable of, until it was too late.

"You should make your way to the Temple now," Hecuba

said, examining Penthesilea carefully, as if assessing her handi-work. "I will take you there. The King is waiting."

Outside, night had fallen, shadows shifted as a draught played with the flames of the lamps. Whether it was cold or not, Penthesilea was not aware.

"He is inside, waiting for you," Hecuba said, when they reached the Temple.

She took hold of the Queen's hands, clasping them tightly as if they were the dearest of friends, causing Penthesilea to flinch in surprise. Yet Hecuba seemed not to notice.

"He will purify you of this deed," she said. "You have nothing to fear here."

And with that, she dropped her hands and turned away.

It was a small temple, in comparison to the size of the walls that surrounded the citadel and not a place where the citizens of Troy came to worship or lament. This was a private sanc-tuary for the King to pay his respects to the gods, an intimate and personal space, and he was allowing her access to it.

The temple was sparsely furnished. Lamps had been replaced by tallow candles, the fat of which burnt with thick smoke that weaved lazily to the ceiling, filling the air with a pungent aroma. A large bowl had been placed on top of the stone altar, with a single cushion on the ground in front of it. Had the place been emptied for her, Penthesilea wondered. Had all the silver and gold and extravagant offerings been removed? It was not beyond the realms of possibility.

King Priam stepped out of the shadows. He, too, had changed his gown and now wore one of solid-blue fabric, with no adornments except for a heavy gold necklace made of jointed plates, which hung so low on his chest it might almost have been armour. He offered none of his characteristic smiles and the twinkle in his eyes had been replaced by an air of solemnity. He crossed to the altar and knelt over a small box that had hitherto escaped her notice in the gloom.

The piglet he withdrew was dark pink in colour and, judging by the viscous blood that coated its skin, could not long have left its mother's womb. Its mouth moved constantly as it opened and closed it in the futile search of a teat from which it might suckle warm milk. Gesturing with his head, the King indicated for Penthesilea to take her place on the cushion.

As she lowered herself down, the piglet finally let out a squeal of terror. It squirmed in Priam's hands, fighting helplessly against his grip. Such small lungs, yet the sound cut through the air.

Priam, however, seemed not to notice. He held the animal with complete calm, seeming unconcerned that it might wriggle from his grasp.

"Your hands," he said, blocking her line of sight to the altar.

Unable to look up at the frail and impotent little creature that continued to protest with its lungs and body, Penthesilea stretched out her hands, turning them over so that the palms were face up.

"Great Apollo, we beseech you. I call on the gods to witness this cleansing. For these hands that have bloodied ..."

Priam's voice faded away as Penthesilea's mind became distracted by the sweat that was causing her robe to cling to her skin. She watched the melting fat from the tallow candles run down to pool then set on the cold surface of the altar. All she could hear were her own words, echoing around her mind. *I have killed my sister. I killed Hippolyte. I pray that the gods will wash her blood from my hands, take the images from my mind that haunt me every night and allow me to die a warrior's death. Let me bring honour to her name and to my father and mother and the Amazon women who deserve a true leader.*

The words spoken by Priam and the squealing, were all peripheral. Until the silence came. Followed by the warmth she felt engulf her hands. She woke from her thoughts to see that the piglet had ceased writhing, and a knife glistened in the King's hand. Blood cascaded over her hands, splattering as it hit the stone floor between the cushion and the altar, more ran down her wrists and bloomed on the front of her pale-blue gown, seeping through to her body.

Her heart started pounding, and a searing pain ripped through her as if it were her blood emptying out, not the animal's. There was a terrible drawing feeling, as if the marrow were being sucked from her bones. Where was all this coming from? No blade had touched her skin. She went to say something, to ask, but her tongue was of no use to her. It had grown thick and cumbersome and refused to let her speak.

Her eyes went back to the piglet. There was no sign of life. Its body was limp, its eyes glazed as if covered by a layer of thinnest gossamer. Priam's head was still lifted towards the heavens and he continued to mutter words of reverence. How was it possible that so much blood could come from such a small creature? The gush gradually became a drip that finally ceased.

Without a word, Priam lifted the limp creature and placed it on the altar.

"Queen Penthesilea."

He gestured for her to stand. As she did so, the already congealing red liquid fell from her hands and over her feet. The dead piglet now lay with its eyes closed. Beside it, a bowl had been filled with hot water, although she did not recall seeing it happen. Petals floated on the surface and the scent of lavender and rose oil drifted with the steam.

Priam stepped back, indicating for her to move to the bowl

and wash her hands. She hesitated. The blood had set in the ridges of her knuckles and was under every fingernail. It had stained every inch of her hands and forearms. It would take more than this to remove it.

"It is time you were cleansed," Priam softly encouraged.

With deep apprehension, she plunged her hands into the bowl. The feeling of relief was instant. The warmth of the water soaked into her fingers and then flowed to the rest of her body, as the scent of the oils relaxed the tension in her chest and she found herself breathing calmly.

"It is done," Priam said.

She frowned. The water had indeed turned red, but she had fought in enough battles to know that blood like this would need to be scrubbed away, or else it would dry in every crease and leave a crimson web on her skin.

"It is done," Priam repeated, with more emphasis. "See for yourself."

Penthesilea slowly withdrew her hands from the water and gasped at what she saw.

Not a drop of blood remained on her skin or beneath her nails. In fact, parts of her that had not even touched the water were now clean. It was all gone. What Priam had said was true.

She was purified.

CHAPTER 53

A servant brought her a towel and led her out of the temple. She could not stop staring at her hands, still unable to believe how clean they were. After some of their most important sacrifices, the blood of horses had caked her skin to her elbows and she had known the stains to remain visible for days. And yet now, there was nothing. It was, without doubt, a gift from the gods.

Unfortunately, Hecuba's robe was ruined. A momentary feeling of guilt turned to one of elation. A dress was easily replaceable. It was a problem that had a solution, a burden that could be lifted almost as quickly as it had descended. And that other guilt, the awful spectre that had shadowed her day and night, its presence had gone. She had been cleansed.

"A bath has been prepared for you, your Highness," the servant girl said as they entered the chamber that she had dressed in. "And the Queen has placed fresh clothes in your room for you to wear at dinner."

"I will not be joining them for dinner," she automatically replied.

It was the response she always offered when asked to stay. But now she realised, with sudden embarrassment, that this was not the same situation. The girl stood, confused and unsure how to respond.

"My apologies," she said, shaking her head. "What I meant to say is that I will require time to bathe before I can join them. Please tell the King and Queen I am grateful for their invitation and will join them shortly."

More satisfied by this answer, but still wearing an expression of wariness, the servant nodded before withdrawing.

Another selection of petals and herbs had been added to the bath. Curls of orange peel floated on the surface as Penthesilea submerged herself in the delicious warm water. It had been years since she had last experienced such luxury. More than seven, for certain. A sense of peace and calm came over her as she closed her eyes and inhaled the fragrant steam. She could feel the change in her. She was cleansed.

"Thank you, Sister," she said to the air. For she knew that even with the gods' good graces, Hippolyte must have played a part in the ritual. She would make her sister proud of her again. She would make all the Amazons proud.

Two more servants appeared to help her dress for dinner in a style that she had never before adopted. Her hair was adorned with flowers, and she was offered a choice of gold necklaces to wear, embedded with jade, garnets or amber.

"Gifts from Queen Hecuba and Prince Hector," she was told.

Her immediate inclination was to refuse. She had not come for gifts. If anything, she should have been the one bestowing every bounty she could upon them. But she knew that acceptance was often the greatest form of gratitude, and so she chose the one that bore the garnets, somehow convinced that this had been Hector's choice.

While she had no doubt that the servants had arranged her clothes and hair in the most suitable fashion, she was hit by a wave of self-consciousness as she approached the dining hall, which deepened as she entered it. Every head, including those of the King and Queen and their children, turned to look at her. She could feel her cheeks turning pink. Had she not, that very morning, held the gaze of over a dozen men outside the walls of the city? But this was different, of course. Then, she had been seated on her horse, armed and dressed for war. Here, she was exposed, in every sense of the word.

In the quiet of the room, a chair scraped against the floor as young Hector left his place beside his father and rushed to her.

"You are beautiful," he said, seemingly astonished. "And you chose my necklace."

"It is true."

Queen Hecuba had moved far more gracefully from the table than her son. She took Penthesilea's hands.

"You do, indeed, put the rest of us to shame. Now come, sit, and tell me what you wish to eat."

She was seated between the Queen and Prince Hector, whose loquacity had not faded even a fraction.

"You wield an axe in battle, don't you?" he questioned her. "Is that so you can strike down more than one enemy with a single blow?"

"I do, and it is."

"And you can stand on your horse when you gallop?"

"I can."

"What of firing your bow with your feet? I have heard that some of your women can stand upon their hands and loose an arrow using only the strength of their toes."

"I cannot do that," she said.

The boy's face fell, momentarily, before she continued, "But my sister, Antiope, was most skilled at that particular trick."

The spark reignited and his questioning continued.

At several points in the evening, Hecuba had to go to the aid of one or more of her young daughters, leaving Priam to take charge of rocking their baby son, Paris. He would dip his finger in the wine and hold it to the infant's lips. Behind all the grandeur and opulence, they were, Penthesilea saw, quite like a normal family.

"Tomorrow will you teach me to use a shield? I want to try and defend myself from you, like you did earlier. Can we do that?"

Priam placed a hand on his son's shoulder.

"The Queen cannot stay, Hector. She has her own kingdom to run, remember?"

Disappointment fell like a shadow across the boy's face, although he held his disappointment in far better this time than in the courtyard.

"I am sure I can spend a little time with you before I have to leave. Provided you do not mind rising at dawn."

"I can wake earlier," Hector answered, with enthusiasm.

"Dawn will suffice," she said, smiling.

When she retired, a little later, Hecuba walked her back to her room.

"There will be servants on duty if you need anything," she said. "Or if you would feel more comfortable leaving now, please do not feel you must stay. I can tell Hector that you were called away to fight. He will understand that."

"I am looking forward to training with him again," Penthesilea replied, finding more truth in her words than she had expected. "And I am grateful to you and your husband for your hospitality. For everything you have done for me."

"We Anatolians must be strong together, must we not?"

Once again, Hecuba took her hands in her own, and this time, Penthesilea did not flinch but rather allowed her skin to absorb their warmth.

"I know that nothing can ever replace what you have lost, but please, if you ever need to, then think of me as a sister, or at the very least a good friend. I hope you will do that?"

A lump formed in Penthesilea's throat.

"Thank you," she said. "I will."

She slept more soundly that night than she could recall doing for years. The nightmares had gone and her mind was filled with sweet dreams in which she and her sisters rode victorious together again, over the steppes. And then she felt the rough sand of the Black Sea under her feet as she walked to the water to bathe and let the waves lap over her.

When she awoke, the feeling of peace remained with her. She stretched out, easing the muscles in her neck and back, as the chorus of birds confirmed that it was well past dawn. Noting that another of Hecuba's beautiful robes had been draped across a chair, she gathered her own clothes: her tunic and trousers. After donning her full armour, she made her way through the maze of corridors that led to Hector's training ground.

The Prince was there alone, practising drills with his shield, just as he had seen her do the day before, ducking down to his knees then rolling over and springing back up with speed, to avoid an invisible strike.

"You should move your left foot back a fraction when you do that," Penthesilea said. The boy stopped mid-motion, a wide grin spreading on his face.

"I thought you had left. Mother said you might need to depart for a battle in the night."

"I will have to go very soon," she said. "But first let me see how you are defending yourself with that left arm again. It looked a little weak to me, compared to your right."

The boy soaked up her words like a sponge, absorbing every piece of advice she offered him, never needing to hear an instruction twice. His speed was phenomenal, as was the accuracy. But as much as she would have liked to stay longer, she also wanted to leave before the sun grew too strong. The quickest way back to Pontus was to cross the desert, but even skirting around it, as she intended to, meant traversing arid land where water would be hard to come by.

She walked with Hector and King Priam to the great gates of the citadel. When they reached them, the guard who had stopped her the day before was waiting with her quiver of arrows and axe. When she had fixed the axe to the side of her horse, she held out the quiver to Prince Hector.

"Here," she said. "Take it."

"You mean that?"

"I do."

With an air of disbelief, he took it from her and ran his hand over the leather, before pinching a feathered arrow with his fingertips.

"Do you see this, Father? Do you? These are the arrows of the Amazon Queen, herself. With them I will be invincible."

"I think it requires a strong archer and not just a strong arrow, to be invincible," King Priam replied, diplomatically.

"Then I shall practise all day. All day and all night."

"I know you will, my son."

With Hector now absorbed with his new weapons, Penthesilea turned to the King.

"I have so much to thank you for," she said.

"You have my blessings. As I said, if ever I were in need, I am certain you would come to help me."

"I would. You have my word."

"Which is all a king could ever ask for."

As she rode slowly away from Troy, Penthesilea found a pleasure once again in simple things, that had been missing for so long. The sound of the wind in the trees. The birds of prey, circling their targets high in the clear sky. Even the green of the grass and the trees was more vibrant. None of these things had meant anything to her since Hippolyte's death. Maybe even before that. Perhaps since her sister had been abducted by Theseus.

And when she reached Pontus, and the citadel appeared on the horizon, she allowed the wind to whip at her tunic and sting her bare skin. She drew in a breath that filled her lungs and held it there until she felt herself quiver.

This was her home. This was Themiscyra. And she would make it great again.

PART VI

CHAPTER 54

*F*or years they worked, training young women who had only been children at the time of the battle of Athens, passing on their skills and lifestyle so that they might never be stolen by the capriciousness of time. They traded what they could for new horses, which they bred and rode as soon as their spines were strong enough, while their mothers were milked to make cheese, which they ate salted and covered with a scattering of nuts. In their forges, they made weapons of the highest quality.

They trained, they farmed, they told each other stories, spending the nights around fires with their youngest girls, recounting all the tales they could recall of Ares and Otrera, of Queen Hippolyte and Princess Antiope. They told them of their battles, of their hunts, of the laughter they had shared together. The same stories were repeated nightly and often by Penthesilea herself. Her dream was that each girl should be able to recount the lives of their ancestors. It would be a way to honour her sisters, which she hoped would be passed down from generation to generation, ensuring the Amazons' permanent place in history.

Yet new births were infrequent, and those mothers who had been lucky enough to bring forth a daughter often chose the nomadic way of life, rather than returning to Themiscyra.

"They are still training them in our ways," Melanippe assured her. "They are still turning young girls into warriors. But this place holds too many memories for them. There are too many shadows lurking within these walls. Perhaps, when there are more of us, they will return."

"Perhaps," Penthesilea replied, understanding all too well how the hallways that had once resonated with laughter now seemed to feel suffocating.

She, herself, had borne no children since before Hippolyte left. It was true, she was far older now than when she had first gone to lie with the Gargareans, but there were women of a greater age who were still able to carry children. Two years after her return from Troy, Cletes fell pregnant. Celebration was in the air, tentative but hopeful. But the baby was lost. It would have been a girl.

Still, they carried on. With more than fifty strong women in Themiscyra, and as many again out on the steppes who could be called upon to ride to the battlefield, they were able to ensure that their supplies never ran empty, and on the rare occasions that they found themselves in need, they were able to trade. The land continued to supply their requirements, just as it had always done, but with their depleted numbers it proved impossible to harvest all they produced each season, and much rotted in the fields or on the vine, a feast for the ants.

The once grand buildings of Themiscyra were beginning to crumble into disrepair and some areas were left to the elements. The women no longer had any need for the huge dining halls or the vast arenas where they had once watched one another spar and train. Vines had taken hold of some of the smaller turrets, smothering the windows and covering the stone with a curtain of green.

They stayed in the smaller one-and-two-room buildings that were easier to maintain, although Penthesilea promised herself one day, when their numbers returned, they would rebuild the rest of the citadel. Bigger than ever.

Despite all the space now available to them, she and Cletes would often sleep out on the steppes in the warmer weather, under nothing but a thin canopy of fabric, or even less. On such occasions, they might have been out hunting for the day, travelling too far south to return within the hours of daylight. Sometimes, in Themiscyra, Penthesilea woke in the night to find sweat drenching her skin and her breath quickening. It felt as though the walls were closing in. Cletes would rise with her and suggest a walk along the beach to watch the moon reflecting on the water.

At times they would meet with the nomadic women, to watch them train their daughters, often with hawks. They filled their time and their minds and the years slipped by, almost imperceptibly.

Only when the first strands of grey appeared in her hair did Penthesilea realise how much time had passed since her youth.

"Pluck them out!' she had insisted to Cletes, whose hair had retained the same ebony hue throughout the years, the effects of age seemingly applying no more to her than to a goddess.

"I like it. I think it looks regal."

"I was a Queen long before my hair turned silver," she countered.

This was a physical sign. Soon others would follow. Stiffness in her limbs, lethargy in her mind. How long after the first grey hair did one become incapable of ruling? Two decades? Three? She knew these thoughts were folly, yet they plagued her nonetheless. Laughing, Cletes reached up and plucked the offending strand, causing a sharp sting.

Penthesilea often thought about herself and Hippolyte in their younger years, when they had seen the miracle of life in everything from the rising of the sun to the birth of a new foal. They used to feel the invincibility of youth when they would ride in the shallows of the Black Sea, the waves crashing around their steeds, the briny taste of the spray filling their nostrils. The taste of pure, unadulterated happiness. There were other memories, of course. Ones she tried to suppress, for fear they would allow the darkness to seep out from the corners of her mind and consume her once again. When such images did recur, she forced her thoughts, instead, to the legacy that her sister had left behind. And not just the Amazons, but Hippolytus, too.

At night, lying next to Cletes and feeling her warm breath on her face, Penthesilea would also think of Hippolytus. Where he might be. What aspirations he had. Whether she would recognise him if she saw him in a busy agora or in the heat of a battle. He would be a young man now, and no doubt Theseus would be considering his need of a wife or, rather, his own need to build more alliances. Then again, perhaps this would not be the case. It was rumoured that Theseus' young wife, Phaedra, had borne him sons, too, although, if the tales on the breeze were to be believed, they were insipid and sickly.

As well as thoughts of her nephew, images of Antiope took root in her mind. She could see her sister, hair billowing, as she galloped through the long grass. And in the beating of the waves, she could hear her euphonious laughter and the harsher, more strident tone that she had employed on the battlefield. She thought of her sisters constantly. And, occasionally, she thought of Priam.

During those first few months back in Pontus, she often considered the Trojan king and the gift he had granted her so unselfishly. Each moment of joy she experienced, she knew she owed to his grace. Each night with Cletes, was a reminder of his kindness to her. She also thought of the boy, Hector, a man as the years went by, whose name was now spoken of in the same breath as those of herself and her sisters. And although her ruminations on the men of Troy faded over the years, they returned with a vengeance when news of war arrived.

Troy and King Priam found themselves under siege from King Agamemnon of Mycenae, who had rallied the combined might of Greece on behalf of his brother, King Menelaus. Despite his wealth and standing, Menelaus had been powerless to stop his wife, Helen, leaving Sparta with Hector's younger brother, Paris. Some claimed that it had been her choice, that she had been overcome with passion and lust at the sight of the young hero, who must have seemed all the more attractive when compared with the bloated brute that her husband had become. Others insisted that was not the case, that it was Paris who had become so enamoured with Helen that he had snatched her away in the night. It was a story that bore echoes all too uncomfortably familiar for Penthesilea. Either way, the outcome was the same.

A thousand ships. That was what she had heard. A thousand ships had set sail for those Trojan sands, to declare war on the gracious King Priam.

"The Greeks cannot get into the city."

All the women she spoke to offered the same opinion on the matter, regardless of whether they had seen Troy with their own eyes or not.

"The walls are impenetrable. The Trojans will win. There is no way they can be defeated."

She took their words at face value, trying to find comfort in them, yet all the while assailed by apprehension. She felt something in the air, like a distant storm that, for now, was being kept at bay by a favourable wind, but would eventually come crashing down on them.

From everywhere came rumours of Achilles, the young warrior, both undefeated, and so they said, undefeatable. Upon hearing these, Penthesilea would scoff, for she had learnt from bitter experience that no man or woman was invincible. Besides, for every tale of Achilles' prowess, there was another of Hector's. He was now the leader of the Trojan army, a prince known for his justice as much as his fighting ability, but one who was as skilful with a sword as any man ever seen in Anatolia. This made her smile to herself as she recalled their brief sparring session. She wondered if he ever thought of her when he sent an arrow flying or jabbed his spear into someone's breast.

"We should go and help," she said one evening to Melanippe.

They were dining out by the sea, feasting on fish caught by one of the youngest girls with her spear and then cooked on a small campfire.

"It was my arrangement with Priam, as you may recall. That I should offer him aid if ever he needed it."

"I thought the arrangement was that if they were ever in such dire straits that they were worried for their safety, then you should go. No one has any real concerns for Troy. Everyone knows of Priam's supremacy. They have held the city for more than five years now, while the Greeks camp outside their walls in squalor on the sand, miles from their homes and kingdoms which are probably being usurped even as they fight another man's war. Priam could hold Troy for another fifty years, Sister, believe me."

Penthesilea pressed her lips together. She pulled more white meat from the bones, before bringing it to her mouth. Then hesitated.

"I have heard tell of a prophecy, Sister. One given by the great seer, Calchas, who said that the war will last for ten years. Do you think that is possible? That it really could continue for so long?"

"If the siege continues in the same manner, then why would it not be possible? The Trojans have food within their walls and the Greeks receive their supplies by ship. Do you see?"

She did. She thought exactly the same thing.

Five more years, but then who would win?

"We should wait," Melanippe said, resting her hand on her knee. "If they truly need us, then we will talk of this again. For now, you have your own women here to think of."

And Penthesilea agreed.

The years passed. The sun rose and set; the moon waxed and waned. More children were born to the Amazons, including, at last, a daughter to Cletes. Other women bore several sons who were returned to their fathers. The horses grew so great in number that most were left to roam. They could often be seen, standing majestically in their herds, the morning mist rising around them. Only a fraction were broken in for riding.

Patience was what was needed, Penthesilea now realised. If the Amazons were ever to return to their former strength, it would not be yet. Perhaps not even in her lifetime. But perhaps in that of Cletes' child, Antianeira, whom she loved more than she could ever have imagined. Each day spent with her helped her understand Hippolyte's reluctance to leave Hippolytus. If only she had been blessed with this wisdom all those years ago.

News of the Trojan war reached them like scattered leaves on a breeze. It seemed there was dissent in the Greek camps, not only amongst the soldiers but also between the leaders, Achilles and Agamemnon, a feud galvanised by the plague which Apollo had sent upon them.

"Perhaps the Greeks will give up," Cletes said. "They have lost many men."

Penthesilea did not share her optimism.

"If they were going to do that, they would have gone already. Agamemnon is tenacious, he will not retreat after waiting so long. He will not leave without a victory, for one side or another."

Cletes nodded and said no more.

It was in the ninth year of the siege of Troy that Penthesilea spoke about it again. Dusk was settling on the steppes, bringing with it a hazy warmth that cloaked the land. They were seated on the crumbling steps of what had once been their arena. The distant gentle lapping of the sea could be heard faintly as they stitched patterns into new trousers. But while Melanippe's mind was lost in the task and the rhythmic motion of her needle, Penthesilea's could not rest. Placing the leather down on her lap, she lifted her head.

"I want us to go to Troy," she said. "We have stood on the side-lines long enough. The war is predicted to end soon, and this Achilles is still strong. I believe we may be the key to ending it, Sister, and doing so in favour of the Trojans. We should leave. Soon. I will tell the women to ready the horses tomorrow."

Given that she was Queen, she expected Melanippe's immediate agreement, but instead, her sister frowned.

"I do not think we should interfere," she replied.

Penthesilea flinched as if she had been slapped.

"Not interfere? It is a battle. Interfering in battles is what we do. It is our very calling."

"Small battles, yes. Small wars. Not ones of this size. We have seen before that we can be beaten and this army is bigger than the one in Athens was. Countless times bigger. And look at our own numbers now. If we join the Trojans and things do not go their way, then it would be the end of us. We would never be able to regain our strength."

A fierce heat started to rise within the Queen.

"Are you truly serious? You would run from a fight? One that I am obliged to support? Without Priam, who knows where I would be? I would certainly not be here, within the walls of Themiscyra. You and I both know that."

"So we must all pay the price for what you did?" Melanippe demanded. "This obligation is yours and yours alone. If you had not gone to Priam, then we would have continued as we were."

The heat was spreading out of control.

"Was it not you who said I should go to him?"

"Yes, for your purification. To aid you. Not to damage what little remains of us. I know how this sounds, Sister, I do. And I wish I could find an easier way to say this, but the fact remains that you promised you would ride into battle to aid Troy and Priam should he need it. You did not promise us. You did not promise the Amazons, and our women should not be held accountable for your bad decisions. We cannot win this fight. This will be Athens all over again, but this time, none of us will return!"

CHAPTER 55

*R*age was consuming her. Her fingers flexed into claws and twitched, as if they needed to fire an arrow or swing an axe. She had stormed away from Melanippe, astounded by her stubbornness. How many insults had she spewed at her supposedly with the voice of reasonable concern? Had she not implied that Penthesilea's presence in Pontus was not required? That the women would have done perfectly well without her? That her purification had brought no benefit to the Amazons? She was their queen, not Melanippe. Perhaps the years of being left to rule had gone to her head. Did she think that, by having Penthesilea ride out alone to Troy's aid, she might resume the role of queen and fight only when necessary or preferably not at all? Did she not see that under such a rule, the name *Amazon* and the fear that it invoked would slip into memory?

No, it could not be. She would not see that happen. She would gather all the women together, including the nomads and all those girls who had yet to draw their first blood and proclaim themselves true Amazons. She would call them all to her, and they would fight under her command.

She paced outside the citadel that night, knowing Cletes would lie awake without her by her side, yet unable to bring herself inside the walls where her sister slept. She finally took her bow out onto the steppes, to where an old hide was pinned to the trunk of a long-dead tree. It was used as a target for the younger children. By daylight, you could see that hundreds of tears had reduced the pelt to mere strips of leather. But at night it stood as a dark shadow, in front of the darker ones of the swaying trees.

The night was cold. Without pausing, the Queen raised her weapon and emptied an entire quiver into the target, each arrow a fraction higher than the last, knowing even without looking, that she had created a vertical line of feathers. The women would come with her to Troy.

By the time she retreated to her chamber, the moon was a fading disc, slowly descending in the wake of Selene's chariot, and the stars were disappearing. It would soon be morning, and she had still not slept.

"I take it your discussion with Melanippe did not go well," Cletes said, unable to stifle a yawn as she sat up in bed.

Penthesilea dropped down beside her, running her tongue along her teeth, trying to hold back the words that wanted to free themselves from her lips.

"She does not think it would be right for me to lead the Amazons to Troy's aid. She does not believe it would be to our benefit or that we are under any obligation to King Priam to do so."

Cletes' dark eyes glimmered in the pale light,

"You must try to understand her views," she said, as gently as she could.

Penthesilea leapt to feet. Her blood, that had only recently cooled, once again pumped with angry fervour.

"Surely you do not side with her? You think she is right?"

"Penthesilea, my love, I did not say that."

"You said I should understand her viewpoint."

"Because she does have a valid point. Our numbers are small. Dangerously so. She does not wish to see the legacy of her father and her sisters wiped out."

"And you believe that I do?"

"Of course not. And neither does she. But surely you can understand her fear? The battle would be far greater than in Athens, with more men against us and fewer Amazons to challenge them. And there, we were fighting to restore the honour of our stolen queen. In this situation, we are not the aggrieved party."

Penthesilea snorted, but Cletes continued.

"Consider, before Athens, when did we ever ride out with all of our good women? Never. There would always be those who remained behind to defend Themiscyra and the children and those too old or injured to fight."

"But there are none who need defending now," Penthesilea countered.

"Exactly."

Melanippe's disagreement was one thing, but Cletes? Penthesilea was the Queen and she wanted to do this. Surely that should be enough reason? Cletes found her arm and brushed it gently with her fingers.

"I understand that you owe Priam for the life he returned to you," she said. "But you are Queen, and you know that it cannot be your desires alone that must be considered here. Your women look up to you and rely on you to make the right decisions for them and their children."

She was in turmoil. Her head throbbed and her stomach was churning. She wanted this so badly, but they were both right. It was not what the Amazons needed.

"Then what should I do?" she asked, returning to sit beside Cletes. "How can I do this? I must go to help Troy."

"I know. And I am certain that there will be those who will wish to accompany you. So gather everyone together and ask them. Do not command them. Thank the ones who offer to fight with you, but rejoice in private. And show no animosity or ill will towards the others. Tell them you understand and accept their decision."

This was a fair solution. Hippolyte had never forced a woman to fight if they did not feel able to. Yet she was still troubled.

"And if no one wants to ride with me?" she asked.

"Then you and I will go into battle at Troy, side by side," Cletes replied and placed a kiss on her forehead.

"And what of Antianeira? What if neither of us returns?"

"Then she will tell our stories, just as we have taught her to do."

It was decided. Penthesilea sent word the next day that all the nomads and tribeswomen were to return to the steppes to hear their Queen speak. And they were to bring their weapons, for she had a request.

On the day when it appeared that all who could answer the call had arrived, neither Penthesilea's heart nor feet would cease their skittish movements. She muttered to herself and wrung her hands as she paced back and forth,

"We leave tomorrow morning. It does not matter if it is with fifty or just the two of us; we leave then," Penthesilea said to Cletes, although it was for her own benefit as much as anything.

Cletes nodded.

"As you wish, my love."

Cletes' loyalty and support were overshadowed by the continuing tension between the Queen and Melanippe. The animosity was so intense, they would start bickering as soon as they caught sight of each other. Penthesilea knew she would not be able to look her sister in the eye when the time came to address the women, for fear of what she might say.

Dressed in full war attire and seated on a chestnut mare, she fastened her zoster around her waist and slid her knives and sword into it. She positioned her quiver so that it lay flush to her thigh and strapped her bow to her back and her axe to the side of her horse.

"Penthesilea, it is time," Cletes said.

She felt both determination and sadness as she rode into what had once been their magnificent arena. Over a hundred women were waiting there. Some of them were girls so young that, standing, they would not have reached the flanks of the horses upon which they sat. Others were so old that their skin, loose and paper-thin, hung in folds down their faces and necks. A hundred women, where once there had been thousands.

"Amazons," she called out to them. "Thank you for coming here to me. I expect that many of you will know why you are here."

Murmurs drifted around, but she did not stop to listen closely enough to pick out any words.

"As we are all aware, a war has been raging in Troy for nearly ten years. The Grecians have gathered in huge numbers and thrown all their might at the great stone wall of the city, to no avail. They have attempted to starve the people into submission. That too has failed and still they stand strong. And yet, in my heart of hearts, I feel that they need our help and that we are to be the decisive element that will allow Prince Hector and King Priam to claim victory over these invaders."

The women studied her silently, knowing that there was more to come.

"You may or may not know that I have sworn my allegiance to King Priam. He helped me at a time when my life was in complete and utter darkness. He saved me, in fact. And although he could have demanded anything of me in return, either to increase his wealth or his standing, he asked for nothing. He gave his help willingly and freely.

"I tell you, as a queen, as *your* Queen, that he is a good and honourable man, who cares not only for the family he loves but also for his citizens. And if his son, Hector, has turned out to be half the man and warrior we have heard tell of, then they will be well commanded. But that does not mean they do not need our help. And I have a personal obligation to go to their aid and fight for them, just as I would do for you.

"Even though I am your Queen, I will not order you to join me in this venture. But," she paused for a moment, "I will humbly ask if there are any women here who would travel with me to Troy. Who would ride and face the Grecians alongside me? I ask if any will be willing to defend a city respected by my father, Ares, God of War. I cannot promise that you will return. But still ... will anyone come and fight beside me?"

Her question hung in the air like crystallised breath on a winter's day. Horses tugged against their riders and looks were exchanged. Many eyes were averted. Girls who had never fought before and those who remembered, all too vividly, how close they had come to losing their lives in Athens.

From the back of the arena, a single voice called out to her.

"I will ride with you, my Queen!"

Cletes had dressed in her war clothes, a cap strapped to her head and boots laced up to her knee. She looked nearly twenty years younger, Penthesilea thought, like the girl she had fallen for all those decades ago. Despite her dire situation, she could not help but feel a fresh blossoming of the deepest love within her.

"You have my sword, too," said an older woman, Thermodosa, who stepped forward.

"And you have my bow."

Amina, the next to speak, had been just a girl when they had ridden to Athens. Too young to fight, she had stayed behind with the other children. Now, she was a fully grown Amazon woman, ready to fight beside a queen who had barely ruled her.

"Thank you," Penthesilea replied

"I will ride with you, too."

Evandre drove her horse forward. She had been injured in Athens. It had been only her second battle, but unlike so many, it was not her last. She had been strong then. And she looked even stronger now.

In the end, more than thirty women agreed to ride with their queen. Melanippe was not among them.

"I feel no ill will towards you," Penthesilea told her, finding her words truer than she had anticipated. "I understand, Sister. Your place is here, with those who remain."

Melanippe lifted her head, tears shining in her eyes.

"If you see our father, give him my blessings."

"I will."

The women moved among one another, offering hugs of farewell and gifting weapons. Several young girls looked longingly at Penthesilea, including her own beloved Antianeira, wishing they could go, too. During her first reign as queen, she would have allowed them the chance to test themselves and prove their worth. But not now. Not anymore.

"My Queen, may I say something?"

Penthesilea turned and found Klonie standing there. The same Klonie who had ridden with her to Athens all those years ago, when she had first searched for Hippolyte, and then a second time, for the battle with Theseus. And now here she was, standing only a little less tall, wishing to go with her to what might prove their greatest battle ever.

"Of course. Please. What is on your mind?"

She drew in a deep breath through her nose, which warned Penthesilea that she was unlikely to be happy with what she was about to hear.

"The Grecians, they are on the shore? All along the beach?"

"With their numbers so great, there is likely to be barely an inch of sand to spare," she replied.

Klonie nodded, taking a moment longer before she spoke again.

"Then we may find it difficult to penetrate their army. If we ride across land from Anatolia, we will arrive facing their greatest line of defence, close to the citadel."

"What other option is there?"

She understood what the woman was saying. If the Greek soldiers were arrayed close to the wall, they would have to use all their energy fighting through them to reach the gates of Troy, from where they could offer the most protection to Priam.

"We could take a boat. That way, we would arrive behind the army and surprise them in their camps with an attack from there. We could strike at their generals and cause havoc moving quickly before their numbers can overwhelm us. We need not sail far on the ship, just from Hellespont. They would not suspect it was us, for we have never been known to travel by water before."

Unease rippled through Penthesilea. Journeying by sea was not the Amazon way. In truth, it unnerved her. Their lives were lived on soil not water. In addition, the sea was Poseidon's realm, and he was Theseus' father. That alone was enough to fill her with foreboding.

"I cannot ... this battle will be hard enough. What if something goes wrong?"

"Such as?" Klonie countered. "It would only be a small vessel. I have made several such trips over the years. I am certain that, for the right price, I will be able to find a captain who will take us."

"Small ships succumb more easily to the swell of the sea or are blown off course. No. I understand what you are saying but no."

The women, who had gathered around them, stayed silent, as Klonie's head bowed in disappointment.

"What if we divide our numbers?" Cletes said, breathing new life back into the conversation. "We are already too few to meet the Greeks head on, if we are going to rely on fast strategical strikes then maybe attacking in two groups on two fronts might help us be more effective. My Queen, you could lead the women who would prefer to travel by land, and I take the rest and finish the journey by boat?"

The look that then passed between Cletes and Penthesilea was not one of an Amazon and her Queen, but of the dearest of friends and so much more. This was how they had always communicated, and in that instant, no one else's opinion mattered more to her.

"You believe it will work?" Penthesilea asked.

"I do. I think it a wise way to proceed."

Cletes had been right about calling the women together and speaking to them. She had been right about going to seek purification. Almost every good decision Penthesilea had made had involved her. It would be arrogant to ignore such a coincidence.

"Then that is what we shall do," she said. "We will split up. Those who wish to ride to Troy on horseback, I will lead. The rest of you will go with Cletes and Klonie, along with our supplies and extra weapons."

The women seemed pleased with this arrangement and nodded in agreement.

CHAPTER 56

In the end, only twelve women rode out with Penthesilea. There was a strong wind at their backs, as if the gods themselves were willing them on and blessing their journey. The morning sky was filled with light coral clouds and there was no hint of rain on the horizon. They rode silently; there was no need for words.

It was not until they had been travelling for some time and a light sweat glowed on her horse's coat, that Penthesilea realised she had not turned around for a final glimpse of Themiscyra before it disappeared from view. She had not looked back lovingly on her home and uttered a silent prayer to the gods to keep all who remained in its walls safe. But she would see it again. Her father would ensure it.

When they reached the Sea of Marmara, they rested their horses, checked their weapons and ate. There were stalls set up along the roadside, and they bought from these roasted chest-nuts and fish on skewers, cooked over hot coals until the skin bubbled and blackened. Their hunger abated, they found a suitable place to sleep and gather their strength. Cletes and the others would have left Pontus by now. They had stayed a little longer in Themiscyra, assembling provisions and loading them on their horses. Gods willing, they would arrive at almost the same time.

As the women slept soundlessly, fingers curled around their daggers, their animals tore at the long grass. Penthesilea, who had remained awake on guard, noticed a group of men standing nearby, huddled together, their hands moving rapidly as they spoke. She had seen enough of the world to recognise when war was being discussed, and the noises they made only confirmed her suspicions. She pushed herself off the ground and went across to them.

"You," she said, looking at the one who had been the most animated. "You have news from Troy?"

He blanched at the sight of the Queen and stepped back. Only her eyes and lips were visible beneath her metal helmet. These were less comfortable that their usual leather caps, but they had chosen them for their strength.

The man stuttered, struggling over the same syllable several times before managing something coherent.

"Y ... y ... yes. Yes. There is news. They are saying that Hector has done it. He has killed the warrior, Achilles. The Greeks cannot possibly win without him. Now it will soon be over."

A long low whistle came from Penthesilea's lips, as an image of Hector the boy formed in her mind. He had killed Achilles, arguably the greatest warrior the Greeks had ever known. He would become part of history now, never to be forgotten. There would be celebrations behind those mighty walls tonight. Perhaps the enemy ships were already leaving.

Offering the man no thanks, she immediately returned to her women.

"Come," she said. "Ready your horses. We should leave. We still have another day's ride ahead of us. We will camp on the mountains behind Troy. You can rest then, before we attack at first light."

The closer they came to their destination, the thicker a sense of anticipation hung in the air. Excitement radiated from each and every one of them, Penthesilea included. Yes, there were only thirteen of them, but in truth, these were the strongest women Penthesilea still had at her disposal. They were the ones she would have chosen to ride with her. She had grown up with several of them and could anticipate their thoughts, as they could hers, in the heat of battle. The younger ones had her same spirit and fervour. Even tired, they could defeat hundreds of strong able men, fresh to the fight. And the Greeks were hardly that. Ten years away from home, waging war, would have taken its toll on them, the more so after the sickening news of Achille's defeat. They would slice through them, one by one. They may be few in number, but their arrival would be the final boost the Trojans needed to push the Greeks back once and for all.

Three days after leaving Pontus and with an amber-tinged sky above them, they crested the final hill that brought Troy into view and drew to a sudden halt. Gasps came from her women in quick succession, and the Queen had to stifle her own astonishment. She had seen the gargantuan structures that formed the walls and citadel of Troy before, but never could she have imagined the sight down on the shoreline. There was row upon row of triremes, like the Heracles had travelled in to Themiscyra, all those years ago. Their number was so great, their sails had formed a new horizon which stretched as far as the eye could see to the north and south, rising and falling as if the sea were breathing and the ships were its skin.

"I have never seen such a sight before," Amina said, with a trembling voice. "Have you my Queen?"

"No, I have not. No one has."

Seeing no obvious lookout points, they slowly walked on, hoping to see weak spots, on land and sea, from which they could cause the most damage to the Greek army.

As they drew closer to the city, they became aware of an affray at the great gates.

"Are they fighting?" Polemusa asked.

The Queen strained her eyes to see more clearly, but it was too far away to make out. Certainly, noises could be heard echoing off the walls, but they did not seem like the sounds of battle. She knew those well enough; she had ridden or run into such situations hundreds of times, albeit against a lesser foe, but it had always been accompanied by the sonorous clang of metal, as sword struck shield. Where was that sound now? No, this was something different.

It was the sound of cheering.

"We must get closer," she called to the women, spurring her horse into a gallop. "If there is a battle beginning, we should strike now."

"What about our plan to wait for the others?"

"If we have already engaged them, then when Cletes and the other women arrive they will have a better chance of catching them off guard."

Anticipation had been replaced by a powerful surge of energy that drove her onwards. Her horse's hooves beat hard on the ground, more compelling than any war drum had ever been. The women kept pace at her side. They were only thirteen and yet they were an army.

They rode to a rocky outcrop, from where they could see the whole length of the beach. Men were gathered a short distance in front of the city gates, but as she had expected, they were not fighting. They were watching something. Dust spiralled up into the air, masking whatever it was that held their attention. Was someone trying to catch a stray horse? No. Only a chariot could raise that much dust. An announcement by the king, perhaps?

"We need to get even closer," she said. "I must know what is happening."

But ahead of them, the only way forward was via what was left of a narrow cliff path. It had become weathered by the relentless pounding of waves during storms at high tide. The remaining stones were decorated with seaweed and shone green with algae. It was too dangerous, a disaster in the waiting. Not even their brave horses could go this way.

Frustration boiled over in Penthesilea as she searched the landscape for an alternative route, but there was nothing. Yet they were so close. The tents of the Greeks, no doubt full of fat, bearded kings tending their gout, were such a short distance away.

"Wait here," she said and dropped to the ground.

Axe in hand, she jumped down onto a ledge, where she landed surely enough, only to take another step and have her foot skid on the slime. In less than a heartbeat, she had righted herself, but now she realised how exposed she was. If any Grecian emerged from his tent and looked up, he would see her there on the cliff face, as helpless as she had ever been.

She dug her axe into a large rock at her feet and, using it as an anchor, scrambled down the loose stones to the next ledge. Repeating this action, she slowly descended, until she reached the welcome relief of solid ground. She then moved stealthily along the beach, her footsteps muffled by the soft sand.

The leather-clad tents were densely packed. Men were

walking back to them, laughing and slapping each other on the back. They were happy, cheering, talking of wine. She quickly slipped back, observing them from the cover of a huge boulder and waited, for what she was not sure, but was certain she would know it when it came. And come it did.

A man left the group he was with and came towards her position, then began relieving himself against the side of her hiding place. As he emptied his bladder, she slipped behind him and, pressing her knife against his throat, dragged him back and out of sight of his comrades.

"If you scream, I will end you now," she said.

She felt the rise and fall of his Adam's apple, scraping against the edge of her blade and heard his breath rasping as she constricted the air flow to his lungs with her other hand.

"Do you understand?" she hissed.

His head bobbed in the tiniest of nods, and she reduced the pressure on his windpipe by a fraction. Whether in panic or just feeling this was his one chance to escape, he grabbed the wrist holding her knife and pulled it away from him. But as he twisted out of her grip, she tripped him with her foot and he fell forwards into the rocks. In a heartbeat, she was on him and, grabbing a handful of hair, pulled his head back and dug her knife in deep enough to draw blood this time.

"Don't move!" she ordered. "I can run this blade through your vocal cords before you even draw breath to scream."

His whole body was shaking, every muscle in spasm. It was a miracle the Greeks had got this far, she thought, if this was the calibre of their men.

"Tell me," she said, flipping him onto his back. "What was that? The dust we saw. What was it?"

The man spluttered an unintelligible sound and then went into a coughing fit. Silencing him with an elbow to the stomach, she loosened the knife a fraction, and a single word came out. A name.

"Achilles," he said.

She was stunned. Achilles was still alive? It was not uncommon for rumours to become confused as they travelled. But the Sea of Marmara was not far from there. Surely the men she had spoken to couldn't have been so badly mistaken.

"What was he doing?" she asked, increasing the pressure again. "What were people watching? Where was all that dust coming from?"

The man's wheezing had transformed into a shallow sobbing. She felt her hand becoming wet as tears fell from his bearded face. He disgusted her.

"H ... he killed Hector. He was dragging his body around, behind his chariot."

"What?"

Penthesilea's dagger fell away from his neck, although he was at least wise enough not to try to escape again. This made no sense. They were two of the greatest warriors. They would want to prove themselves by fighting on their feet, swords and shields in their hands. No decent man used a chariot, unless it was for the purpose of entertainment.

"He tied him to the chariot," the man said, still whimpering. "Achilles tied him by his feet, and dragged him around, for what he had done to Patroclus. For killing his cousin."

The air froze in her lungs, and she struggled to regain her poise.

"This is a war! Are you are telling me that Achilles did that because Hector had killed a man?"

He nodded.

Rage filled her. To humiliate a warrior after death. The idea was simply unthinkable. And to do it to a man such as Hector!

That sweet little boy, who had thought only of protecting his king and his people, no talk of glory or fame. Who had looked upon her gift of arrows as if it were more precious than every gem in Corinth combined. And Achilles had done that to him.

"That is all I know. I swear to you."

She nodded. He was telling the truth and knew no more. With a flick of her knife, she opened his throat and blood flowed on to the pale sand.

Penthesilea's mind became detached from her body as she numbly scaled the rocks back to her women. They were where she had left them, still learning what they could about the terrain.

"What did you discover?" Amina asked, as she mounted her horse. "What have you learnt of our opponents?"

"I learnt what the gods have called me here to do," she replied. "I am to kill Achilles."

And with that, she pulled on her reins and kicked her steed into a canter.

CHAPTER 57

*T*heir euphoria was long forgotten. It had evaporated like morning mist in the first rays of the sun. What they were facing was no normal foe, but an enemy whose lack of mercy extended to denying human dignity. These were animals, beasts who deserved to be slain and skinned like the Nemean Lion.

They lit no fire that night, for they could not risk drawing attention to themselves, and although it was not cold, Penthesilea found herself longing for the warmth of Cletes beside her. For her gentle touch and soft laugh.

She did not sleep. Instead, she mentally rehearsed her movements, envisioning all the possible ways she might kill Achilles. An arrow in the heart. A spear to the belly. Her axe sweeping through the tendons of his neck. It did not matter how it was achieved, only that it would be she who would do it. No hero defiled a corpse as he had, dragging Hector through the dirt. She could only imagine how the coarse earth must have ripped at his flesh, tearing it from his bones. She would ensure Achilles suffered the same dishonour. Even Theseus, whom she despised, would not have met such a fate at her hands, and she dreamed of his death almost daily. This man's end, she craved.

Early the next morning, they found a less precipitous route down to the beach, where they watched the battle resume. Observing their opponents fighting was not an unusual thing for them to do before joining in. They could note the way they fought and their weaknesses and better devise a plan to bring about their demise. Yet today, Penthesilea did not study the Grecians. She sought, with ever-increasing frustration, just one man.

"Should we not fight?" Thermodosa asked. "I worry that the Trojans will be lost without Hector to command them. Is that not what we are here for?"

Penthesilea barely heard. With the same focus as that of a hawk circling above a vole, she was scanning up and down the shore, searching through the blur of bodies for one in particular. Sunlight reflected off helmets and there was the crash of metal upon metal as men fell. She might never have laid eyes on Achilles, yet she knew, with absolute certainty, that the moment she spotted him, she would know him.

The battle wore on, and despite Thermodosa's concern, the sides seemed evenly matched. For every Trojan soldier Penthesilea saw fall, a Grecian met the same fate. It was no wonder the war had ground on for so many years if this was how it had been waged.

By the time the heat of the midday sun shimmered in the air, she was growing impatient. In less than a day, she had learnt exactly how this so-called hero operated. Having defiled an honourable man, he then sent his men into battle while he was probably lounging in the cool comfort of his tent, no doubt in the company of women he had taken as slaves. His name alone was enough to bring bile rising to the back of her throat.

If I cannot go to him, then he will have to come to me, she thought, unable to stand it any longer. Raising her sword, she signalled for the attack to begin.

The battle cry of the thirteen women rose high above the armies with a volume that belied their number. Their hooves thundered and their steeds snorted as arrow after arrow flew from their bows.

"It is the Amazons!"

The cry went up, whether from a Greek or Trojan, it mattered not. Men turned pale with shock and fear as they rode into the affray, slicing down every Grecian in their path.

"Bring me Achilles!" Penthesilea shouted, as her axe cut through three breast plates in a single swing. "It is only Achilles I want! Bring him to me!"

Men backed away from her. Some dived onto the sand and scuttled away like crabs on their hands and knees to avoid her blade. Reverting to her bow, she brought an end to all who tried to escape her. Men fell by the dozen, her fellow Amazons' arrows as deadly as her own.

Once they had seen which side the women were fighting on, the Trojan men, who had retreated towards the wall in silent awe, now joined them, moving with a rhythm that told of many years spent in combat together. Following the commands of the women without question or hesitation, grouping and regrouping on their word, they began to turn the tide of this particular battle, stunning the Greeks with their newfound ferocity. Yet Penthesilea's main target was still eluding her.

"Bring me Achilles! I will show him the same respect he bestowed upon Prince Hector!"

Her muscles burnt as she moved with a speed that she had not achieved since her youth, her father's blood pumping through her veins.

"Bring me Achilles!" she cried again, and then the terrorised Grecians parted, and someone stepped forwards.

She had never seen a man of such stature before. He was more colossal than even the greatest of the Gargareans. His arms and legs bulged with muscles, and veins coiled around them like snakes. Each step he took shook the earth. The Trojans now retreated behind the mounted Amazons. Penthesilea moved her horse forward. She knew from his size alone who it was she faced.

And it was not the man she wanted.

"Ajax, son of Telamon," she said.

She dropped to the ground, her shield and axe in her hands. Her horse turned in a circle, churning up a ring of dust.

"It is not you I plan to kill today. I seek only Achilles."

"Queen Penthesilea. I am afraid that will not be possible."

He offered no other words but lifted his bronze shield with one hand and swung his sword at her with the other. With so much weight behind each strike, her shield rattled, causing her bones to tremble. And yet, no matter how he tried, all he could do was make contact with her shield, except on those occasions when he swung too wildly and struck the sand instead. There was no lightness to his feet, no finesse or refinement in the way he prepared and executed each strike. He was a man used to winning every fight he ever entered through brute force alone. Every fight except this one.

"Bring! Me! Achilles!"

Each word was punctuated by another smash of her axe, until with one final swing, she knocked the immense warrior to the ground. Before he could right himself, she was straddling him. Lifting her weapon high above her head, she swung it down at his breast plate, stopping only as the two metals met. His eyes bulged with fear as he stared up at her.

"I will kill you," she hissed. "Or you can fetch me Achilles."

The instant she stepped over him, Ajax scrambled onto his hands and knees and then raced away towards his men.

"Fetch Achilles!" he yelled at them. "Fetch Achilles!"

As she waited, amidst all the noise and chaos, Penthesilea closed her eyes and breathed in a deep lungful of air. A strong breeze was blowing from across the sea, the scent of an impending storm clear and strong in the cold crisp air. She remembered watching as a child as the clouds darkened out to sea, long before they reached the land. She and Hippolyte had loved waiting for those first few drops of rain that splashed on the skin, before the downpour arrived along with the thunder and lightning.

In that moment, she could feel her sister there beside her. She could feel Hippolyte, and Antiope too. She had not been able to avenge their deaths, but she would fight for them today, as well as Hector.

Hushed whispers alerted Penthesilea that someone was approaching. She opened her eyes and readied her axe.

Though not as imposing as Ajax in size, this man exuded a different kind of strength. People parted around him, just as they always had when she or Hippolyte arrived somewhere. His walk was closer to a swagger than a stride, and several blond curls showed from beneath his helmet. She grimaced at the cocksure confidence which oozed from him. This man was the very antithesis of Hector. His arrogance reminded her of another man. At least she could rid the world of one of them.

"I do not believe we are acquainted?" Achilles said, swinging his sword in a circle.

"I can rectify that," she replied.

Penthesilea made the first move. She swung at him from a distance, a difficult action and something her opponents rarely anticipated. Yet Achilles did. He saw her axe coming and dodged it with ease, causing her to tumble past him. Immediately regaining her balance, she spun around and struck out once more. Once again, he avoided her blow. Her breaths were coming thick and fast as she lunged and struck out again, and then again. But her blows weren't finding their target. Her opponent was always just out of reach.

Achilles twisted away from her next blow and hit her with his shield as she went past, sending her tumbling to the ground. The sand grazed her knees and elbows but, with one push, she was on her feet and swinging for him again, and this time, her axe found his shield. But it was not enough and he did not seem to be tiring at all, while she had already used a lot of her energy fighting Ajax.

She suddenly found herself on the defence, her attacks few and far between. As she shook her head to stop the sweat from running into her eyes, Achilles took advantage of this momentary distraction to strike again. The tip of his blade sank into one of the plates on her arm. With a guttural yell, she twisted away, wrenching the metal apart.

A trickle of blood ran down to her elbow. It was only a nick. It would heal quickly. Yet even as these thoughts flashed through her mind, so did another. The only person who had ever drawn her blood before had been Hippolyte, and that had been enough to mark her out as Queen of the Amazons.

Heart pounding, Penthesilea staggered back on the sand, placing more room between her and her opponent than she had ever needed in a fight before. Her axe was no use now. He had dropped his sword and plucked a spear from the sand, and she would not be able to get close enough to deliver a fatal blow. The spear tip glinted in the sun, showering the sand with a thousand reflections, like constellations moving against a yellow sky.

How could she reach him? Hippolyte would have known what to do. This battle would already have been over if it had been she who was fighting Achilles.

Penthesilea's mind drifted to her sister. To the brightness of her smile and her eyes, which, even in death had shown compassion. She knew she would hold that memory in her heart for ever. Even if she lived for a thousand years, it would shine as brightly in her mind as it was now.

It took her a moment to realise that the glint she could see was not coming from her sister's smile but from Achilles' spear, moving through the air at speed towards her. She tilted her head and frowned, as if she had all the time in the world to consider this object hurtling in her direction and then twist her body away.

Yet she did not. And the shining tip plunged into her chest.

Death on the battlefield was an honourable gift for an Amazon, and it was such a gift that Penthesilea received that day. She lay on the yellow sands of Troy, Achilles' spear in her chest, her heartbeat growing fainter until finally it was still. Some say that Achilles removed her helmet and fell instantly in love with her. That he wept for the loss of his equal, longing to spend just one more moment with her.

But, in truth, he felt no desire for the Queen; it was the look on her face that he envied. The slightest of smiles on her warrior lips, as if she had peacefully slipped away and was now exactly where she wished to be.

The twelve women who had travelled to Troy with Penthesilea fought on valiantly, their arrows and swords dispatching many Grecians in the name of their queen. But it was not enough. The enemy's numbers were overwhelming. One by one, they fell, warriors to the last.

EPILOGUE

$\mathcal{A}$nd what of the remaining Amazons? Those who had stayed in Pontus and those who had travelled with Cletes to sail to Troy?

The remaining Amazons bid farewell to Themiscyra and made their homes on the steppes with the other nomads. Melanippe continuing to teach the ways of the Amazons to the nomads. No longer did she ride to war, but found contentment in the simple life, camping under the stars and bathing in the rivers. She grew crops and hunted rabbits. As the years passed, the younger children grew to know her simply as Melanippe, another nomad, but a woman of extraordinary age who could shoot an arrow or ride a horse with greater skill than any person they had ever met, and who could weave magical tales of the gods and the warrior queens and princesses. They did not realise she was one of those of whom she spoke. That she was a daughter of Ares. And that was the way she preferred it.

As for Cletes, her boat never reached the shores of Troy, but was blown off course by a fierce wind that ravaged the sails and tossed the vessel until its ropes snapped and its mast splintered.

One by one, the Amazons on board were lost to Poseidon's swell. All except for Cletes herself.

Through some unfathomable grace, she was swept onto a distant shore, a place where the Amazons were creatures of myth and legend. Knowing there was no way for her to ever reach home again, she eked out a life there, never disclosing her true identity. After some years, she married a king and became a fair and compassionate queen, always loyal and faithful to her husband.

But in her heart, there would only ever be one true love. Penthesilea. The last Queen of Themiscyra. The last Queen of the Amazons.

THE END

ACKNOWLEDGEMENTS

It takes far more people than just myself to get a book our of my head and into the hands of you, the reader, but this one was a beast!

Firstly I need to extend a heartfelt thank you Adrienne Mayor. Although I have never met her, or even conversed with her, the release of her fantastic book, *The Amazons* six months after I starting writing this, proved an invaluable reference throughout writing this book, although I did apply some poetic licence at times in the interest of narrative flow. For that I apologise, but if you ever read the book, I hope you'll understand.

Then my editing team. This is the largest book I have ever released and as such, required so much work from so many. To Joel, Emma and Carol, thank you for all the work you did getting the book into shape. And to my amazing team of proofreaders, Kath, Lucy, Jane and everyone else for spotting those stubborn errors that would otherwise make it to the final draft. I would be lost without you.

To those family and friends, who celebrate every little win with me; your support and belief has helped me get this far.

To my readers. You are amazing. Without you I'd be ranting crazily into the void.

And then to Jake. My first reader, biggest fan and harshest critic. (And long suffering husband.) The hours you spent to get this book ready has made all my others pale in comparison, and I know that at times it took as much from you as it did from me. I do not have words to express how grateful I am for everything you have done to help bring my vision to life here and for everything you do for me every single day. Thank you.

COMING SOON

CHILD OF OLYMPUS

A mother's love knows no bounds, in this world or the next.

**After centuries of imprisonment, Demeter wished only for a life of
quiet contentment, watching over the humans from her home upon
mount Olympus. But even for a Goddess, the is a price to pay for
peace.**

Tricked and defiled by those closest to her, Demeter flees her life as an
Olympian and takes her daughter to live with amongst the mortals.
There Demeter vows to keep Core safe from all the sufferings she
herself had endured at the hands of her family. But can she keep her
promise, or will her immortal brethren find yet more ways to make
them suffer?

If you enjoy tales with Greek gods, heinous betrayal, and formidable
parental bonds, then Hannah Lynn's latest mythological retelling will
blow you away with its haunting and powerful portrayal of Demeter.

**Daughter to a Titan, Sister to the King of the Gods, and Mother to
the Queen of the Underworld.**

ABOUT THE AUTHOR

Hannah Lynn is a multi award winning novelist. Publishing her first book, Amendments – a dark, dystopian speculative fiction novel, in 2015. Her second book, The Afterlife of Walter Augustus – a contemporary fiction novel with a supernatural twist – went on to win the 2018 Kindle Storyteller Award and the Independent Publishers Gold Medal for Best Adult Ebook.

Born in 1984, Hannah grew up in the Cotswolds, UK. After graduating from university, she spent 15 years as a teacher of physics, first in the UK and then Thailand, Malaysia, Austria and Jordan. It was during this time, inspired by the imaginations of the young people she taught, she began writing short stories for children, and later adult fiction.

Now settled back in the UK with her husband, daughter and horde of cats, she spends her days writing romantic comedies and historical fiction. Her first historical fiction novel, Athena's Child, was also a 2020 Gold Medalist at the Independent Publishers Awards.

STAY IN TOUCH

To keep up-to-date with new publications, tours and promotions, or if you are interested in being a beta reader for future novels, or having the opportunity to enjoy pre-release copies please follow me:

Sign up for newsletter
HERE

Or visit
Website: www.hannahlynnauthor.com

REVIEW

As an independent author, I do not have the mega resources of a big publishing house, but what I do have is something even more powerful – all of you readers. Your ability to offer social proof to my books through your reviews is invaluable to me and helps me to continue writing.
So if you enjoyed reading *Queens of Themiscyra*, please take a few moments to leave a review or rating on Amazon or Goodreads. It need only be a sentence or two, but it means so much to me.
Thank you.

Printed in Great Britain
by Amazon